CHRISTMAS IN PINEVILLE

2ND EDITION

DEBRA ELISE ROMANCE COLLECTION SERIES

DEBRA ELISE

Redeeming Scrooge / Debra Elise

Chasing Noel / Debra Elise

Zesting with Zane / Debra Elise

Tangling with the Mountain Man/ Debra Elise

Rescued by an Outlaw / Debra Elise

Tangling with Santa / Debra Elise

Tangling with the Grinch / Debra Elise

Print ISBN 979-8-9929331-7-8

CONTENTS

ZESTING WITH ZANE

TANGLING WITH THE MOUNTAIN MAN

RESCUED BY AN OUTLAW

TANGLING WITH SANTA

TANGLING WITH THE GRINCH

WANT A FREE BOOK?

Sign up for my newsletter and get your copy of >>> TANGLING WITH MY EX.

Gage

A former marine with attitude, PTSD, and fantasies his wife didn't want to be a part of.

Toni

I asked my ex to leave so he could heal, to discover what would make him whole again.

Now our daughter is getting married. I haven't seen him in four years. A weekend together, pretending to get along for the sake of our family, testing my sanity and my new-found desires.

I've dreamt about the things Gage described. Could I do what he wants, what he needs?

Maybe it's what I needed all along, too.

ABOUT

****IN THIS SECOND EDITION, 2 NEW STORIES HAVE BEEN ADDED - REDEEMING SCROOGE & TANGLING WITH THE GRINCH****

Love Always Finds a Way in Pineville, Idaho.
This is never truer than during Christmastime.

In this 7 novella collection, you will find stories filled with *steam, surprises* and **magical** holiday, ever afters.

Stories in this collection include:
<u>From the Rescued by Love Series</u>

REDEEMING SCROOGE - A meddling aunt, a pixie, help a party planner and a card carrying scrooge with their steamy second chance (later in life) - *new!*

CHASING NOEL - A steamy snowed in, enemies to lovers billionaire baseball team owner, an interior designer & a surprise baby (later in life)

REDEEMING SCROOGE

A PINEVILLE WORLD CHRISTMAS NOVELLA
(RESCUED BY LOVE SERIES)

ABOUT

Sophie McMannis owns a party planning company and lives for the holidays.

Grant Conrad, a card-carrying scrooge, is also a former all-star baseball player, womanizer, and her aunt's boss. When he steals a kiss at midnight on New Year's Eve, he has no clue who she is. She knows exactly who he is and can't compromise Aunt Kathryn's job--no matter the full-body shiver he induces.

In between arguing over a stolen kiss (but was it really?), a box full of decorations, and the commercialization of the holiday, they fight against a mutual desire (not very convincingly neither saw coming.

Can Grant overcome his aversion to Christmas and convince Sophie that a womanizing scrooge can be redeemed? Anything is possible with the help of one meddling aunt, a pixie, and plenty of mistletoe.

PROLOGUE

*N*EW YEAR'S EVE

SOPHIE MCMANNIS SPOTTED her aunt's boss as soon as he walked into the ballroom. Rumor was he hated the holiday season, a real-life Ebenezer Scrooge so, she was a bit surprised to see him attending the New Year's Eve party.

Tonight's event was part charity fundraiser part a reason to party for the city's elite. She'd never been as a guest, but after working her ass off to build her party and event planning business the last few years, she'd finally scored the contract to design the gala of the season.

She scanned the room full of men and women in holiday colors with a sparkly dress scattered here and there. Her gaze is drawn to the broad-shouldered former baseball star as he worked the room with ease, no sign of his staunch scroogie-ness on his handsome face. She'd managed to avoid meeting Grant Conrad for the six years her Aunt Kathleen had worked for him.

Tonight wouldn't be the night to end that streak. She didn't need his kind of negativity even though he may have starred in one or two of her fantasies during her college days. That was a time when you couldn't open a magazine or turn on the TV without seeing his face or his half-naked form in an ad form sports cream or a men's fragrance. He'd since retired and now owned a successful sports management company.

She'd heard first-hand accounts from her aunt about Grant's dislike of Christmas. Aunt Kathleen had been so excited when he left for a two-week vacation every year to avoid, as he referred to it, the 'hub-bub' of the holidays.

But Sophie lived for the holiday's; any holiday. And she couldn't fathom anyone hating them. She'd built her business by planning and creating dynamic holiday-based events. And she was allergic to the haters, the avoiders, and the scrooges. And, Mr. Grant was the scroo-giest of all scrooges she thankfully never had the displeasure of meeting.

She would not ruin her night by exchanging words with the dynamic man she'd maybe, once in a while drooled, okay lusted, over because tonight's event at The Resort in her hometown of Pineville, Idaho was too important to her business and to her personally. It served as a charity benefit for the Children's Cancer Center and Harmony Hospital. An organization that was part of her heart and her family's past.

So what if it was also an excuse to work on New Year's Eve. The perfect built-in excuse to not have a date to kiss at midnight. As much as her aunt, who was more mother than auntie, complained about her lack of interest in finding a man and her near-constant hints at wanting and some babies to spoil, she didn't have time to invest in a relation-ship right now.

And she was fine with her single status. Just fine. Her company was growing, she'd recently hired an assistant to work with her full time, but even with Evie's help, she had little personal time. She certainly didn't have time to stand still as Grant Conrad, uber-rich and hunky ex-baseball superstar, turned heads and induced fantasies as he roamed the room with his bored-looking date.

Sure, he was built like a Greek god, but he probably bored his dates to death with endless sports talk. She often wondered how Aunt Kat continued to work for a man who, by his own account, lived and breathed sports. As far as she knew, her aunt never watched a baseball game in her life or any other sport. But her aunt was a master sergeant at heart, and Sophie imagined she kept Grant on track and organized. And he paid her well, which earned him some brownie points in her book.

"Sophie, who are you staring at? Anyone I know?" Evie bumped into her shoulder and looked toward the tall drink of water standing off to himself in a corner of the room. *Tall drink of water?* Jeez, her aunt's vintage euphemisms were taking up space in her subconscious again. However, she had to agree with the statement. He was hard to miss and even harder to look away from.

Darn it. She was supposed to be checking the champagne supply, not getting caught gawking at Grant. She turned her attention to her assistant and raised her arm toward the cheese bar. "The brie is almost gone, and I think I'll have the caterer put out more grapes and water crackers."

Evie let out a snort, "You can fool some people some of the time, but you can't fool all of the people all of the time. You were checking out Mr. Hottie. Lord, I wish he was still playing. That man could fill out a uniform…and whoever invented baseball pants…oh, my, I think I need some ice water."

Evie was an excellent assistant, but she tended toward the dramatic, especially when cute guys were involved. And Sophie didn't need a visual of Grant in baseball pants or out of them for that matter.

As she finished her thought and turned back to Evie, her gaze collided with the subject of their discussion. A vision of Grant in nothing but a pair of baseball pants, top button undone, his heavily muscled shoulders, abs, and arms chiseled. Was he still as cut five years after his last game in the league?

He was staring at her with an intense, questioning gaze. Perhaps he was used to women fawning over him, and her unreadable stare was unexpected. She shook her head and broke the link. Now was not the time to get caught up in whatever that moment was. Besides, he had a date. She wasn't here to find a guy but to do what she loved, creating an unforgettable experience for her client and their guests.

"Sophie, Hi. The room looks A-mazing. And the caterer you found is causing a stir with his scallion pancakes, and the fig with bacon and chile is almost gone." Amber Wyatt, one of her closest friends, was helping her out with the champagne service. She managed the front office for a local psychologist, and Amber had been there for Sophie in the beginning when her payroll was tight to help out when she needed an extra set of hands. And although her business was doing now well, she could still count on Amber in a pinch when one of her part-time employees were sick.

Plus, she didn't have to worry about Amber's professionalism when she served guests. Amber wasn't looking to snag a date, or a hook-up, like many of her college-aged employees did. Her gorgeous friend was expert level at deflecting unwanted attention from men who thought the staff was fair game. But Sophie worried that Amber had shut herself off from anything long-term; then again, so had she. But they each had their reasons.

Unfortunately, Amber's reason was the friendship ending kind having had a crush on one of their mutual friend's brother since they were teens. Losing a friendship over a guy was a line no one wanted to cross. Sophie just wished Amber would find someone else, someone to show her how great a person she really was, not just a pretty face.

Sophie shook herself out of the unwelcome melancholy and gave her friend a grin and quick side hug. "So, you don't think it has anything to do with the woman offering up the savory treats?" She watched her friend blush and roll her eyes. "Soph, stop. I'm here to help you, not find a date. Besides, look around. No one is here solo. It's New Year's Eve, and the only available men are either too young or too old for us."

Sighing, Sophie nodded and scanned the room and had a funny comeback on her lips when her gaze landed on Grant--again. Not that she was purposely looking for him. His gaze was locked on her, and when he noticed her attention, his gaze traveled down her body; warning bells sounded along with a full-bodied shiver.

She broke the eye contact, "Amber, could you do me a favor and go into the kitchen and ask for another bucket of ice for the shrimp? I need to address um…a situation."

Her friend looked over to where Grant stood still staring at Sophie and let out a low whistle. "Situation, huh? Damn, Sophie. Are you keeping him a secret from me?"

"What? No. I don't even know him. Well, I know of him; Aunt Kat works for him, but I've never met him. And I'm positive he doesn't know who I am." She adjusted her necklace and turned toward Amber.

"Really, because the way he's looking at you says different. If a man looked at me like he wanted to pick me up and spread me out on the nearest--"

"Amber…*Ssh!*" Sophie felt her face flush. She glanced around to see if anyone was close enough to hear their conversation.

"I'm just saying that man wants you. And he looks like he knows what to do with you once he gets you." Amber patted her on the shoulder. "Close your mouth before the drool drops out. C'mon, go see what's what. He's the hottest guy, no, not guy. I meant man---all man, in this room tonight. Hell, in the whole city. Yes, he has a revolving door to his bedroom, but you should definitely go for it. A night of hot sex never hurt a girl; in fact, it may just--"

"What has gotten into you?" Sophie whispered.

"--and oh, my lord, those shoulders. Makes you wonder how big the rest of him is." Amber winked.

SOPHIE LET OUT a frustrated groan and smoothed her hands over her hips. She briefly closed her eyes—wrong move. Amber's description of Grant's body created a naughty flash image of him in her bed. *Whoa.* All of her girl parts took notice and perked up as well. Between Evie and Amber going on and on about Grant and his hot body now, Sophie couldn't stop wondering what was hidden under the tailored suit jacket.

In his playing days with the United States Baseball League and before his arm injury, he was the league's heartthrob thanks in part to his bare-chested photos. And he had all her favorites: wide-shoulders, muscular arms, and...*oh, Hell, get over yourself, Sophie.*

For years, Grant's image had been splashed across every sports magazine cover on the market. The only difference from then versus now was the sexy gray at his temples.

Amber let out a heavy sigh, "Maybe I'm just tired of being politically correct and pretending I don't have a libido, or maybe it's the glass and half of champagne I indulged in. Either way, my new year's resolution is to get real about what I want."

Sophie took in Amber's confession or rather her declaration of intent. She held Grant's gaze. She refused to squirm under his visual onslaught of seduction if that's what it was. But there was no way she'd fall under his spell. Let him look; he wouldn't be touching anytime soon, especially since he brought a date. He really was the womanizer everyone labeled him.

"You know what, Amber? Good for you. And after we're done here, let's go out and start the new year off right. Let's meet up with Reese at her club later, and you can tell me all about how you decided to 'get real.' She said she would save a table for us."

Grant chose that moment to acknowledge their staredown, or whatever it was, and dipped his chin. Her lips thinned, but so did her nipples. Damn, he wasn't giving up. The ridiculousness of the moment shook her. She was working and getting paid well to make sure this night was a success for the hospital. Spending her time flirting was not on the night's agenda.

Ready to concede, lady luck paid her a visit. Grant's attention was hijacked by an overzealous party guest dressed in a dark red and black suede tux wearing a party hat. She glanced down at her smartwatch, the best investment she'd ever made and the only concession to glam she'd made in her outfit. The crystal-encrusted wristband gleamed in the semi-dark room. It read ten forty-five, and the screen also flashed a countdown reminder.

She scanned the buffet tables again. The guests were still nibbling. "Amber, I'll go into the kitchen. Could you go over and double-check the serving dishes on the hot table and text me if there's anything that needs replenishing?"

"Oh, but--"

"It's okay. I need to check on the champagne supply one last time before the countdown toast by the hospital's CEO." Sophie grabbed the lifeline she gave herself and made a beeline for the kitchen. However, Grant was in her peripheral vision, and she was weak. He seemed to be tolerating the man bent on relieving some past baseball moment and deftly avoided an arm simulating a pitch. But his gaze was once again locked on her. His date still nowhere to be seen, and now she was more confused than ever. Did she look like someone he knew? Did she look easy? The longer she thought about it, her anger increased.

Whatever was drawing his attention to her, shrimp and champagne were calling her name. Grant Conrad could take his lady-killer notoriety and lavish it on someone else, like his poor date. Besides, he was neither her type nor in her league.

She smiled, then softly chuckled at her own joke as she placed a hand on the swinging door into the kitchen. With a smile still upon her lips, she glanced back towards the main room and whether she intended it or not, and that would be something she'd think about later--much later, her gaze landed on the man she was spending way too much of her time on.

His eyes widened, and a flash of a smile lit up his face. She averted her gaze as quick as she could and hurried through the doorway. The clinking of glassware and the steady hum of voices in consultation greeted her. She found the sous chef and asked for more of the mini-shrimp cocktail to be taken out and chatted with two servers she knew from past events.

The champagne for the party was stored in a room off the back of the kitchen. The vintage had been chosen by the hospital's volunteer committee. She'd been impressed at their choice. Maybe after she ensured everyone had a glass at midnight, she'd have some herself. Until then, she needed to make sure her mind was clear and focused on the agenda from this point forward and not the hazel-eyed male who kept invading her thoughts.

Back in the ballroom, she found Amber and Evie and went over the final items on the schedule, a short speech by the founder of the charity and, hopefully, an even shorter speech by the infamously long-winded CEO of the hospital.

The next hour sped by, and at eleven forty-five, there was no sign of the hospital's CEO, but she located Mrs. Bette Lancaster, the founder of the charity. Unfortunately, she was in deep conversation with Grant.

She was beginning to wonder if she'd pissed off her guardian angel. She believed she had one. She also believed in Santa, leprechauns, and fairies and found herself but often found herself at odds with fate. Right now, she didn't know what to believe in regards to Grant and his interest in her. She made her way across the room toward them, perfectly aware that his eyes were locked on her as he also spoke to Mrs. Lancaster. She took quick peeks around the room, looking for his date. When she located the socialite, she was thrown off her stride.

The woman was locked in a heated conversation with the CEO of the hospital. Their body language indicated familiarity, but when Grant's date turned away from him, and the CEO grabbed her by the waist and swung her body into his and planted a passionate kiss on her lips, for a split second, she felt sorry for him. Grant, not the CEO. Damn it. She did not have time for drama. She looked at her watch, less than ten minutes till midnight.

Sophie made a last-minute change to the agenda. Screw the agenda. She'd make it work without the hospital's top executive. Mrs. Lancaster and Grant were now both looking in her direction. No doubt, they noticed the scene behind her.

"Sophie, dear. It seems Henry is busy with his fickle ex-girlfriend. No worries, I can speak for both of us."

The self-assured woman just became her hero. Sophie typed a quick text to Evie requesting the microphone. She held out her hand, "Thank you, Mrs. Lancaster. I know Henry couldn't have asked for a better spokesperson. If you follow me, I have the perfect spot for you to speak to the guests." Amber nodded toward the podium located at the north end of the room. Grant's voice startled her. His low timbered tone sent a thrill through her. "I don't believe we've met. I'm Grant Conrad."

Steps away from freedom, Amber looked over her shoulder, unsure for the first time in a long time how to handle herself. To be rude was pointless and would not go over well in front of the charity's president. But time was not on her side. She really wanted to know why her? What was so special about her that he'd spent the night seeking her out, sending her heated glances?

"It seems your date is leaving with another man." As soon as the words were out of her mouth, she wanted to reel them back in and swallow them down with a glass of champagne. Damn, now he knew she'd taken notice of with whom he'd arrived at the party.

"Larissa? No worries, I knew her goal was to make Henry jealous, and I played along. Thank you for your concern over my feelings. But I was hoping we could have a moment to meet before..."

She tuned him out. *Wait. What?* Mrs. Lancaster was waiting for her; it was now five minutes to midnight, and the wait staff was almost done delivering the champagne, and he wanted her attention--now. A loud murmur of anticipation filled the room. If she didn't turn around now, the speech might not happen, and who would take the blame? Not happening.

"Perhaps another time. I need to make sure the rest of the night goes smoothly. Excuse me while I assist our speaker." Her heart pounding, she went to turn toward the podium, which thankfully was less than ten feet away. But he stepped in closer and gently touch her arm.

"You can pretend all you want, but I've been on the receiving end of your beautiful brown-eyed gaze. And I have to admit; you're the most interesting woman in the room tonight. You not only dazzle in that dress, but you also handle yourself well under pressure. I admire that. I'm a man who goes after what I--"

Confusion and temper warred, she looked around to see if they had an audience, but everyone was in their own world. In a loud whisper, she responded. "Really? Well, sorry, but I'm not a member of the groupies you seem to attract wherever you go. Now, I've got work to do." She looked down at his hand on her arm and back up into his dumbfounded gaze.

His eyes narrowed, but he said nothing. She spun around on her spiked heel only to hear that Mrs. Lancaster had begun to address the room with just three minutes to midnight. Evie had come to the rescue and assisted the woman as she started her speech.

Sophie fumed. The man had an ego the size of Alaska, and he'd done what few people had ever managed to do--get her to miss an agenda item for one of her events. Statue still, she forced a smile and listened to the words of one of the community's most beloved and generous benefactors. She was acutely aware that Grant continued to stand feet behind her. The goosebumps on her arms and the tingle on her nape refused to leave no matter how much she willed them away—damn man.

She glanced at her watch, a minute and a half to go. The crowd clapped in unison; Mrs. Lancaster serenely smiled. The woman was a pro. She knew Sophie's attention had been snagged, and yet she ended her speech with time to spare.

She was so grabbing every last bottle of champagne leftover that she could manage to haul out later. Never had a man driven her to drink, but Grant was no ordinary man and one she needed to stay away from.

With a cleansing breath, she moved to the podium, stood behind her new hero, and listened as Mrs. Lancaster prepped everyone and started the countdown as she lifted her glass to toast in the New Year. The pop of balloons and squeaks of noisemakers filled the room. Still on sensory overload, Sophie stepped back and stumbled. She caught sight of a shiny black men's dress shoe and ran her gaze up the attached leg and further up to a broad chest and into the hooded stare of Grant Conrad. When had he gotten so close?

With quick movements, he'd captured her elbow and guided her further back with him as he maneuvered them behind the arch of black, white, and gold balloons. Her breath caught in her throat. Grant steadied her with a firm yet gentle grip on her shoulders. The gazes he'd sent her earlier were no match for the dark, sensual look he focused on her now.

When his eyes zeroed in on her lips, she licked them.

He groaned. "So, do you want to be the only people in the room who don't kiss at midnight?"

Speechless, she didn't look away, couldn't. The heat from his body enveloped her. The sharp words she gave him moments ago may as well have been in her head. She doubted he was turned down often, but now the need to feel his lips on hers overwhelmed. Sophie fought the twin urgings of leaning in and pulling away. As the seconds ticked by, her attraction to Grant made the decision easy. She lifted her face, and he swooped down, captured her mouth, and sucked then softly bit her lower lip.

A low moan filled her ears, but from whom she wasn't sure. Lost in the pleasure-pain of his bite, her body swayed into his. Sophie ran her hands up his heavily muscled arms and circled his neck. He wrapped her up in steel and deepened the kiss. His tongue swept between her lips, dueling with hers before he

Notes of *Old Ange Syne* echoed in the distance. Again, someone moaned. It was her. The sound snapped her out of the desire-filled fog they'd created cocooned away from the others. *What the what?*

Grant pulled back from the kiss she shouldn't have given while wanting to beg him for another. "Happy New Year."

His husky voice penetrated all her nerve endings, and his smile inspired a half-dozen naughty things she imagined his mouth doing to her beyond kissing.

Happy. New. Year. Yes, it was. And parts of her were very happy at the moment, but she was supposed to be working, not losing herself in a kiss with a virtual stranger. And he couldn't know who she was…her aunt could never know. Dammit. This wasn't who she was. She didn't kiss men she didn't know, no matter how they made her knees wobble or her breasts ache and her nipples hard. And now, her lips were swollen.

She lifted her fingers to touch them, stepped out of his arms, and pushed down the panic. Not because she was afraid that Aunt Kathleen would find out or that her client, Mrs. Lancaster, would notice, but because she wanted another devastatingly wicked kiss. *Lord, had she ever been kissed like that?*

"Um, yeah. I ah, have to get back to work, and this was…not smart. I've got to go." Sophie made a beeline for the kitchen, her go-to temporary haven. Cowardly? A hundred percent. But necessary.

He didn't call her back or follow her. But she swore she felt the heat of his stare bore into her backside and follow her across the ballroom. With every ounce of self-preservation, she kept from looking over her shoulder to see if the tingling sensation she experienced had indeed been from his hot gaze.

What was she feeling besides attraction? She should be fuming that he stole a kiss; well, not stolen precisely. She'd reexamine the moment later. Much later. She pushed through the swinging door to the kitchen and stood off to the side, and narrowly escaped being run over by a couple of servers, trays full of champagne.

She pounded her head lightly onto the wall. There was no way she could face him again without him finding out who she really was. Her duties were done for the evening; there wasn't much left to do other than clean up after the guests. Most of them would continue their celebration in the hotel's lounge, where a band had been booked for those that wanted to dance the night away. She stayed in the kitchen and texted Evie asking her to let her know when he left.

Evie: FUNNY YOU ASK. AFTER YOU TWO KISSED HE WALKED PAST ME WITH A FROWN ON HIS FACE, PICKED UP HIS OVERCOAT AT HATCHECK AND LEFT. CAN'T WAIT TO HEAR ALLLL ABOUT IT.

Sophie didn't respond. She felt her face flush. There went any hope of keeping Evie, and Amber for that matter, from grilling her later. Considering they were all single, her kissing one of the city's most eligible bachelors on New Year's Eve was going to be hard to live down.

But she didn't feel too bad about running away because they were so not going to be a thing anyway. Besides, she didn't have room or time in her life to redeem a scrooge--no matter how he made her toes curl.

CHAPTER 1

$\mathcal{E}$LEVEN MONTHS LATER

GRANT CONRAD HATED Christmas like a kid hated broccoli. He refused to celebrate the holiday and typically took off on a beach vacation. This year, however, he needed to close his deal with Kemper & Associates by the end of next week, two days before Christmas.

And that meant going to their end of year party where the official announcement of his sports management company's buyout would be made. Kemper believed in good cheer, and all the trappings of the holiday and ending the year with a warm fuzzy for his employees had become…tradition. Grant could care less, but he needed the sale finalized to move on to his next chapter in life: becoming an owner of a national sports franchise.

He stood at his office window and scanned the decked-out streets and storefronts of downtown Pineville, Idaho. The light posts were wrapped in green and red garland. The cheery color combo was a yearly reminder of the season he did his best to ignore.

His go-to-date Larissa Saldana had just informed him she wouldn't be attending with him. One of the most important nights of his life, and she'd bailed. Oh, he knew she'd been using him for quite some time to make her ex-boyfriend jealous, and now it seems her efforts had finally paid off. When she'd excitedly informed him, she and Henry were now engaged; he hadn't been the least bit jealous.

The emotion just wasn't in him. Annoyed as hell, well, that was a different story. Now he needed a last-minute date. Grant had decided a long time ago to never allow himself to become attached. He'd definitely earned his bachelor status and had no plans of changing anytime soon, if ever.

Larissa's parting shot still rang in his ears, "Don't worry, Grant, just check your list of women. I'm sure you'll find another date in no time."

A few hours later, he slammed the phone down and proved her prophecy wrong. No one was available. Plus, he'd had to cross several women off his 'list' who either laughed or cursed him for his last-minute request.

"Kathleen, I need you," Grant called out to his long-time assistant, stood and began to pace the office. Packing boxes prevented him from working off his frustration as he walked back and forth. Kathleen had been with him since day one of his company, and she often thought of solutions he wouldn't have. And even though she acted more like a disapproving mother at times, she never missed an opportunity to chide him for his revolving door of women. Even with her reprimands, he thought highly of Kathleen. There was no doubt she'd be going with him to the Outlaws organization.

Women were great; he loved women. Worshipped them in bed and received zero complaints until today. Hell, he didn't have the time, or desire, for a long-term relationship. Friends with benefits suited his lifestyle, and he'd never received any pushback until now.

Going over his list again, it struck him that he didn't really consider any of the women he dated a friend. As he read more names, it began to sink in that it had never bothered him because he knew they felt the same toward him.

But he wasn't about to show up at the event without a date. It had become an essential part of his image. Tirelessly so because going solo would cause unwanted attention. It would be like waving a red flag in front of every mother with an unmarried daughter in attendance. He wasn't going to let the endless questioning of when he was going to settle down dominate his evening.

Kathleen walked in as he hung up from another fruitless phone call. In her mid-sixties, a foot shorter than his six-two frame, her silver-gray hair swept back in her signature look with a ribbon tied around her long hair at the back of her nape. She had a timeless look about her and was the one woman he had complete trust in and admiration for.

This afternoon her face was drawn into an impish grin as she waited uncharacteristically silent; excellent strategy considering his mood.

"You look proud of yourself. You have good news for me, or are you getting ready to ask me for another raise?" He teased Kathleen regularly about her negotiation techniques.

"I found you a date."

"Great, you're a lifesaver and just what I needed to hear. Who is it? Did Sharon call back?" She was the only woman on his shortlist who hadn't responded. He'd left what he hoped was a persuasive voicemail.

"No, actually, you don't know her," Kathleen answered.

Grant frowned. "You expect me to take a blind date?"

"Yes. And you won't have to worry about Sophie falling for your charming ways either. She understands it's strictly business."

Grant studied his assistant and returned her grin. Who was he to argue? He was a desperate man at this point, and he'd take Kathleen if she hadn't already turned him down.

"All right. I'll bite. Who is it?" He sat and waited for the big sell.

"My niece, Sophie." She raised her hand, effectively shutting off his big fat no.

"Before you say no, hear me out."

Grant laughed. After all the reprimands concerning his dating life, she was setting him up with her niece. There had to be a catch.

"I can't believe you'd trust me with a member of your family. Wait, isn't she still in college?"

"Graduated four years ago. She's twenty-six and owns her own business. And right now, you don't have much of a choice. It's either Sophie, or you go solo." Kathleen said.

Grant couldn't believe this was happening. He had to stoop to taking his assistant's niece, who'd probably never been to a society event in her life. He'd be forced to stay glued to her side in fear she would say or do the wrong thing. Dammit, maybe he should try Sharon again. He wasn't beyond pleading at this point.

"I know you're worried she may not be used to going to these fancy parties, but I can assure you, she knows her way around rich people. I told her, this is a big night for you. She's not going to embarrass you."

"Really? Are you're willing to stake your job on it?" He ran his hand over his jaw and let it sink in that Kathleen's niece might be his only choice.

"Grant, give me some credit. I know you, and I know Sophie. Besides, I can ease your mind that she won't be falling for you or expecting further dates."

He clutched his chest and mimed removing an arrow from his heart. "Gee, thanks. How can you guarantee she won't? I'm quite a catch, haven't you heard?" Grant laughed for the first time that day.

Kathleen rolled her eyes. "She's too smart for that, and she knows all about your reputation. She's focused on her own career the same as you. She's not looking for a husband. Plus, you're not her type."

Maybe this could work. No expectations, no messy ending. "Wow, thanks, Kathleen. After such a glowing recommendation, I can't wait. Do I at least get to meet her before Friday?"

"I'm afraid not. She's booked solid for the next couple of days. However, I have her business card, which has a nice picture of her. So, it won't really be a blind date. You'll know what she looks like before you pick her up."

Kathleen placed the business card face down on his desk and turned to leave the office. She paused at the doorway. Her eyes crinkled as she smirked. "Oh, and you're welcome, Grant. She'll be the perfect date for you. She's low maintenance." She closed the door.

Loud chuckling emanated from the outer office at their shared inside joke about the women he dated.

He could say no. Should say no. But he couldn't afford to spend any more time finding a date. Kathleen had presented him with the perfect solution. He pictured her niece as the same no-nonsense, comfortable shoe wearing, reading glasses-on-a-chain career woman as Kathleen. Low maintenance. Just what he needed.

He picked up the card for a look at Sophie. His eyebrows rose as the face smiling back at him was none other than the siren he couldn't seem to banish from his thoughts.

Sophie McMannis was the woman he'd couldn't take his off and kissed a year, no two years ago, at midnight on New Year's Eve. A scorching, promise-filled kiss he hadn't been able to forget or duplicate since.

He hadn't turned into a monk over her walking away from him, but he'd definitely slowed down in the female department. He thought it had more to do with working on becoming an owner in the USBL, but maybe it was because finding that spark again with another woman had become

She was also the only woman to walk away from him after he made his intentions clear. She'd successfully avoided him by escaping to the kitchen. He'd admitted defeat and left without getting her number or a chance to apologize for stealing a midnight kiss. Not that he was sorry for the kiss.

There had been something about her that had kept his gaze glued to her and her curves that evening. And he hadn't felt the least guilty as his date for the evening had gone home with her ex-boyfriend leaving him free to pursue someone else.

As he scanned her features in the tiny photo, his grin widened. So, was Kathleen adding matchmaker to her long list of skills? He should be mad, but he couldn't muster the need to call out his long-time employee. Oh, he didn't have plans on taking her to bed. He wouldn't cross that line with Kathleen's niece. But he did want another kiss.

He looked at Sophie's picture again. He'd worked hard that night to get close to the woman who still months later he couldn't shake the memory of that night. He was venturing into dangerous territory, but he couldn't shake how she felt in his arms, how her lips felt under his and how impressed he was that she walked away. Hell, being turned down had never happened to him.

And if wanting something you couldn't have should have been a red flag, he ignored it.

SOPHIE LOVED CHRISTMAS. Her party event business boomed from Labor Day till New Year's Eve. She designed one-of-a-kind parties for the rich and not so famous. This year was no different. Although she'd lost the bid for the Kemper & Associates gala, she was busy with plenty of other high-profile functions to ease the sting of missing out on the sought-after event.

She was so busy that she hadn't had a chance to return her aunt's early morning voicemail until lunchtime the following day. Sophie knew Aunt Kathleen would understand. They'd spoken about Sophie's crazy schedule over the weekend, which led her aunt right into yet another lecture on her lack of a dating life.

Sophie had given up trying to convince the woman who'd raised her after her parents' tragic car accident that she was not ready for marriage and babies. In fact, she might never be ready. She liked her life, but Aunt Kat was determined. Sophie loved that her aunt wanted her settled and happy with a husband but now was not the time.

Sophie had set aside twenty minutes for lunch between frantic phone calls from her clients, one of whom wanted to know if they could rent real reindeer. Promising them, she would give it her best shot, *but, yeah, not going to happen this close to Christmas*, she called her aunt.

"You want me to go where? With who? Aunt Kathleen, have you been into the whiskey again? I have three major parties this week and two the following week. I just can't. Besides, he's your boss. I don't want to date your boss and mess things up for you." Sophie rubbed her temple and fought off a migraine.

Her aunt knew nothing about her brief encounter with Grant last New Year's Eve. There was no way she would agree to help him out now. She'd long ago chalked up his kiss to too much champagne, on his end, and being caught up in a weird dynamic with his date who'd ended up with another guy that night. So, no, she wasn't going to tell Kathleen what had happened between her and Grant--ever.

Plus, by her aunt's own accounts and the gossips in town, he was a womanizing scrooge. Two things she couldn't get past, given her business and her own love of Christmas. And she was still mad at herself for letting down her inhibitions with a guest during an event she oversaw. She counted herself lucky no one from the charity committee had caught them.

"Aunt Kathleen, you've complained for years how he's anti-Christmas. Why would I spend my time with a man who has publicly blasted my favorite holiday? And you've told me enough about him and his legion of women to fill a tell-all book. No, absolutely not." There, two valid reasons to turn down her aunt without feeling any guilt at keeping her secret. Almost.

"Sophie, you owe me."

Those three words made her stomach roll. Her aunt played dirty when she had to. And Kathleen was calling in the long-held favor Sophie herself had instigated. There was no way she'd go back on her word. Darn her sneaky aunt.

She let out a heavy sigh, "Alright. Have him email me the details. I'll have Evie take over the party I have scheduled that night."

The happiness she heard in Aunt Kat's voice took away the sting of embarrassment she still felt from that night. It also was a good reminder that her aunt had taken her in and given her shelter and love when she needed it most. She'd do anything for that woman.

After she hung up, Sophie banged her head on the desk. Bad move. Now she really did have a headache. She could only pray that Grant Conrad had forgotten about their midnight kiss. A kiss that had very likely ruined her for anyone else.

GRANT DIDN'T BELIEVE in fate, but he did send out a quick thank you to whatever entity was responsible for bringing Sophie McMannis back into his life. He should be mad at her. She'd had to have known who he was that night as her aunt had worked for him for over six years.

So why hadn't she said anything? Unless she'd been as drawn to him as he had been to her. And when he'd asked a few of his friends at the party to find out her name, it hadn't connected the two of them anyway. They had different last names, plus he'd forgotten the first name of Kathleen's niece the few times he remembered her discussing Sophie.

He shouldn't be thinking of her now. One woman shouldn't be taking up so much real estate in his brain right now. He had just received the final contract from his lawyer, and the sale of his company had finally become real. His focus needed to be on it and not on a woman he kissed once and needed to be off-limits.

But he was beginning to no longer dread the upcoming party. The thought of seeing Sophie again sent a rush of excitement through him. Something that had been missing as of late. He enjoyed a challenge, a worthy opponent. When he thought of the women he tended to date, he realized they been carbon copies of each other.

Where had the excitement of seeing Sophie again come from? And when was the last time he honestly looked forward to being with a woman that hadn't only involved getting naked? There couldn't be any naked time with Sophie McMannis. Her connection to his assistant ruled that out. But it didn't mean he couldn't have a bit of fun.

An hour later, he'd sent off a ridiculous email, which included instructions for their date. He outlined how she should dress, nothing too low cut, and how she should act, polite, and not discuss politics or religion. He included a list of people he'd be introducing her to for good measure. He chuckled as he hit send.

Her reply didn't take long, and unlike his multi-paragraph email, Sophie's contained three words.

Find someone else.

Well, at least she didn't use the other F word. His plan hadn't been to piss her off so much as to get back at her for keeping her identity a secret from him. He didn't have time to continue the back and forth and closed the email without replying. He'd pay her a visit in person later today when he had a meeting downtown not far from her business.

He was meeting with Thomas "TS" Scott, the billionaire owner of the Idaho Outlaws. They were the newest franchise in the United States Baseball League. Today, they'd be finalizing any loose ends before Grant joined the partnership group. His dream of team ownership was so close, and it included the potential to bring future sports teams into the group, either in Pineville or elsewhere in the US.

The money he'd make from the sale of his company, along with investments he'd made during his career, gave him the financial leverage required to make his dream a reality.

He drove down Main Street toward the restaurant known as The Club and did his best to block out the festive decorations and window displays. Instead, he focused on the meeting with TS, and Blake Anderson, the Outlaws' manager. He and Blake had bonded during their rookie year chasing girls before he'd been traded to another team. They'd kept in touch through the years. Still, when Blake had moved to Pineville after taking on the manager position with the team a couple of years ago, they'd tried and failed to make their schedules work. Hopefully, that was all about to change when he became part of the organization.

He snagged a street-side parking spot in front of the busy restaurant, which happened to be one of his favorites. It was also owned by one of the Outlaws player's wives, and she always kept a table or two available for a player or the team owner. Another perk he could look forward to. Maybe he should bring Sophie here to discuss their upcoming date?

Where the hell had that come from? And when did he ever worry about where he would take a woman to dinner? Months of celibacy had obviously done more harm than good.

A light snow had begun to fall; he shrugged out of his overcoat, brushed the snowflakes out of his hair, and greeted TS and Blake. The three men, oblivious to the stares from the other patrons, shook hands and traded back slaps. After they each gave their drink and lunch orders to the waitress, Grant dived right in. "How are the trades going?" He'd been disappointed that he couldn't officially participate in building the upcoming season's roster until after the sale of his company was complete. He understood the conflict of interest clause the league had, but that didn't mean he liked it or couldn't work around it.

"It's coming together. We're almost there. We've been interviewing for a couple trainer positions as well as checking in with a few players who are making noises about moving across the country."

Grant had heard the rumors. Many in the league were still skeptical of a team full of older players, men who'd had issues in their personal lives that sometimes affected their performance on the baseball diamond; the bad boys of baseball had become an unofficial tag when speaking of the Outlaws.

Then there was living in an area of the country that was new to professional sports. Many thought the smaller market would eventually fail, but so far, they'd proven all the critics wrong.

Initially, Grant was concerned when the team's star player, Maverick Jansen, had had some dustups with the media when the team had first relocated from Boston. However, once he'd settled into Pineville and met his now-wife, Kelsey, and the VP of public relations, the outlook for the club's chances of winning a championship had drastically improved. Actually, it seemed the bad boys on the team were all finding love in Pineville, even TS and Blake, both of who'd recently married and become fathers. Grant was still having trouble seeing Blake as a family man.

The waitress delivered their drinks. "Sir, would you like anything else? Water, an appetizer, or…" He was used to flirting waitresses, and he'd noticed her quick glance at his left hand. "No, thank you. I'm fine." Grant turned his attention to TS and Blake. Both men wore wide grins.

"What?" He knew what was coming.

"You're not safe anywhere; it seems." TS chuckled.

Blake looked back at the retreating waitress. "She is a bit young for you. But if you're looking for--"

"Screw you, Anderson. I can get my own women. Just because you're all happy and tied up in domestic life now doesn't mean everyone is looking for the same thing." Grant knew he'd pay for the comment, but if you couldn't tease an old friend, then what was the point.

"I think he's jealous, TS. Poor guy, all alone. No one to come home to and crawl into a nice warm bed at night with. I think he needs our help." Blake and TS shared a look that spelled trouble for Grant.

An image of Sophie moments after he kissed her on New Year's flashed. Her lips swollen, her eyes heavy and questioning. He shook his head, not ready to examine why her face would come to mind as Blake and TS gushed about married life. "Look, I'm happy for both of you, but not every guy wants those things. And right now, my focus is on one thing. Team ownership."

"A quarter ownership." TS reminded him. "And I know exactly how you feel, Grant. Less than a year ago, man, I was you. But I'm not going to paint a rosy picture about marriage and fatherhood. It was a tough thing wrapping my head around at first. But both Noel and Carson are my world. Being a father has made everything else that much sweeter, you know?"

Shit. Not liking the switch to discussing family and sharing their feelings, Grant shifted in his seat. He should have ordered a double.

"Look, I get it. But when you're ready, you'll know. Or maybe it'll hit you over the head like it did me and then, well… then you're asking yourself why you resisted it in the first place." TS and Blake shared a look, then Blake added, "And Grant, it's the best, man. God, we didn't have a clue in college, did we? But, when you know, you know."

Grant didn't want any part of this conversation, "Yeah, I'm happy for you guys, but let's get back to our partnership. I received the paperwork from my attorney, and in less than two weeks, the sale of my firm will be finalized. What else do you need from me? I want to make sure I'm up to speed the moment it's a done deal."

TS's expression turned thoughtful, and for a moment, he thought the Outlaws' owner was going to tell him he'd changed his mind.

Grant let out the breath he wasn't aware he'd been holding. He'd had this dream for so long, he couldn't believe he was this close to realizing it and if... nope, not if, when. When the ink was dry, he wanted to be ready

T.S. took a sip of his drink, and the look disappeared. "A large part of my decision making is based on gut feeling--"

"But," Grant interrupted.

"No buts. A lot of people think that making money, being successful is being in the right place at the right time. That's part of it, no doubt. But it's also about instinct. Choosing the right people to help you achieve the goal and more. And in case you were wondering, I still believe you're the right fit, and I'm looking forward to building this team with you and more. So, relax. Enjoy your drink."

Grant nodded. He'd learned that the personal connections he had with his clients were what had helped him to create one of the most successful sports management companies in the country. And now he was ready to bring that to the Outlaws.

Their food was served, and after a few bites of the delicious meal, TS continued. "There's little left to do really. Now we just wait until your wire transfer is complete. After you hit billionaire status for a day, maybe two, you become cash poor and a quarter owner of a United States Baseball team."

Grant laughed. "I'm still a bit off the billionaire mark, but I'll get there."

TS held up his glass, and the three men toasted. "Here's to the Scott-Conrad Group, may we achieve all we set out to conquer."

"Amen. And amen to me keeping my hard-earned money in the bank while you two losers' foot all the bills." Blake took a sip of his drink and laughed. "And now that I have to negotiate my next contract with the two of you instead of just TS, I think now's a good time to mention I'm going to have another mouth to feed. My salary isn't nearly enough for a family of four. And Christmas is coming up too, so maybe you each could throw in an extra million or two."

Grant held back a groan at the mention of Christmas. He kept his mouth shut on that topic since everyone thought he was a scrooge anyway. Besides, he was happy for Blake and his wife, Caris. He didn't begrudge others from wanting marriage and parenthood. He just never saw himself as needing either one.

They'd adopted a little girl last year from Puerto Rico, where Blake's mother was from. However, he didn't realize that they were still trying to have their own child after Caris's infertility issues.

"Man, that's awesome news, congratulations." TS slapped Blake on the back and signaled the waitress. "This news deserves another round."

When the fresh drinks arrived, Grant joined TS in raising his glass, "To the Anderson's. And Blake, better you than me. Fatherhood suits you. I mean that. But you're going to have to do more than impregnate your beautiful wife to increase your already seven-figure salary, like say win next year's pennant race?"

"C'mon, Grant. Just wait till you find the *one* and start making babies. Kids are the best, but they're not cheap. And I'll take you up on the challenge you just put out there and expect you to pay up when it happens." Blake drained his glass and set it down with a loud bang. "Man, I can't wait till your scroogie-ass gets knocked over by a woman. I'll be the first one to help you up and say, 'I told you so.'"

"That'll be a long wait, my friend. The women I date know I'm a poor bet in the relationship department. The bachelor's life is the best life. No expectations, no drama." Grant finished his drink and checked the time. It was nearing five p.m., and if he left now, then he should be able to catch Sophie--catch her off-guard, that is. He had plans for her, and none of them included the happily-ever-after TS, and Blake tried to convince him he needed.

No, his plans for Sophie were definitely more naughty than nice.

CHAPTER 2

Grant hadn't felt this level of anticipation overseeing a woman since, well, college when his hormones ruled his decisions. He parked in front of Sophie's building, impressed with the location. She must be doing well. The rent wasn't cheap in this section of town.

He entered the renovated church and smiled at the receptionist. "Hello, is Ms. McMannis available?"

Sophie came out of the backroom and cut off Evie's response.

"Ask someone else. I changed my mind."

"Nice to see you again, too, Sophie. It's a shame we didn't share contact information last time we met. Makes me wonder why you didn't tell your aunt when she asked you to be my date."

"That's between myself and my aunt. I didn't want to cause her any awkwardness at work. Listen, my answer remains the same. Ask someone else."

"I wouldn't be here if there was someone else available to take to this damn party," Grant muttered. This woman had already gotten under his skin, been under his skin for months. And now that they were face to face again, he didn't want to let her out of his sight. He'd question his motivations later.

"You have a funny way of handling your dates, Mr. Conrad. Do you always send out such a detailed expectation list, or am I just special?"

"It was my way of breaking the ice. Once I saw your business card, I realized you'd kept some information from me when we met. Think of it as an icebreaker." He took in her appearance. Her hair hung loosely around her shoulders. Dark and wavy, he fought down the urge to run a hand through one of the silky curls. He took a step closer as she eyed him warily. Her scent washed over him, a hint of peppermint and something undefinable. It made him wonder if he kissed her now would she taste like she smelled.

"Why doesn't your aunt know we've met before?" Grant asked.

"Because she doesn't need to know, and I don't need to explain myself to you. Now, if you'll excuse me, I need to finish a project in the back."

She turned to her assistant and spoke as if he'd already left. "Evie, can you call Marlene and let her know I'll be there soon. I'm almost finished with the special garland." Sophie, without so much as a good-bye, stalked from the front office toward the back room.

Grant followed her and admired the sway of her hips. He rarely took no for an answer, and he couldn't recall a woman saying it to his face. "You know, you could give me a second chance. I'm not used to begging, and I really could use your help."

"You really have a problem taking no for an answer, don't you? Did Santa put you on his naughty list, and now you're trying to redeem yourself?" She stood her ground, hands on hips, hips he wanted to get his hands on again and fell just a little in love right then and there. *Whoa.*

There had been too much talk about love and feelings at lunch. He needed to rethink his decision to go out with the niece of his best employee. An employee he didn't want to be hurt because he messed things up with Sophie.

But damn this woman, if he were looking, would be perfect for him. She stood up to him when others rarely did. She was gorgeous, smart, and presented the very thing he couldn't resist—a challenge.

"Look, let me buy you dinner tonight, and we can start over. Sophie, if Kathleen likes me, hell she's put up with me for six years, then I can't be all that bad, right? Give me a chance. I'll be a perfect gentleman. I promise."

"It's eleven days before a major holiday—my busiest time of the year. I can't just put everything on hold because you want to play nice. I've already told you; I have plans."

Grant hated this conversation. Every year he received the same excuses from staff members, business associates. Work still needed to be completed, no matter the commercialized hype.

"C'mon, Christmas is just another day. I understand you have a business to run, but...uh oh, what did I say?" As soon as he said it, he knew he'd stepped in it.

Her lips thinned, and her body went rigid. The air in the room took on a frosty heaviness. *Dammit.*

"I said, I have plans," Sophie said.

"Break them." Hell, why not double down. The air between them filled with an undeniable current of attraction. He wanted, no needed, so for some indefinable reason to have her pick him over her plans. What was it about Sophie he just couldn't walk away from?

"Not these plans. I need to drop off some decorations for a very important client. And what is your deal with Christmas anyway? Santa bring you coal when you were a kid, and now you have to ruin it for everyone else?"

Again, with the Santa crap. Grant held back a curse, "Look; I'm not here to discuss my opinions on Christmas, which is an over-commercialized, made-up holiday by toy manufacturers. You agreed to a date, and I'm here to make sure you follow through on your promise. My level of Christmas spirit is not up for debate."

Wrong thing to say. She recoiled as if he'd stomped on her favorite toy.

"Who are you to come into my place of business and make demands? One shared kiss gives you zero rights with me."

"It was one hell of a kiss though wasn't it, Sophie? C'mon, It's after five o'clock. Finish your project tomorrow. I'm sure whoever they are, they can survive one more night without whatever fluff it is you have in that box."

SOPHIE SEARCHED for something to throw. She paced around her storeroom and took in one deep breath after another. Grant had her tied up in all kinds of knots. She heard the words come out his mouth, but her attention had been focused on his lips, on that kiss. Damn, it was almost a year ago, and she still couldn't get that night out of her head. And now he was here, in her space, and it made him think of things better left alone. Then on top of it all, he just didn't get that what she had to do was just as important as his business.

After reading the ridiculous email he sent her, she knew the best thing to do was back out. She'd deal with Aunt Kat's disappointment later.

She still didn't understand why her aunt had made this--him, the requested favor Sophie had made her promise she would ask for one day when she'd discovered how much debt her aunt had gone into to pay for college.

She'd known that money had been tight in the beginning. But she'd thought her parents' life insurance would be enough to cover her degree.

Kat had given her a home where she felt loved and never a burden. Sophie owed her, she wanted to fulfill her promise, but he was making it nearly impossible.

It made her sad, and his words had gone straight to her identity. She lived for the holidays. The tradition, the memories she tightly held onto. Not sure he meant to personally hurt her, but now she felt compelled to find out why he was a card-carrying scrooge. No one developed that level of hatred over something without a good reason.

"Sophie, let's just move past this silly conversation and call a truce. I'll take you to dinner, and we can discuss the party."

"Silly?" The tiny bit of empathy she'd begun to feel vanished. She eyed a small vase on the shelf above him. She immediately dismissed the idea of smashing it over his big head; she wasn't that quick. "Tell me something, Grant, are you always this rude, or is it just the season that has you acting like an asshole?"

"That's an interesting description. And, no, I don't typically go out of my way to be an asshole, no matter the time of year."

"You really don't like Christmas, do you?" Empathy returned. And something else she didn't want to name.

He remained silent and continued staring at her as if she'd never spoken. Sophie was now positive he was hiding something when it came to Christmas. Something she knew about first hand because of her own personal tragedy. The difference being instead of hating the holiday, she'd embraced it.

When she lost her parents to a car crash on Christmas Eve, she chose to honor her parents by treasuring the holiday each year. It was her mother's favorite time of year, and she'd always gone overboard with the decorations and baked a ton of cookies.

Her mom's pure joy stuck with Sophie, and she didn't want to lose it just because she lost them. Exhausting herself to near collapse to make her client's events memorable also brought her joy. And she wasn't going to disappoint tonight's special client. Not for him.

"All right, I can compromise. I'll take you to drop off your decorations, and then we'll go to dinner—"

"To discuss your wonderful list of do's and don'ts?" Sophie interrupted.

"Ah, now the truth comes out. You're mad because I thoughtfully sent you an email about what to expect at the gala. This isn't your typical dine and dance, end of the year party. A business deal, mine, will be announced that evening, and I need someone with me to keep the society hens away. I can only accomplish that by having a date. It's business, Sophie, not pleasure."

He could have fooled her. A hint of desperation and the interest in his eyes made her think otherwise. "Mr. Conrad, I feel sorry for you."

"Why? And drop the Mr. Conrad bit. I think we're on a first-name basis, don't you?"

Taking in a slow breath, she counted to ten before she spoke.

"You've managed to bring what should be a joyous time of year to its lowest common denominator. Just another day. Another opportunity to make money when, in truth, it should be a time to embrace the true meaning behind Christmas."

"And, Ms. McMannis, what would that meaning be?"

"You'll have to figure that one out for yourself. But guess what? I've changed my mind; I'm willing to compromise. You can take me to dinner, but only if you come with me to my appointment. If I don't leave now, I'll be late."

"Sophie, that's—"

She held up her hand to cut him off. "Just business, right? If you want to convince me to go to the party with you, do it while we eat— later. But right now, I'm not about to disappoint my newest client, and I could really use some help with this heavy box." She smiled sweetly, daring him to say no.

Sophie picked up the boxful of mistletoe-laced garland for the pediatric cancer ward and her special patient, thrust it into Grant's chest, and walked through the exit. She left *Mr. Scrooge* to follow her —or not. But, if a man ever needed a dose of Christmas spirit, it was Grant Conrad.

If she couldn't get through to him, maybe the children could.

Challenge accepted. He carried the box to his car and managed to open the door for her. He glanced at her as he plugged the address she'd given him into the GPS. She was just as gorgeous as he remembered. The night they met, her dark brown hair had been pulled up and had him itching to take it down during their kiss. Today, it was down. And he had an urge to lean across the seat and mess it up. In the time since he walked into her shop, his initial attraction for her had doubled. Once he convinced her to change her mind about the party. First, he had to avoid any further discussion on the merits of the holiday he'd grown to despise. And he needed to stop daydreaming about getting his hands on her.

Right now, she was throwing off icy waves of indifference, and he needed a new tactic to warm her up. The best way to do that was to separate the smart, sexy, and currently pissed off Sophie from her business-suit-encased curves. His new objective was to remind her how well they fit together.

Used to making split decisions in business, he relied on his inner radar when it came to his company, so why not use it with Sophie? He hadn't needed to woo a woman in a long time. He may be a bit out of practice, but she had no idea what she was up against when he decided he wanted something. And he wanted Sophie McMannis.

Not paying attention to where they were going as he mentally plotted his plans for Sophie, he thought the GPS voiceover said something about a hospital. When he heard it repeat Harmony Hospital was located on the right, he turned to Sophie and asked for the address again.

"It sounds like I entered the wrong address. Could you—"

"No, this is the place. The entrance to the underground garage is up ahead. If we hustle, we can still make it in time." She said.

"In time? In time for what? Are you visiting a sick friend before you drop off the decorations?"

She sent him a bright smile. Damn, she was beautiful when she wasn't mad at him. He'd have to make sure he gave her plenty to smile about later that night.

"Um, something like that," Sophie answered. She pointed toward a space next to the elevator. "Look, there's a perfect spot."

Grant said nothing to her evasive comment. Why would she want to go here, and why not just answer the simple question?

He followed her with the box of decorations as she made a phone call.

"Hi, Marlene, I'm on my way up. Is she up for this?"

Why would she have to check on the readiness of her client? Did she think so little of him that he'd refuse if she'd been up-front with where they were going?

He'd help her deliver her box of Christmas fluff, play nice with whomever she was there to meet, and wine and dine her before taking her back to his place for a night of—

"That sounds perfect, Marlene. Thank you for setting this up. See you in a minute."

Sophie put her cell away and faced him with another dazzling smile. "So, I guess I should let you know what's going on."

"You didn't need to hide from me where we were going. I'm sure the doctors and nurses will appreciate all your efforts. Are you decorating their breakroom or—"

"Um, no. We're not here for the staff, Grant. We're on our way up to the pediatric cancer ward. Each year I bring decorations based on the requests of the children. This is my final delivery. They had a little girl admitted earlier in the week, and well, I need to make sure her room is the way she wants it for Christmas."

"You're doing this…" he nodded down at the large box, "all for one little girl?" Grant asked.

"Why is that so strange? I'm not going to let her feel left out. Besides, it's Christmastime."

Grant again marveled at her attitude toward the holiday. Never would he spend time fulfilling the needs of someone for such an over-rated day, but he had to admit, seeing Sophie's smile made him decide on the spot he could make an exception this one time. Damn, he had it bad for her.

"You don't look like you think this is a worthwhile endeavor." She said.

"It's not that. I was just wondering about all this effort for one child when you're obviously busy with other projects so close to the holi-day." He followed her to the elevator and tried to read her body posture. Had he totally messed up his chances with her?

"I believe children need happy Christmas memories. And that's hard to do when you spend it in the hospital, battling cancer. It can quickly become a depressing time for the child and their family. And I do everything I can to make sure it's not."

"Ah, so you're a do-gooder. Once a year, you spread holiday cheer to the sick to make yourself feel better. I can appreciate it," Grant stated.

Sophie's eyelids dropped, and the smile that had previously lit her face turned into a thin line. Sophie went from happy and relaxed, too stiff and business-like before his very eyes.

Calling himself every kind of fool, he silently watched as she turned away from him and stepped into the elevator. She punched a couple of buttons and focused her gaze on the lights above the door as they crept upward toward their destination.

Yup, he really stepped in it. His mind scrambled to come up with something to make it better, but he had nothing. He thought his childhood memories of a depressed mother and absent father buried deep enough to no longer affect his daily life. However, Sophie's empathy for others had triggered something in him. He needed to get a grip on his emotions and his words.

"Mr. Conrad, I'm not sure what your agenda is, but I'm not falling into a pointless discussion with you on the merits of the holiday and how I choose to celebrate. You obviously have some darker issues buried beneath that handsome face of yours, so why don't you just give me the box? I'm this close to…no, you know what? You can leave. I'll call a cab to take me back to my office."

The look on her face left no doubt what she was about to say and do. She looked as if she would have no problem smacking him and in front of witnesses no less. He definitely had an outlet for all that pent-up emotion. He just wished she wasn't related to Kathleen. And he was on the verge of no longer caring about it and doing everything he could to convince Sophie to channel all that energy with him in bed.

"You're dismissing me? After one stupid comment? Okay, don't answer that. I know it was a low blow, and I…I apologize for questioning your efforts. I simply don't get all the hubbub over a holiday that really doesn't mean anything and, in my opinion, brings families together under false pretenses with expected gift-giving. Christmas is for—"

"Don't finish that sentence. I'm already beyond pissed. Don't give me a reason to punch you in the nose." Sophie huffed.

So much for getting back on her good side. Man, he sucked at this. "All right… all right. I get it. No more talk about why I can't stand this holiday." Grant shifted the box to rest on his hip and grabbed Sophie's hand. "Please, let me help you out here, and then we'll go grab something to eat. We can talk about anything you want, except Christmas. Truce?"

Sophie opened her mouth to answer him. Unfortunately, her answer became lost in the ping of the elevator bell; the doors opened on the fifth floor, the pediatric cancer ward. Grant looked directly into the faces of two nurses standing behind the counter situated across from the elevators. He flashed a smile, "Ladies, hello," and waited for Sophie to step out of the elevator.

The nurses returned his smile and called out a greeting to Sophie. He'd given her no choice but to let him off the hook unless she wanted to make a scene, and Grant didn't want that any more than he was sure Sophie did.

Under his breath, he asked, "Are you getting out, Ms. McMannis? Looks like a couple of nurses are waiting for you to decide. You can castrate me later. Right now, let me help you.

Sophie stepped out of the elevator, ignoring him.

Grant locked onto her backside as her hips swayed and suppressed a groan. How was he going to handle spending time with her without touching her?

She spoke with the nurses while he debated on his next move. Sophie, on the other hand, had no trouble pretending he wasn't right next to her.

Damn, it was going to be a long night.

CHAPTER 3

$\mathcal{W}$as there ever a man in existence who'd figured out the mind of a woman? If there were, you'd think the bro-code would have been activated, and it would have been shared world-wide. Fanciful thinking aside, he was a bit shell-shocked over why he continued to take Sophie's dismissal of him. What made her different from any of the other women he wanted? Women who'd barely held his attention for longer than it took to exchange small talk and seduce them into his bed?

She was his anti-type. A woman who didn't fall for his charm and wit. It had been forever since he'd been turned down. So long, in fact, he couldn't remember a single instance. And she didn't merely turn him down; she slammed the door and put him in his place. She'd threatened bodily harm, and he… liked it. Then she'd waived a red flag and ignited his win-at-all-costs mentality.

Well, game on.

He decided to ignore her ignoring him, placed the box on the end of the counter, and took a long look around the children's ward's open layout. An odd mixture of silence and noise from TVs came at him as he began to stroll down one of the three corridors.

He noticed most of the doorways to the patient rooms were already decked out in red, green, white, or silver garlands. Some had hand-drawn reindeer or Santa Claus cut-outs taped to the doors. There were dancing elves on the walls between each room. One lonely doorway was empty of the festive colors. Drawn to its clean lines, he walked toward it and stopped at its threshold.

He could hear the beeps and whirs of the machinery located next to the hospital bed, a bed-sized perfectly for a child—a child who was nowhere to be seen. Grant paused. For a moment, he questioned his motive in entering the room. He shrugged. He was here, and curiosity won out.

A trail of wires and clear tubing led to the floor. Leaning over the bed, he noticed a blanket tucked underneath and heard maniacal laughter. Concerned, he stepped back and bent down for a closer look and came eye-to-eye with a pixie. There was no other description that fit the tiny girl. The pixie wore a purple headband around a perfectly round, bald head with wide green eyes.

"Hi," the pixie said.

"Hi, back." Grant smiled.

"Are you a doctor? You don't look like a doctor?"

"No, my name's Grant Conrad. Why don't you think I'm a doctor?"

"Because your shoes don't squeak. All the doctors and nurses have noisy shoes."

Grant thought about it, and she was right. His shoes didn't squeak. "Well, then I'm definitely not a doctor. Or a nurse. What's your name?"

"Lily Ann Dupree."

"Pleasure to meet you, Lily Ann Dupree. Can I ask you a question?

"Sure." She turned her head to the side and smiled.

At that moment, Grant lost a little bit of his heart to the pixie hiding under the bed. "How come you're hiding under here? Isn't it cold on the floor?"

"Not too cold. I have my blanket. See? And besides, I like it down here."

"Hmm, kinda like a fort?"

"Yes! Oh, you understand. No one likes me to be down here, but my mom has to work late, and the nurses aren't supposed to be back for a bit, so I hide out down here… away from the noise."

"The noise?"

"Yeah, you know those machines I'm attached to. Too noisy." Lily Ann wrinkled her nose.

He cleared the sudden lump in his throat. "Ah, I guess that would annoy me, too. But it's kinda hard for adults to have a conversation with you when you're under the bed."

"There's plenty of room. C'mon, I'll show you." Lily Ann, the Pixie, scooted her blanket, iPad, and herself further under the bed, making room for Grant. "See, even someone as big as you can fit right here."

Lily Ann pointed to a spot barely big enough for another child her size.

He was sure his six-two frame wouldn't fit but didn't want to hurt her feelings.

"You'll have to get down on your belly because you're too tall to sit on your bum like me, see?" Lily Ann encouraged.

He squatted down for a better view of the enchanting child who had no qualms about talking to a stranger.

Charmed didn't come close to what Grant felt. This wisp of a girl, far from home, attached to machinery, opened her heart to let a stranger into her sanctuary. "That's very kind of you, Pixie, but you don't know me. Where are your parents?"

"My momma's at work, and I don't know about my daddy. He's been gone for a while. Hey, you called me Pixie, but I said my name's Lily Ann," she giggled.

Pushing aside the ache her words caused, he kept his response light. "I know, but you look like a little pixie hiding in a deep, dark forest. Besides, don't all pixies have pretty headbands and wear flowing white dresses? So, to me, you're a pixie."

Squeaky shoes sounded down the hallway, and Lily Ann's gaze turned downcast. She let out a dramatic sigh.

"That's the nurse. Guess I need to get back in bed. It's probably time for my medicine."

Grant was torn. This little girl had captured his imagination and kick-started his protective instincts. First, Sophie threw him off balance, and now Lily Ann. Maybe he could negotiate a compromise with the nurse.

He got back up on his knees, braced his hands on the bed to pull himself up, and readied himself for a negotiation. He locked eyes, not with the nurse, but with the woman who did wild things to his pulse. Draped in greenery, she held a step stool in one hand and a stapler in the other. Gone was the tight-lipped look of moments ago, now replaced by a soft smile—for him.

"What?" He grinned. "You've never seen someone talk to a pixie before?" he asked.

"No, this would be my first time," Sophie said.

"Well, allow me the pleasure. Ms. McMannis, I'd like to introduce you to your very first pixie, Miss Lily Ann Dupree. Miss Lily Ann, I mean, Pixie, I'd like to introduce you to Ms. Sophie McMannis. She's here to decorate your room. Right, Sophie?"

Lily Ann giggled. "I'm not really a pixie, but Mr. Conrad says I look like one."

Sophie walked through the small room and searched. "Where's the pixie, Grant? I hear her, but why can't I see her?"

More giggles escaped from under the bed.

Grant looked to the doorway and received a wink from the nurse as she entered the room.

"All right, sorry, everyone, I need to break up the fun. Lily Ann, it's time for your next dose. Back up on the bed, please."

"But I'm having fun!" Lily Ann sniffed.

"I know, sweetheart, but we've talked about this before. And your mom just called and said to begin without her. She's stuck in traffic. Now let's get you all settled and ready, my brave girl."

"Okay," Lily Ann whispered.

Grant noticed the little girl's lower lip tremble as she came out from under the bed. He helped her up and gave her a big smile. "Could I stay? I've never seen a brave pixie before?"

"Oh, yes, please!" Lily Ann pleaded with the nurse.

The nurse looked first at Grant, then at Sophie. Worried he was about to be thrown out, "I'd like to—"

"Um, Marlene, he's with me. He's my, ah… intern and wanted to help decorate Lily Ann's room."

Damn, she was quick on her feet. He liked that in a woman. Grant turned away to hide his smile, handed Lily Ann her blanket, and tucked her in.

"An intern? Girl, bless you. I wish I had an intern who looked like him. Sure, I guess it's okay, Ms. McMannis. You do so much for the hospital to brighten our kids' rooms and spirits. But the next time you bring one of your interns, you give us a warning so we can freshen up a bit, okay?" Marlene sent Grant another wink and pushed her cart closer to Lily Ann's bed.

Sophie reached over, tugged Grant's suit jacket, and mouthed, "thank you." He wasn't sure what compelled him to this room or to stay and interact with the brave Miss Lily Ann the Pixie, but he was glad he'd followed his impulse.

Sophie had opened him up to all types of new emotions today. He may still struggle with the craziness of Christmas, but one thing he understood was the loneliness of a child and needing someone to make you feel special.

After the nurse administered Lily Ann's medication, Sophie went back into her party planner mode and issued directions. But all he could think about was getting her into a dark corner somewhere and kissing her till they both couldn't remember why they'd argued earlier.

She'd placed the stepstool underneath the doorway and handed him the stapler. "I'm going to position the garland, and I need you to put a staple in between my hands, okay? Then we'll finish off with the snowflakes I brought to hang from the ceiling."

Grant couldn't argue with that idea, especially since it put him at eye level with Sophie's full breasts. He grinned, "Yes, ma'am," and did what he was told to do. Maybe her bossiness carried over into the bedroom.

From the bed, Lily Ann began singing a Christmas song while they hung the garland.

"You know, Ms. Sophie, I like the garland with the little white ball flowers. What are they called?"

Sophie froze with her hands still over her head, the garland hanging down one of her shoulders.

She looked at him. A plea for help in her eyes.

"Yes, Ms. Sophie, what type of flowers are you holding?"

He was enjoying her discomfort, darn him. She stuck out her tongue and turned towards Lily Ann. Wrong move on her part. He shifted with her and placed his hands on her hips.

She took a moment and tried to forget he was touching her. It didn't work. "Well, actually, it's not a flower, Lily Ann. It's called mistletoe. And it's a traditional plant displayed at Christmas." Her insides began to heat. Her mouth went dry, and her heart picked up speed. Why couldn't he be five two and bald?

"Ooh, I've heard of mistletoe. That means you need to kiss Ms. Sophie, Mr. Conrad. It's a tradition."

Lily Ann's innocent demand spurred Grant into action. He turned her to face him. She couldn't meet his gaze.

"That sounds like a great idea, Pixie. I wouldn't want to miss out on such a time-honored tradition. Ms. Sophie, pucker up."

Not giving her a chance to step down, Grant grabbed Sophie's waist, swung her down to the ground, and placed his lips firmly upon her startled mouth. It was a chaste kiss but, when she slammed her lips shut, he began to nip at them until she relaxed with a sigh.

He ended the kiss before she was ready. When she opened her eyes, he looked a bit dazed. She certainly was. He also looked a tad smug because he knew she wouldn't make a scene in front of Lily Ann. She'd save that for later.

Since they had an audience, she gave him a small smile and cleared her throat. "Um, okay, now that we have that tradition taken care of, we need to finish up in here so Lily Ann can get some sleep."

"Aw, but I never get visitors. Can't you just stay until my mom gets here, please?"

"Yes, please, Ms. Sophie?" Grant asked.

"I'd like to meet your mom, Pixie. Does she look just like you?" He added.

"No, she has brown eyes and brown hair, silly. I'm bald, but I used to have blonde hair. But when it grows'd back, it might not be blonde. It might be darker. But that's okay because then I will look like my mom. Except for the eyes though, 'cause mine are green," Lily Ann stated.

So matter of fact for someone who'd been through so much.

A look passed between them. A moment where they needed to know they weren't the only one struggling to contain the tug of raw emotion over Lily Ann's answer. Who could say no to a pixie all alone in a hospital bed?

"Well, I guess we can stay. I'd like to meet your mom too," Sophie said.

CHAPTER 4

Grant's emotions were still on a roller coaster when he and Sophie exited the elevator back into the parking garage.

Whatever the future held for Sophie and him would work itself out. But making sure Lily Ann had a joyous Christmas experience this year had become his new priority. He was confident he could pull it off without falling too far down the commercialized holiday's hyped-up black hole. Although keeping his reputation as a Scrooge had just become harder.

He assisted Sophie onto the passenger seat. Neither of them had said much since leaving Lily Ann's room. After he pulled out into traffic, he felt more than saw the question in Sophie's gaze.

"Thank you for coming with me this evening, Grant, but I'm feeling pretty wiped. Could we postpone dinner? I'd be up for meeting for coffee to discuss the—"

"No kid deserves to go through the battle she's fighting. Hell, she's what, eight? And the nurse, Marlene, told me it's her second go-around. Shit, life just isn't fair." Grant revved the engine. He couldn't take his anger and frustration out on Lily Ann's cancer, so he took it out on his car. The light turned green. He sped away, tires squealing.

"Slow down, please. I changed my mind. Let's stop for a quick bite, okay? Look, there's a cafe on the corner." Sophie pleaded.

He ignored her request and blew through the next light.

"Are you insane?! Grant Conrad, slow this car down now. Better yet, pull over and let me out. I'll find my own way back to the office."

Grant continued to ignore her shouted requests.

Sophie reached over, punched the start button, and punched him in the arm when nothing happened.

"What the…? Are you nuts? Do you want us to crash?" Grant shouted.

"Do you?" she challenged.

Grant eased the car into the nearest parking lot and rolled to a stop. Breathing heavy, he gripped the steering wheel and let out a short laugh. "Jesus, Sophie. Forgive me, please. I'm so sorry. I've never…. I mean, this is not like me; usually, I'm…"

"Cool and calculated?"

"Yeah, something like that." He relaxed his grip and sat back in his seat.

"I guess it's just been a long day, you know? I've never been around someone who has cancer, and for it to be such a small child…"

Plus, no one stands up to me, and I usually hate that. But not you. For some twisted reason, I find it a hell of a turn on. And I…you've got me all tied up in knots. Do you know that, Sophie?" Grant shifted toward her, desperate to touch her. "You reappear in my life just when I don't need the complication of a woman. And then I meet Lily Ann, and her attitude just blows me away. You…" He ended his speech before he gave too much away. And, screw it. He'd show her how he felt.

Grant captured Sophie's stubborn chin and locked her in place. Ignoring the voice that kept repeating, *you don't have time for this, run!* He feathered kisses along her brow line and whispered, "How 'bout it, Sophie? Take the leap with me. Let's see where tonight takes us." He waited for her to pull away or tell him off. When she didn't, he did what he'd wanted to do all night. To devour her until neither one of them could think.

She returned his kiss and threaded her fingers in his hair, bringing him in closer. Her response was more than he could have asked. It was perfect. And it scared the hell out of him.

He'd never allowed himself to feel anything for the women he slept with. He always made sure they knew going in that it was only a physical connection. But not with Sophie. She'd managed to get under his skin and chip away at the shield around his heart. And it'd only taken a few hours.

He kissed her as if he was a teenager again, racing against the curfew clock to get one last kiss in. The kiss continued until neither of them could breathe. When he came up for air, a dam broke inside him. He began to chuckle and rained kisses on her beautiful face.

"Care to share what's so funny."

He laughed harder at the stern look on her face.

"Listen, I'm not taking your laughter as a compliment, Grant. Maybe we should go back to the hospital and pay a visit to the staff psychiatrist."

Real worry laced her words.

Guilt sprung up. "Sorry. I'm … sorry. This entire day has been full of firsts, and I'm still adjusting. Plus, I find out you've been hiding in plain sight all along." Grant pulled her back toward him as far as the console would allow. "Give me a chance, Sophie." He whispered, "Attend the party with me. Please?"

"And then?" she asked.

"And then, after all the nonsense of the holidays, we could explore what's happening between us."

"Nonsense, huh?" Sophie pushed out of his arms and settled back in her seat.

She turned her gaze out the front window. She stared for so long without saying a word; he worried she'd never speak to him again. He glanced outside to find out what had fascinated her. The world had turned into a fairyland with twinkle lights entwined on the lampposts, their glow glittering on the storefront windows. Snow continued to fall lightly. The outside of the car looked as surreal as it felt inside.

"Grant, I'm not sure we would work, short-term or otherwise. Then there's Aunt Kat, and well spending any more time together could just lead us on the road to nowhere."

She continued before he could answer, "This has happened… too fast, and I want to make the right decision—for both of us. Can you give me a couple of days?" Sophie asked.

"A couple of days isn't going to change my mind. But if that's what you need. I can be reasonable. Don't look so shocked. I have many sides you haven't seen—yet."

He waited a beat. He'd hoped for another smile. A chuckle. Anything. Instead, she remained silent.

He started the car to take her home. "Whether you agree to attend the party with me or not, I'm not letting this go." He pointed his finger between them. "You and I need to finish this without having the favor you owe your aunt hanging over our heads. And Sophie?"

"Yes?"

"Have you wondered yet why Kathleen set us up?"

Her face scrunched up, and he wanted to drop a kiss on the wrinkle that appeared on her nose.

"No, well, yes. But I'm sure it's nothing personal. She was just doing what a good assistant does, and besides, we're as different as two people could be. I mean, I don't like sports, and you hate Christmas and--"

Grant took the hand she was waving in the air to make her point and brought it to his lips. He placed a soft kiss on the back of her hand. "I'll give you two days to decide. Then I'll call you, okay?"

She nodded and tugged her hand free.

He started his car and before he pulled back out onto the street. "Oh, and Sophie," he made sure to make eye contact with her as he reversed out of the lot, "hiding behind our differences is off the table. Because everything in my world is negotiable."

CHAPTER 5

*W*ith an hour to spare, and instead of calling, Sophie texted Grant.

I'LL GO.

Because, of course, she would. She'd given her word. And she texted to avoid her own feelings, and she didn't have a free night before the party to have the dinner he wanted, but mostly she didn't want to hear his voice. She'd been thinking a lot about him, and hearing him speak with his deep, rumbly, sexy voice made her want things she shouldn't.

He may think nothing of having revolving bed partners or the fact her aunt worked for him, but she couldn't do that to Aunt Kat nor herself. So, she was surprised when he called her each night around ten thirty for the past week.

She began to look forward to his call after she'd removed her make-up and slipped into her comfy sweats and an over-sized, super soft, long-sleeved Henley t-shirt.

Each night he'd provide her with a bit of trivia about who would be attending the gala, and then they'd end up going off on tangents. And some barely veiled sexual innuendos, from herself as well, which left her hot, confused, and very excited to see Grant again in person.

They debated which restaurant had the best rib-eye steaks in town or which Star Trek movie in the new franchise was better. They even discussed Aunt Kathleen and the reason why Sophie had been raised by her after her parents were killed in a car accident. Still, nothing was said about why he hated Christmas.

It was strange to have conversations with a man who'd kissed her only twice and melted her insides each time; the first was heady, full of desperation, and the second--sweet, on the verge of chaste but no less devastating to her self-preservation. Then to not discuss their attraction. Not once did he try to talk her into a hook-up. It was unexpected. Grant Conrad was a nice guy for a died-in-the-wool scrooge.

As she drove through downtown Pineville, she took in the sparkle of ornament-wrapped wreaths, red and green—everything. She recalled their conversation. It had been late, and the huskiness of his voice had made her want to see him.

She could have seen him, but she didn't want her hormones to take over. She was enjoying the build-up of anticipation for their date tonight. She continued to use work as an excuse. And she was super busy, so she hadn't technically lied.

There was a last-minute party she agreed to design, and then there were the reindeer she somehow managed to book for her best, although far from a favorite client. The client's unlimited budget had convinced the local ranch owner to haul his herd into town last minute.

With all that behind her, she needed some insider information on Grant Conrad. And she had just the person—her Aunt. The problem was how to ask without raising Kathleen's suspicions. The business-only date had now turned personal, compelling her to know if Grant had the capacity to change just one little thing. Alright, a big little thing, but it was a deal-breaker.

Whenever she needed guidance, Aunt Kathleen zeroed in on what she couldn't. Her solutions always worked. It was her superpower. And she needed some of that power today.

So, she'd turned over the only event scheduled for the day to Evie, confident the holiday brunch was in good hands. She stopped at the high-end dress store she would never have stepped foot in had it not been for Grant.

The evening dress with its low back was more daring than she would have typically worn, but last-minute shopping wasn't her friend this time of year. But secretly, she loved it. It made her feel sexy, and she couldn't help to wonder how Grant would react when he saw her. The contradictory feelings were driving her insane.

Maybe she shouldn't have stayed away from him? What was that stupid saying, "*distance made the heart grow fonder*?" But in her case, distance and nightly phone calls made her body want him in a desperate way that was new and exciting. She'd begun thinking way too often of how he'd look naked in her bed. How his lips and hands would feel as they touched and explored and…ugh, she should just jump him tonight and find out. Lordy, was this what men went through when they were hot and horny for a woman? Or did it have to be the right person to feel this intense ache and need for someone? She'd never fantasized to this extent over any of the handful of guys she'd been with. And lusting over Henry Cavill didn't count since he was totally unobtainable.

Could she sleep with Grant once and then move on? Would she be able to look her aunt in the eye again? Maybe he'd changed his mind? Perhaps she was going cuckoo for cocoa puffs over something that wasn't ever going to happen. *Get a grip, Soph. It's one date. A few hours with the man. Keep it in your pants and deal.*

A blaring horn snapped her attention back to reality. Lack of sleep had taken over her brain cells and turned her into a carnal version she didn't recognize but really wanted to meet. One day. Not today or with Grant. But maybe she should start saying yes to Amber and Evie's invitations for a girl's night to O'Malley's Pub. They all could use a night to let loose, and you never knew, prince charming hung out in bars just like all the other guys, right?

Sophie waved to the guy behind her after he blasted his horn a second time and turned into the parking lot between the salon and deli on Sherman Avenue. She'd made a hair appointment since she sucked at up-do's and asked her aunt to meet her. She'd had always loved her long hair, but it took hours for her to style. And for an event like this, she needed help taming its thick mass.

As she walked into the salon, she breathed in Christmas. White and red candles stood sentry on the check-in desk. The scent of peppermint floated in the air. Memories of baking candy cane kiss cookies with her mom washed over her. She sighed and relaxed for the first time all day.

She was under the dryer, curlers covering her head, when Aunt Kathleen finally arrived.

"Sorry I'm late, dear. There were some last-minute changes to a contract Grant needed. But we got it done. This deal means everything to him."

Her aunt had never shared specific information about her job before. Uncomfortable knowing the intimate details of Grant's business, Sophie debated. Should she change the subject or allow Kathleen to give her some insight into how? Curiosity won. She kept silent.

Aunt Kat sat in the chair next to her and patted her hand. "Don't you worry, he'll be in a better mood at the party."

"Better mood? What happened?"

"Mr. Kemper wanted to structure the payout with a longer time frame. Grant hit the roof. I don't think I've ever seen him so mad."

Shoot. This was not what Sophie wanted to hear hours before their date. Yes, she'd wanted her aunt to give her a peek into Grant's personality, but this information struck her as intrusive. She knew her aunt would never compromise her working relationship with her boss by giving out sensitive information, even to her.

A tinge of guilt struck her. She pushed it aside and told herself she'd stop aunt before any more business-related information was shared. Her interest rested solely on how to approach Grant's aversion to celebrating Christmas. Because if she were honest, that was the last thing holding her back from sleeping with him. But what if she had read his signals wrong. Maybe his default setting was to flirt with all women. Her old insecurities crept in, making her rethink how she should approach him tonight. Keep it business-like or bring out the seductress she wanted to be?

"Aunt Kathleen. Would you say Grant's response was typical? Or is he more… oh, I don't know… reasonable when it comes to obstacles?"

Her aunt stopped rummaging in her purse and tilted her head. "Obstacles happen every day. So, no. Not typical in the least. This one would have prevented Grant from being able to finance his dream."

Dream? Sophie had no idea. Of course not; they'd spent zero time speaking about hopes, dreams, the future. Their time together had been spent arguing, hanging out at the hospital with Lily Ann, and kissing.

"What dream?"

Kathleen stopped rummaging and set aside her purse. "Becoming co-owner of the Idaho Outlaws. He didn't tell you?"

"No reason to. We're…" We're what? Beyond their physical attraction, they had nothing in common except her aunt and a favorite steakhouse.

However, anyone watching the network news or reading social media in the last month knew about the Outlaws. They were the former Boston Patriots bought by uber-billionaire Thomas Scott. He'd renamed the team the Outlaws and moved the organization to Northern Idaho a couple of years ago. They were now considered one of the best teams in their division.

And now Grant was going to become a team owner? He'd be busier than ever now and would have even less time for… what, a relationship? Would he want to see her again after tonight? What would it mean for them? Awesome, now she was thinking of them as a couple. A few kisses, and her brain was a tangle of emotions when it came to him. Not smart.

She could only handle one problem at a time. She decided to focus on the immediate issue. Grant's Scrooge-like stance on her favorite holiday. If she couldn't get him over his hatred of the holiday, she didn't see even see them having just one night together, let alone anything long-term.

"Would you say he's willing to change his mind when presented with a different viewpoint?" Sophie rotated her cell over and over in her hands. She bit her tongue to keep from adding anything further.

"I'd say yes. His business wouldn't have become the success it is without being flexible. His negotiation skills are legendary."

Sophie released the breath she held with a loud 'whoosh.' Her aunt locked eyes with her.

"You okay?"

"Yes… yes. It's just getting hot under the dryer." She fanned herself and let out a nervous laugh.

"Why do you ask, Sophie? Wait. You're not going to cancel your date, are you?" Kathleen's lips formed into a frown.

Damn. She hated it when her aunt gave her that look. She never wanted to disappoint her. Kathleen had taken her in, raised her as her own, and never looked back. Sophie owed her so much. Guilt crept back in. No more questions about Grant. She'd come up with her own solution based on what her aunt already shared.

"No. It's just, well, since we'll be spending some time together, I was curious." She made a show of looking at her watch. "Look at the time; I think the hairdresser forgot about me. Thank you for coming to hang out with me."

Her aunt's frown didn't go away. Sophie began to worry. It wasn't like Aunt Kathleen to keep secrets.

"You know, Sophie, I should have told you this sooner, but if you're worried about me, don't. Grant is taking me with him to the organization. He's going to set up an office in the stadium and take over the running of player relations and public relations."

"I had no idea. Why didn't you say anything?"

Her aunt continued to flip through the fashion magazine, unaware of Sophie's churning emotions.

"Well, I didn't think you'd be interested. After a year of searching for the right buyer, and once Grant found Kemper & Associates, it happened quickly once the negotiations began. Plus, you've been so busy, sweetie. Don't worry about me.

"I'm looking forward to the change. It's all good, and bonus, I'll be able to get you game tickets." Kat winked.

Wow, the things you learned in a beauty shop. Sophie let the news sink in.

Grant couldn't stop smiling. The deal was done with Kemper & Associates. With Sophie at his side, tonight's announcement would be the icing on a very large cake. And TS had phoned him with the best news. The league had officially acknowledged him as co-owner of the Outlaws, and the wire transfer had been cleared.

He planned to give Kathleen a huge bonus for her assistance with the contract payout's last-minute hiccup. He was so damn happy; he didn't mind the silver and gold fluff in the condo's elevator as it took him up to his penthouse. He had a ton to accomplish in a short amount of time.

An image of Sophie's face slammed into him. Damn. What did he want to do? What did he want from her? Them? He'd already fallen for her smiles, her laugh, her stubbornness. All of it. Without realizing it, she'd worked her way under his skin and parked. Waiting for him to pick a direction. The destination, his choice. His bed or her heart.

He called the car service and canceled. He punched the lobby button in the elevator and caught his reflection in the mirrored wall. Not recognizing himself, he studied his image. What he saw was a different guy—a man with a new purpose and a man who wanted a chance with Sophie.

Her building wasn't far from his. Two blocks over, one block down, in fact. He found a rare parking space right in front. He now wished for a bit more time to settle his nerves. Excitement at seeing her again and sharing his news brought another grin to his face.

A knock sounded on his passenger window. He blinked at the woman peering into his car and forgot his own name. Sophie straightened and waited. Shit, he needed to get out of the car.

He indulged in a long look and let out a low whistle. The black and white laced dress hugged her curves, raised his temperature and his cock. She looked...edible. The hemline stopped mid-thigh, and when she turned to adjust her wrap, he almost bit his tongue. The back plunged to the small of her back, his weakness.

Grant exited the car and prayed she h notice the evidence of his desire for her.

"What happened to the car service?"

"I changed my mind." He hesitated inches away from her. If he touched her, he wasn't sure he could keep it casual. The doorman was staring with unapologetic curiosity. Not the best place for seduction.

"You look nice." She said.

"You look … gorgeous." He wanted to say hot. Smokin' in fact, but he'd save that for later. In private. He took her arm and stepped toward the car. But she beat him to the door handle. When she reached down, he sucked in a breath. Her backside brushed against him, a barely suppressed groan. Sophie froze at the contact.

His gaze locked on her back as the dress had stretched a bit wider at her movement. His fingers itched to trail down her creamy skin. He didn't dare.

Public.

Doorman.

Wrong time.

He gave her room to move and helped her in the car. He pinched the side of his thigh the entire drive over to the hotel. They exchanged pleasantries about their day. Didn't help. The air in the car crackled with energy. Not helpful. When they arrived at The Resort, he turned his keys over to the valet, and they walked without speaking to the elevator.

Inside and alone, thank god. He gave in to the need to have his hands on her. He turned, stepped closer, and gently placed his hands on her upper arms. The desire he fought was mirrored in her eyes. Good. "Thank you for being here with me, Sophie."

"You…you're welcome." She licked her lips.

Days of not seeing her, only speaking on the phone, discussing politics to which pizza crust was the best, New York style, of course, had been the craziest foreplay. Each day he couldn't wait to speak to her, hear her voice, imagine what he'd do to her if he were there. "Dammit, this elevator ride is too short for what I really want to do." To his own ears, his voice sounded rough, thick with desire. He wanted to kiss her. He knew if he did, they'd never make it to the party.

"And what's that?" Sophie's words rushed through him, igniting yet another layer of want.

"Everything."

They stared at each other until a discreet cough broke through the silence and reminded them where they were. The elevator doors wide open.

"Grant. We've been wondering where you were. There's plenty of people here eager to see you. This must be your date, Sophie, right?"

It's a good thing Steven Kemper was paying him a boatload of money; otherwise, Grant would have pushed the 'close door' button on anyone else.

The thought took him by surprise; business had always come first for him. Women would and could wait. Not so with Sophie.

Without taking his eyes off Sophie, "Steve, let me introduce you to Sophie McMannis. Sophie, this is Steve Kemper. He and his partner are now the proud owners of my company." He eased back from her and gave himself an inward shake. He needed more than a moment to get his erection under control without further embarrassing both of them. But he promised himself as soon as possible after the dramatic announcement Kemper wanted to make, then they were out of there.

"Nice to meet you, Steve. Congratulations." She held out her hand.

Possessiveness surged through Grant. He wanted to grab her hand, keep her from touching anyone but him. He had it bad, and they had barely arrived.

"How about I get you both a drink. I'll introduce you to my wife; she's already at our table, and dinner should be served soon." Steve led them to a secluded area near the stage.

On the way, they were introduced to people he's never seen again. His resentment at being kept from Sophie's attention grew and worried him. He focused on the decorations hoping to gain some control over his unexpected feelings.

Ice blue bows and ribbons graced the backs of the chairs. Snowflakes were projected onto every flat surface, dancing in rhythm to the music a quartet played Christmas music. For once, it managed to soothe rather than grate on his nerves. And it made him want to take Sophie in his arms and stay locked with her on the dance floor the rest of the evening. So much for control.

Grant nodded to several acquaintances, nodded to a few of his employees. Former employees. And he attempted not to stare at his knockout date. He wasn't ready to look at Sophie again. He feared if he did, he'd drag her into a corner and destroy her carefully crafted hairdo.

If the dress hadn't gotten his attention, her hair would have. In the muted light of the room, her hair shone. Her long hair had been pinned up with a few sections of curls left loose, tiny rhinestones woven throughout.

He wanted to dive in and touch. But he didn't. He held her chair as she sat and checked his watch. He noticed her face light up as she spoke to Steve's wife when she explained what she did for a living. He found himself half-listening to Steve as he droned on about his plans for Grant's company. Former company.

When the emcee called them up on stage, he couldn't get up there fast enough. Sophie watched him as he accepted Steve's handshake. He was overcome with a feeling he didn't often allow himself—pride. He didn't remember giving his speech. He must have. Everyone clapped. His employees, former employees, cheered. Not only did they get to keep their jobs, but he'd given each a going away bonus.

With the announcement over, he stepped from the stage to get back to Sophie and spotted her speaking with a woman he'd briefly dated last year. Damn. What was she doing here?

He'd just made it back to the table to hear, "You'll just be another name on speed dial."

Dammit, dammit, dammit. He looked back at Sophie and found her gaze following the jealous woman as she disappeared into the crowd. Sophie had kept her cool, but he could tell by her hooded look that she was pissed. But at him or someone who he hadn't thought of in months?

Since the meal was done, there was nothing left to do but

socialize or leave. Neither moved. They played out a silent argument of heated gazes and stiff body movements as he was approached from all sides.

Grant suffered through the slaps on the back, the handshakes from friends and colleagues, and the cool gaze Sophie directed his way. Yeah, she was pissed at him.

Shit, he was unable to break away from the people around him. Over the noise, he raised his voice, "I'm almost done." But he wasn't sure if she heard him. He kept his gaze on her as she made a beeline for the exit.

Grant did his best to accept the congratulations and requests for lunch or drinks. He understood that his friends would want an inside track to tickets. It was bound to happen; he just didn't want to deal with that aspect of big-league ownership right this minute. But what he wanted had left.

Sophie was not a jealous person. She had nothing to be jealous of. They'd shared kisses. One which fed her nightly dreams and one under the mistletoe. Both devastating in two distinct ways. Both left her wanting more.

Grant owed her no explanations for the vile woman who'd made it her mission to ruin Sophie's evening. She wasn't running away. She'd simply left to use the restroom, freshen her lipstick. She kept telling herself that as she paced the foyer outside the ballroom until searching for calm and the backbone to go back in, join Grant and pretend everything was fine.

She turned her attention to the decorations. Her artist's eye loved the mixture of the old and new Christmas ornaments. Antique toys were scattered under a flocked tree adorned with blue and silver ornaments. The entire area was decked out with matching garland, and mistletoe hung above doorframes of the various hallways leading off the lobby.

She avoided those areas and continued to pace. She was still debating on what to say to Grant when he found her.

"You didn't leave."

"No, I didn't. I thought about it, but that would have been rude. I might be pissed off, but I'm not rude."

"Look, for what it's worth, I'm sorry. That woman was someone I—"

She held up both hands. She so did not want to hear what he had done with that woman or anyone else. "You don't have to explain. Really. We both had a life before we met. It's just that she reminded me of why I should have kept this date strictly business."

"Did you want tonight to be more than just a business arrangement, Sophie?"

His low tone and soul-piercing gaze ramped up her pulse rate. She rubbed her neck and sighed. She'd never experienced a catfight, not that it had been, but it made her feel... sad and disappointed. Disappointed in herself for thinking she could somehow change Grant's mind on Christmas. No, that wasn't right. She'd thought she could change his mind about women.

"I'd somehow convinced myself that I was different." But it didn't matter. The woman she'd never see again, fingers crossed, didn't matter either. And neither would any explanation from Grant. He didn't owe her anything. She accepted there'd be no 'them.' "I'm ready to go whenever."

"Not yet. I wanted to share a few things with you before we left your place earlier, but I messed that up by lusting over you the minute I saw you in that dress."

She didn't know that one word would have the power to flip her feelings. A low hum sounded in her ears, and her nipples tingled upon hearing 'lusting.' She clasped her hands together and twisted. A throbbing began between her thighs. Her mouth went dry at the thought of him wanting her the same way she'd imagined them together.

Grant's gaze zeroed in on her mouth as she licked her lips. His groan left her breathless; the full-throated response amped her need for him. What had been an agonizing decision was no longer an issue.

"I've bought into a baseball team—the Idaho Outlaws. Once I sold my company, I had enough capital to fund my dream and … and, oh, Hell, it's happening at the same time I found you. My timing has never sucked this bad, but I don't want to take you home and say good-bye. Not tonight."

He ran his hands through his thick, short hair and managed to look sexier than he ever had. She didn't want to say goodbye either. She'd take this one night and worry about later…later.

Grant started to speak again when a group of people entered the foyer, loudly laughing. They didn't seem in a hurry to move on. He took her by the arm and guided her into an alcove behind the tree.

"That's better."

"Better for what?"

"This." He leaned into her and gently pushed her up against the wall. He placed his hands on either side of her head and captured her mouth with his. He sucked on her bottom lip, captured her tongue, and consumed her.

If a fire broke out now, there would be no way she'd stop. She'd happily deal with the consequences because, at that moment, he owned her. Her body wanted more. She wanted everything he was willing to give; nothing else mattered.

Sophie wrapped her arms around his neck and pulled herself as close as she could. Their bodies conformed to each other. Her limbs went week as she was rewarded with the hard length of his erection against her belly. The dark corner was her salvation as she ignored the sounds of the party. He broke their kiss to trail open-mouthed kisses along her jaw, nipped her ear, then blew softly to soothe the pain, but the action created an intense pleasure she wanted again. She lifted her chin to give him better access. He chuckled and repeated the action, sending shivers straight to her clit.

He went lower, lavishing her neck with open mouth kisses before re-capturing her mouth. When neither could breathe, he placed his forehead on hers. The sound of their ragged breathing echoing off the surrounding walls.

She needed to touch him. Anywhere. Everywhere she could. She placed her hands inside his dinner jacket and ran them along his chest. Holy mistletoe, he was cut. She knew he'd been in great shape during his playing days and hadn't thought he would still be now. She greedily moved down to his ribs. Hello, six-pack.

She wound her hands under his shirt and up his back. Well-defined muscles greeted her. Lost in exploring his body, she jumped when she felt his hand caress the underside of her breast.

"Do you want me to stop?"

"God, no!" Her plea sounding husky and unfamiliar.

"Good, because I don't think I can."

He began to rub his thumb over the rock-hard tip of her nipple and blew softly into her ear. She let out a squeak as the sensation traveled through her. Her core spasmed, and her thighs softened. No longer did she care where they were. She wanted him. Now.

The only thing that mattered was having him inside her. She wound a leg up against his thigh and rotated her hips. He let out a moan, grabbed her hips, and pulled her into his erection.

"Yes." She rasped out.

He held her gaze, "God, you're beautiful, Sophie... I can't wait to be inside of you."

Grant reached under her dress and cupped her bottom. He traced tiny circles on her skin. Close to her opening. Closer to where she wanted him to touch. But he moved his hand back and chuckled in her ear. Even his chuckle turned her on.

"Touch me, Grant." She whispered.

"Where?"

"You know. Don't make me beg."

"A little begging never hurt anyone, Sophie. Where do you want me to touch you? Say it."

He growled the command.

It left her breathless.

"Please... please touch me—"

"I know I saw her leave the ballroom, Steve. Sophie must be in the ladies' room. I'll check."

As if a bucket of ice had been dumped over her head, she stilled her movements. Mortified, she closed her eyes and waited until she heard the door close across the hall. She let her leg fall and patted down her dress.

"You can open your eyes, sweetheart."

Grant was a hell of a sight. His hair was a mess from her fingers, his jacket was on the floor, and his lips were swollen. She imagined she looked similar. She placed her head in her hands and groaned. "I can't believe…" Shaking her head, she couldn't finish.

"Sophie, it's alright. She didn't see us."

He scooped up his jacket and put it back on. She needed a mirror, but the only room with one was the very one Mrs. Kemper was in. Looking for her.

What was she doing? Never had she ever…not in public anyway. And probably in private either. *Holy crap*. Her legs shook from the rush of endorphins as her body begged for more. He'd muddled her brain again, and she'd enjoyed every minute. Still, the interruption was just what she needed, what her practical side was shouting at her needed to happen—stupid practical side.

Now she knew how it felt to be with Grant. A front-row seat to what it could be like to be thoroughly loved by the most eligible bachelor in Pineville. Damn. Trouble was, a night wouldn't be enough, now would it?

"Sophie, you okay?"

"Sure. Yes…I think I'd like you to take me home. I'm not sure I could go back in there after…well, after." What more could she say?

"When can I see you again?"

Confused by the question, she hesitated. She wanted time to answer, but considering all the things they'd just done, his request wasn't unreasonable.

"I'm surprised you're not asking me back to your place. Isn't that how these things go?"

Where had that come from? She sounded bitchy. Alright, a lot bitchy. But she'd just had the hottest experience of her life, and she was a bit cranky it had been interrupted. Very cranky.

"I'm sorry. I'm not sure why I said that. I guess I just don't want you to think I do that sort of thing with every man I go out with."

"But I do, huh? You think I do this with every woman I take out?"

"I didn't say that. I meant I don't want you believing I'm easy." Ugh, how did their conversations always end up twisted around? "What we just did was great, but it was a moment. And this was only for tonight. I think maybe we need to call it a night."

"You don't sound too sure about that. And I'm not going anywhere, anytime soon. Sure, I'll be traveling once the season starts, but Sophie, what just happened, how we both got lost…I hope you know that's special and hell, let's just say that doesn't happen as often as you think it does. But it's your call."

Her call? Well, that was not the response she expected. He wanted her but would wait. She wanted him, but she needed time. And she needed to put as much distance between herself and his talented hands and wicked mouth as she could. Because now that the moment was over, she knew if they did sleep together, it wouldn't be enough.

"Thank you for giving me some space to think it over; however, I'd like to go home for now." This time she made sure to sound convincing. His mouth lifted at the corners, but his eyes bored into her. He knew she still ached for him. But he didn't try and talk her into his bed. Grant took her home. Walked her to the door and kissed her on the forehead, "I'm just a call away, Sophie."

There was still the matter of his boycott on Christmas. He'd given her options, but could she live with his feelings in exchange for more, for a chance at something neither had seen coming?

CHAPTER 6

Sophie slowly came awake after spending half the night fighting with her sheets. She buried her head under her pillow at the sound of her cell playing Jingle Bells. She flopped over to her back and ran her hand over the nightstand, grabbed the phone, and croaked out, "—'ello."

"Good morning, dear. Just checking in to see how last night went."

Last night. Right. Her. Grant. The date. "Um, yeah. It went…well." She and her aunt had a close relationship, but there was no way she was confiding how she and Grant almost had sex behind a Christmas tree in the foyer outside a ballroom full of hundreds of people.

"There's a nice picture of you two on the society page."

Picture? Oh, crap. She sat up, scrambled out of bed, and fell. Her feet were encased in the top sheet. The cell landed at her side. Calm down, Soph. Breathe. Surely the Daily Post wouldn't have printed a picture of them while they were… Oh, God. No. Just no.

A loud voice rose up from the carpet. Aunt Kathleen was yelling her name. She grabbed the cell, "Sorry… sorry, Aunt K. No, I'm fine. Just tripped over my own feet."

"Um, what are we, uh I mean what am I doing in the picture?" Fingers crossed one of her boobs wasn't showing.

"It's a really nice candid of you two. It looks like your dancing. You're smiling up at him. You two make a nice couple. I don't know why I didn't think of this sooner."

"Think of what sooner?"

Silence. And then… did her Aunt just say 'shit'? She heard throat-clearing, then more silence.

"Aunt Kathleen, what aren't you telling me?"

"It's nothing really. You know I should let you get some rest. It's early, and I—"

"Spill it."

A huge sigh came over the line.

"Alright, but you have to admit you like him. Why just looking at the expression on your face in that picture—"

"For the love of baby Jesus, tell me what you're keeping from me?"

"Oh, Sophie, it's just that… well, I kind of fibbed when I said Grant didn't have a date for the party."

"Define fibbed."

"It's true that his original date canceled. She's engaged now, you know, and it was for the best. Anyway, after he called some of his other, um… friends, only one hadn't returned his call. Or he thought she hadn't returned his call."

Sophie wasn't sure how to respond. And she was still lying on the floor, staring at the ceiling as she listened to her aunt's confession. Maybe she should sit up for this.

"Are you trying to tell me one of his many—er, friends, did call back and accept his invitation? And instead of telling him, you offered to set him up with me?"

"Well, it all worked out. Besides, Sharon wasn't his type, or at least not the right one for him."

"And I am?"

"Of course, you are. And it's time you both put your private lives first. Before you know it, you'll be fifty and have no one to come home to."

She banged her head against the floor. Her aunt wanted grandnieces and nephews. Kathleen hadn't had any children of her own, and she'd never married… and shit. She didn't want Sophie, or Grant, to end up like her. Alone. But she didn't have to be. And wasn't; she dated plenty. And she didn't seem lonely—quite the opposite.

Sophie had always thought her aunt wasn't the type to marry. She'd never once talked about any regrets. Maybe she'd been wrong about assuming her aunt was content being single.

And now she was left with a pretty big choice. Get angry at her well-meaning, match-making aunt for lying to her and to Grant, or let her off the hook since she kinda sorta wasn't mad. But what would Grant say when he found out?

"Okay, maybe we should discuss this—after Christmas. I need to get into the office for a while and make sure my team is on track for tonight's events. I'll see you tomorrow. We're making dinner for Christmas this year, right? I found this great wine. I think you'll really like it."

"You're not mad?" Kathleen asked.

"No. I'm not mad. And I'm not all that surprised. It's just that if Grant and I were to continue dating, there's a pretty big hurdle we have to overcome."

"Christmas. I know. But if anyone can get him to loosen up about the holiday, it's you."

"Well, thanks for the vote of confidence. Look, I'm going to be late if I don't jump in the shower. I love you, Aunt Kat."

"I love you too, Sophie. Oh, and sweetie, my money is on you."

Sophie sat on the floor long after her call ended. Should she tell Grant what her Aunt had done? What would his reaction be? She didn't want to be responsible for getting Kathleen fired.

So that meant it was all on her shoulders. Did she want to pursue what had happened between them last night? The fire between them was undeniable. And she'd witnessed first-hand his softer side with Lily Ann. One she'd never have guessed hid beneath his thousand-dollar suits and his drive to become an owner of a professional baseball team.

Why would a self-described scrooge get his slacks dirty, providing a moment of silliness and laughter in a young girl's day, and still maintain his loathing for the holiday? Unless… unless he secretly craved an experience that was typically out of reach for him.

Something was holding him back from allowing Christmas into his life. Maybe she could figure it out in time to give whatever was happening between them a chance. There was no doubt they had an intense sexual connection. Last night proved that.

Before she could change her mind, she texted Grant and asked him to meet her at the coffee shop in his building. He'd told her he would be packing up the last of his personal stuff today and moving it over to the Outlaws stadium. She began to formulate a plan as she got ready. After all, what good was a party planner without one?

Sophie spotted Grant sitting at a table in the back. He was speaking with the waitress. Or rather, he was listening as she flipped her hair and flapped her lips covered in neon-blue lipstick. No, that wasn't nice. Her lips didn't so much as flap as they smacked as she chewed her gum and spoke at the same time.

She marched over, pulled out a chair, and did her own hair flipping. She stared at the waitress who'd frozen at Sophie's arrival. The look on the woman's face sobered. She offered Sophie a smile and left the table without so much as a backward glance at Grant. Damn. Another flare of jealousy. She'd leave the waitress a nice tip.

"Grant, I've thought about what's happening between us, and—"

"So, you do agree something is happening?"

"—you try my patience, like right this minute.

I agree something is going on. I mean, especially after last night." She cleared her throat. She was hot. Lord, she was sweating. She shrugged out of her wool coat. Better.

She caught his gaze on her chest, and the desire she saw locked her in place. Immediately she was thrown back to last night and Grant's whispered words. "God, Sophie, you're so beautiful... I can't wait to be inside of you."

"Sophie? Sophie?"

She shook her head and looked, really looked at the man sitting across from her. Instead of desire, a look of concern framed his face. It made her want him even more.

"I, uh... I don't want to miss out on what could be, well, you know ... uh, and even though you're my aunt's boss and a scrooge...."

"Whoa, slow down. I can't keep up," Grant leaned forward. "Take a breath."

She did. Then another.

"I want... I want to give it; I mean us a chance. I'd like you to go to the hospital with me tomorrow and attend the kid's Christmas party." Sophie chewed on her lower lip and waited for his answer.

"What time?"

"Two o'clock. Listen, I know it's short notice, but... wait, what did you say?" she asked.

"I said, what time? I'd be happy to go."

"You'll go? Just like that. No promises or arguments about celebrating a silly holiday?"

"Nope."

Grant looked like he was enjoying keeping her off balance. Like he had last night when she crawled all over him. Her face heated at the memory—again. She had to quit doing that.

"I'm not going to promise my opinion will change overnight about Christmas, but if it's important to you, I'll go. I also don't want to miss a chance at something ... you know, with you." He winked.

Sophie liked his response but needed him to know what he was up against. "So, you'll go and not make any comments, even if I ask you to wear a reindeer headband?"

His half-laugh, half-snort, was kinda cute. But he didn't say no. Maybe a little pained at the thought of looking silly, but she had hope. "The staff will be dressed as elves, and there'll be a Santa. You'll have to pretend it is real in front of the kids." Hmm, still no protesting. "You think you could pull that off, Ebenezer?

"Hey, I did alright at last night's party. I don't remember making one comment about the snowflakes dancing on every surface and the ribbons and garland attached to every table, door frame, and chair backing. So, I think I can behave myself at a kid's Christmas party without ruining it for everyone."

"Well, the two are not the same, not really." She said.

"How so?"

"Well, for one, the party last night was for the privileged. Don't get me wrong, the cause was worthy, plus you made your announcement, but it's not the same as celebrating with friends and family. It wasn't about Christmas. Not really. It's just an excuse to dress up and feel better about oneself by writing a check," Sophie replied.

"I'm sure the charity, the guests, and Steve and his partner would disagree with you," Grant said.

"I'm not worried about what they think. I'm worried about you," Sophie answered softly.

"Why is it so important to you? I've held my beliefs for years. What makes you think you can change my mind overnight about Christmas by attending a kid's party?" Grant asked.

"I saw how you interacted with Lily Ann. And I'm pretty sure you didn't fake any of it just to impress me. Did you?"

"No."

"Well, I think I'm a pretty good judge of character, and besides, miracles can happen—especially at Christmas." Sophie paused and went for broke. "I liked seeing that side of you. Maybe, with a little more exposure to the real meaning of the holiday, you and I could…"

"Could what, Sophie?"

She reached for her glass of water. Dammit. This conversation wasn't going according to her plan. It could have something more than the intense attraction she frequently thought about. Like maybe an exclusive relationship. Why couldn't she own her desire and speak it out loud?

"I know what I'd like to do, Sophie. And it has nothing to do with the holidays or parties, but everything to do with how I feel when I'm around you."

She swallowed the last drop of water. He was not making this easy. "We've been in each other's company less than half a dozen times. Don't you think we're moving a bit fast?" Sophie asked.

"Not at all. When I see something I want, I go after it. And you, Miss McMannis, are at the top of my wish list. I'm not willing to go slow and wait through weeks of polite dates and all the usual rules of getting to know someone. That hasn't been my style in a long time. But I know everything I want to know about you, and my goal is to make sure you feel the same way. I've spent enough time with women to know what I don't want and enough time with you to know you, and whatever is happening between us is worth pursuing."

"Well, that's quite…. um, thanks? I think. Not sure I'm thrilled with being some type of goal to be pursued. Not very romantic." Sophie took her hand out of Grant's and sat back. "What happened to giving me some time?"

Grant recaptured her hand and laced his fingers with hers.

Sparks traveled up her arm. Dammit. She was mad at him, yet her body betrayed her. Did she need romance?

"Forgive me, Sophie. I'm not used to wooing. My dating life has been…"

"Business-like? From what I hear, all your relationships are nothing but emotionless attachments, Grant. Women tend to like being treated as special, unique. We want to know you put us first, not as an afterthought when you have an itch to scratch or need a date to a function."

"Sophie, I'm not looking for… Hell, I'm not sure what I'm looking for. But I'm serious when I say I'd like to explore whatever this is between us. What happened last—"

"Should have never happened. It must have been the wine or…" The fact she hadn't been intimate with a man in a while almost leaped out. That wasn't the reason, and they both knew it.

"Don't lie to yourself or to me. You wanted me just as much, Sophie. If it hadn't been for the interruption, I would have discovered just how wet for me you were. You can't deny how what's happening."

Until that moment, Sophie had been holding out hope. Maybe, just maybe, he did want more from her than sex. Not that there was anything wrong with that. She just had to figure things out once and for all. Did she want a few nights of incredible sex, or did she want a chance to see if they could have something more?

It didn't help that her mind kept wandering to his rock-hard abs and chest. All she needed to do was close her eyes, and the sensation of her hands on him last night returned. Then there was his broad shoulders and toned arms. She'd spent the night wondering what it would feel like to be underneath him and all the things that followed.

Shocked that the first thought of him was his physical attributes. Sophie let that sink in for a moment. She'd never gone looking for happily ever after from the men she'd dated. If the sex was good, bonus. But she hadn't been ready to settle down. Not until now.

Yet here she was presented with the absolute wrong man for her, and she couldn't stop dreaming about him naked. Scrooge or not, he was the sexiest man she'd ever met. But that one little flaw would be hard for her to overcome.

"Differences aside, Sophie, we fit. I feel different, for the better, when I'm with you. Plus, you make me laugh."

"Excuse me?"

"I know it sounds weird. I've spent some time thinking it over. 'Why, Sophie. Why her?' Besides the obvious chemistry and the way you respond to my kisses." He grinned.

"You're blushing. I like that I can make you blush, Sophie."

She was in trouble. At his words, she melted on the inside. Her insides tingled, and she was back to picturing him naked.

"You make me laugh, Sophie. No one else does. But don't get me wrong. I like other things about you too."

"Like?"

"You're smart, sarcastic, strong-willed. You have the biggest heart I've ever seen and the softest lips I've ever kissed. When we're together, all I think about is how can I steal another kiss or get my hands all over you."

Grant rubbed her palm with his thumb, and she was on fire. The tingle in her core turned into a squeeze. She raised her free hand and asked for another glass of water as the waitress passed by.

Suddenly faced with what she wanted, she panicked. "Last night was a mistake." She blurted out. What if her plan didn't work? What if she fell all the way, and he was still whole-heartedly against Christmas?

"No, it wasn't. In fact, the only thing I regret about last night is that it embarrassed you." He said.

"I wasn't embarrassed."

"No?"

"No. I was—confused?" She wanted to take the word back as soon as she said it. Dammit.

"Confused?"

Uh-oh. She'd struck a nerve. He released her hand, sat back, and crossed his arms. He stared at her. He kept staring until she started to squirm in her seat. Dammit, she wasn't a bug under a microscope to be figured out.

"I don't think you were confused at all, Sophie. I think you were turned on and would have let me take you standing in that corner if Steve's wife hadn't walked by. Confused? No. It scared you. It scared you that you could forget about everything around you—except us."

Ding-ding-ding. Give that man a prize.

But not yet. Deep down, she knew he was hiding something, and she was determined to find out the real reason he despised Christmas. And if her instincts were wrong? Well, she'd just worry about that later.

"Can we call a truce on the personal front for today? I didn't come here to debate last night. I shouldn't even be here now. I have a luncheon and a dinner to coordinate and oversee."

"Why did you ask me here?"

The plan. She couldn't tell him about the plan. Well, not all of it.

"I promised to go back to the hospital tomorrow for the party. If you still want to pursue this,"—she waved her hands between them—" then I'd like you to be there."

His brown eyes darkened. His intense gaze almost made her

confess all. He had entirely too much power over her senses. She hoped she'd have the same effect on him tomorrow.

"Sophie, you can't use the kids at the hospital as a shield from what you feel for me," Grant said.

She didn't reply. She couldn't. If she did, she'd spill everything. Her plan, her need for him, and that having him go with her had nothing to do with the kids but everything to do with getting her Christmas wish to come true.

CHAPTER 7

Grant arrived at the hospital at two o'clock, as Sophie asked. He had a feeling that his stance on celebrating Christmas might be an issue between them, but he didn't think it would be a deal-breaker. Today might be a test, but a sexy as hell party planner wasn't going to change his mind. He'd have fun letting her try.

The atmosphere in the children's ward was festive and not at all what he expected. Wouldn't all this commotion tire the kids out?

He looked around but didn't see Sophie. Christmas carols played, and various members of the nursing staff greeted him wearing the predicted reindeer headbands. He hoped he wouldn't be asked to wear one. He drew the line at wearing ridiculous headgear even when kids were involved.

He caught a glimpse of a sleigh down the hall packed with toys. Still, not sure where he should go, he felt someone come up behind. Not just anyone, but his someone. Damn, he was already thinking of her as his. He turned and looked down at Sophie and barked out a laugh.

"What are you wearing? That is the most hideous thing I've ever seen."

"It's an ugly Christmas sweater. I tried to find one in your size, but no luck. But I'm sure I can come up with something around here to get you in the festive mood."

"Um, no thanks. I'll pass."

"Spoilsport."

"Bah, humbug." He grinned.

"Shh, don't let the kids hear you say that."

The head nurse, Marlene, came up and gave Sophie a hug. "Sophie, I'm so glad you're here. We're kinda in a pickle. We seem to have, ah, forgotten to book a Santa."

"Oh, no. Wait. Let me think. I'm sure I have someone in my contacts I could call."

"You're a lifesaver. We have a suit. We just need a body to fill it."

"Got it. I'll be right back." She turned back to Grant. "I'm going to the lounge to make some calls. I'm so sorry about this. Hey, maybe you could go visit Lily Ann, and I'll meet you there?"

Oh, Sophie, you think you're fooling me, but I'm onto you. He almost laughed out loud; she was so cute as she gave him an innocent smile. Innocent my ass. "Sure. If you don't have any luck, maybe we can call Kathleen. I'm sure she'd be up for tracking down a substitute Santa."

"I, um, oh no, that is… since it's Christmas Eve, she was going to spend it with a few of her friends."

"Yes, but I'm sure for you, she wouldn't mind."

"Don't worry. I'll come up with someone. Now, just go visit Lily Ann and let me worry about this. Please?"

"All right, but I'd like some time after the party so we can finish our discussion from yesterday. I think I've come up with a solution." Grant winked at Sophie and gave the nurse a salute.

He walked down the hallway towards Lily Ann's room and whistled. He was enjoying himself. And on Christmas Day. Huh, maybe the joke really was on him.

CHAPTER 8

Twenty minutes after Sophie left to make her fake calls, she smiled to herself on a superior acting job. She met a maintenance staff member at the storage room where various costumes were kept and hustled back up to the children's floor.

When she entered Lily Ann's room, she found the nurse, Lily Ann's mother, and Grant all gathered around Lily Ann's bed laughing as the little girl was mimicking, whom she didn't know. Seeing the smile on Lily Ann's face and of those around her touched Sophie. Grant looked relaxed, and the best part was he didn't seem to realize the de-scrooging process was well underway.

He glanced over, and his smile widened. *Focus on the plan, Sophie.* Not his handsome face. There was still a lot to accomplish before the party ended. She listened to Lily Ann continue her story. The little girl wore a pretty, pink scarf and matching knitted cap with sparkles and tiny sprigs of white flowers. The set appeared to be new.

The little girl looked exactly like a pixie as she beamed with love and happiness. When the laughter from everyone began to fade, Sophie stepped into the group, leaned in to give Lily Ann's mom a hug, and kissed the tiny girl on the forehead. "I love your new scarf and pretty hat, Lily Ann. Did your mommy make them for you?"

"No, Mr. Conrad brought them for me. He said a pixie wasn't really a pixie without flowers in her hair, so this was the next best thing since I lost all mine!" She bounced up and down on the bed while she spoke.

Sophie looked over to Grant, who shrugged and gave her a sheepish grin.

"I saw the set in the shop next to the coffee place we met in. The color had Lily Ann's name all over it. So, I bought it." He tweaked Lily Ann's nose, sending her into another fit of giggles.

He'd bought an honest to goodness Christmas present, although he probably wouldn't label it as such. Surely, he wouldn't turn down her request to fill in and play Santa, right?

"Grant, that's really thoughtful of you." She cleared the lump that had formed in her throat and soaked in Lily Ann's joy at receiving Grant's present.

She turned to the others, "If you don't mind me stealing Grant away from the party, I need to speak with him in private."

She held out her hand and waited for him to accept it. When he did, she swore she could hear gears clicking into place. Her body flared to life at the simple touch, and her heart picked up its pace. She wondered if he would always have this effect on her.

When they reached the hallway, Sophie pulled him around the corner and led him to the nurses' station. "Thanks for coming with me. I need the support. I wasn't able to find anyone to come on such short notice to play Santa, and now, I have to give them the bad news."

She looked at Grant out of the corner of her eye to judge his reaction. He raised his eyebrows but said nothing. What did that mean? Was that a good sign, or was he ready to spout out some nonsense about Santa?

Taking in a deep breath, she readied herself to lay it on thick. "Hi, Marlene, I'm back. I'm afraid I don't have good news."

"Oh, no, don't tell me. No Santa?"

"Well, not necessarily. We have a costume, and I guess I could wear it, but it's two sizes too big. I'd probably trip over the boots every other step." She paused, peeked up at Grant, and carried on.

"I guess we'll just have to hand out the gifts and tell the kids there was a bad snowstorm at the North Pole."

"That's such a shame. These kids deserve some happiness, especially during this time of year." Marlene stepped up the drama.

"They're such troopers with their treatments, and they've really been looking forward to Santa. It's just so sad we can't give them that."

"Couldn't one of the male doctors do it?" Grant asked.

"Oh, I wish they could, Mr. Conrad. But everyone is either on-call or their home with their own families. We didn't plan this very well. Such a shame the children have to miss out on having Santa." Marlene looked at Grant with the saddest puppy-dog eyes Sophie had ever seen.

"It's okay, Marlene, no need to beat yourself up." Sophie looked at Grant too, but she couldn't compete with Marlene.

He looked from Sophie to Marlene and back to Sophie. "Okay, you two. Knock off the sad eyes. Suppose I don't offer to play Santa. In that case, I solidify my reputation as the town Scrooge, but if I step into that outfit, I'll be reviled and kicked out of the National Grinch Association for life. I can't win either way."

She held her breath, crossed her fingers, and even her toes. Would he disappoint them? She'd use Lily Ann if she had to. She just hoped she didn't have to.

"I can smell a set up a mile away. I'll play Santa on one condition. You, Miss Sophie, have to wear this, and you'll be my special helper." Grant leaned over the nurses' desk and grabbed a green headband. He held it out to Sophie with a dare in his eyes. "Put this on."

She looked down at his hand, and for the second time that day, she felt herself flush. "You want me to wear a headband full of mistletoe?"

"Looks that way. What do you say, Sophie? You wear the headband, and I'll wear the damn suit and make this the best Christmas party these kids have ever seen."

Well, how could she argue with that? Besides, it looked like she'd be getting something out of this deal as well. More kisses from her very own and devilishly handsome scrooge turned Santa.

Best. Day. Ever.

Three hours later, Sophie considered her plan a success. Watching Grant interact with the children and the staff did something to her insides she wasn't prepared for. He made each child feel special as he handed over a handpicked gift with their names on it.

How could he not be swayed, even a little, by the joy he brought today all in the name of Christmas? He'd have to have a heart of stone not to absorb the happiness and love these children radiated toward him when he bent over their beds or wheelchairs and gave them his undivided attention.

Hell, she had trouble holding back tears on several occasions, and when he entered Lily Ann's room, she almost did lose it.

"Santa, you came. I knew you would! Oh, Santa, I love you!" Lily Ann bounced on her bed as her mother attempted to settle her down and rest. But there was no holding Lily Ann back from her one-on-one time with Santa.

"HO-HO-HO. Why, hello, Lily Ann. One of my elves told me a pixie lives under your bed. You must be a very special little girl to have her very own pixie."

"Oh, Santa, I'm the pixie! I play under my bed whenever I can, and my new friend Mr. Conrad said I looked just like a pixie, so he started to call me Pixie. Look, he even gave me this pretty scarf and sparkly hat with tiny flowers."

"He sounds like a very nice man."

"He is Santa. He's the best. 'Cept he's not here right now. Momma said he had to make a business call. Whatever that is."

Sophie glanced at Grant and received a wink and a grin.

"But you came, and now I can tell you my Christmas wish," Lily Ann said.

Sophie cleared her throat and stepped closer to the hospital bed. "Go ahead, Pixie, tell Santa your wish."

"Well, Mr. Conrad had such sad eyes the first time I met him when he told me he doesn't have any family to celebrate Christmas with, so that's my wish. For Mr. Conrad to get his very own family. You know, so he's not alone when he wakes up Christmas morning next year."

Sophie covered her mouth to keep from crying out. What a precious child. To think of asking for a wish for a grown-up while she was in the hospital fighting for her life. She looked over at Grant and searched for any change in his expression. It was hard to tell what he was thinking under the thick beard and bushy fake eyebrows.

"Well, that's very nice of you to think of your friend, Lily Ann." Grant's, aka Santa's voice, full of restrained emotion.

"Yeah, I think he's lonely, and he told me he doesn't really celebrate Christmas, so that's my wish. What do you think?"

"Hmm, I'm not sure about that one. Wouldn't you like something for yourself?"

"Oh, but Santa, you *haaave* to find him a family. He's really, really sad."

"Why do you think that, Lily Ann?"

"Because anyone who doesn't believe in Christmas must be sad."

A child's logic was so simple. Sophie decided to step in and help before Lily Ann began asking for something else Grant couldn't promise her. Santa beat her to it.

"Lily Ann, I must say you're a very smart little girl. And I will do my best to find something special for your friend. Now, I need to go next door. I think I have one more toy to deliver before I have to head back to my workshop. Merry Christmas, Lily Ann."

The look Lily Ann gave him was uncertain at best. She looked like she wanted to argue, but a huge yawn escaped, and instead, she laid back on her pillow. "Okay, but make it super special. Merry Christmas, Santa. Tell Mrs. Claus hi for me."

"I will. You rest so you can get better and escape this joint." Grant winked at Lily Ann and left the room.

Sophie noticed Lily Ann's face was all scrunched up. "What's wrong, Lily Ann? Are you feeling okay?"

"Oh, yes, it was funny what Santa just said. You know to rest up so I can 'escape this joint.' Mr. Conrad told me the same thing the other night."

"Hmm, that is strange. It seems both Mr. Conrad and Santa are very smart. So, I suggest you follow their advice." Sophie walked over and gave Lily Ann a hug and a kiss on her cheek. "Sleep well, little Pixie. I hope all your wishes come true."

Halfway to dreamland, Lily Ann mumbled an "uh-huh" and snuggled down into her blankets, still wearing the scarf and hat from Grant. Sophie said goodbye to Lily Ann's mom and wished her a Merry Christmas.

More hopeful than she'd felt in a long time, Sophie sent out her own wish to Santa. After today, how could Grant not see the joy in Christmas?

<h1 style="text-align:center">CHAPTER 9</h1>

Grant couldn't believe he'd been able to hold it together when Lily Ann told him, Santa, her wish. He tried to remember when he was as young as Lily Ann when Christmas had been joyous for him, and how he looked forward to Santa leaving him presents. It had been so long, but the memories, as faded as they were, brought a smile to his face.

He hadn't allowed himself to recall that time of his life, and he found it didn't hurt quite so much since he met Sophie and Lily Ann. But his feelings on Christmas were still clouded in pain. He pushed them away and decided to focus on the new memories made today.

The kids had been fun to interact with, and he stole kisses from Sophie when he was sure no one was looking, which only proved to frustrate him. He found himself adjusting the too tight Santa pants several times.

He folded the suit and put it in the bag to give back to Marlene and went in search of Sophie. With a renewed determination to get her into his bed and bury himself deep and keep her there until they'd both had their fill. Then later, much later, he'd open up about how his interaction with Lily Ann made him rethink a few things. And if he really wanted to be in her life, she deserved to know why Christmas has haunted him since his childhood.

After checking all the places Sophie could be, he found himself back in front of the nurse's station. He spun around to retrace his steps and nearly mowed her down. She reached out to keep from falling and laughed. Before he could say anything, she reached up and grabbed his shoulders, pulling him down and kissed him. Unlike the chase kisses they'd snuck in without the kids seeing, this one was all heat and just naughty enough that he wished they were already back at his place.

She ended the kiss and hugged him tightly. "Thank you, Grant. You didn't have to do what you did, but I'm glad you did. The kids and Lily Ann loved you."

Grant wrapped his arms around her waist and pulled her in closer. "How about we go back to my place, and we can thank each other--in private."

Sophie hesitated before she answered him. "I'm hungry. How about we go for dinner? There's a new restaurant not far from here I've been dying to try." She turned to the nurse, who was not being very subtle in her eavesdropping. "Marlene, thank you for letting us take part in the party. I'll be back next week to help remove all the decorations. But make sure you let all the families know they are welcome to keep whatever they want, okay?"

"It's you and Mr. Conrad we need to thank. You both are such a blessing to these kids. Thank you so much. Merry Christmas."

"Merry Christmas, Marlene." Grant gave her a hug.

The nurse blushed.

Sophie gave her a big hug too. "Merry Christmas."

"Okay, she's gone. Now it's our turn to leave. We can take my car, and I'll have someone pick up yours tomorrow. You ready to go?"

Should she listen to her body, her heart, or to her head?

"I can tell you're overthinking, Sophie. Just jump in with both feet and take a chance."

What began days ago as a "business only" arrangement had bloomed into something neither of them had expected. Her plan to teach this handsome Scrooge a lesson in Christmas spirit had turned into something entirely different.

She'd fallen all the way today. There was no denying that she was in love with Grant.

He held out his hand, and Lord help her, she took it. She crossed her fingers; she was making the right decision.

CHAPTER 10

Grant parked his car in the garage and escorted Sophie into his house. She immediately noticed the lack of color as they entered through the kitchen. She followed him to the living room and looked around. The home reminded her of a hotel. No personal touches, framed photos, and no big surprise--no Christmas decorations. She wondered how much time he spent here.

"How about we sit and have a glass of wine." He massaged her shoulders and nibbled her earlobe. "I promise not to pounce on you right away unless that's what you want me?"

"Um, oh, that feels good. But uh, yes, I'll take a glass. Thanks." Sophie let out a long sigh and walked over to the couch.

He brought her a glass of Merlot and put his feet up. "I know what's going through that pretty little head of yours, Sophie."

"Really, because I'm having a hard time thinking, so if you could help me out, I'd appreciate it."

"You're thinking to yourself, 'How'd I get so lucky to be sitting here with the most eligible and hottest bachelor in the city?'"

"Ow! C'mon, you know you are." Grant rubbed the spot Sophie had punched.

"Okay, how about this. You're questioning your attraction to a man who seems a hopeless case when it comes to Christmas with his scrooge-type behavior and his womanizing ways. Former ways, I might add. And if that weren't enough, this guy is going to start traveling for his job, and long-distance relationships are hard. How am I doing?"

He reached over, captured one of her curls that had escaped her clip, and gave a playful tug. He was giving her an out. Did she want to take it?

Sophie set her glass aside without taking a single sip. "As much as I want you, and by that, I mean have sex with you. Like, right now. What happens next? For me, the whole Scrooge thing is a pretty big problem. Most of my business is over the holidays, Grant. But here's the main thing, Christmas is more to me than just a holiday."

"I know. Compared to my holiday issues, you amaze me with your ability to embrace it even though you lost both parents right before Christmas." Grant paused. Ran a hand through his hair and turned sideways on the couch, facing her. "It's way past time I explained why I feel as I do."

Sophie crossed her fingers, made a wish, and waited.

Grant took a large drink of wine. Sometime during the last few hours, he'd realized he couldn't lose this compassionate, driven, and sexy woman.

"What if I told you I wasn't always a Scrooge? That there was a time when, like any kid, I waited impatiently for Christmas. That I believed in Santa?" Grant picked up her free hand and began rubbing his thumb on the pad of her palm. He felt her shiver and waited.

"I guess I'd say, 'No way. You? Really?'" Her eyes crinkled, and she chuckled.

Grant laughed along with her, but soon he didn't feel like laughing. "I'm an only child. Did you know that?"

"Maybe. Aunt Kat may have mentioned it."

"My mom had three miscarriages after she had me. The last one was right before Christmas when I was eight. I didn't know exactly what was going on, but I did know she desperately wanted another baby, and so did my dad." Lost in his memories, he appreciated when Sophie remained silent.

"Two days before Christmas, Dad brought Mom home from the hospital. She locked herself in their bedroom and refused to come out. They fought almost non-stop throughout the day and into the next. I was home from school, so of course, I heard everything; our house wasn't that big.

"They said nasty things. Each blaming the other for Mom not being able to carry another baby. I guess Dad decided he'd finally had enough. That night, he came into my room and told me he was leaving for a while, and I needed to make sure Mom didn't stay in bed too long. He gave me some cash and left. It was Christmas Eve, and I…" He stopped, rubbed his neck, and took a long drink from his wine glass.

"Hell, I was eight, and my parents couldn't keep it together long enough for one more god damned day. But I did what he told me to do. Took care of mom until she felt better. We didn't have a Christmas that year. And my dad never came back. They divorced, Mom had to support us, so there wasn't always enough for presents in the following years either. By the time I was a teenager, I could care less about Christmas." His hands had balled up. He flexed them and worked out the kinks. Sophie grabbed one and held tight.

"What happened to your dad? I mean, did he visit you, pay child support?" The stroke of her fingers along his skin settled his nerves, turning into an entirely new sensation.

"He did, in the beginning, but he'd remarried about a year after he left us. Visits and money became scarce. Last I heard, he was in Minnesota with his fourth wife."

When he stopped speaking, she didn't rush in to fill the silence. Instead, Sophie placed her hand on his back and rubbed small circles up and down. Her touch helped. She leaned in and kissed his cheek. He didn't need words of sympathy, and she somehow got that. His respect for her grew. *God, she'd been worth waiting for.*

The unexpected thought took him off guard. Was that what he'd been doing all this time? Waiting for someone to break down the walls he'd built?

He continued. "Mom passed a few years ago. But I made sure she had a good life once I started earning money. Hell, the happiest day of my life had been when I signed my first contract, called her, and told her to quit her job. I bought her a house before I bought mine. She never had to work a day again."

A weight lifted from him as he told Sophie about his parents. He couldn't let her think she was simply another in a long line of empty encounters. He wanted what was happening between them to last.

He reached around her and lifted her onto his lap, and held her tight. Sophie wiggled and settled in and began to fidget with one of his shirt buttons. His body reacted instantly. Her eyes widened as his erection pressed against her cute little ass. He did his best to ignore his need for her. He wanted more from her than just her body, and he wanted her to know that upfront.

"Grant, thank you. I know it couldn't be easy for you to talk about such a painful time. It means a lot to me. No one could blame you for your feelings toward Christmas. But...."

"But?"

"Sorry, I didn't really mean to say but. I couldn't help but wonder if playing Santa tonight had stirred up those awful memories, and if so, I'm truly sorry because it wasn't my intent, and well I..."

"I know, Sophie, you set me up hoping to show me the true meaning of Christmas, right? You know, I was already halfway thawed once I spent some time with Lily Ann. Putting on that Santa suit, as itchy as it was, got to my eight-year-old self and reminded me there was a time I loved Christmas."

He sat back and pulled her against his chest. He anchored his hands on her curvy hips and pushed her down on his erection so there would be no doubt how much he wanted her.

"And then there's you."

"Me?"

"Yes, my very own Christmas siren, luring me to the dark side, or rather the light side of the holiday. Sophie, it's because of you that I realize I need to move beyond that angry little boy. What I saw in those kids' eyes, and then hearing Lily Ann's wish, it humbled me. You made it happen, and I want to properly thank you, but I'm having a hard time taking you seriously." Grant slid his hands up Sophie's sides, under the camisole she wore beneath the ugly Christmas sweater. He began kneading the soft flesh below her full breasts.

"Um, okay, that couldn't be more confusing. Care to explain?"

"Babe, it's simple. Your curves drive me to distraction, but the mistletoe headband needs to go." He lifted his chin up to indicate the object she was still wearing.

"What? Oh, yeah." Sophie reached up and patted the headband. "I don't know. Maybe I'll keep it on. It seems to be working for me." She trailed a finger down his chest, ending at his belt buckle. She bit her lip and smiled. "That is unless you know, it might distract you."

"Hell, no. Come here." He tugged the hideous sweater over her head, taking her camisole with it. He watched as she peeled off her bra and let out a low groan. Damn, he was a lucky man. He cupped her breasts and flicked both thumbs over her pretty pink nipples.

Sophie closed her eyes and let out several tiny moans. Her response thrilled him as he took a rock-hard nipple into his mouth and sucked until she moaned louder, the sound of his very own Christmas siren.

She pressed into his erection, rotating her hips. He lifted his hands, cradled her head, and brought her face to less than an inch from his mouth. "You're still wearing too many clothes."

"Me? You still have all yours on. Maybe you need to do something about that first, hmm?"

With quick movements, Grant pulled his shirt over his head. Buttons popped and bounced off the coffee table. He lifted her off his lap and laid her down on the couch, and captured her lips. She met his intense need and tangled her tongue with his. She was beyond perfect for him.

Sophie arched her back and dug her nails into his scalp, and consumed him equally with her lips and her own need. *Damn.*

Before he lost all coherent thought, he whispered into her ear, "Sophie, I want to bury myself so damn deep in you I can't see straight. If that's what you want too, tell me now; otherwise, I'll wait until you're ready."

She gifted him with the sweetest sigh and a throaty 'yes' that went straight to his cock. He stood and removed the rest of his clothes and then helped her remove her slacks and red silk panties. "Why, Ms. McMannis, had I known you were wearing these as you marched around the hospital, I would have found the nearest broom closet and happily pulled them down with my teeth and…"

"Naughty, naughty boy. But I don't think you would have. Not with a floor full of children waiting to see Santa.

She took the mistletoe headband and tossed it over her shoulder. "So, is it safe to say your scrooge days are over, Mr. Conrad?"

"I believe it's safe to say you've had a hand in redeeming me, Ms. McMannis. And it's only fair that you're rewarded. Name your prize." Grant wiggled his eyebrows.

"God, you're corny, but I love you."

Grant froze at her words. He hadn't been expecting them, but he'd take them. No one had said those three little words to him since before his dad left. He wasn't quite sure what he'd done to deserve this woman who'd cracked through his Grinch-like façade and discovered his true self, but he was not letting her go. Ever. "Sophie, I--"

She shushed him and lifted her hips. "You don't need to say them back just because I said them. And for my prize, I want you. Inside me. Now…please."

"Well, since you asked so nicely." He pushed off the couch, "Hold that thought. I'll be right back."

"Wait…what?!"

He ran upstairs, grabbed what he needed, and was back less than a minute standing in front of a wide-eyed Sophie.

He absorbed the heat in her eyes and the small 'O' on her full lips as her gaze locked on his erection. He rolled on the protection as she watched, then took the final steps to the couch. It was his turn to be awed as her legs fell open. For him. But he didn't want to rush things. No, he wanted to savor their first time. He needed to taste her and make real his broom closet fantasy.

"Grant." Her husky plea was his undoing. He fell to his knees, grabbed her hips, and pulled her to the edge of the couch. Her squeal, then sigh as he leaned down and trailed open mouth kisses on the inside of her thighs sent a surge of warmth through him.

He paused, "I think you'll like this prize better." He circled and feathered a thumb over her swollen clit, blew a soft breath, and licked his prize. Secure that she'd enjoy his substitution. By her throaty moans and a sexy drawn out "yes" and "more," he was correct. Grant increased his pace and was rewarded with more sweet moans as she cried out his name.

He watched as she rode out her orgasm, and when the rocking of her hips slowed, he dropped kisses along her stomach, under her breast, then captured her lips in a slow, open-mouthed kiss.

She ran her hands down his back, broke their kiss, and let out a soft laugh, "Grant, that was...perfect."

Her laugh wound its way around his cock and his heart. Damn, he loved this woman. "Just wait, I'm nowhere near done with you yet."

He entered her slowly, his eyes glued on hers. He thrust inside her, filling her the way she'd filled the cracks in his heart. His forehead fell to hers. "Damn, I want to go slow, make this good for you, but I need you... next time, baby. I promise, nice and slow."

Her answer was to wrap her legs around his waist. The grin on her face and the lift of her hips urged him to move inside her again. He began to thrust until he'd wrung another moan from her. They rocked into each other, and when she fell over the edge, he soon followed, shouting her name.

Their deep breaths mingled; their fingers intertwined. He brought their joined hands up for a kiss and didn't want to wait a moment longer.

"Sophie."

"Hmm?"

"I love you."

Her smile lit up her face, and his heart burst.

She sighed and wound her arms around his neck and brought him tight against her body. "Did you know that it's a well-known fact that a true scrooge is allergic to mistletoe?"

"Really?"

"Definitely. And I knew you couldn't possibly be one from that first night in Lily Ann's room. You stood much too close to her mistletoe garland without breaking out in a rash." She wiggled against him and nipped his earlobe. "In the end, it probably wouldn't have mattered if you were a life-long grinch or not because once I saw you sitting on that cold, hard floor connecting with a little girl you'd never met, my heart was yours."

Grant was rarely at a loss for words. But for Sophie, he would gladly change his ways.

Grant and Sophie entered Pineville's most popular ice cream parlor, Main Street Scoops, six months later. Before they had a chance to locate her, Lily Ann found them. In an instant, they were enveloped by a sweet bundle of giggles and short, bouncy white-blond curls. The pixie they'd met last Christmas, Miss Lily Ann Dupree. She chattered non-stop as she tugged on Sophie's arm, leading her to the table in the old-fashioned shop where her mother sat patiently with a smile that matched her daughter's.

Grant held out their chairs, but Lily Ann wasn't done with her welcome. She turned her smile on him, and as any proper pixie would do, she beckoned him to her level for a quick peck on his cheek.

"I'm so glad you made it!" She patted Grant's face and wrapped her arms around his neck for a hug. She whispered in his ear before she bounded over to her chair.

He grinned as he noticed Sophie soaking in the sight of the young girl who exuded pure joy. Sophie choked back a sob, and he found himself looking away to clear his throat and compose himself.

This young, courageous girl had no idea the important role she'd played in bringing them closer together. As far as Sophie knew, today's plan was to present Lily Ann with an offer to attend an Outlaws game, watching from the owner's suite. But that took a backseat once the ice cream was served, and she began to recite all the highlights of her last six months.

"And when I got to ring the bell at the hospital, Mama cried, and the nurses threw pixie-dust in the air. It was pink and purple, mostly, oh, and you wanna know the *bestest part?*" Lily Ann, now up on her knees, wiped cotton candy ice cream from her chin and stared expectantly at them both.

Grant cleared his throat once more and reached out to wrap his hand around Sophie's. "What would that be?"

When Lily Ann had been in the hospital, she'd been a shining light of optimism. Then when she'd used her wish to Santa on him to have a family, he'd vowed that whatever she or her mother needed, he'd make sure they'd have.

Lily Ann looked between them and threw out her arms, "I get to play with my friends again. Isn't that awesome?"

Grant, Sophie, and Lily Ann's mom all nodded their heads, unable to put into words what her joy meant to them; they listened and marveled at her enthusiasm.

Today would be all the more special as she would help him with a very important task and surprise for Sophie.

While Sophie was occupied discussing which American Girl doll Lily Ann would take to her playdate tomorrow, Grant signaled her mom and handed her a box under the table.

"So, Lily Ann, now that you're in remission, Sophie and I want to invite you and your mom to an Outlaws game with us. We'll sit high above the field in the owner's box, and you can eat all the hot dogs and ice cream you want. Actually, we were hoping to make a weekend out of it. We have some tickets to Silverwood Theme Park, and you can spend the day on the rides or in the waterpark. Sophie really wants to ride on their steam train through the forest."

As Grant listed all the things she could do, Lily Ann's eyes widened and filled with tears. He hadn't thought he'd ever experience this level of happiness from doing something so simple as giving tickets to a ball game or amusement park, but he was wrong. This little girl, their Christmas pixie, had once again shown him it's the little things in life that mean the most.

"Oh, Mama, can we? Can we go to a baseball game and Silverwood, and wait," she turned her saucer-sized eyes to Grant, "Can I ride a roller coaster? I seen the commercials for the Thunder Terror. It looks scary, but I can do it. I know I can. Can we Mama, please?"

Lily Ann's mom had begun to laugh and cry at the same time. She used her napkin to wipe her tears, "Well, I don't know about you getting on something called the Thunder Terror. But maybe we could—"

"Mrs. Dupree, it's my, it's our treat. All of it. Think of it as an early Christmas gift." Grant looked from Lily Ann, who was hopping from one foot to the other, to her mother. Maybe he should have cleared it with her first. What if she said no?

Lily Ann's mom mouthed thank you to both he and Sophie and wiped fresh tears from her cheeks. Grant let out a relieved breath and prepared himself for the next surprise—this one he had discussed with Lily Ann's mom.

Lily Ann let out a *"woo-hoo"* and hugged her mother, "It's okay, Mama, I know those are happy tears."

She next hugged Sophie and came over to him, but before he could hug her, she slapped her hand over her mouth, "Oops, almost forgot." She swung around to face her mother, and at her mother's nod, she took the box Grant had brought and danced around the table and placed it in front of Sophie.

"This is for you, Miss Sophie. Mr. Grant told me that Santa called him and wanted me to give this to you. I'm pretty sure it's because of my wish for Mr. Grant to have a family. And I think it'll only come true if you open the box."

"Why, thank you, Lily Ann." Sophie turned to him, her eyes sparkled, and he marveled again that she'd chosen him. A man who once believed relationships were for suckers and Christmas for fools.

During the last six months, she'd been beyond understanding as he'd flown all over the country as he transitioned into his new role with the Outlaws. She'd stuck by him and accepted his grumpy moods and, more importantly, was willing to tease him out of them in the most inventive of ways.

He'd been trying to figure out the right occasion to ask her, and then fate stepped in. Last week, the phone call from Lily Ann's mom saying she was officially in remission gave him the solution he'd been looking for. He knew that the little girl just had to be part of his proposal to Sophie.

He cupped Sophie's cheek and looked into her shining brown eyes, and saw his future. Their future. "Sophie, you've put up with me and my scroogie-ness since the very beginning, the late-night phone calls, and canceled dates when I couldn't make it back to town, and you've shown me what it means to be a part of something bigger. You've shown me that family matters and that love is worth fighting for, especially when life gets in the way."

He picked up the box and held it out and watched as Sophie's eyes grew as big as Lily Ann's, unshed tears fell freely down her beautiful face.

"Hurry up, Mr. Grant. Ask Miss Sophie. Hurry, she's crying!"

Laughter rang out, and Lily Ann's mother shushed her and gathered her onto her lap.

"Yes, Mr. Grant, hurry," Sophie whispered.

"Sophie McMannis, would you do me the honor of becoming my wife?" He opened the box and waited.

"I'll say yes on one condition." She peeked over at the glowing little girl with ice cream on her chin.

"Name it."

"Instead of a flower girl, we need to have a pixie carrying a basket of mistletoe at our wedding."

Grant leaned in and stole a quick kiss from his bride-to-be with a murmured promise of more later. Her sweet sigh and flushed features warmed him inside and out. How lucky was he to have Sophie McMannis in his life, loving him, accepting him, faults and all?

And now, he had another question to ask.

He looked over into Lily Ann's smiling face, "Looks like your second wish came true, Pixie. What do you say, would you like to be in our wedding?"

"Oh, yes, please."

Sophie McMannis, party planner extraordinaire, had her dream wedding one year to the day from receiving Grant's email asking for a 'business only' date.

The wedding was, of course, Christmas themed. Her meddling aunt was her matron of honor, and there was a sweet, green-eyed pixie flower girl. She would now have two favorite days of the year to celebrate her love of Christmas and the Scrooge who stole her heart.

CHASING NOEL

A PINEVILLE WORLD CHRISTMAS NOVELLA
(RESCUED BY LOVE SERIES)

ABOUT

Thomas "TS" Scott isn't sure what to do about Noel Snow.

He owns a real estate empire and a baseball team.

She hates sports.

She's an in-demand interior designer with a vision.

He gave her dream job to someone else.

Sparks don't just fly whenever they're within five feet of each other—they explode.

Just in time for Christmas...

A snowbound cabin brings them together for the short-term.

Two months later, their soon-to-be baby reunites them.

Will they overcome their pasts and open their hearts to a love that's been simmering for years?

The chase in on.

CHAPTER 1

$\mathcal{N}$oel Snow couldn't believe what she was hearing. Did one of her friends just dare the man Noel had sworn never to speak to again, one Thomas "TS" Scott to "*stop strategizing and go after the woman you've been chasing and kiss her senseless?*"

Oh, no. Not happening. There was no way she was letting TS anywhere near her, let alone kiss her. All of her friends knew how she felt about him. Why would they think that telling the owner of the Outlaws baseball team to kiss her was a great idea?

It wasn't like they didn't know the reason she was mad at him in the first place; he'd given a job she desperately wanted to someone else —after he led her to believe she would get the job.

She and TS kissing? In front of all their friends? Not happening. So what if her heart was racing and she could feel her body respond to the idea with an enthusiastic, *yes, please*. Nope, not going to happen.

And no one needed to know that she'd like nothing better than to have him kiss her and other naughty things that would make her ninety-five-year-old grandmother blush. And no one, not even her group of girlfriends, knew she'd had TS on her mind since he moved back to Pineville.

And for sure no one needed to know about the dreams she'd been

107

having of TS and her together either. Where after he awards the interior designer position for his luxury condo project to someone else, he gives her the lamest explanation—ever, and she was like "oh, okay" then the dream turns into the hottest sexual experience of her life.

If only she control her dreams. Or her heart. It pounded wildly at the thought of TS' lips against hers. And other body parts.

Who the heck was she kidding? She wanted him. That fine line between love and hate had never been thinner than today. But she wasn't ready to forgive. Maybe not ever.

She looked at her girlfriends, Kelsey, Lara, and Caris, who had just moments ago been enjoying their joint baby shower when Blake, Caris' husband, dropped the challenge.

All eyes remained on Noel. "Um, I don't think that's—"

She froze as she watched TS put his drink down and close the distance between them.

"It's about damn time."

Cheers echoed Blake's statement.

Traitors. Every last one of them. Noel took off and headed for her car.

"Noel, wait."

She ignored TS's plea and prayed he didn't follow.

"Blake, that wasn't fair."

Noel heard Caris's words as she rushed past the couple.

Blake added, "No, but they both needed the push. Plus, it'll be fun to watch the chase."

Chase? Like she was some prize to be won. Screw that. Noel left the backyard where the shower had taken place and was a couple steps from her car when she heard him call her name again. He was close, too damn close.

She stopped and faced TS. If they were going to have it out, she wanted it over quick, no witnesses. And no kissing. "I said all I wanted to say to you TS when you backpedaled out of the job offer. I don't have anything left to say except goodbye."

"I've been thinking about you, Noel. A lot." TS loosened his tie as he moved closer into her personal space. So close that she backed up and bumped into her car. He was so close she could count the freckles on his nose.

He lifted his hands to steady her, but she waved him off. She didn't know what she'd do if he touched her. She remembered the last time he'd touched her, when they'd walked down the aisle together at two weddings and when they'd danced at the receptions. She remembered how it felt to have those hands on her, his arms around her, and on her lower back just last winter. It had been torture.

Thomas "TS, to his friends" Scott was her enemy. A heart-stopping-frustration-inducing-chiseled-jawline-stubborn-assed, broad-shouldered-hunk-of-a-man in a three-piece suit who she'd had a secret crush on, since forever. Once simply friends because of their shared friend circle, he'd become her enemy when he gave the job, she wanted—she deserved, to someone else.

But he was still her fantasy.

And he was close, too damn close. So close she was able to inhale his scent. The musky, earthy smell was uniquely his and dangerous to her senses. His hazel eyes were mesmerizing, the blues and greens swirling together, and she knew she could quickly become lost in his intense gaze.

"Don't you want to know why?" TS asked.

She licked her lips and caught his gaze zero in on the movement. She felt a flush creep up her chest and warm her neck. Her eyelids fluttered shut, and images from her dreams, of them together—naked, began playing in her mind. *Noel just get in the car. Say you don't want to know why.*

But her hormones wanted to know why. Her heart did too, and then her mind totally rolled over and took a nap.

"Why?" Her whispered tone surprised her.

He flashed a crooked grin, and her pulse rate leaped. That damn crooked, sexy smile of his was her catnip. At that moment, she knew it didn't matter what his answer was. They'd been dancing around each other for months—ignoring the sparks, the insane chemistry, something was about to give.

Breathless, she waited for his answer. She wasn't naïve. She knew this unbearable attraction was mutual. Obviously, since he was staring her down like a mountain lion stalking his next meal. And there had been a time when she thought she wanted from him what her girlfriends had found, but reality had burst that bubble long ago. She refused to let history repeat itself; she'd learned from her mother's pain. And then there was his reputation. He never dated the same woman twice. He was the king of one-night stands.

Now all grown up and wiser, well wiser than her mother had been, she'd take the moments. Moments of joy, accomplishment, and most definitely pleasure. And pleasure was staring her in the face. There was just one little thing they needed to get over. It was big but she wasn't sure enough time had passed for her.

"You drive me crazy, Noel. Plain and simple. What is it about you that has me thinking about kissing that sassy mouth of yours, night and day, when I should be working? It pisses me off, and I think you feel the same. The need, the heat, and I know you're pissed off at me too. But dammit, I want you."

He rubbed the back of his neck and ran his hands through his hair, then placed them on his hips. He reminded her of a gunslinger waiting for his opponent to make a move. "And since I don't give up easily, here I am, laying it all out. You, me, one night."

And just like that, her blood cooled, and the typical hum of desire she felt around him vanished. The reason they were at odds, pissed off at each other, reared its ugly head. The job she wanted. The position he made it sound like she would get when she interviewed for the position of interior designer for his luxury condominium community on Lake Coeur d'Alene.

He told her he loved her designs and the fact she was all about local flair, design and sourcing materials from the Northwest was essential to him. In the end, he chose a celebrity designer who wanted to bring the French Alps to Idaho. TS had fallen for the glitz and glam of aligning himself with Henri what's his name. Well, maybe he should make out with the French guy.

But most of all, she hated that she'd got her hopes up. Hopes of branching out into more significant projects, hope for a project she could add to her portfolio and take it with her to other, broader markets in the Northwest. She had wanted to leave Pineville for a few years now, but on her terms and after she'd achieved more of a name for herself in the industry. Yet all she ended up doing was wasting precious time believing in a job that had never been hers to begin with. TS had done what no other man had done since her father walked out on her family all those years ago. He'd made her feel like a fool for putting her faith in someone who had no intention of returning it.

She hated that her body betrayed her every time she saw TS; whenever she was forced to be around him thanks to their friends. It was maddening and a bit heartbreaking since in one form or another, she'd been in love with him since middle school, and that just made this moment suck all the more.

He wanted her in his bed, and he was arrogant enough to think she'd eventually end up there. He knew how to push her buttons, she'd give him that, but sex was easy. And she was afraid—afraid it wouldn't be enough. She'd want more.

Noel shook her head. The longer she remained silent, the more leverage he achieved. She opened her mouth to tell him to take a hike. But before she could he placed both hands on either side of her trapping her between him and her car. He leaned in until they were chest to breast. And she let him.

"Don't say no. I can see the wheels turning. Don't hold one business decision over my head as an excuse to turn down what I'm offering. What, I think, we've both wanted for a long time." TS put his mouth next to Noel's ear and whispered, "If I thought we could get away with it, I'd take you right here. Tell me you want me too. If not here, then come home with me."

His whispered words excited her. His breath against her ear created a shock of electricity that traveled to her middle and settled hot and heavy. The wickedness he promised was so damn close to one of her fantasies she thought one taste wouldn't hurt.

Maybe just one kiss.

Then she could walk away. Prove to him, to them both that she was the stronger one. That his decision hadn't broken her.

She'd burned for him every time they were within feet of each other. And dammit she wanted to burn now, if only for a moment, then she'd walk away.

All she had to do was lift her chin and turn her head and offer him her lips. But she didn't. She placed her hands on his head and greedily took what she wanted. His lips soft, firm and their warmth fed her need.

TS' low growl vibrated against her breastbone as she pressed in closer. She wanted this; every moment seared into her memory.

Breath mingling, she opened her mouth and sucked in his tongue. Twin moans erupted as they took turns devouring each other. Her hands outlined his chest, then rested on his shoulders. She gripped tight as TS slowed the kiss, sipping then licking her swollen lips.

His hand kneaded her breast, caressing her heated flesh through her blouse. She sucked in a breath as he flicked a thumb over her hard, sensitive nipple. A rush of warmth filled her at his touch. She deepened the kiss and pressed herself into his erection and groaned.

Too much. Not enough.

In the back of her mind, she knew she needed to end this now, before she did something even more stupid, like letting him take her against her car, in front of Luke and Lara's house.

It took everything she had, but she loosened her grip on his shoulders and pulled back. "Wait, wait. We need to stop."

She straightened and gave him a soft push back. The only sound between them were their heavy breaths. She couldn't look at him. Not yet. She fixed her rumpled clothes and twisted her hands in front of her.

She cleared her throat, "That's all I can give, TS." When she found the courage to look him in the eye, she inwardly groaned. His eyelids were heavy with desire and his lips as swollen as hers felt.

"I... I'm sorry. I shouldn't have done that. I'm not a tease, TS, but I can't. I can't do this. And I can't go home with you—sleep with you."

Confusion clouded his gaze for a moment before it was replaced by anger. "Don't tell me this is your way of getting back at me for giving Henri the job, Noel. Is it?"

She shook her head, "Of course not. It's just. It's... it doesn't matter. It was a great kiss, but that's it, that's all that can be between us. I'm not built to have sex for the sake of sex, and our situation is complicated." She snorted and let out a sharp laugh, "We share the same friends. We run into each other all the time, and we're godparents to Mari..."

"And you're still mad at me." TS moved away from her.

Far enough that she no longer felt his heat. She missed it.

He no longer looked at her, focusing his gaze in the distance. "I'll take your word that you're not playing games with me, Noel. After all I don't really have a choice, do I? But it doesn't change how I feel about you. So, if you ever change your mind and want a good hard fuck, give me a call."

He didn't go back to the party. Back to their friends and the celebration they both ditched because of this stupid attraction neither one wanted. Good damn hormones or pheromones or whatever the hell it was about him, that drew them together.

She watched as he strode to his car, and like a scene from a cheesy rom-com movie, he peeled out and roared down the road.

She deserved his anger. She shouldn't have kissed him, and was equally mad at herself, but she'd made the right move.

She rubbed her chest and stood for a while, replaying what had just happened; the explosion of passion had almost—almost convinced her to say yes to anything he wanted.

She drove home slowly; to the only male she let into her life, her heart; her cat Thaddeus. Her beloved Bengal was as unique as he was predictable. All he wanted was food, a place to sleep in the sun, and a good belly rub from time to time.

The same could be said about TS, minus the predictable part. She hadn't seen this coming.

Maybe it was time to reconsider moving soon rather than later.

CHAPTER 2

THANKSGIVING

TS spent most of the day watching Noel; how carefully she avoided him and how she went out of her way not to talk to him.

He tried to never relive his past, let alone obsess about it, but every time he was around her, he kept thinking about that damn kiss.

Noel had walked away, leaving them both unfulfilled. And she'd managed to keep him at arm's length ever since. But he was a gambling man, and with the holiday season and some free time, an opportunity was knocking at his door.

Timing was everything, in business and in life, and he was going to go after what he'd wanted—Noel in his bed, fulfilled and satisfied.

Perhaps then he could get past the non-stop wanting whenever they were in the same room.

He wasn't sure if it was fortune or folly that they shared a group of friends who spent a ton of time together. Wives and girlfriends hung out during the Outlaws games, then everyone came together for dinners at The Club, weddings, baby showers, BBQs, and holidays. Then there were the parties and game nights during the offseason at Maverick and Kelsey's.

And Noel was always there. Tempting him by simply being herself.

As she was today. He was drawn to her laugh, to her spirit. He admired her protectiveness of everyone she cared for. She was definitely the mama bear of the group—Kelsey, Lara, Caris, and Reese were the benefactors of her generosity.

Noel mothered her tribe and the men who loved them. He, on the other hand, seemed to take on the role of an outlier. He was tolerated by her at best. But when two people had the type of chemistry they did, pretending it wasn't affecting them, in his opinion, was a waste of time.

And so, he did his best whenever they were together, to find a way to remind her of what almost happened between them.

He'd do it with a look or a touch that was longer than necessary. A smile or a gaze that was longer than polite or platonic but not too long to make it obvious to others, namely their friends. The game had become, in a word, frustrating, and he was ready to speed things up.

TS needed to make sure Noel's expectations were the same as his. Because there had been too many love connections among their friends. And this was one epidemic he was determined not to catch. First Maverick, their best pitcher, then Luke the starting catcher and then his team manager Blake. And he was sure it was only a matter of time before Connor and Reese became engaged.

He didn't want love, didn't have time in his life, and thanks to his parent's dysfunctional relationship believed it wasn't for him. Since he was seventeen, he'd worked non-stop building his first app, then his company, and it snowballed from there. He'd achieved everything he'd written down that long-ago night during his junior year in high school.

In the past fifteen years he'd done more, created more, made more money than he'd ever dreamed. More than the old man and then some. Unfortunately, his father had died before TS had finalized the purchase of the Outlaws.

He'd wanted to rub it in the bastard's face, but a heart attack had denied him that chance. Owning a pro baseball team had been the only dream he'd ever shared with the old man then regretted it ever since. Thomas, Sr. never failed to belittle TS' dream and reminded him every chance he got that TS got lucky with the 'tech thing'.

He shook off the memory. The past was past, and he had plans for his future. A scaled-down future. Between the Outlaw's second season in Pineville and the condo project, he'd come to realize those were the only things that mattered.

So, he'd begun selling off his other businesses. He planned to slow down. Take more vacations, enjoy the life he'd built for himself instead of putting it off for just one more company, one more challenge.

But today, the challenge he set for himself was a smart, if sometimes snarky woman whose curves and soulful grey eyes kept him up at night. He was done waiting, he was done playing—the real chase started now.

"Kelsey, come sit. Mari will be fine, she's handled a house full of people so far, and if she wakes up fussy, I'll take care of her. You need a break from being super Mom." Noel popped Mari's pacifier back in and dropped a kiss on the silky-haired infant before Kelsey put her down for a nap.

Everyone had moved into Maverick's man cave to watch the football game while Noel had stayed with Kelsey while she nursed baby Mari who was now asleep thanks to a full tummy. For a moment, a deep longing came over Noel—for a child of her own. She'd begun to rethink her decision not to marry, to maybe someday have a child.

Her parent's marriage had been happy, in the beginning. In the end, her father had left, and Noel had been forced to care for her ill mother and younger brothers. It had not been a stellar advertisement for happily ever after and so at an early age, she made a promise that she'd never put herself in the same position. To her, marriage seemed unnecessary and offered guaranteed heartbreak.

But now that her friends had babies, she found herself thinking maybe she could be a single mom. When she looked over at Lara to see her feeding Andrew, a whisper filtered through her mind, "do it, Noel."

She watched as both Kelsey and Lara put down the babies in the nursery, and a louder voice urged her to consider what she'd miss out on if she didn't have a child of her own.

Kelsey switched on the baby monitor and picked up the remote.

"Okay, let's go join the party. We should have an hour before someone needs a diaper change."

Noel chuckled and followed them. She still had a smile on her face when she entered the man cave, and the first person she saw was TS. He was standing in the back of the room, talking to Blake. She quickly averted her gaze but not before she noticed the heat in his eyes. He flashed her a crooked grin, damn him. He finished the drink in his hand and made his way over to her.

Kelsey whispered in her ear. "Looks like someone's on a mission."

Noel closed her eyes. Did anything get past her bestie? It was eerie how tuned in Kelsey was to her group of friends. *Lucky me*. Noel sighed.

As nonchalantly as she could, she changed direction and sat down on the smaller of the leather couches. TS filled the space next to her, and a shift in energy and heat blasted her as his muscled thigh brushed hers.

Noel looked toward Kelsey and sent her a silent SOS by rapidly blinking. When that didn't work, she mouthed, "Help me."

All she got was a wink and a sly smile. What the heck? She whispered, "Traitor," then faced the TV and pretended to be interested in the game.

She closed her eyes and sent out a silent prayer to whatever higher power was available at the moment. When she opened her eyes, TS was still there. He offered her a drink and leaned back into the comfy couch, which she belatedly realized was a love seat, and stretched out his long legs.

Maybe her prayer hadn't been specific enough.

"You don't mind, do you?"

Another crooked smile, and she wavered. She was tired of ignoring him. It had become a job she didn't want anymore. She might as well accept he wasn't going away and make the best of things.

He was sending out all kinds of signals today. Clearly, TS hadn't forgotten their hotter than hell kiss. Dammit, why did he have to be so tempting? Pheromones, it was those damn pheromones again.

Alright, Noel, you can handle this. She searched her brain for a neutral topic— she was, after all, great at small talk. She'd had to be in her line of work. But before she could open her mouth to break the tension-filled air, the Skyhawks scored and everyone in the room roared to their feet, including TS.

He bumped her arm, and the wine in her glass splashed down her front. Instant mortification overcame her. She knew what she would find when she looked down. The blouse she was wearing was silk. A hiss of breath had her eyes flashing to his. TS's attention had also been drawn to her shirt or rather to her chest.

An all-over body flush hit and lord help her, her body responded to his intense gaze, and her nipples stood at full attention. Seconds ticked by as a crazy standoff developed. When his gaze began to travel up and locked with hers, the heat she thought she saw earlier paled in comparison to what was now swirling in his eyes. She needed to do something. She croaked out a barely audible, "excuse me."

Then she ran like a coward.

At the door, she pulled on her coat while Kelsey tried to convince her to stay. She begged off, saying she wasn't feeling well. Technically it wasn't a lie since the feeling's TS stirred in her were going to be her undoing if she stayed any longer.

FOUR DAYS AFTER THANKSGIVING, and TS was still thinking about Noel. And her eyes and her body's reaction after he spilled wine on her blouse and how her nipples had puckered under his gaze. He got hard every time he thought about it.

He'd asked Lois, his secretary, to send her a replacement. The next day he received a very short, polite thank you via text. It made him hopeful because he knew she was avoiding him for the very same reason he'd decided to kick his campaign into high gear to get her into bed—undeniable, all-consuming attraction.

There'd always been something about Noel Snow. When they were teenagers, he began to see her as more than Kelsey's shy friend and he'd thought she was starting to feel the same way. She had a wit he appreciated and grey eyes he wanted to get lost in. Then her mom had become ill, and she missed more school than she attended. Then she stopped going.

Around the same time, his mom had run out of ideas to torture his father, so she uprooted him right before his junior year. But he never forgot about Noel. He hadn't returned to Pineville until several years ago to buy the land for the Outlaw's stadium.

And he hadn't seen his mother since he left for college. His one salvation back then had been his talent in coding. Determined to prove his father wrong, he finished high school on-line and spent all his time developing a home security app. It had been his ticket to Silicon Valley and his first million.

He never looked back after that. TS's wealth had far outpaced the old man's, but it hadn't been enough for him; he needed more, more businesses to acquire, more real estate to develop. But he realized that acquiring more things wouldn't banish his father's spiteful words. "You want what I have boy, make it your damn self," had been his father's favorite refrain whenever Thomas Sr. was deep in the bottle.

TS loosened the death grip he had on the steering wheel. Shit. He hated it when he went down the rabbit hole that was his childhood. He relaxed his hands and turned his attention to the scenery as he drove to Maverick and Kelsey's. He'd been invited for lunch, but really all he cared about was seeing Mari. The little girl had captured his heart the first time he held her. He loved kids, other people's kids. As much as he'd love to have children, he knew to do it right meant two parents and for him, that wasn't ever going to happen. He was happy with a night or two with a woman who understood there was no chance of long term with him. He'd seen enough bitterness in his parent's marriage to convince him he wasn't built for long-term, to him, love was an illusion.

As he continued to make his way through downtown traffic, he marveled at how much growth had taken place. He loved this city by the lake with its art-friendly atmosphere; there was a giant moose sculpture from a local children's book penned by a local author on the corner of Main and Front that never failed to bring a smile. He passed the remodeled City Park at the base of the ever-popular Tubbs Hill edging the east end of the lake with its hiking trails, and a small cove where locals ventured to climb upon the rocks jutting out of the lake.

The more daring would launch themselves off the rocks, as he had done hundreds of times, and swim in the warm waters on a late August evening. It all made him feel connected again to the place he'd forsaken in order to find his own way.

He was glad he'd returned home. That he'd built his dream where his father had ruled—and been universally hated. Money didn't guarantee people would like you. TS had to work hard during the building of the stadium. One of his most satisfying moments had been when he won over the city council members who remembered his father.

They were going into the third season in Pineville, and Outlaw fever had steadily grown. He and Blake and the scouts had worked hard in putting together a balanced roster of players. He wasn't sure how much longer he'd remain general manager. It all depended on when Blake felt he wanted the role, and that would depend on if they could find someone to fill his shoes. He had an idea that Maverick may want the job once he retired. TS planned on planting that seed today.

He pulled into the driveway and laughed. Christmas was still a month away, but that hadn't kept Kelsey from putting out the giant blow-up reindeer and Santa in their front yard. He knocked on the door and was ready to tease her about it but was greeted by a stressed-out Maverick holding a crying Mari.

"Come on in. Kelsey's sick. Probably nothing, but she's napping, so no lunch unless you don't mind frozen pizza, or I could call for delivery or—"

"Maverick slow down. You uh, want some help?" TS nodded at the still upset Mari.

"Really, I mean that would be awesome, man. She's upset because I was singing to her, and she might need a diaper change. I haven't checked yet." A look of gratitude filled Mav's face.

"Sure. Besides, all women love me." TS shut the door behind him and followed Mav into the kitchen.

"I could put her in the bouncy seat, she loves it, I think. She's only a month old, and I'm not sure she's made up her mind if she likes me yet."

"Mav, just hand over the baby. And quit worrying about if your daughter likes you. I'm sure she does. Leave the worry for when she's a teenager."

Mari's wailing increased. TS held out his hands. "If I can handle the whiny tabloid press, I can handle my goddaughter." He raised his eyebrows and waited.

"True. Okay, but if she spits up or poops on you, you've been warned." Maverick put Mari in TS's arms.

TS settled the baby in the crook of his left arm and used his right hand to gently rub her head and brow. He began to softly sing, "*You are my sunshine, my only sunshine.*" She stopped crying, and with eyes wide, intently watched his mouth as he continued to sing. At least he thought she was watching him sing, she could be pooping for all he knew.

When he was done with the song, she let out a huge yawn. He looked up at Mav, "Point proven."

Mav was shaking his head, "man she's not a woman; she's a baby. And if it's true that all women love you, then how do you explain Noel, hmm?"

TS pretended he didn't understand the question and handed the now asleep baby back to her father. "She needs a diaper change."

"Aw, man. Why didn't you notice before she fell asleep? I'll be right back. There's beer in the fridge. I'll meet you downstairs, give me about ten minutes."

It took twenty, and TS had finished his first beer and opened a second. He reasoned he wasn't going back to the office, and it was the only lunch he was going to get since he didn't trust Mav with anything except microwave popcorn.

TS handed Maverick a beer as he collapsed in his favorite chair.

"Okay. Baby's asleep. Mama's asleep. Let's talk about you and Noel." He took a long drink and sighed. "Kelsey tells me you two shared a kiss a few months back, but she's still mad about you giving the interior design job on your condo project to that French guy. So, what's going on?"

TS didn't discuss his love life or rather sex life with his friends, but Noel was a special case, and maybe getting another guy's opinion might help. "Do you really want to talk about this? Don't you want to watch ESPN? Or we could watch game tapes?"

"Look, I've been there, okay. Remember what I went through with Kelsey? Let me return the favor, okay?"

Why the hell not?

"I still need to smooth things over with her concerning the job, but the thing is I can't stop thinking about her. As in—I haven't seen another woman in months—and short of telling her I want to take her to bed, again, and risk getting slapped in the face, I'm out of ideas. I'm pretty sure she's interested, and from what I can gather, she's not looking for anything permanent. And fuck, I can't believe I'm telling you any of this." TS took another pull on his beer.

"No, it's good. I've been watching this show. It's healthy, and shit for men to share stuff like this with their friends. Makes us better husbands and fathers. You know all the crap women love."

TS didn't know if he should find out more or punch Maverick for telling him he watches daytime TV.

"Right. Well, I'm not looking to be either one. I just want to get Noel into bed, out of my head, and get back to normal. Did your show say anything about how to do that?"

"Actually, no. But I have an idea. And if I didn't think Noel was into you, then I wouldn't feel right telling you this. And before you ask how I know she's into you, remember who I'm married to. Kelsey has been trying to figure out a way to get you two together for a while now."

Well, that laid to rest his worry that Kelsey might be upset if he pursued Noel. But the only 'getting together' he wanted to do was the horizontal kind. But he wasn't going to tell Kelsey that. And if he and Noel did get together, she'd know upfront and agree it was a one-time thing.

"Okay, what's your idea?" TS asked.

"I happen to know that Noel is going be spending a few days before Christmas at a cabin the girls have co-owned since their college days. And weren't you telling me not that long ago how you wished you could take a vacation and get away from it all, you know disconnect. Well, this place doesn't have wi-fi or electricity. It's got a generator and a couple fireplaces. It's about ninety minutes out of town—just far enough, ya know?"

TS smiled. Away from their regular routine and their nosy friends. It just might be the solution he was looking for. And if she wasn't interested, then it wasn't so far out that he couldn't drive back home the same day.

He grinned at Maverick, "tell me more."

CHAPTER 3

"*Y*ou sure you want to go out there—alone?" Lara asked as she fed Andrew. "If your brothers get wind that you went out there, during winter, they're not going to be happy; at you or us for letting you go."

Noel rolled her eyes at Lara. "The forecast is calling for clear and cold temps now through Christmas. No more snow predicted. I'll be fine."

They were hanging out at Kelsey's and making Christmas cookies. Noel didn't bake, but she was happy to be the official taste tester. So far, the brown butter salted caramel snickerdoodles were her favorite. They weren't traditional Christmas cookies but Lara had found the recipe on Pinterest, and Noel was in love. They were almost as good as sex, and since she hadn't had any in a long time, she reasoned the cookies were worth the calories since she was currently in a dry spell.

"I'll be fine. I need a getaway, to be honest. There's nothing like being alone, with no distractions to bother me while I reset. I'll be back the day before Christmas, early in the morning. Both Zane and Hayden will be in town that afternoon, so they won't know, or need to know that I was gone."

She snuck a few more cookies and put them in a zip-top bag. "What?"

"They're your brothers, not mine. So, if you want to incur their wrath fine."

The doorbell rang, and Lara's dog, Zander, raced to the front door and barked.

"Good boy. Thank you for protecting us." Lara gave him a rub and opened the door.

Reese, Caris, and Valeria entered. The little girl ran over to Noel and wrapped her chubby arms around her leg.

"Auntie No-No. Pick up."

"Valeria, ask nicely." Caris sent Noel a wave and waited for her daughter to follow through.

Noel looked down at the toddler. "What do you say, sweetie?"

"*Pweese.* Pick up." She lifted her arms and waited.

"Much better." Noel brought her up for a kiss on the nose and cuddled her close. This was almost reason to stay and hang with the group and eat more cookies and talk about what everyone had been hinting about to their husbands for Christmas.

But it wouldn't solve her problem. Staying at the cabin would hopefully give her the time and space to decide what came next. With her business and with TS. Because she knew something between them had to give, and soon.

"Okay, munchkin. Auntie No-no has to go-go before it gets too dark. I'll see you at Christmas, okay?"

"Kissmas! Pesents. Yay!" Val scampered out of Noel's arms and took off after the dog.

They all knew she was thinking of leaving the area, taking her business to a bigger city. There were several larger interior design firms in the area, and she'd been having trouble competing. And then she didn't get the job on TS' condo project, and then there were her feelings about him that were all twisted and unresolved—lots of reasons to leave. She felt a fresh start somewhere else might just be what was needed to take her to the next level in her career.

"Noel, before you go, we wanted to give you something. It's not a Christmas present. It's something to help you decide your next step." Kelsey dragged a wrapped box out from the pantry.

Noel laughed and looked around at her circle of friends as she took the cork board out of the box. At the top were the words, There's No Place Like Home stenciled in black letters. She teared up at the thoughtfulness and love of her friends. She knew they didn't want her to leave, but they'd support her no matter her decision.

"Thank you. This is perfect. I'll take it with me to the cabin." They knew she loved to make vision boards, and their gift was extra special since they also loved to tease her mercilessly about her slight obsession. She hugged everyone, and when she got to Kelsey, her friend didn't let her go. "While you're gone, be open to new possibilities, oaky?"

Noel thought Kelsey's statement a bit odd, and since they'd been friends for a long time, Kelsey also understood how important it was for her to be alone for a while.

"I'll see you at Christmas." She hugged Kelsey tight then grabbed her bag of cookies. It took her another ten minutes to get out of the house. Val wanted another hug, and then Zander had taken off with one of her boots.

She took her time on the drive out to the cabin. A light snow had begun to fall. So much for the forecast. Her SUV was equipped with all-season tires, and having grown up here, she knew conditions could change in an instant.

The sight that greeted her when she turned onto the private drive instantly made her smile. Memories from college. Late-night girl talks and midnight skinny dipping in the nearby bay littered her mind. This was the perfect place to decompress and think about what came next.

She walked into the main room and scanned the area. The furniture was covered in sheets. They'd all been busy with their lives to make the hour-long drive to freshen the place up in well over a year. She packed away the food she'd brought with her and made a cup of tea.

She carried her cup out to the back and stopped at the edge of the overhang, where the property sloped down to the sandy beach and the water beyond.

Crisp cold air fanned her face. She took in a breath. The scent of the Ponderosa Pine took her back to less complicated days. But soon the freezing weather forced her back inside and into the kitchen to make dinner. Later, she tidied up the house and put the sheets away.

The cabin had four bedrooms, two masters on either end with the great room and kitchen in between, and two bedrooms upstairs. She took the room with the view of the lake.

She'd turned on the generator earlier, but she loved this room because it had a wood-burning fireplace. Luckily there was still half a cord of wood stacked behind the house. She lit the kindling and soon was adding logs until she had a nice blaze going.

She decided not to wear the sleep set she brought since the room was toasty warm. In her tank top and undies, she grabbed her tablet. She pulled on her favorite socks and crawled into the over-sized four-poster bed and selected a cozy mystery that had been on her to-be-read list for months

After a couple hours of reading, her eyes wouldn't stay open. She must have finally drifted off because she woke out of a dead sleep to a loud rattling. Then she heard a man's voice, cursing. She wanted to run, but where would she go? Her heart pounding, her mind flashed to a horror flick she and about a billion other people had seen

An unsuspecting woman, all by herself in a remote cabin, wearing hardly anything and with nothing to defend herself expect her tablet and a cold cup of tea.

She stayed still. Maybe she'd been dreaming. There'd been a break-in at an antique store in the book she was reading, maybe she just had an overactive imagination. She waited a couple more minutes, but no more noises. Then she remembered. Years ago, Kelsey had brought a baseball bat and hid it in the closet.

God, she hoped it was still there. She moved slowly and tried to be quite as she got out of bed and walked to the closet door. When another noise came from the kitchen, Noel no longer cared if she was quiet or not.

She wrenched open the closet door, found the bat and swung it up onto her shoulder. Damn, it was heavy.

Another curse echoed down the hallway.

Dammit, she needed her cell, but there was no service. Shit, her brothers were going to be furious.

Footsteps pounded down the hardwood and grew louder as they approached her door.

She raised the bat and prayed.

TS headed down the hallway of the cabin toward the master bedroom. He opened the door and took a step into the room.

"Don't move or I'll shoot."

"Shit, Whoa, what the fu—Noel?" TS ducked as the bat swung and missed his shoulder.

He spun around and caught Noel as she stumbled backward.

"Oh my god. TS!"

Stunned, he watched as she let the bat drop to the floor then let out a few curses of her own.

"Dammit, what are you doing here?" Noel shouted.

"First things first, sweetheart. Is that thing loaded?" TS laughed long and hard.

She smacked him on the shoulder she'd missed with the bat. "I thought you were a bad guy or a… a hungry squirrel or something."

"A squirrel? I'd love to see a squirrel drive an SUV and haul the stack of wood I just brought in. What are you doing here?"

"I asked first." She lifted her chin in defiance and picked up the bat and put it back in the closet before she collapsed on the bed.

"Maverick told me about the cabin and that it hadn't been used in a while. I was looking for a place to spend a few days before Christmas, to you know recharge, and disconnect. He didn't tell me I'd have a roommate. Don't get me wrong, I'm good with the arrangement and the view."

"Wait a minute, what view? The curtains are closed."

"You're uh, …" He pointed toward her.

Christ, TS couldn't think. She was wearing a tank top that hid absolutely nothing and a lacy pair of panties. "Hell. Noel, you keep looking at me like that... damn, what you do to me. What is it about you that keeps me on a low boil? No one has ever come close to messing me up as you do." TS forced his gaze to remain on her face and not on the breasts he now imagined exposing and paying loving attention.

"Ha. You're seeing things. I'm looking at you like I always do." Noel crossed her arms.

"Exactly." TS let out a groan. She may have thought she was covering herself; instead, the movement ensured all the blood from his brain emptied and headed south.

He loved pushing her buttons. And she had many. TS was ready to test them all. Tonight.

He stepped further into the room and in a low voice whispered, "you know I'm not such a bad guy, Noel."

"I never said or thought you were, it's just..." Noel let out a breathy sigh.

She smiled, then laughed. Hope bloomed in his chest.

"Listen, we both can't stay here, and since I'm already settled in, you can leave."

"If that's what you want, I'd be happy to; however, Mother Nature changed her mind and dumped almost a foot of snow, and she's still going. I barely made it up the lane. I'm not going anywhere tonight, actually this morning since it's after three a.m."

"But, what about calling—"

"No service. This blizzard isn't letting up anytime soon, so you'll have to put up with me. I have some ideas on how you could do that if you'd like to hear them." He should feel bad about not being able to leave at her request, but he wasn't. He doubted he could get very far anyway considering how hard he was. Maybe she'd agree to help him out?

"TS, do you expect me to believe that in the six hours since I feel asleep, that there's enough snow outside to keep you from leaving?"

"I don't expect anything from you, Noel. All I can ever do is take what you're willing to give. But in this case, yes. You need to believe me. Check for yourself, the snow has drifted up to the porch, and the steps are barely visible."

Her facial expressions jumped all over the place, from desire to disbelief to uncertainty. He wasn't above taking advantage of the situation, but he wasn't going to talk her into anything she didn't want. And he was pretty sure she noticed how she was affecting him, his erection hadn't backed down no matter how he tried to picture something else, anything else, and oh, Hell.

She turned and walked to the window. She was killing him. Her ass was perfect, he couldn't take his eyes off her as she flipped the curtain aside and peered into the storm raging outside the cabin.

"Dammit. Okay, you're right. I um, didn't turn on the baseboard heater in the other bedroom, but I'm sure it'll warm up in no time once you turn it on. The room is on the other side of the kitchen—"

She'd turned back toward him and froze. He watched as she warred with herself. The desire was back on her face, in her eyes. She twisted her hands in front of her, then dropped them, then wrapped her arms around her waist.

His heart rate sped up as she licked her lips and continued to stare at him. The only sound in the room was the howl of the wind and their breathing.

"Noel, I know this isn't how you thought things would go, but I for one am damn glad the storm hit. I've wanted you for a long time. Hell, I know you know that, and that damn kiss at the baby shower… you were just as turned on, right?"

Instead of answering him, she dropped her arms and started to walk toward him. Either she was going to throw him out of her room or—not. Hell, he hoped it was door number two.

CHAPTER 4

*N*oel didn't care how or why TS was here. Yeah, she smelled a setup, but she was done denying herself. She wanted TS more than she wanted her first cup of coffee in the morning. She'd take the unexpected storm as the universe telling her it was time.

Time to get her groove back, and it was more than time she and TS found out if the sparks they'd been setting off whenever they were together were the real deal.

"You know something TS, you talk too much." She stopped halfway across the room and crooked her finger at him.

It would be so easy to keep pretending she didn't want, didn't crave his touch in the middle of the night. Screw easy. She no longer wanted to dream anymore about what being with TS would be like. She desperately wanted to experience what he had to offer.

TS flashed the crooked grin that never failed to send a shiver through her. He closed the distance between them, backed her into the wall and leaned into her overheated body. She wrapped her arms around his neck, her body pressing back into his.

"No one's ever accused me of that before. I hope you're ready for me, Noel. I've wanted you for so long that once isn't going to be enough. I don't think it'll be for you either. I plan on burying myself balls deep into you—all night.

"TS, you may be the most arrogant man I've ever met, but I'm done denying myself and you. I've thought about you too. And what it would be like to have you inside me, driving me crazy as I scream your name."

At her words, he let out a deep groan and devoured her lips. It was at that moment she grasped what this meant as his kiss consumed her. No more yearning, no more nights of frustration, and wishful thinking. She began to tremble from the deep need he created.

He took her hands and pinned them above her head and wrapped one hand around her wrists and held her in place. His erection throbbed against her belly as he ran his hands up and down her back. His hot, open-mouthed kisses along her neck and collarbone drove her slowly crazy.

Her palms began to itch, she needed to touch him—everywhere his gaze had touched her flesh earlier. Enveloped in his arms, she pleaded for sanity. "TS, please. I need to touch you." Her voice hoarse from desire, she wiggled one arm free and covered his erection through his jeans and whispered. "These have got to go—now." She reached for his zipper.

Noel found herself tossed onto the bed and watched in a daze as he stripped out of his clothes in record time. He covered his toned body over hers. She ran her hands over his heavily muscled arms, his shoulders and back, around to his stomach where she lightly tickled the skin over his taut abs.

TS sucked in a breath as she caressed him lower. She reached out to grasp his cock again when he took both her wrists in her hands and placed up above her head—again. He seemed to have a preference for keeping her hands off his body, but she needed to touch him, or she'd go insane. "TS, please?"

"Not yet, sweetheart. I'm going to learn every inch of you first before you get your turn."

Noel sighed as he lowered himself on her, she opened her legs, and he settled in between her thighs. At the intimate contact, something inside of her broke open. She couldn't name it, it scared her even as it brought her a sense of contentment she'd never experienced.

Noel wrapped her ankles around his back and pressed into his hard length. He rocked his cock into her and ground his hips until she thought she'd weep with gratitude. This. This is what she knew it would be like. Feel like.

"Sweetheart, if you're going to change your mind about this, say it now, or..."

"TS, this is what I want. We both knew from the first kiss... I ... I never thought… but from the moment I touched you, I knew. I knew this is where we'd end up."

"Damn, Noel. No more talking like that, or I'm going to come right now. I've wanted this for too damn long. I promise I'll take it as slow as I can. Until I can't. Then I'm going to erase every memory of any other man you've ever known."

He took possession of her lips and her thoughts. He took his time, and it was driving her mad.

When they both ran out of breath, he began dropping kisses on the top of her breasts. God, she burned for him. When his tongue swirled around one nipple, she arched her back, desperate to get closer.

Sounds of pleasure escaped her as he thoroughly loved her breasts. When he moved and started a trail kisses down her sensitive abdomen to the edge of her curls, she began to move her hips, desperate for his touch.

"Yes." She moaned. Her voice sounded foreign to her; husky and needy. She let out more sounds as he moved his tongue closer to exactly where she wanted it.

He didn't disappoint. He licked and suckled her clit until she thought she'd go mad.

He teased and caressed her, bringing her to the edge of frustration as she lifted herself closer, searching for release.

"Is this what you want?" He slipped a finger inside her and began to stroke slowly, torturously until she felt the first divine pressure of a climax building.

"More." She pleaded. She didn't want it to end, but she couldn't wait and lifted herself up once again, begging for his kiss. His mouth covered her again. His tongue back where she wanted it most.

"Please, TS, oh my God, that feels so good. I need...." She lifted her head from the pillow and watched as the man who was creating delicious sparks of heat inside her looked up at the same time.

She rotated her hips and rode his tongue as her climax exploded through her, sending tendrils of heat throughout her limbs. He continued the pressure, and the climax continued to build before it burst deliciously sharp. So intense her pleasure, Noel screamed his name. When he placed another finger inside her and found the exact right spot, the sensation sent her over a second time. She cried out again then felt herself float back down to the bed.

TS stretched his body up and over hers and guided himself into her. He set a slow pace as he captured her lips, kissing her, teasing her. She let out small groans each time he pulled out just to the edge before plunging deep.

"You feel so damn good." TS turned her over and guided her up onto her hands and knees. He reached around and caressed her breasts as he slipped two fingers into her. She cried out his name again as he flicked his fingers and pumped them in short strokes, bringing her to another orgasm. When he took them away, she whimpered, and he chuckled.

"You like that? Jesus, Noel, you're so wet for me."

When he nipped her ear lobe, she almost came again as he entered her at the same time. TS set a steady rhythm; she never wanted him to stop.

He came with a shout of her name and stayed inside her as he shuddered. He kissed and softly scraped his teeth against her neck until his body stilled.

They fell to the bed in a tangle of arms and legs. He brought her overheated body on top of his and stroked her hair while their breathing returned back to normal.

"Noel?"

"Hmm?" She wasn't sure she could form a coherent word.

"No regrets?"

She was silent for a moment too long because he pinched her butt.

"Ow. Bully. You fishing for a compliment?"

"I think I just proved myself very well, actually. I'm more concerned with... how you're feeling?"

TS was a complicated man. Being sensitive to other's feelings was probably something new to him, and she thought him sweet and…and oh, my Lord, that was the best sex she'd ever had. How stupid was she to have turned him down before?

But she wasn't going to let him know. It would be her secret. Besides, she wanted him to 'prove' himself at least once more before the night was over, and they went their separate ways.

"It was good. I feel… good."

"Good!? I'll show you good." He placed his forearms on either side of her face and kissed her stupid. He lined up all their good parts and, in a well-satisfied and raspy voice, added, "Hope you're not too sore for round two."

She smiled to herself. Oh, yes, she was definitely looking forward to round two.

NOEL WOKE up to the smell of ambrosia.

Coffee.

Strong coffee.

She sat up and yawned, stretching her arms above her head. The first thing she was aware of was all the small tugs and tingles her muscles produced. Some underused and others, well the loose-limbed feeling made her smile. It was the second awareness that made her freeze.

A man was standing in the bedroom doorway, leaning against the doorjamb wearing unbuttoned Levi's, and holding a cup filled with the one thing she couldn't live without.

Maybe she'd let him back under the comforter with her. "If that cup is for me, you're about to get lucky again. After I drink it." She realized too late her top half was bared to his gaze. She knew because he wasn't smiling at her comment. He was locked on her breasts. His gaze was at half-mast, his erection pushing through the opening of his unfastened jeans. Yeah, she'd forsake her coffee for more of him.

"Um, I hope you have more condoms because I hadn't planned on having marathon sex while I was here." Coffee forsaken, she flipped the comforter to the side, making sure he knew she was up for what his body was signaling he wanted.

"We're not going anywhere today. The snow has stopped falling, but we're going to have to dig our way out to the main road, eventually."

"Um, okay." At the moment she didn't care if they were going to be here for a month. She just wanted him back in bed. Now.

He set the coffee on the dresser and ditched his jeans.

Noel sucked in a quick breath. Damn, the man was built. His broad shoulders and muscled arms and chest were swoon-inducing. And she'd had the pleasure of learning every inch of him last night and a just a couple hours ago. If he was offering a round three, who was she to argue?

Before she could say his name, he was back on the bed leaning into her. He captured her lips and made her forget what he'd already done to her because this time he devastated her. And she matched him kiss for kiss, touch for desperate touch. This time was different. They knew now what the other felt like, tasted like, sounded like when they came.

This time it was a race to see how much pleasure they could wring from the other. Luckily there would be no loser in the silent, sensual contest.

They spent the rest of the day napping, eating, and making love. No thought was given to leaving. At one point, they dragged out a deck of cards, and TS suggested they play strip poker, but since she was wearing his shirt and he had changed into just a pair of sweats, it was a short game.

The next morning Noel woke up after being thoroughly and oh so, spectacularly satisfied. This time there was no coffee perking up her senses. Instead, she listened for sounds of TS since he was no longer in bed with her.

It was quiet. The kind of quiet you only found in the woods far from other humans. She'd missed that stillness. Maybe in the late spring or early summer, she'd take another long weekend and come back; if she were still living here.

The air had cooled in the cabin. Naked, she made a dash for the bathroom down the hall and turned on the shower. Warm water sprayed out. At least it wasn't cold. She stepped in and washed her hair. As she rinsed out the conditioner, she heard the front door slam. TS's boots stomped down the hallway.

"Noel?"

She called out, "in the shower." A thought that he might join her warmed her head to toe. When he called back that he'd be in the kitchen, a sense of disappointment took her by surprise.

They'd just spent hours in bed, consuming each other. She shook her head and scolded her greediness. She knew this prelude was all about working each other out of their respective systems.

It had been inevitable considering how long she'd been thinking of him. It was over, they'd go back home, back to their lives, and if all worked as she was planning, she'd no longer have to see him whenever their friends got together. In six months, maybe nine, she'd be in another city. Away from the temptation of TS.

And far enough away that she wouldn't have to see him with other women.

The door rattled from a knock, and she jumped.

"Hey, you still breathing in there?"

"Yes. Yes, I'll be out in a few minutes." She grabbed a towel and wrapped it around her dripping hair and took another and covered her shivering body. She caught her reflection in the mirror and noticed her face was covered in light red scrapes from TS's beard. Her lips were slightly swollen. She wondered if he bore any marks created by her desperate need for him?

It was unlikely she'd find out. She opened the door to find him standing outside.

"Uh, hi."

"Hi, back."

Well, this was awkward. They were standing staring at each other without either saying another word. Noel had to bite her tongue from asking him what he was thinking. Too dangerous, too personal, and what they'd just done had to remain simple. Just sex. Asking for anything more would be foolhardy. And Noel was no fool. She reminded herself she wasn't looking for happily ever after. She'd take what they did and keep it tucked away.

Because she knew he had no room for her in his life.

Noel knew he was consumed by his real estate projects and the baseball team he owned. For years in public and in private, he made it known that marriage and kids were not on his radar. In fact, he often mentioned he didn't see himself having either. She knew a little about his upbringing; it hadn't been a happy home. In fact, Kelsey had mentioned to her once that he never took friends to his house when they were kids, and she had only met his mom once. His father had no interest in him.

Unfortunately, she could relate. Perhaps that was part of the draw between them. Like found like.

TS cleared his throat, "I made some scrambled eggs, and there's fresh coffee."

He said the magic word. Bless him. She could use a gallon at this point.

"Great. I'll just, uh, go change and be right out."

He nodded and stepped aside to let her pass. "I'll hit the shower. I already ate."

"Oh, oh, good." Noel turned to the bedroom and listened as TS shut the door, and the shower was turned on.

She grabbed some clean clothes from her overnight bag and dressed in record time. She towel-dried her hair and wound it up in a bun on the top of her head. She pulled on a pair of thick socks and padded out to the kitchen.

Noel inhaled her first cup of coffee, poured a second, and served herself some eggs. She was toasting a bagel when TS walked into the room. His unique scent reached her, and she took in a deep breath. Dammit, she was turned on again. How was that possible after having had—she didn't' know how many orgasms—but it was a lot, more than she'd ever had.

"Hey. I'm going to hike out to the end of the drive and see if I can get cell service. If I can, I'm going to get someone to come plow us out. Shouldn't be more than four, maybe five hours and then I'll be out of your hair." He reached around her and refilled his coffee cup.

Noel didn't move. She felt a bit numb. Last night, and this morning had been a whirlwind of emotion and physical connection. And just like that, he placed any notion of a romantic spin on their time together out of reach.

He shrugged into his ski jacket, took his cup of coffee, and walked out into the bright day. She watched through the window as he hiked through the snow-covered driveway until she could no longer see him.

She kept herself busy while he was gone. She changed the sheets on the bed, tidied the kitchen and thought about finishing her book. But that's as far as she got, thinking about it. Screw it.

Noel pulled on her snow boots and jacket and went out to the back of the cabin and found an old shovel propped up against the siding. She attacked the snowdrift that had built up against the back door to the master bedroom and created a path between it and the kitchen door.

That's where TS found her. Hair plastered to her temples from sweat and mumbling to herself. God, she hoped he hadn't heard her. She'd been giving herself a pep talk. Actually, she'd been trying to convince herself she could act as unaffected by what they'd done as TS had earlier. But she'd quickly come to the realization that it was going to take more than an hour of her practicing how to act to cover up all the feelings he'd unleashed, if ever.

"There you are. The plow is here, and I wanted to say goodbye before I left."

She adjusted her sunglasses, thank god she remembered to bring them and leaned on the handle of the shovel. "Wow, that was fast. I guess it pays to have connections."

"No, it pays to have money." TS grinned.

His smile stole all coherent thought, but she didn't have one of her usual snarky comments to throw back at him.

"Well, yeah, I guess it does. So, you're welcome to stay…" Lame, so lame. Noel regretted the words.

"That's nice of you, Noel. But I know you wanted to be out here alone. Wanted time to recharge, right?"

She nodded and looked away. Recharge, yeah. She got some of that alright. Noel pasted a smile on her face. "I guess I'll see you around then."

For a moment, she thought he was going to kiss her. But he took a step back and rubbed a hand on his neck. "Noel, look, I wish… I think we both got what we wanted. It's been building up between us for a long time, and I know I'm never going to regret it. It was great. You're great. But, it's no secret that I'm not looking for…more."

He looked at her expectantly. She knew what he was looking for. He needed her to say she agreed.

"Of course, TS. It was great, and I, I don't have time or room in my life for more either. I've got a lot on my plate. My business is growing, and please don't worry. I'm not the clingy type. I… it's just that it happened so fast. Didn't it? This whole thing was just so unexpected."

She meant what she said. Her life had no room in it for a relationship or expectations from someone else, or love. Because this definitely hadn't been about love.

"Right. Yeah, fast." TS stayed where he was for another beat. Put his hands in his pockets and rocked on heels.

When he reached up and took off her sunglasses, she braced herself. She knew he was going to kiss her one last time. Should she let him?

He didn't give her an option. His kiss overwhelmed her, and his touch and scent were forever stamped in her brain. Dammit.

He pulled back. No charming grin this time. His gaze held emotions she couldn't read. He brushed a stray piece of hair off her face, turned, and left.

CHAPTER 5

The day after Christmas, Noel needed to tell someone about her time at the cabin with TS.

"You know how when you've had really great sex? I mean can't-stop-thinking-about-it sex?" Noel paced the room without waiting for Kelsey to answer and kept going.

"When your body quakes and shivers hours a day even after you've had it. Bam!"

"Bam?" Kelsey put Mari back in her cradle. She ran her fingers through her hair. "Hold it right there. What are you doing right now? Are you telling me that you and TS have finally hit the sheets?"

Finally? Noel had thought it would never happen, but Kelsey's question hit her hard. Had she been that obvious? Hiding her real feelings for TS, even from her best friends, had become second nature. *Maybe she wasn't as good an actress as she'd thought.* How much did she tell Kelsey? And why the Hell was she running her mouth now about sex?

Probably because she couldn't stop thinking about it. It'd been both the best night, well two nights of her life and the worst. The worst because she'd finally admitted to herself, she wanted more, and now she knew. Knew what it was like to be with TS; to be well and thoroughly made love to by a man. For her, it had been beyond just the sex, but they'd made an agreement, she couldn't afford having second thoughts.

The sound of snapping fingers brought her back to the present. Kelsey had moved to stand in front of her.

"You still with me, Ms. Snow? You can't just drop a bomb and then go silent. You're referring to TS. Oh, my God. You are! When? Wait. The cabin? Tell me everything."

Kelsey grabbed Noel's arm and marched her over to the couch. Mari had fallen into a milk induced baby coma and was sweetly sucking her thumb. Noel had never envied a child before, but she wanted that bliss. To fall asleep without worry or memories of something that couldn't be.

"Noel, you know I'm going to get it out of you eventually. Stop staring at my baby, she's not going to save you by waking up. Did you or did you not have sex with TS when you two were snowed in at the cabin?"

She took in a long deep breath and met Kelsey's intense gaze. She thought for sure Kelsey would be upset with her. After all, TS was like a brother to her. And she'd always been fiercely protective of him when it came to his personal life. And now, Noel would still be a part of that story whether she wanted it or not.

But lord, there was so much between them she couldn't get over. Better to let it all out now, move on, and let it fade to the background. She had a business to build and spending any more brainpower on what could never happen was a waste of her time.

The one thing she'd give him credit for was that as soon as the fun part was over, he'd gather her close and hold her. Rubbing her arm and back, she'd drift off until the need for each other became too much. It was as if they both wanted to pack a lifetime of passion into their time together. And it would have to be enough for her. She'd make sure.

"Okay, yes."

Kelsey squealed. What the hell? Were they back in high school?

"But."

"Oh, don't say but. You two have been circling for at least the last two years. It's about damn time. We all were rooting for you."

Noel managed a strangled, "We?"

"Yup. You would always clam up whenever TS's name came up, or you'd make sure to become scarce whenever you two were in the same space. It was pretty obvious, sweetie. I had hoped maybe… well, you know. Then that whole thing with the interior design position for his project went to someone else."

"Gee, thanks for the reminder."

Kelsey grimaced. "Sorry. But you know what they say, 'time heals all wounds.'"

"I thought so too. That's why I slept with him. It just seemed… inevitable, you know?"

"You're preaching to the choir. Same for Maverick and me." Kelsey grinned then gazed down at her daughter. "And for us, it worked out. Better than I could have ever hoped it would. Maybe— "

"No, there is no maybe for TS and me. One night, well two days actually and done. We both agreed. That itch has been scratched."

"Then why did you ask me about having had great sex?"

"Because you're my best friend. And so is Lara and well Caris and Reese too, but you and I, we've always been … closer. I might tell them too, but I needed to tell someone and that someone had to be you."

"Because I'm also friends with TS." Kelsey handed her a tissue.

She hadn't been aware she was crying. Silent tears had appeared, and she wiped them away and blew her nose. "Yes, because he's your friend too. And because he's always been a pain in my ass. Ever since we were kids, but that didn't stop me from sleeping with him, and I wanted you to know. To know I'm okay and to not get mad or anything at him. Okay?"

Mari snorted. The baby was still asleep, and when Noel looked down at her, the little imp had a smile on her face.

"This kid is so like me already; it's scary." Kelsey adjusted the pink blanket with baseballs and bats all over it, she chuckled. "TS gave her this blanket. He's been spoiling her since the minute she was born." She turned back to Kelsey. "Noel, even with all you've told me and really it hasn't been much other than the mind-blowing sex, I think you two would be good together. Hey, don't roll your eyes. I'm serious here. We've all been secretly hop—"

"Hoping? For what? To complete the set of happy couples?" As soon as she said the words, her chest tightened. Dammit.

Kelsey sat back and crossed her arms. She didn't answer her stupid question. Thank God.

"Okay, Mom. Stop with the hairy eyeball. I'm sorry. And I'm happy for all of you. I am. You and Maverick, Lara and Luke, Reese and Connor, and Caris and Blake. I am so flipping happy for all of you. But you know that's not for me. It never has been. You know better than anyone why. So, please let this go."

Her best friend still didn't say anything. She didn't look mad or upset. She looked... sad. And if there was one thing Noel hated was having those around her to be was sad. She had enough of that emotion as a child and teenager.

"I'll let it go. But I think you're wrong about one thing, Noel."

"Really? By all means, don't hold back."

"Noel, I love you and all the other girls as if you were my sisters. I think that's why we're all so close. Because we found the sisters we always wanted but never had. But I'm going to give you this advice whether you want it or not."

Noel braced herself. If there was one thing she hated, it was advice. Advice about her personal life anyway. "Alright, I'm listening. But I'm not agreeing to anything."

"Be open."

Huh. Not what she expected. "Be open to what?"

"Everything. Be open." Kelsey stood up, hugged her, and walked out of the room. "I'm going to grab a shower since you're here. I haven't washed my hair in two days. Take care of your goddaughter and enjoy the moment. I have a feeling come Monday you're going to need to be very open."

What the ...? "Kelsey Marie, you get back here. What are you talking about?"

Noel stared at the spot where Kelsey had disappeared for a long while. Dammit, she was up to something.

CHAPTER 6

"**S**o, I hear you and Noel finally, uh did the horizontal mambo, and then you let her get away?"

Kelsey Sullivan, now Kelsey Jansen, was the only person in his life who'd dare question him, well except for Noel. And he wasn't about to discuss his sex life with her even if he really wanted to know what Noel had told her.

"Gee, good afternoon to you too, Kelsey. And I'm not going there. I'm working because you see that's what I do in my office. So, if you don't mind…"

"Mind? Me? Nope, not a bit. Okay, how about we discuss why you and Noel made that ridiculous agreement of spending just a night together and how two smart people could be so stupid?"

He'd hoped the one night; actually, two would have been enough. A week later, he knew the time they spent at the cabin would never be enough. Now he just had to decide if he was strong enough to put himself out there and ask for more.

"TS? Hello? Boy, you two are a pair, aren't you?"

Which question to answer first? Kelsey's words weighed heavy. Did he want to be a pair? Could he succeed in a relationship with a woman the way he had in his business life? His messed-up childhood had shaped or better yet warped his views on love and marriage. Until Noel. She'd managed to twist his thoughts, his cold heart, in a direction he couldn't have predicted.

"Thomas Scott, stop tuning me out. If you don't want to talk about Noel and what happened, fine."

Shit. She was so not fine. Must be sleep deprivation. Had to be. TS couldn't stand the thought of Kelsey being mad at him.

"Pardon me, I didn't want to interrupt, but TS your interviewer is here from Pinnacle Sports Magazine. Should I have him wait or…" Lois gave Kelsey a warm smile, handed TS the reporter's business card, but gave him a frown.

TS knew that look. Lois had been with him since the beginning. First, as a receptionist at the first tech company, he started, then the office manager than his personal assistant when he sold the tech company making him the youngest billionaire in America. She knew him better than anyone. And she didn't hold back on her opinions.

"So, I heard what Kelsey said about you and Noel and if you want to know what I think—"

"No, Lois. I really don't."

"Too bad. I've watched you avoid anything permanent in your personal life for too long. Noel is a lovely girl, and you should stop acting like being alone is okay. It's not. You need someone like her. You deserve to be happy, TS." Lois finished her short speech and crossed her arms.

"Christ, is there anyone in my life that doesn't have an opinion about this?"

"No."

"No."

Kelsey and Lois answered simultaneously.

He looked between the two women who'd been in his life the longest. They'd always had his back. They'd always let him know when he'd crossed a line. They were the only ones he let in. But even with them, he'd held back, didn't share the dark spaces from his past, a childhood that had cemented his bachelor for life attitude.

He looked down at the card Lois handed him. Shit, now he had to deal with this. The reporter, the Sports Pinnacle, the nation's leading magazine on professional sports, had sent wasn't one of his biggest fans. In fact, the guy had written an article shortly after TS bought the Outlaws railing against him as a spoiled rich boy using his daddy's money to be a part of the sport TS could never hope to be a player in.

Proof that the hack had done little to no research on his past or the accomplishments he'd achieved on his own, without his father's wealth. Damn, he did not want to deal with this now, but if he put him off, then the chance of a less than favorable article was guaranteed.

"I appreciate that you two have my best interest at heart, but I'm a big boy, and I can handle my own love life."

"Well, alrighty then. But you better do it quickly because Noel's going to move her business out of state if you don't do something and I mean a big something. So, I need you to get your act together and—"

"Move. What? Wait, when?"

"Oh, so that got your attention. Well, good. Because since your stupid decision to sleep together just once, both of you have lost your minds. Noel thinks she's ready for a new start—somewhere else. She also thinks she's too damaged to find love, to be in love, etcetera, etcetera. Which is ludicrous, by the way. So, you need to fix this. Now." Kelsey walked over and stood next to him.

Whoa, love? This was not about love—at least on his part. And he was pretty sure if Noel had those feeling's she wouldn't have agreed to just their time at the cabin and no more.

When did things get so complicated? He looked at Kelsey and took in her disapproving glare. "You practicing for when Mari's a teenager and walks in the door after curfew with that look?" He asked.

"You wish. I know you, TS. And you haven't been happy for a long time."

He opened his mouth to refute the claim. She cut him off before he could speak.

"I'm talking on a personal level. Purchasing the Outlaws, building the condos on the lake, plus all the other company's you buy up, that's business, and it should make you proud. But those are just things, TS. They're not going to keep you warm at night or bring you contentment into your golden years. Only love can do that. And that, my friend, is what you're missing. What you need. So, swallow whatever pride you've been holding onto and pick up the phone and ask Noel on a real date."

"Since when does one have to do with the other? I'm not looking to marry Noel or anyone else. End of story.

"You're wrong, TS. This is about love. It's about opening yourself up to the possibility. You can't hide your feelings from me. I know there is something there between you and Noel. Take a chance."

He wanted to ignore her plea, but he wasn't going to argue with Kelsey. There was no use. She already knew why he didn't believe in love. The safe thing to do was let her think he would consider it "What aren't you telling me. What did she say to you about our time at the cabin?"

"Not much. But enough to know that there's something worth fighting for. You both think you're each better off alone. And that's crap. Work out what's keeping you from being happy and believing that you'll be no different than your parents were. Just because they failed at love doesn't mean you will too."

She hit on TS's biggest fear. No wonder she was the only one he let get close to him. "I'll think it over. That's the best I can do right now, Kelsey."

Long after Kelsey left, TS sat in his chair, staring down onto the field. His very own field of dreams. He'd accomplished quite a bit in a short amount of time. But was he willing to put himself, his heart, on the line? Did he really see a future with Noel? He knew he wanted her but forever was a damn long time.

CHAPTER 7

NEW YEAR'S EVE

$\mathscr{N}$oel heard excited squeals and giggles as she stood on Caris and Blake's front porch. Today was the fifth time she'd come to sit with the toddler. They'd been blessed with her adoption last year, and the family of three had blessed Noel with the joy of spending time with Valeria on their date nights.

She was eighteen months old and was ruling the household. She charmed everyone who met her with wide-eyed brown eyes and infectious giggles.

Caris had been having fertility issues before Blake, then Valeria came into her life. She had been so happy when their whirlwind love story played out with the hippies of endings by becoming a family.

Noel was happy for Caris and all her girlfriends. She didn't begrudge her circle their happiness. They'd earned, no deserved, every bit of joy in their new lives. And the fact that each was wrapped up tight with an Idaho Outlaw the irony she was now involved, correct that had a brief hook-up with TS wasn't lost on her. Apparently, they all had the same type.

They were all going to get a big kick out of her sleeping with TS.

But she'd long ago made up her mind that having a family of her own wasn't a priority. She was determined after watching her mother go through continued betrayal by her father then take him back again and again simply because she didn't want to be alone had been a painful lesson to learn at a young age.

Noel had wished it had been her mother that had left her father than the other way around. The day her father walked out on them, she'd vowed to never let a man close enough to ever treat her that way.

She was happy in her new role as 'Auntie' of three and counting. She received all the fun and unconditional love without the loss of sleep or the cost of orthodontia and college.

The mini fireball rounded the corner of the entryway and let out another round of giggles. "No-No, Auntie No-No." A blur of dark brown curls made a beeline for Noel. She pressed her cherub face against the window next to the door and grinned.

"Valeria! You do not go to the door by yourself." On the toddler's heels, Caris appeared with a sippy-cup in one hand and a hairbrush in the other.

Noel noticed Caris looked like she'd just stepped out of a magazine even though she'd put in a full day at work and been wrangling her energetic daughter while also getting ready for a date with her husband. Her soothing tone as she reprimanded Valeria was perfect in her profession as a psychologist and washed over Noel, making her feel calm just by being in the same space as her. She secretly wanted to be Caris when she grew up.

"Yes, sweetie. It's Auntie Noel. Now be a good girl and stop kissing the window. Oh, no licking, either." Caris picked her up and opened the door.

"Welcome to chaos. Hope you're ready, she's gotten her second wind." Caris led the way into the front room and handed the toddler over.

"Are you kidding? Auntie No-No came to play. Isn't that right, Val?" She rubbed noses with Valeria and twirled her around and was rewarded with more giggles.

"Well, don't say I didn't warn you. Her pj's are on the dresser, she'll need to put on the nighttime pull-ups, and yes, I know you know the routine, sue me."

Noel wasn't insulted. Caris was a mom. A very organized, type-A mom, but she was loosening up ever so slightly.

"Don't worry. I won't let you down, Doc. Now you go grab Blake and get out of here and ring in that New Year right. We girls have serious business to attend to, don't we Val?" She swung the toddler like an airplane and gently landed her on the couch.

"Again. Again! No-No."

Noel fell down on the couch and laughed. "In just a minute, sweetie. I need to take my shoes off and— "

The front doorbell rang, and Caris excused herself. Blake walked into the room, and the little girl immediately jumped off the couch and threw herself into her daddy's arms. From number one to two just like that. Guess she couldn't blame Val. Blake was one of the best guys she knew, and he'd taken to fatherhood quicker than any man she'd seen. Caris was very blessed. And it didn't hurt that he was fine to look at. In fact, all her girlfriends had become just as lucky.

A familiar voice tickled her ear. She turned to the entryway as Blake, with Val, in tow greeted the man she'd done her best to stop thinking about.

"Hi, Noel."

"TS."

Nobody said anything else. She wasn't sure how to act. They hadn't said, well she hadn't said anything about them except to Kelsey. Had TS told Blake? And why was he here?

"You didn't have to drop off the paperwork, TS. I could have picked it up next week."

Blake took the folder TS handed him, and with Valeria still on his hip disappeared into the back of the house.

"TS, we were just going out. It's New Year's Eve." Caris moved into the room and crossed her arms. "Don't you have plans, either?"

TS wasn't listening to Caris. He was looking at Noel. And Noel was trying not to react to the heat in his gaze or the grin on his face. The one that melted her insides—every single time.

Caris moved to block TS's view of Noel. "Listen, we don't get out often, so when Blake comes back, no baseball talk."

He leaned around Caris and gave Noel a wink. "Yes, Ma'am. No baseball talk. Promise. Is it okay if I talk with Noel? Is that allowed?"

Noel couldn't gauge Caris's reaction since she was still looking at TS. Did Caris suspect anything? Caris could read people better than anyone she'd ever met. But then again that went along with her job.

"Sure. But Val is the priority. Don't monopolize Noel's attention, okay?"

"Sure. I've got ah, a couple interior design questions I want to ask her. Since she's here." He offered Caris his best grin.

"Mm-hmm." Caris turned to Noel. "Make sure you boot him out before Val gets sleepy."

And when TS wasn't looking, she mouthed, 'later' to Noel. Well, that just proved her point. Nothing got by Caris.

Blake came back in the room, handed Val off to TS, and grabbed his wife's hand. "Let's get before they change their minds."

She watched as Blake and Caris said goodbye and gave loud smacking kisses to Valeria that had her giggling again. The toddler waved bye to her parents and patted TS on the face.

"Sketchy." Valeria rubbed TS's face.

He looked confused.

Noel burst out laughing. "She means scratchy—your beard." She pointed to his face.

"Ah, yes. I'm very sketchy." TS rubbed his cheek against the little girl's. Then he waggled his eyebrows. More giggling.

"All right, you two. Enough. I think we should read a book. Val, could you go get me your favorite book, sweetie?"

"Book. Down." She pointed to the floor and waited.

TS took the order and set her on her feet.

They both watched her race out of the room.

"We have less than a minute before she returns. What sort of question could I answer that the one you hired, can't."

He unleashed another grin. This time it was not so innocent. And was full of wicked intent. "Well, it dawned on me that I hadn't given you a good reason why I gave the job to someone else and not to you."

"TS. You don't owe me—"

"Yes, I do, Noel. Give me five minutes. Then I'll leave. Please?"

She wasn't prepared for this or for him.

"Alright." Noel still wasn't sure what was going on, but she'd play along.

Before he could explain, Valeria came running back in the room with her favorite book. It was about bunnies, and she knew it by heart, which she found out last time when she skipped a page on accident and the little girl shook her head and made her read the page.

"Hey, how about you read the book to Val, and I'll go get her milk?" She hadn't expected him to jump at the chance to read the bunny book, but he was just full of surprises.

He grabbed Val's hand, took the book, and sat down on the couch. She crawled up into TS' lap and snuggled in. Noel felt a twinge of something she'd couldn't put her finger on.

While they were busy discussing the carrot patch, the baby bunny was lost in, she found the milk and warmed it in the bottle warmer. So many extra gadgets needed for a little human. She was pretty sure her mom never had one of these. When the milk was ready, she found TS and Val on the floor on their stomachs playing with the toddler's favorite stuffed animals. A bunny and a bear that was outfitted in Outlaw colors.

They were whispering so she couldn't make out what they were saying. She stood back and let them have their playtime. Kelsey had told her how good TS was with Mari. Not that she thought TS wouldn't be, however before everyone started having babies, she'd never pegged him for the fatherly or even the fun uncle type. Apparently, she was wrong.

When Val let out her second yawn, Noel decided to step in. "Okay, little one. Time for milk, then bed." She bent down and scooped up the sleepy girl and met TS's intense gaze.

She shook her head at him. "You're insatiable."

"It's your fault." He sat back, then pushed off the floor to stand.

He was standing too close. Her pulse picked up, and he was still staring at her like she was his favorite, stuffed bunny. Ugh. This was getting a bit complicated. She hadn't expected him to show up in her life like this. Now he was reading bedtime stories and playing on the floor with their friend's toddler and wanting to apologize to her.

She needed him to leave before she broke the babysitter's main rule—no boys allowed. It didn't matter that Caris and Blake knew he was here. It mattered to her. And she needed to guard her heart.

She broke eye contact and sat down and gave Val her milk. Soon the little girl was nodding off, and she carried her into her room. She got her off to bed and found TS still sitting in the same spot as when she left.

"I know you think I'm going to ask you to make out, but I'm not. Well, I might if you ask nicely." TS paused, flashed her a smile then went back to pacing.

She hadn't either until he brought it up. Great now she couldn't *not* think about it, or them together. "TS, what did you want to say?"

This was a side she hadn't seen yet—an uncertain TS.

"I gave the job to someone else, not because I believed he could do a better job, but because I was selfish. I wanted you in my bed, and I couldn't have you and be your employer at the same time."

He walked over and took her hand, "And now that it's happened, I thought the time we had together would be enough, but… I realized it's not. Enough. I'm not even sure what enough is, but I was hoping we could figure that out together."

Damn right, it hadn't been enough. Noel knew she'd never feel the same about any other man's touch after having TS worship every inch of her body. But what he was suggesting was…crazy. She couldn't come up with a better word or a good response.

"What we had at the cabin was great, I mean beyond great, but you… me, our past. I thought we agreed we're not the type of people who are looking for long-term, a relationship. I'm not sure—"

"Just don't say no, not right away. Think about it. I'm leaving on a business trip tomorrow then I'll be back at the end of the week." He caressed her cheek and ran his thumb along her bottom lip.

"Hey, it's New Year's Eve, and I know it's nowhere near midnight, but I was hoping maybe we could… for good luck… may I kiss you, Noel?"

His husky whisper went straight to her happy place, and she nodded. It was New Year's Eve. Everyone should have someone to kiss, right?

He placed a light kiss on her lips and rubbed once then a second time. He pulled back much too quickly. The kiss was everything; it tore her apart and put her back together, and it was not enough. She wanted more, more than he was looking for—she was in big trouble.

Noel followed him to the front door. Her thoughts in a jumble. Whatever this was between them was getting complicated. She didn't want complicated. It was the exact opposite and not what she signed up for. Deep down, she knew this was a bad idea, but she still wanted him.

"I'll be in touch when I get back from LA. And maybe we could have dinner… or just talk. I'm open to whatever."

CHAPTER 8

JANUARY

"If I never have to look at another curtain tassel, it'll be too soon." Noel plopped down on Kelsey's over-stuffed love seat, kicked off her heels, and leaned down towards the baby cooing on the pink sparkled unicorn blanket at her feet. "Hand her over, I need some baby therapy."

"What's this blasphemy? Aren't you worried I could turn you into the National organization of Interior Designers or whatever?" Kelsey picked up her daughter and handed her into Noel's outstretched arms.

Mari settled into her arms and gave her a wide-eyed look. Her goddaughter never failed to soothe whatever stress she heaped on herself. She sat the baby on her knee, face to face, and marveled at the miracle Kelsey and Maverick had created.

The little imp held her gaze and tilted her head. The look she gave Noel was as if she could see straight to her soul. "What do you see, Mari? Give me your wisdom." Noel whispered the question, not expecting her to answer but wouldn't be shocked if she did.

Kelsey snorted. "Don't let her fool you. She may look all Zen now, but come three-thirty-two in the morning she morphs into a demanding baby lion with a roar to match."

"Is that true, Mari? I won't believe you're anything but a perfect angel." Noel cuddled the baby against her shoulder and took in a deep breath. Ah, her favorite scent, baby powder, and lavender lotion were a heady mix.

If she pictured herself at all as a Mom, it was with a baby that looked a little too much like TS. She quickly banished the dangerous image and contemplated how to bring up the discussion she had with TS the other night.

"Since you're here, do you mind if I go take care of a few things? I just fed her, and I promised to keep her awake until Mav gets home. I checked, and the plane landed about twenty minutes ago, so barring a chatty reporter or two he should be home by nine." Kelsey didn't stick around for a yes as she left the living room.

That meant so would TS. Would he call her? Did she want him to? She did not have time to moon over a guy, and this was why she chose to not get involved with anyone. She'd been cursing him all week since he'd put a glimmer of hope in her mind that maybe they could work things out. Be a couple that had great sex, maybe become each other's plus-one, then go back to their corners and do their own thing. It could work. Or it could be nothing but heartbreak.

"So, kiddo. What should we do?"

Mari let out a hiccup and a toot at the same time. The actions startled her, and the typically calm baby let out a wail. Big fat tears fell down her cheeks, and Noel's heart tightened.

"Oh, no, sweetie. It's okay." She spoke in a sing-song tone and placed the baby on her shoulder and rubbed her back. "Auntie Noel will make it all better." Mari didn't seem to agree with her and kept up the sniffling and hiccuping.

Alright, she needed the big guns to handle this. Noel leaned further back into the cushions and turned Mari, so she was cuddled into the crook of her arm. "I have the perfect song. My mama sang it to me when I was little." Before she began to sing, she closed her eyes. Her mother's smiling face appeared.

Loretta Snow's skin had been sun-damaged and lined from too many cigarettes, but she always had a ready smile and a kind word; for everyone. Her voice raspy from smoking, she would sing to them every day. Her younger brothers pretended they didn't like it but would complain if she stopped.

She sang whatever was popular at the time, but at bedtime, there was only one song she would sing, and today Noel would sing it for the first time since her mother's passing.

Noel dried Mari's tears and gave her a quick kiss on the nose. It distracted the baby into silence.

"*I'll be there for you...*" She sang a bit off-key, and as her mother did, she left out the first verse but poured all her heart into the chorus. *Friends* had debuted when Noel was four or five, so she hadn't watched the show when it was first on, but her mother had. And her mother had fallen in love with the theme song and made it a lullaby for her kids.

When she finished the last round of the chorus, she knew she was in trouble. Mari's eyes had closed, and she was making the cutest little sucking noises as if she were still nursing. The sound of the front door opening and closing echoed throughout the room.

"Uh, oh. Daddy's home." Noel tickled Mari under her double chin and called her name. "Time to wake up the princess. You don't want Auntie Noel to get in trouble, do you." No luck.

Darn it. Kelsey was not going to be happy.

"Hey, Noel. Nice to see you escaped from your dungeon." Maverick always made an entrance, even in his own home. He dumped his duffel bag, bats clanged loud enough to wake the dead or a sleeping baby. Neither happened.

"Now, hand her over nice and slow, and I won't tell Kelsey you let her fall asleep."

He took possession of his daughter like a pro and made the transfer without waking her. Mari snuggled into her daddy and let out a sigh. Noel swore her ovaries cried out at the sound, and then Mav had to top off the moment with the broadest smile she'd seen on his face since Mari was born.

"God, she's beautiful. You know Noel, I have no idea what I did to deserve her and Kelsey, but I'm damn glad to have them both." He kissed the baby on the top of her silky head and kept grinning.

At that moment, she was envious of her friend's life. She had it all. A career she loved and could work from home when needed, a precious daughter and a loving and yes, sexy, and handsome husband. It was a life anyone would be thrilled to have and one not many ever experienced.

Noel's eyes welled, and she turned away from Mav and Mari and found Kelsey standing in the doorway, giving her an odd look. It wasn't pity, more like she knew what she had and wanted the same for Noel. And she loved her for it, but she knew her past would always keep her at arm's length from any man who came too close to offering what Mav gave to Kelsey.

She didn't understand why she was suddenly so melancholy, it wasn't like her, or it hadn't been in a long time. She'd worked hard on her attitude over the years and had come close to perfecting a positive outlook over the sad and disillusioned teenager she'd been. She should be happy, dammit. She loved her career, great friends, and she was looking forward to growing her company.

So why did seeing her friends happy and content make her feel anything else? It must be sleep deprivation. She'd only been averaging five to six hours a night lately, and she'd lost a few pounds due to skipping meals. Maybe all she needed to get her attitude back in positive territory was a healthy meal, a good night's sleep and before she could name anything else, TS' face popped into her memory and how'd he looked as they rolled around that oversized bed.

Hmm, maybe that's all she needed; to get laid. A woman had needs, and there were worse ways to get her groove back. Like chocolate or bacon mac n' cheese. And two days of pretending that she didn't want to take TS up on his offer or what she thought was an offer to continue what they started at the cabin was long enough. She'd been achy and if she were honest a bit horny lately. For him. Only for TS.

"Hey, handsome. How was the conference?" Kelsey walked over to her husband and kissed him as she wrapped her arm across the baby he held.

"Hey, yourself. Thanks for keeping her up."

Mav and Kelsey were lost in their moment. Noel felt like the third wheel she was and quietly gathered up her shoes and purse and tiptoed out of the room. She peeked over her shoulder at the picture the happy family made. Yes, she was jealous, but her happiness for them outweighed the heaviness she felt whenever the green-eyed monster lifted its ugly head.

A soft voice followed her out of the room. "Girls night, next Friday. Be there, Ms. Snow. I know where you live, and I'll hunt you down if need be."

Noel smiled. Girls' night at The Club was just what she needed.

Or to get laid.

It was going to be interesting to see which one would happen first.

"OUCH. DARN IT!" Noel pulled the tray full of roasted sweet potatoes out of the oven. They were perfectively caramelized, and the scent of cinnamon wafted through the kitchen. She loved to cook but rarely did since it was only herself.

He'd called, and she suggested dinner at her place. Glancing at the clock, TS would arrive in ten minutes. It was a date. Sort of. It was definitely a prelude to needing the box of condoms she bought today.

She set the oven to warm and put the potatoes back in then double-checked the chicken breasts she had on low on the stovetop. Rosemary and garlic chicken were her go-to dish when she wanted some comfort food. And she wanted to impress.

And the truth that she wanted to impress TS made her smile. She deserved to be happy. Not the happy type of happy that came with couple-hood, but maybe contentment-happy was enough. And someone to have great sex with, dinner here and there and then a friendly goodbye when one or both of them decided it was over.

A text from Kelsey brought her back to the present. She pulled up the article Kelsey wanted her to read and sat down hard in the chair closest to her.

She jumped when the front doorbell chimed.

"Darn it." Noel untied her apron and went to let TS in. The hit piece she'd just read on TS made her wonder why he didn't call her to cancel. Had he even seen it yet?

She opened the door. His face said it all. Yeah, he'd read it.

"Hi." She stepped back to give him room. Lots of room.

TS stood there, staring at the space between them. "Something I said?"

"No, I … well, I just read the article on The Pinnacle's website. Are you okay?"

"Neve better. What's that I smell? Cinnamon?"

So that's how they were going to play it—pretend it wasn't out there. Because after all, they weren't a couple.

She motioned him in, and he followed her into the kitchen. "Smells good."

"You already said that." She removed her apron and tossed it onto the counter. "Look, we can do this another night if you need to handle this."

He didn't respond, and for a minute, she didn't think he would. "I'm a good listener, TS." She wanted him to let her in. It scared her that she'd begun wanting things from him she had no right to, but he needed a friend right now.

"What do you already know? About my parents. Has Kelsey ever told you what a messed-up pair they were?"

She hadn't, and from the anguish, on his face, she wouldn't have had to. "Very little. I know that they didn't get along, always fighting and that you never invited friends over to your house."

"Yeah. The article did a pretty good job of digging into my mom's background, and you don't need to dig deep to know my father had money and was disliked in the community. But what the reporter didn't know was how he spoke to me."

She knew his father had died years ago. Heart attack or something. And she knew TS hadn't returned for the funeral. She didn't judge him for it. If she knew her father had died, she'd be the last one to attend his funeral. Huh, they had more in common than just great sex.

"He didn't want me. And he sure as Hell didn't want to marry my mother. But she blackmailed him. Back then, it was still taboo to knock up a part-time hooker and grifter." He locked eyes with her as he said those heart-breaking words. As if he was daring her to look down on him.

The article had mentioned the grifter part. It seemed his mom was still active. But not the other part. And certainly not the unwanted angle. She stepped closer to him and put her hand on his chest.

"I wish I had the right words to help you heal. I can understand the unwanted part. Our father left my family when the going became too tough after my mother's diagnosis. But you have to know that his words came from a dark place. Sounds to me like his role models sucked. And he took it out on you."

He removed her hand from his chest and leaned back against the kitchen counter and crossed his arms. "Is that supposed to make me feel better? That he was part of some messed up crappy parenting cycle and just passed it on to me. Because being told you'll amount to nothing every day of your life is fucked up, Noel. There is nothing anyone can say, not even you, that will change how I feel about him. Ever."

His voice held controlled rage. She wanted to take it away, make everything better. Her heart ached for the little boy who only wanted to be loved and instead received nothing but spite from a wounded soul who made no attempt to rise up and become a better man.

Noel knew he wasn't mad at her. All she could do was be there for him.

"I would never ask you to change who you are or how you feel. What I said was meant to let you know I understand. And because I think you need to hear it, tell you that no one has control over how you feel about yourself. Your father made a choice. He stayed in the cycle, stayed bitter, and did nothing to make sure his child had a better relationship with his father then he probably did."

He didn't say anything, but she had a bit more to say. Her need to take care of him was getting stronger; the more time they spent together.

"You probably don't want to hear it, but I'm sorry that reporter dug up your past and is making you relive it. But don't let it have power over you. You're a better man than your father ever was, TS. Don't let him ruin what you've worked so damn hard to accomplish."

She didn't know if she'd gone too far. He was notoriously private and probably didn't want to have to share his hurts with her considering their relationship or lack thereof.

Noel waited for him to tell her he had to go. Instead, he let his hands fall to his sides. His face no longer showed any signs of anger. What she did see created a swarm of butterflies in her stomach.

"Thank you, Noel. I needed to hear that. You're a good friend."

The look he was giving her made her feel anything but friendly. It was downright predatory. And lucky her, she was the prey.

"We can talk more about what a shitty childhood I had and how I feel about a slimeball reporter tracking my mother down. But I'd rather handle other things. Namely you. You have a problem with me handling you, Noel?"

She watched as TS's gaze roamed over her body. He did it twice, and when he paused on her chest, then looked up and locked eyes with her, she forgot her own name.

A part of her knew he was looking to blow off steam. That what they had was exactly what he was silently asking for. But another part wanted to open her arms and take him in and tell him it was going to be okay.

Her voice was shaky as she answered, "No." Not from uncertainty but from the pent-up desire, she'd been holding onto during the past four days.

"Good. Turn off the oven, Noel." He commanded.

She understood this was about sex and nothing else. His tone turned her on, the need in his eyes compelled her to do as he asked.

She turned around and switched off the heat. Not wanting to waste time, she quickly ran through her menu to make sure nothing else needed to be done. Everything else would keep while they… attended to other needs.

"TS, I want you to know— "

"Later, Noel. Right now, I need you."

His words carried a level of desperation she recognized and their husky tone full of promises she wanted fulfilled. Now.

Before she could turn back around and walk to him, he was behind her and pulled her into his chest. He laid a hand on her stomach and pushed her into his erection.

"Tell me you're not turned on right now?" He feathered kisses along her neck and jaw. She melted into his form and arched her back, trying to get closer.

A sense of Deja vu overcame her as an insistent buzzing sound came from his jacket pocket. She smiled at his groan. He kept kissing her neck as the tone played on.

"TS, are you sure you don't have to answer that?"

"Do you want to know what I've been imagining?" He spoke in her ear and nibbled her lobe. She squirmed against him and clutched the counter.

Noel nodded her head and pushed her body as tight as she could to his, which gave him a better view down the top of her dress where it billowed. She heard him suck in his breath. He'd discovered she hadn't worn a bra.

She knew he was getting a full view of her breasts as she felt her nipples hardened, waiting for his attention.

His hand roamed under her blouse, he cupped his hands under her aching breasts and flicked his thumbs over their rock-hard tips. It was her turn to groan.

He removed her blouse and turned her around to face him and tipped up her chin to bring her gaze even with his.

"First, I'm going to suck your nipples until you're on the verge of coming. They're so pretty and needy. Just for me. I fucking love that I do that to you, Noel. Next, I'm going to slip my fingers inside your panties." He followed up his words with action.

His middle finger entered her and began to lightly stroke her. All the while, he held her gaze.

"I'm going to bring you so damn close to the edge you'll think you're going go mad. Then, I'm going to lean you back onto your table and spread your thighs and sink my tongue into your hot, wet core and make you come, screaming my name."

Noel let out a small gasp.

"Finally, I'm going to enter you. Slow at first. In and out until all you can think about is coming again, around my cock. Then I'm going to—"

"You know something, TS?" She grabbed his hand to stop his movements so she could think.

"What's that, sweetheart?'

"You talk too much. Shut up. I need you inside me. Now." She crawled up his body and hooked her legs around his waist and swallowed him whole. Her tongue dueled with his as they fought for dominance.

He chuckled. "I think I've heard that before. And soon. First, I want to taste."

She watched as the man she was on the verge of falling in love with, held her aching breasts reverently in his palms once again. He leaned down and took a nipple in his mouth and suckled until she grasped his head and brought his lips to hers in a kiss she never wanted to end.

He grabbed her hips and aligned her soft form against his hard body. He rubbed his cock against her and lifted her onto the table. He pushed the dishes out of the way and laid her down as if she were the most fragile thing in the world.

"God, I want you so damn much. I want you to remember every touch of my hand. Every lick of my tongue. You deserve to be well-loved because I'm going to make you hard and fast after you come. So, hang on."

Oh. My.

"Yes. Please, I just need to feel you inside of me."

TS nipped her lips and sucked her bottom lip into his mouth, cutting off her plea. His tongue stole into her mouth, consuming her. She wrapped her arms around his neck and lifted her hips and rubbed herself against his erection.

For a moment, she thought he'd take her just the way she wanted. Fast and hard. His hands traveled up her ribs, skimming her breasts, and captured her arms up above her head.

She moaned as he broke off their kiss. "Dammit, TS. Please? I—"

He ignored her once again and did as he pleased. And promised.

"I want your eyes on mine. I want you to watch as I worship you. I want to see you come undone as I lick you and make you come."

Noel almost came from his words. She'd never experienced such an erotic moment in her life.

"Can you do that for me, sweetheart?"

She nodded.

She couldn't speak. Her skin felt two sizes too tight. She needed relief, and only TS could provide it.

"Open your eyes, Noel," TS ordered. His voice, huskier than she'd ever heard, brought her ever closer to the edge.

"Keep your hands above your head. No touching until I give the okay."

She was beyond caring that he was issuing orders. If he was bent on pleasuring her, who was she to argue?

TS traced his fingers, feather-light, along her neck and collarbone, dipping lower onto the swell of her breast and circled a taut nipple without touching the aching point. He was testing her. Lost in the flurry of emotions he made her feel, she gave herself and her body over.

He paid attention to every inch of her body, licking and biting, then kissing the sting away. When he reached the top of her thighs, she was ready to implode. No longer could she hold herself still. She wantonly tempted him and opened her legs wider.

"TS." She whispered. Longing threaded her plea. She watched him as he loved her body, then begged, "Please."

TS placed the tip of his tongue on her clit and pressed the swollen bud. The light touch after his methodical attack on the rest of her body did her in. Her orgasm slammed into her. The joy of it brought tears to her eyes as he used his tongue to mimic what his cock would soon be doing.

This. This is what she'd wanted since their time together at the cabin.

He was relentless and continued to lick and suckle her until another orgasm crested. She rode the wave for as long as she could. Her limbs loose, Noel absorbed the tiny electrical impulses and cried out his name.

TS kissed her stomach and trailed his wicked tongue over her belly button. It was too much, it was not enough. She wrapped her legs around his waist. "Oh, God. TS, now, inside me, now!"

He rolled on a condom and entered her. She could have wept at the contact, and maybe she did as he thrust his cock in and out, slow at first, then fast and hard as promised.

He held her tight as his strokes went deeper and deeper still. Damn his request, she placed both hands on his shoulders, and she matched his pace and met each thrust.

He called her name, "Noel. Look at me."

When she did, TS' body shuddered, and with her name on his lips, she watched as he came apart in her arms.

CHAPTER 9

FEBRUARY

TS' feelings concerning Noel had been all over the place since Christmas, Hell since they were two gawky teenagers. In the beginning, he was just damn glad she wasn't looking to him for her own happiness and that her expectations were the same as his. But lately, he'd begun coming up with excuses to see her, and it just wasn't for sex.

Tonight was the perfect example. He'd asked her to attend an event with him. He'd told her it would benefit them both professionally. What he hadn't told her was that he couldn't imagine going without her.

He and Blake had just finished a round on the handball court when the team's manager stopped and smacked his head.

"Dammit, I just remembered. It's date night."

TS took a drink from his water bottle. "How the hell do you forget something like that. I must be overworking you." And why did men have to schedule a date when they were married? Wasn't it a given?

"It's not that. Man, I'm sorry. But she's ovulating."

TS couldn't have heard him right. "Ova-What-ing?"

"We're trying to get pregnant. She takes a test and when it's the right time, we— "

"Spare me the details." TS didn't need to know everything about his friend. "Go. Join the merry band of baby-makers. Might as well, it's an epidemic around here."

Blake laughed and slapped him on the back as he walked off the court. "Don't worry, TS. One day you too will be at the mercy of the baby God's."

Watching as Blake whistled his way off the court and down the hall toward the shower rooms, TS shook his head. Poor bastard. He didn't say anything because hey, the world needed people to operate, but he wouldn't be one of its procreators. At least that part of the damn article that had been true.

He'd never hid his feelings about becoming a father, but now that they were out there, he felt…judged. No one had said anything to him directly, but whenever one of his friends started talking about their kid when he was around, they apologized for boring him. They hadn't done that before the article. It bothered him. Maybe it was time he told them how he enjoyed all the new additions, and how it had made him begin to think…maybe. Maybe he could have what Mav, Luke, and Blake had found.

He gathered up his towel and water bottle and headed to the showers. He had a date too. With Noel. He grinned and thought about the last time they'd been together.

Dinner had been ruined. Noel had been a bit put out, but after he'd returned with takeout, and they'd ate their fill, they then took their time being filled up by each other.

TS had thought his plan for friends with benefits was foolproof. But he was beginning to think he was the fool. He knew he should end things before…before Noel ended up hurt. He'd never been with a woman this long before. He told himself it was a simple matter of chemistry; they craved each other.

But … dammit, why'd there always have to be a but? Because he knew she wasn't the one he needed to worry about being hurt. It was him. He wasn't ready to label his feelings for Noel as love, but what he felt for her was more profound than any other woman he'd been with.

He didn't trust love. But he was quickly beginning to trust Noel with more than just his physical needs.

Noel smiled as she listened to TS softly snore. They hadn't lasted long at the charity event. TS made some lame excuse to the organizer then practically dragged her out of the building. When they walked through her front door, he took her in his arms and carried her up the stairs.

They didn't make it halfway. It was the first time she'd ever had sex on a staircase. The rug burns were worth it.

She'd wondered throughout the short time they were at the party he had brought her. It had been the closest they'd come to being a couple in public. He introduced her as his "close friend," but to her, it was a start. She didn't want to get her hopes up, but she'd already sort of had. And she knew better. Had learned often enough during her mother's cancer journey and her father's abandonment that hope was a fickle friend.

Whatever their ending was, TS had outdone every lover she knew. Not that there were many, but she was now good and truly ruined for anyone else. They devoured each other. And every time they were together, she thought it couldn't possibly get better. And every time she was proved wrong. She worried that the growing attachment she felt was the Big L. Because, in the beginning, it was all about the orgasms. And to prove her point as she stretched and let out a low moan when her over-sensitized flesh rubbed against the bedding. Yup, ruined.

Dammit, dammit, dammit. Who was she kidding? Could she really claim it was because the sex was great? If only. Because then she could blame the hours she spent with him on something else, anything instead of her own choice, and need for him.

There she said it. Well thought it anyway. She looked over at TS's profile. In the early dawn, his face was bathed in partial shadow, his brow line and lashes highlighted by the rising sun. Her fingers itched to touch his stubbled cheeks and rub her thumb along his lips. Lips that had brought her immeasurable pleasure.

No, she wasn't ready to voice her true feelings out loud. She'd given TS a part of herself she'd never given another man. Her vulnerability.

How was she going to dial it back in when the full light of day appeared and highlighted the real her, the one she kept closely guarded not just from him, but her closest friends?

How would she keep herself from begging him to become a part of his life for as long as he wanted her?

CHAPTER 10

$\mathcal{N}$oel rolled over and found herself alone. She squinted at the bedside clock. Five-thirty. So much for pillow talk. She curled up and shut her eyes. Maybe she could fall back asleep, get another forty minutes, and worry later about TS sneaking out of her bed.

A rumble in her stomach was the first sign something wasn't right. She took in a deep breath to settle the sudden nausea, but her system wasn't having it. She bolted out of bed and barely made it to the toilet bowl.

Fifteen minutes later, she stood at the bathroom sink splashing water on her face and taking small sips of the cool liquid. She felt her forward. She wasn't hot, but to be sure she searched for a thermometer. The last thing she needed was the flu. There wasn't any room in her schedule to miss even one day of work.

Later after her shower, she felt a bit better. She made some toast, skipped the jam, and downed some coffee. She was going to be late if she didn't kick it into gear. But at least the nausea had left. She dressed in record time and made it to her office just as her assistant pulled up.

The day was full of phone calls and a visit to a new client's home, but no word from TS. Not that she expected him to call or text. They weren't dating; she reminded herself.

A memory from last night made her smile. He'd been so sweet to her at the party. He genuinely wanted her to have a good time. And didn't that just add to her newly admitted messy feelings.

Her cell rang, and her heart rate went up. She looked at the screen. It was Kelsey. Dang, it was silly to get all excited every time her phone went off.

"Hey. What's up?"

"Just making sure you're going to be at The Club by seven. Girls' night, remember."

"Yes, Mom. I remember. I'm just finishing up a meeting with the paint contractor. I'll be there."

"Good. If you need a ride, call me. I'm designated driver tonight."

"That doesn't seem fair. What happened to cabbing it?"

Kelsey let out a snort. "I'm still breastfeeding. One drink for me otherwise I'll have to pump and dump, which I don't want to do. The guilt is bad enough, but Aunt Flo is in town and my breasts can't take the misery of the breast pump. So, no worries, you can drink for me."

Oh, the joys of being a woman. Noel's own breasts twinged at the thought. One positive aspect of never having kids was she would never have to go through that particular scenario. Her periods were tough enough as it was and… *Oh, shit.*

Kelsey changed the subject, but all Noel could do was respond with a couple 'uh-huhs. Her mind raced. What day was it? When was her last period? Damn, damn, damn. She was late. She was never late.

She ended the call with another promise to be on time and stood staring at her shoes. The poor contractor walked off after he repeated his question twice, and all she could do was manage an, "I'll call you tomorrow."

After the man left, she fast-walked out to her SUV. She got in but didn't start the engine. It had been what two months since her last period, two weeks before… Christmas. Why hadn't she noticed before now?

She softly banged her head against her steering wheel and played out her days since her last period. What the Hell was she going to do? Maybe it was stress. Yeah, she'd heard stress could mess with your cycle, except perhaps… it wasn't.

Her tires screeched as she pulled out of the parking and headed for the closest pharmacy. She bought five pregnancy tests and a bag of chocolate. She avoided eye contact with the cashier.

She debated texting Kelsey or Lara. They'd know how it felt to be pregnant. But then she'd have to tell them why she was asking, and she wasn't ready. This could not be happening. Was the universe playing games with her?

Her friends were forever making fun of her whenever she made a vision board to help her plan out major events or goals in her life. Like a remodel and design for a client, a wedding, or when she'd organized the joint baby shower last year for Kelsey and Lara.

Then there had been the one she'd done when she was working on the initial bid for the condo project. The job she wanted more than anything, but TS had given to someone else … then she ended up with him, just as he had hoped. As she had wanted. Shit, it had worked.

Dammit, if this was the Universe messing with her plans, it was so not funny. She'd been a bridesmaid—twice. Kelsey and Lara had zoomed past her into grownup-land; got married and knocked-upped all in the span of a year. Then Caris had eloped with Blake and adopted the most adorable baby girl ever.

If she wasn't careful, she'd have an anxiety attack along with nausea. She was just a block from home, she could do this. She repeated that thought as she parked in the garage. She took in some deep breaths hoping it would settle her stomach and her racing thoughts.

She wasn't pregnant. They'd used protection. She was currently the proud owner of an entire box of condoms in her night-stand. He had condoms at the cabin too. Every damn time.

Noel went into her kitchen and made some tea. Tea would settle her nausea. It'd go away, and she wouldn't feel like puking her guts out.

Crackers, she needed crackers.

She turned to the cupboard where she kept them and whoa. Too fast. She leaned to one side and caught herself on the wall.

Nope, not pregnant. Just stress.

She waited for the water to boil and took her cup to the table and sat down. She blew on the hot liquid and nibbled on a cracker.

Much better. See, she didn't need to take the five tests that were still in the shopping bag on the far end of the counter, mocking her. The tea was doing its magic, and she felt much better.

Noel desperately searched her memory. She knew she had a period in January, she must have. Never in her adult life had she missed one —ever.

Sure, her life had been crazy, but to forget the monthly cramps and PMS induced chocolate binges? There was no way she'd just breeze through a month without either of the two happening.

Lord, she missed her mom. This was one of the few times in her life she could have used a good cry in her mother's arms, and a dose of Loretta Snow's no holds barred opinion.

Noel smiled. Her mother had never been a shrinking violet. She wore her emotions openly, and if you weren't clear on how she really felt, she'd tell you. Tears welled again. She grabbed a tissue and wiped off her ruined eyeliner.

Her mom had been opinionated until the very end. Between treatments and her naps, her mom had watched all the news channels. She was stoically independent in her political views, and she'd argue with the right and the left TV commentators.

Noel couldn't watch a news show without thinking about her mom. They were the few good memories from the last few months of her mom's life she had. There hadn't been too many towards the end. Her brothers had struggled to deal with what had become inevitable. Their mom wasn't going to recover.

She'd dealt with it by tutoring online every spare hour she had. The extra money made the difference between eating tuna or chicken. And she'd happily given up sleep as long as it meant her mother would stop worrying. And asking Noel to track down their dad. That was one thing she wouldn't do for her mom. Ever.

She tucked away her memories of being a caregiver and surrogate mom to her brothers instead of being a typical teen. Yes, she'd readily filled those roles. Being needed had, in a weird way, filled her up. But remembering served no purpose other than to weigh her down and prevent her from believing she could achieve a life without responsibilities.

Apparently, old habits had been hard to break since she was staring at the possibility of one hell of a responsibility in the face.

She still wanted to ensure that everyone in her circle was happy and living the life they wanted. But what she wanted more than anything was to be wanted for herself and not what she could do for anyone. And she wanted TS to want her for her, not just for sex whenever they both had the itch.

Another wave of nausea had her sprinting for the bathroom.

After she was done, she splashed cold water on her face and brushed her teeth. She caught her reflection in the mirror. A hollow laughed escaped, followed by a second that made her sound like a loon. There was no getting around what she needed to do.

She walked back into the kitchen and grabbed the bag filled with the pregnancy tests dumped out the chocolate, and dry heaved at the thought of it—dammit.

Back in her bathroom, she took out all five out and followed the instructions. One after another, she lined them up on the countertop without looking at them. Then she waited. Five minutes went by and she still hadn't looked. She paced in her bedroom. She waited for another five minutes.

The tests had to be ready by now, but was she? Nope. But she was running out of time. She'd need to leave soon for girl's night. She scooped up the tests and closed her eyes. When she looked down at the death grip she had on five plastic life-changers, she let out an unladylike snort.

Five plus signs burned an impression onto her retina. Even when she closed her eyes, she could still see them.

Her latest vision board hadn't included today's surprise.

World rocked.

CHAPTER 11

$\mathcal{N}$oel arrived at The Club five minutes early. Proud of herself, she gave herself a pep talk before she got out of her car. Tonight, she'd put on her best smile and pretend everything was fine. She had years of practice under her belt.

"Noel! I can't believe it. You're on time." Kelsey stood up from the booth in the back corner to let her in. It was their favorite spot, and thanks to Reese, it was always available for their nights out.

"I was just telling everyone that Mari held onto her rattle today, when she moved her hand and the toy made a noise her smile made me cry. Oh, she was so proud of herself." Kelsey's face, flush from her excitement, turned to Noel.

"I wish you could have been there. All of you. Darn it. Maybe I should set up a surveillance camera twenty-four-seven, so no one has to miss all the excitement."

Noel joined in as everyone laughed at the absurdity of Kelsey's wish. She would've loved to have been there to see little Mari discovering something new. Her goddaughter had a massive piece of Noel's heart. And now Noel would have her own baby to share silly moments about.

A waiter showed up at the table and teased Reese about slacking off. It allowed her to wipe away a stray tear. Great, her hormones were already kicking in. Then a moment of panic hit her. She couldn't have any alcohol pregnant. How was she going to get out of ordering her favorite, a glass of Merlot?

Would one drink harm the baby? She had no idea, but she didn't want to take any chances. When the waiter paused and looked at her for her order, she asked for the wine and a glass of water. If she were lucky, no one would notice if she left the wine untouched.

The talk turned back to kids as three of the ladies at the table were moms. She and Reese looked at each other and shrugged and joined in when they could.

Twenty minutes later, Noel's wine sat on the table, taunting her. She'd asked for her water to be refilled twice. So far, no one had said anything. And they were still discussing baby stuff. She'd tried twice to change the subject, but it always circled back around to the babies. Was this what she'd be doing once her baby was born?

"You know, maybe we could talk about oh, I don't know, my wedding instead of how to get spit up out of a silk blouse?" Reese said sarcastically. She softened the question with a big smile.

Noel could have kissed her. She would have happily discussed baseball then keep talking about diaper rashes and sore nipples from breastfeeding. All the things she'd probably need to know about, but not today. Today, she needed a diversion from how her life would soon change. Planning a wedding fit that bill.

Except she wouldn't be. Reese's mom wanted the job.

"I'm sorry, Noel. You know you would have been my first choice, but my mom is insisting on handling everything. Now that she's retired, she has a lot of time on her hands. And she's already driving me nutty, but I can't say no. Please don't hate me." Reese reached out and placed her hand over Noel's.

"C'mon, I'm not going to hate you. For long." She sent Reese a wink. "To be honest, I've got three high maintenance projects keeping me busy. My assistant has taken over the rest of our client list, and I guide her when I can, and TS and I get together whenever we're free..." *And oh, shit.* She just said that out loud. Her and TS, in the same breath.

A look passed among the group. A look that said they all knew something she didn't know, or they already knew. Dammit, they'd already known about her and TS. Of course, they did, because they were all thick as thieves.

"Um, about TS. So, how's that working out. You two seeing each other a lot, huh?" Lara giggled as she asked the question.

So yeah, her friends knew she was seeing TS. She looked at Kelsey and waggled her finger at her. "Couldn't keep it a secret, huh?"

"I didn't have to say a word. Every time you two are in the same room, it's fireworks. It's been that way, well ever since he moved back. But honey, since the holidays, you two can't keep your eyes off each other and well it's—"

"That obvious, huh?" Noel sighed.

Caris gave her a reassuring smile then added for the group, "Okay, let's get this out in the open. We're not mad that you didn't tell us about you and TS. And don't be mad at Kelsey. She didn't say anything until we guessed."

"We're happy for you. All of us." Lara added.

"But?" Noel asked.

"There's no, but." Lara smiled then looked down at her drink.

"Um-hm." Noel wasn't going to make it easy for Lara or for any of them. She wanted to hear what they had to say.

"Okay, there's a but. We were just wondering why you're keeping it a secret?"

A wave of concern hit her as four sets of eyes stared at her. She took a sip of wine. One little sip wouldn't hurt the baby, and she needed the fortification to tell them about her and TS's arrangement without letting it slip that oh, yeah, I'm knocked up too.

Noel played with the wine stem of her glass. "TS and I hooked up right before Christmas, at the cabin. It was supposed to be just a one-time thing, you know. And then, well we decided to do the friends with benefits thing. Neither one of us is looking for anything more serious.

And well, it's been good." She looked up and found four different reactions.

Caris' face held concern, ever the psychiatrist. Kelsey's she couldn't read, but then again, she had a damn good poker face. Lara had a look of wanting to ask more questions and Reese, well she had that knowing look. The look that said, 'hope the sex is worth the heartbreak' look because I've been there.

"It must be good; you've had a perpetual glow about you for the last couple months."

This from Reese. Then her friend looked pointedly at Noel's wine glass. Busted.

"I appreciate all of your concerns, really. But you know I'm okay with this arrangement. I'm not looking for marriage. And neither is TS. We've both had lousy role models, and when you've lived through it, believing in a happily ever after isn't a thing.

But that doesn't mean I'm not beyond excited for all of you. You deserve what you've found with each of your Outlaw's, and I've become an auntie to three beautiful babies. It's all good. I promise." She paused and took a moment to decide how much more she wanted to reveal to them.

"What a bunch of bull-pucky." Lara reached out and took her hand. "Noel, I think we can agree that all of our guys were resistant to settling down in the beginning. I don't want to see you alone just because you think you don't deserve or can't trust in love or whatever because of your messed-up parents."

Kelsey finished her drink and set it down hard on the table and rubbed her hands. "Okay, here's what I think. You're both scared. I get it, boy do I. You both are so wrapped up in not wanting to get hurt, that you can't see that you're perfect for each other."

She wanted to believe Kelsey and Lara. But they didn't know what she knew. That his mother had become pregnant on purpose and used it as leverage. And now history, at least for TS, would repeat itself.

"Is there anything else, Noel? Maybe a reason why you've barely touched your wine, and you haven't called me for a movie night to pig out on ice cream and chocolate. Not since before, you know the holidays."

Kelsey, Lara, Caris, and Reese could sniff out a lie at twenty yards. So, she wasn't going to lie to them. "I'm pregnant." She whispered it, then cleared her throat. "I can't believe I didn't see the signs. I think I'm at least six weeks."

No one congratulated her. Her announcement wasn't like Kelsey and Lara's. Yes, they'd each become pregnant before marriage, but for them, they knew their guys loved them. Both Mav and Luke had been shocked sure, but they'd both wanted kids. And they'd wanted to get married and were living their happily-ever-after's.

Noel didn't see the same for her and TS. With some guilt, she let her friends plot on how to break the news to him and assured her he would be happy. If not right away, he would undoubtedly come around. After all, they'd each seen how he was with their children. But other people's kids were easy; she wanted to scream. No commitment, no responsibility, no worrying in the middle of the night if you were a good parent or not.

She left the restaurant, not any clearer on what path she'd take with TS. But she'd been given plenty of advice on how to handle nausea. Peppermint tea and pressure point, sea-sickness wristbands thingies. Plus, the name of several pregnancy books.

Noel was grateful to them all. She knew they had her back, but a numbness crept over her as she sat in her car. The weight of her pregnancy hit her hard. She'd never imagined herself as a single mom.

And despite what her friends had agreed upon, she knew what TS's reaction would be. Their friends-with-benefits would turn into resentment, reluctant duty or maybe denial. Not the fairy tale they were trying to convince her would happen.

Would he refuse to acknowledge their child? Would he look at her differently? The similarities to his parent's beginnings... damn, she grabbed the wheel tight. She started to hyperventilate. No, no ... she took in a slow breath and let it out slowly. And did it again.

Her cell went off. It was TS wanting to get together.

For the first, since they began seeing each other, she turned him down.

CHAPTER 12

How do you tell a man whose mother had become pregnant on purpose in order to force his father into marriage, that you're pregnant with his child?

"Sorry, I know we used protection each time, but oops—surprise! You're going to be a daddy."

Yeah, that wasn't going to work. TS was going to shut down on her, shut her out, and what… deny he's the father? Would she have to go through a DNA test for proof?

She may not have thought she'd become a mother, but now that she was, well, she'd get used to it. She did love children, she just never wanted to put one through what she'd lived. Could she do this on her own?

Her cell rang. Kelsey's picture popped up on the screen.

"Hey."

"You come up with anything yet?" Kelsey rushed her words out.

"No. At least not anything worth repeating. Maybe he won't notice."

Kelsey's sigh landed in the pit of Noel's stomach. She knew how worried her friend was, and if the tables had been turned, Noel would have—what? Made the announcement for her? Demand the father

184

marries her friend? What was the right solution when neither party had planned for, let alone wanted to have a child?

She wasn't going to force anything on TS. She just needed to decide how to break the news without starting a fight.

"Right. TS notices everything. You think he's not going to notice when your boobs get bigger, and you're suddenly wearing boat neck dresses?"

She knew Kelsey was trying to get her to laugh, but all her humor had left when she'd read the positive result on the pee stick. All five of them. Humor was not going to get her out of this situation, but maybe a business deal would.

TS spoke fluent corporate speak, and he was nothing if not pragmatic. She'd work up a contract. Give him a multiple choice of custody, a fair childcare estimate and an option clause for a marriage in name only for a set period, then an amicable divorce. She'd ask nothing for herself; only shared financial responsibility.

Even though she hadn't wanted a child, there was no question she was keeping this baby. She'd do her very best to give him or her a life where they'd never doubt that they were wanted. She'd give her child enough love for two parents.

"Okay, then. What are my options? Pretty soon, he's going to find me puking in the bathroom if I continue to sleep with him. Or like you said, he's going to notice my body changing if we continue to sleep together."

Noel walked over to her full-length mirror and ran her hand over her stomach. As much as she'd been puking lately, even she could tell her tummy was a bit rounder.

She didn't have much time left. She needed to tell TS.

Her doctor said the second trimester should be better and the nausea would ease up.

"All this worrying over how to tell him is making me crazy. I'm going over to his office, and I'll just tell him."

"And then what?" Kelsey asked.

"I'll let you know. And Kelsey. Thanks for putting up with me. I don't know what I'd do without you." She called TS' secretary Lois to see if he had any openings for her to come in. Noel reasoned, telling him in his office might ensure less of a blow-up.

***

TS WAS DAYDREAMING. Typically, if he allowed himself to dream, it would be about baseball. That he'd been good enough to play pro, and instead of owning a team, he was on the team. He hadn't had one of those in years. Now his daydreams were filled with Noel.

She'd turned him down last night day, and he was restless. He'd become used to seeing her. Their time together had involved more than hopping into bed. He found himself talking to her about work and last week, they discovered their love of the same crime fiction writer.

Noel had worked her way under his defenses, and he wasn't sure how to handle the new set of emotions that created.

"Hi. Lois said I could come right in."

Noel stood on the threshold, a hesitant look on her face. It produced a sinking feeling like she might be thinking of ending things. "I was just thinking of you. Come in. Close the door." He left his desk but stopped before he reached her. She still hadn't moved.

"Noel? You okay?" He offered her his hand.

She looked at it before she grabbed it and followed him. She sat down in the chair, facing his desk instead of the couch. Not a good sign.

"You look tired. You okay? Have you been sick? I was wondering why you didn't want to get—"

"I'm pregnant."

Her words came out in a rush. Maybe he hadn't heard right. "I'm sorry."

"Me too. I'm so sorry, TS. This is… not what either of us wanted. But I saw my doctor. I'm almost seven weeks. And you're, um, you're the father."

He sat down before he fell down. *Pregnant?* Noel Snow was pregnant with his baby. His heart skipped a beat, and a loud rushing sound overwhelmed him.

She was oh, hell, she was crying. He looked down at the square pattern on the carpet. He opened his mouth twice to speak, but he couldn't, didn't know what to say.

Goddammit. He started to laugh. A low laugh he couldn't control. When he saw the look on her face at his inappropriate reaction, he stopped. Shit. Like father, like son apparently. Except he'd never treat a child of his, the way he'd been treated. A baby. Someone was going to call him daddy. A part of him felt… happy but the rest was terror. And one of the reasons he never wanted to be a father. But now? Now, maybe he and Noel could figure out a way to make it work?

Unfortunately, she knew his backstory, and she was probably scared as hell to what his reaction would be. He needed to handle this… oh my god, he was going to be a father.

"You uh, have already seen a doctor?"

She looked over at him with a frown. She nodded, then stood up and began pacing the room.

"You don't have to say anything. I'm aware of how you feel about kids. And I'm not here to pull what your mother did on your father, I just … well, you need to know."

Yeah, his mother. Of course, she'd think of that. But he didn't believe she was anything like his mother. He was more interested in what she wanted. Did she want marriage, money? Maybe she wanted nothing at all or maybe, she didn't want the baby. That last thought made him ill and he discounted it because he knew Noel. She'd want this baby.

He was, why wasn't he flipping out? He blew out a breath he didn't realize he'd been holding. Hell, had he changed his mind because he had feelings for Noel? Okay, he needed to think, he needed time, yeah, they both needed to time.

"I… don't know what to say. Can I have some time? I need to figure this thing out and—" TS threw his hands out and couldn't finish his the damn sentence. For the first time in his life, he was at a loss for words.

In mid-stride, she looked up at him; her face fell at his words. He'd hurt her. Somehow with his words or the wrong words, he'd failed whatever test or expectation she'd had when she walked in and told him he was going to be a father.

He knew anything he said to her now would sound insincere. He was screwed, no matter what.

"Noel, maybe we each need some time to let this sink in. I, ah, could you maybe give me a couple days, I'll look into setting up a trust fund and then we'll get together and hash it out."

Before his eyes, she schooled her features. He could no longer read her.

"Sure. Whatever works for you. Because it's not like I haven't been puking for two days straight or anything. My god, I thought I had the flu. Nope, just a baby making its presence know. So yeah, I'll set aside my life and feelings for a couple of days while you decide what you want to do about it. Take all the time you need, TS."

Stunned, he watched her walk out his door. It had been open the entire time, and he stood still as she walked to the waiting elevator, slammed her hand on the buttons. She remained facing the back wall of the elevator as its doors closed.

"That went well." He grabbed his phone to call... who? Who was he going to talk to about this?

He picked up a pen and threw it across his desk and watched as it bounced off the wall. He leaned back in his chair and ran his hand through his hair. *Dammit, TS, you totally screwed that up.*

Lois entered his office wearing a frown. Laser-focused, she dropped a stack of papers on his desk and stuck her finger in his face. "You need to fix this." She crossed her arms and stared him down.

"That's what I'm trying to do." His mom may still be alive, but he didn't count her as anyone who gave his feelings a second thought. Not like Lois.

"Well, you sucked at it."

He did. But damn, he'd never seen her really mad before. And never at him.

"I know. But to be honest, I don't have any experience with ... you know, female feelings and—she's pregnant, Lois."

"I heard. You forgot to close the door. And for what it's worth, I think those female feelings you're worried about dealing with are about love." Lois uttered the word he was unable to say.

His secretary's face softened into a smile. Thank God. She wasn't really mad at him. And he ignored her word choice. Not going there.

"Lois."

"Don't Lois me. She loves you. She might not be ready to say it either, but that beautiful girl that you just made cry is having your baby. And you need to fix this situation. Oh, and congratulations, by the way, although at this moment, I think she could do better."

"Hey." He rubbed his chest. Where was she going with this because at the moment all he wanted to do was run? It was the where he couldn't decide.

"She needs you to go after her. Beg for forgiveness and for God's sake, don't say anything more to her about money or trust funds."

"And what would you suggest I do when I catch her?"

"Men." Lois rolled her eyes. "You grab her, hold her, and don't let go. Then you get over your rotten upbringing and forget what your father ever said to you. TS, you need to open your heart to her. She deserves it."

He stood and turned to look out then down at the baseball field. His favorite view. Damn, he loved baseball. It was the only true love he'd ever found. And now he was going to have a kid. And Noel, he was in love with Noel.

He waited for denial to rear its head, but nothing. All he felt was if she wasn't in his life, he'd go back to being someone he no longer wanted to be.

"TS?"

"Yeah?"

"You do too. Love doesn't have to hurt. Your parents were the worst examples someone could have. Falling in love is easy, it's staying in love that takes work. But when you find someone worth fighting for, worth doing the hard work for and with, then it's worth all the pain you ever went through." Lois stepped behind him and placed her hand on his shoulder.

"That's pretty profound. I had no idea you were so smart; well, I did but not about this." He ran his hand through his hair and wished he could take back the last ten minutes. He needed a do-over. "What if I screw it up?"

"Look around you. Look at everything you've created. You built your company without any help from your father, then you sold it and built a corporation most couldn't on their best day. So, take my advice, you won't screw it up. Go after her. She's the only woman you cared enough to let your guard down with, TS. Doesn't that tell you something?"

Was he ready to be the hands-on father she just requested? More importantly, could he trust her with his heart; could he trust himself not to screw things up like his father had?

CHAPTER 13

*H*e found her. Thank God. She exited the ladies' room on the main floor and turned toward the door to the parking garage. He watched her stiffen when she saw him. Shit. He had no clue what he was going to say. And he no longer had the time he wanted to wrap his head around the fact he was going to be a father.

"Noel. I'm not good with relationships and everything that comes with them. I know that's not what you want to hear, but I don't want to upset you anymore than I have. I just, Hell, I don't know what I need. And I didn't even ask what you want. Can you help me out here?"

She'd listened to him but showed little emotion, which was freaking him out. He tried again, "Look, I'm going to be honest with you. I can't make any promises. I've lived so long with the hate and disappointment from my father that it's not going to be easy for me to switch gears and think I can make this thing work."

Her nostrils flared, and she dropped her purse on the floor. The noise echoed off the walls. Dammit, he'd said the wrong thing again. Lois had put too much faith in him. He was screwing things up and fast.

"Our baby isn't a thing, TS. He's going to need both of us, and whether we're a couple or not, all I need you to do is the best you can.

I'm not expecting you to turn into super dad. A child has simple needs. To be fed, clothed and cared for. To be loved and have his parents spend time with him."

"I know this is not what either one of us wanted or expected considering we used protection, but it's real and I'm having this baby."

"How long have you known, Noel?"

"Three days."

He rubbed his face. Okay, so she hadn't been holding out on him. Unlike his mother who'd waited until she knew his father couldn't force her to get rid of him. His gut roiled at the thought.

"Seven weeks. I had a sonogram done. I could show you the pictures if you want. He looks a bit like a blob right now, but the nurse assured me that in another couple of months we'll be able to make out features. They don't usually do sonograms so early in the pregnancy but I needed to see the baby, our baby."

"He? It's a boy?" His voice cracked. He didn't sound like himself.

"Um, no. I've just been thinking of him as a boy. Twenty weeks is when they're usually able to tell the sex of the baby."

"Okay, so seven weeks, huh? That means it happened at the cabin."

She nodded. "If you ask me if the baby is yours, I swear to God I'll kick you, TS."

"What? No. I'm not worried about that. I know the baby is mine."

She looked around and sighed. "Maybe this isn't the best place to be having this discussion?"

It wasn't, but he couldn't let her leave thinking he didn't want their child or her.

"I think you're right about needing time, TS. I'm suddenly exhausted. You didn't say anything when I told you I'm keeping the baby. And if you fight me on this, I'll win. I mean it."

I might not have wanted kids either, but now that I'm pregnant, well, this baby will never know it wasn't wanted. So, you think about how much or how little you want to be involved and let me know."

He looked at her. Really looked at how she was holding up. Yes, she looked tired, but she was so damn beautiful. His heart squeezed at the thought of hurting her any more than he already had.

She was strong and fiercely independent, and if he'd been given a choice as to who would be the mother of his child, it would be her hands down. But he'd be damned if he told her he loved her for the first time in the parking garage.

He just hoped he wasn't making a mistake by letting her leave without him.

A DAY LATER, TS called in the troops. He needed advice and fast.

Maverick, Luke, Blake, and Connor arrived in record time. He had purposely kept the reason from them in the group text. The less they knew he reasoned the more honest their opinions would be when he dropped the truth.

Blake arrived last, and as soon as he sat down with the others in his game room, TS made the announcement. "Noel's pregnant." Sure, he could have eased into it, but time wasn't his friend right now.

To say he caught them off guard was an understatement.

"Whoa."

Luke, Maverick, and Blake's jaws dropped.

Luke was the first to recover, "Did your condom break too? That's how it happened for Lara and me, but hey we have Andrew and it's good, man. Fatherhood is the best."

Maverick elbowed Luke. "Let's all just take a moment. TS how you doing, over there? You look, ah a bit green."

Blake sat back and crossed his arms, "When did all this happen. I thought you two, well, you tell us. What has been going on with you and Noel? Besides the knocked-up part."

TS felt green and nauseous, and his head had been pounding non-stop since Noel walked away from in the garage. Mostly, he was confused. Somewhere along the way, he took to the idea of being a father and it didn't freak him out. What freaked him out was not having Noel in his life or only through mediators and agreed-upon exchanges when they handed off their kid. Which wasn't going to happen—no way in Hell.

"Listen, I asked you guys here to help me come up with a plan. You're all experts, well okay, you have experience with women and babies and I'm pretty sure Noel hates me right now, and I want to fix this." TS ran both hands down his face. He needed more coffee or maybe whiskey. Lots of whiskey.

"She can't hate you too much, she let you see her naked." Luke laughed.

"TS, what about you know, your anti-relationship stance? You sound like maybe that's not the case here. So, we'll shut up," Blake glared at Luke, "and you tell us what you need help with. Whatever you want, we've got your back."

He knew they did, thank God they did. Blake's declaration made him feel ten times less freaked out. "Okay, the meat of it is she wants the baby, but not me. She's all set that we're going to do this on paper. Because, dammit, I never gave her any reason to think I wanted anything more from her. So that's on me, but I need to let her know that's not where I'm at, not anymore."

"Not anymore? As in you used to want to a different woman in your bed every night, but now you only want Noel?" Maverick let out a low whistle. "Uh, oh, gents. I think Mr. Bachelor over here has done the unthinkable."

Three sets of eyes stared back at him, waiting for him to acknowledge Mav's statement. Well, TS couldn't believe it either, but it was true. He didn't know exactly when it happened, but he wasn't going to say it out loud in front of them when he hadn't even said it to Noel.

"Damn, it's true. You're in love. Noel's done the impossible—she's hooked the unhookable, king of the one-night stands, the country's most eligible billionaire who made it known far and wide that marriage was for suckers and fuck you on that one by the way. So, TS now that the mighty have fallen, what are you going to do?"

He deserved the dress down and yeah, Noel had done the impossible. But he wasn't going to let her or his screwed-up philosophy on relationships be the reason she used to give him an out on being in his child's life. Or hers.

"I'm going to convince her that I've changed."

Blake looked skeptical, but he offered what in the end, was the agreed-upon approach. The kiss method, "keep it simple stupid."

It took two days to make it simple. The one part of the plan that wasn't so simple was getting Noel to go to the location where she wouldn't see it, or him coming. And he knew just the person to make it happen.

CHAPTER 14

"*H*ow'd you know I was here?"

TS allowed himself to take in the picture Noel made sitting on a bench at the city park, huddled in a bright red parka, lips blue from the cold. He noticed her spine go rigid as he approached. The bench she chose was located behind the cement wall separating the beach below from the park, and its endless snow-covered acres of grass. To the east was downtown Pineville, with The Resort located right up to the lake's edge. In between was an open-air skating rink with a handful of skaters braving the subzero temperatures.

This was Noel's favorite place, according to Kelsey. A place she went to think over significant decisions in her life. The bitter cold hadn't kept her away and it wouldn't deter him.

The day called for chocolate and flowers, but he'd foregone the typical Valentine's Day offerings and hoped what he had would be accepted. He rechecked his pocket to make sure it was still there. He'd purchased a ring yesterday, an emerald cut diamond solitaire. He planned on winging the actual proposal, but not before he told her what she been waiting to discuss concerning their child and what he needed to say to her—what she deserved to hear.

"A mutual friend ratted you out. And before you get all pissy about it, I'd like you to hear me out—"

"I don't get pissy. I get even." Noel's gaze darted between him and then back out to the lake.

Great, she was determined not to make this easy for him. "Oh, I don't doubt it. How about you postpone getting even for a bit. I'm hoping we can work out what's best for the baby and for us."

The wariness in her grey eyes was still there, but she had stopped looking at the lake and focused a suspicious gaze on him.

"So, you must have had your lawyer work something up, huh? You didn't have to deliver it in person. In fact, I'd prefer it in the future if we not see each other and—"

"You know I'm not your father, Noel. I admit I should have handled the news differently, but I don't run when life doesn't go as planned. Especially when it involves someone I care about."

He paused, waiting for a snarky comment. When she remained silent, he felt a weight lift from him.

"I've had a lot of time to think. About you, the baby, and about us. And something new happened while you were ignoring my texts and phone calls. I realized I missed you. I missed your smile. I missed you putting me in my place, and yes, your snarky comebacks. And yes, I missed how you felt lying next to me, under me and how you taste."

And it's so much more, Noel. It's everything I never knew could be missed. About you turned into an aching and empty space that I never realized had been there. I had spent so many years telling myself I didn't need anything, anyone on a personal level, to feel or to add to my happiness. Everything has finally clicked into place for me and I'm hoping it's not too late."

"Who are you, and what have you done with the real TS?" Noel wiped her tears.

"The new me. A better version. The one who broke all of my rules, let you in. No one else could have done what you did, Noel."

"What do you mean? What did I do for you?"

The need to touch and comfort her increased, but if he did, he wouldn't be able to finish telling her everything that had been building up inside of him since she stopped speaking to him.

"You didn't try to make me into someone else, Noel. You took me warts and all. You showed me with how you treated everyone around you that you still believed in love, no matter how much you denied it to me, you made sure everyone knew no matter how bad things got, something better was sure to come along. You have no idea how incredibly special you are to all of our friends; to me."

If I could go back to that day in my office, I would. I'd come up with the right words to tell you that all that mattered was you. I should have run after you and convinced you that we could work through all the doubts. I'm sorry I hurt you."

He lifted her chin with his free hand and captured her gaze. "It seems I've spent the two years chasing you, wanting you, loving you."

"You what?" Stunned, she opened her mouth to say more, but TS leaned in and touched his forehead to hers

"I want it all. You. The baby. Us." He kissed her, sweet and slow. And when Noel put her hand on his shoulder, pulled him closer, demanded more, he obliged. He kissed her deep until they both ran out of breath.

"Now what?" Noel whispered.

"Noel, I need you. I want our child, and I want him or her to have two parents living together. And—I love you. In case you didn't hear me before."

"I did," Noel whispered. She began to weep.

"Good. Now, please tell me those are happy tears?" TS demanded.

"Bossy." Noel shot back.

"Always. But I have changed in other ways."

"Really? And who's responsible for this miracle?"

"You. You changed me. The very first time I saw you after moving back. It was like a damn arrow to the heart. Well, to be honest, it went straight to my happy place first."

She laughed; he wanted to hear that laugh for the rest of his life.

"All I could think about was you, and how was I going to get this hotter-then-Hell, all grown up Noel into my bed? Not that I had a clue what I would do after I got you there. Because even then on that very first day, I knew.

"Then your name pops up on a bid proposal for the condo project, and whatever plans I had to woo you were blown to Hell. And it was Hell, Noel. Months of torture, then two weddings, a baby shower, and the kiss that sealed my fate."

"And now, fast-forward to this moment, and I'm scared you're going to walk away and keep me from our child all because I pushed you away when I should have held on and refused to let go."

"I can't believe that Thomas 'TS' Scott is ever scared. You eat CEOs for breakfast, TS. I'm not buying it." Noel grinned.

TS held out his hand, and when she took it, he bent down in front of Noel in front of the place she loved the most. "I don't want easy. I want you. It's always been you, Noel. And the fact you're pregnant is a bonus. Every day with you is a bonus and I want you always, will you marry me?"

"Oh, my… I had no… TS, are you sure?"

"Sweetheart, don't cry. I seem to be making you do that a lot and I'm sorry. Please say yes. Say yes so I can kiss you again. Say yes, so I don't have to be a miserable SOB for the rest of my life. Say yes… say yes, because you love me." He held the ring toward her, but she kept her gaze on him.

Noel placed her hands on his face. "I do, I mean I will. I love you."

She brushed away a tear. One of his and cradled his face in both her hands.

"Did you know I'd wished for you, on Christmas?

God, he wanted to kiss her forever, but when they both came up for air, he placed his forehead on hers and brushed the last of her tears away.

"Everything, every moment, every hard thing I've ever been through has led me to you, to us. To our baby." He placed his hands on her belly and couldn't wait to watch her and their child grow. He made a silent vow to himself and to their child that he'd never repeat the sins of his father.

With a love he'd never thought possible, TS whispered, "You were worth the chase, Noel."

EPILOGUE

SEPTEMBER

"Okay, folks, here's a first. It looks like there's some activity in the owner's skybox. Word has it that Outlaw owner and general manager, Thomas Scott, TS to family and friends, is pacing the box and not because of the game. His better half, Noel, is due any day with their first child.

Could be the little tyke might be making his major league debut this evening. Stay tuned, we'll keep you updated as new information comes in."

TS had the most stubborn wife. He continued to pace the room as he spoke to the 911 operator. "Her water broke less than five minutes ago. Apparently, her contractions started around noon today, but she neglected to tell anyone."

He looked over to see Noel puffing through a contraction. A light sheen of sweat bathed her face. She never looked more beautiful.

Kelsey caught his attention. She'd been timing the contractions. "Three minutes. Where's that damn ambulance, TS?"

"I don't need an ambulance, TS. Can't we just—"

"Noel, sweetheart. We're on the top level of a baseball stadium. I'm not letting you walk to our car in the underground garage. You're getting an ambulance." He tried to keep the panic out of his voice. Not sure it worked.

The sound of sirens drifted through the open skybox window. He happened to glance up at the full-screen TV mounted in the back of the room and cursed.

"No, sorry. It's all good. Yeah, we can hear them now." He stayed on the line with the operator and motioned to Grant.

"Get on the horn and call whoever is in charge of the television cameras and tell them to stop showing the skybox. Dammit, I should have installed the privacy glass."

"TS?"

"Yes, sweetheart. What do you need? Don't worry, they're on their way up now."

"Babe, I need you to relax. He's not going to be born on TV." Noel rubbed her stomach. She reached out and took his hand. "You can do this, TS. You're going to be an awesome father."

He hoped she was right. Panic had set in a week ago, and he wasn't so sure anymore. He was just grateful Noel would be their son's mother.

The EMTs arrived, and with efficiency he was grateful for, had his wife secured in the ambulance before any reporters discovered where they'd parked the vehicle.

Thankfully, they'd made it to the hospital in time because forty-five minutes later, their son was born.

Carson Hayden Scott was a whopping eight pounds, fourteen ounces.

Later that night, he cradled his son as the woman who stole his heart slept. He had everything he didn't know he wanted and everything he'd been lucky enough to find. Noel had indeed done the impossible—his secret Christmas wish had come true.

ZESTING WITH ZANE

A PINEVILLE WORLD CHRISTMAS NOVELLA
(TANGLING SERIES)

ABOUT

HOLLY

I'm not prepared for the instant connection I feel when Zane Snow, successful developer, and the brother of my favorite client, arrives at my shop minutes before closing to pick up an order of my famous lemon shortbread. Unfortunately, the order system doesn't show it and the last two dozen are spoken for.

Struck by his movie star good looks, his persistence and something I've never felt before, I do what I've never done. I let a man inside my kitchen. And if I'm not careful, into my bruised heart.

ZANE

They say when you know you know, right? But I never expected a baking lesson from the curvy and gorgeously flustered pastry chef. What do I do when the object of my desire doesn't believe in love at first sight? I jump in with both feet, surprising my family, who see me as the "all work and no play" brother.

I can't get enough of Holly's shortbread, smile, and sweet, addicting kisses. She says she can't gamble on love after a broken heart, but I'm wagering on a Christmas miracle.

CHAPTER 1

HOLLY

"*H*olly? Could you come out front? *Please?*"

My manager's voice carried an unnaturally high pitch to it. Darn it, I'd just begun the last batch of white chocolate and peppermint cookies and then I needed to get out the ingredients for our biggest seller, my grandmother's lemon shortbread.

Once again, it was my bestseller and there were just two dozen left but were already spoken for. Plus, I wanted to give my overnight baker a head start so we wouldn't be caught short handed with only four days left before Christmas. I giggled at my own pun.

"Holly?" Kiersten popped her head into the kitchen. "Um, I'm sorry, but I've kind of got an emergency out front."

Sighing, I brushed a chunk of hair off my forehead, wiped my flour-covered hands down the front of my apron, then blew out a frustrated sigh. The joys of owning your own business had been coming few and far between lately.

Following Kiersten through the swinging doors, my lower belly fluttered as if filled with butterflies as I looked over the front of my pastry shop, Just Desserts. At least that hadn't changed. The thrill of knowing I'd created a successful business doing something I loved.

It had been five years since my grandmother passed, my inheritance had made this shop a reality. When I opened the shop, I put her favorite cookie, and mine, Lemon Shortbread, on the menu between Thanksgiving and Christmas every year in her honor.

It may not scream the season, but since all her grandchildren were scattered across the country, my grandmother would make home-made cookie care-packages at Christmastime. The shortbread quickly became my favorite and when I was older, I managed to charm the recipe from her. Probably because I was the only grandchild interested in baking.

We'd sold out earlier in the day except for the two-dozen going to Harmony Hospital's overnight ER staff. Kiersten had been grumbling all day about delivering it. Not because it had become a tradition, a way to let the hard-working doctors and nurses know how much we appreciated them, but because of who she'd probably run into, the *Doctor McSteamy* of Pineville. One of these days I'd get the whole story about what had happened between them, but for now I couldn't afford any more distractions.

I really wanted to get home at a decent hour tonight, but now it wasn't looking like it would happen. I still needed to prep a few more batches of shortbread. Short an employee this year, I didn't want to get further behind the already packed schedule.

I hesitated to complain because business was good. Almost too good. I either needed to find a new location that had a larger kitchen, or even scarier, a second location.

"Holly, that's Zane Snow. He's here to pick up two dozen of the Grandma's Lemon Shortbread cookies." She pointed to a man across the store.

I looked at Kiersten; she looked at me, then finally to the customer who was standing by the front window, his back to us as he spoke on his cell. I didn't know this customer, but if the stiffness of his shoulders was any indication and the short clip to his words, he was not a happy camper.

Wait. "Did you say Snow? As in Noel Snow-Scott?"

Kiersten nodded. Shrugging, she said, "Sorry. He says he's her brother. Guess he's in town for the holidays and for the birth of his niece. You know, in spite of how it seems right now, he seemed really nice, and he's hot. You should, you know, flirt with him. You could use a date. And bonus, he's not local, so you could finally let loose and have a *really* good time."

While I listened to my manager's ridiculous suggestion, I was paying close attention to his broad shoulders, how his dark, thick hair skimmed the collar of his ski jacket, and how good his butt looked in a pair of well-worn jeans. He had potential, but I was not going to hook up with a customer, or the brother of one of my close friends, just because Kiersten wanted my year-long dry spell to finally end.

Well, the last laugh was on her, because what she didn't realize was that it had been much longer since I had sex, months longer. My last relationship had gone full platonic, ending on good terms.

It had been my fault, really. Ever since my college boyfriend had cheated on me with my best friend from high school, I made sure to pick men who I liked but who didn't necessarily make my heart pound and my body ache. I never wanted to feel emotionally battered and bruised like I had after returning home from culinary school to find them together.

Besides, sex wasn't that important to a relationship. Trust, respect, and real companionship were at the top of my next boyfriend wish list. As I found out all too well, lust and desire faded. I wanted as close to a guaranteed forever as I could get.

"Holly?" Kiersten said my name, humor lacing her tone. "I know, right? Wait till you see the front half. *Delish.*"

Kiersten and I had no business ogling the man the way we were, especially since as soon as his call ended, I'd have to disappoint him. "Quick, tell me what happened."

Sighing, Kiersten walked over to the tablet we used for all our orders, waving her hand over it. "The order isn't in the system. Mr. Snow says Noel made it over a week ago. I think he's talking to her now. I'm sorry, Holly. I don't remember taking the order. Did you?"

If I had, I would have remembered it even if it hadn't been in the queue for today. I knew how much she loved the shortbread and how much she looked forward to it every year. She hadn't mentioned a brother coming into town, or that she put in a special order less than a week before Christmas. But she was due to give birth any day, and as I found out with her first pregnancy, baby brain was a real thing.

"I didn't. I suppose one of the other employees could have. Hopefully, it was just this order that got lost. We don't have time to make up for any more missing orders." Running some quick calculations in my head, I could probably increase the amount of dough I was planning to make tonight and in theory, and with another set of hands, I could get the order filled, even delivering it myself to Noel within a couple hours. It was almost seven and Kiersten had already promised to close up for me but staying would put a dent in my plans to have a meal that wasn't rushed, then a long bath and getting to bed on time for once before I had to be up at five a.m. and start the mad rush to Christmas Eve.

Oh, well, who needed sleep anyway? I'd already scheduled myself a week off after Christmas for the first time since I opened so I could sleep all I wanted then.

"Hello. You must be Holly, the owner."

A voice as smooth as buttercream, and as smokey as burnt caramel, pulled me out of my musings. The first thing I noticed about Zane Snow's front side was that it was just as Kiersten had said, hot with a capital HOT. He had fine laugh lines around his eyes, a dusting of silver at his temples and a dimpled chin. I was a sucker for a chiseled jaw and split chin. But it was his full lips lifted in a warm and very sexy smile that had my mouth going instantly dry.

A furious flutter erupted in my stomach, and suddenly I couldn't put one coherent thought together. Kiersten elbowed my side, but it didn't help. Closing my mouth, which embarrassingly had fallen open, I turned to her, silently pleading for help.

"She is. Holly, this is Zane. Zane, Holly. And she'll explain everything." Kiersten laughed, walking away to help another customer.

Yeah, he wouldn't notice my supreme awkwardness after that little exchange. *Sheesh*, when was the last time a man had made me tongue-tied?

"Hi. Yes, I'm Holly. And you must be Noel's brother?" *Duh Kiersten just told him your name.*

"I am. One of two actually. How'd you know?" His voice sent tingles along my spine.

"Snow isn't that common of a last name and well, that's, uh, why I didn't say anything right away. You both have dark chocolate eyes." *Lame, lame, lame.* I wanted to melt right into the floor.

His smiled brightened, and lord have mercy. My stomach rolled, triggering a full body shiver, resulting in all the hairs on my body standing at attention. Praying he hadn't noticed my reaction, I puffed out a breath. *Get it together, Hols. You've been around handsome men before.*

Pasting a smile on my face, I pointed to the tablet. "I'm so sorry about the mix-up. We had a system update a few days ago. If I'd known Noel had placed an order, I would have made it and delivered it myself."

Zane kept staring at me, the smile never leaving his face. Did he know how powerful that smile was? Did he think the shortbread would magically appear if he continued smiling?

"Great. Noel says you're the best pastry chef in Pineville, and the prettiest. I'm really looking forward to trying some. I know it's almost closing time for you, so I'll pay and be on my way."

His compliment was so unexpected that I missed him pulling out his credit card, holding it out to me.

"As soon as you ring me out, I'll be on my way. We're having a pre-holiday family thing just in case she pops before Christmas."

I couldn't think. It had been so long since a guy had hit on me, words once again failed me. He probably thought I was being rude the longer I just stared at him without speaking.

The longer we stood not talking, staring at one another, the warmer my face and body became. And something shifted in his gaze as I toyed with my apron strings, overcome by what it would feel like to be kissed by him.

The bell over the door rang out, and another customer walked in, breaking the spell.

"Um, well, about that. The shortbread, not when Noel will pop. So, not only did her order not go through, but I'm also completely out of the shortbread. I just feel terrible about it." An idea began to form. I didn't want to disappoint Noel or Zane.

"But I might have a solution. I was getting ready to prepare more dough for the overnight crew to finish up for tomorrow's orders. I'll make enough for her order, then stay while it bakes, but it'll take a few hours before it's ready."

Zane's smile dropped, a deep wrinkle appearing between his brows. He shifted his stance wider before folding his arms.

His movement drew my eye to his trim waist, down his muscular thighs, and back up again. Danger flashed in my mind. I couldn't afford to get caught up in the sexy fantasy my brain was creating while trying to figure out how to spend more time with him, could I?

"That long, huh? Isn't shortbread like a handful of ingredients? Couldn't you make it quicker?"

Huh, so Mr. Snow didn't have a clue about the basics of baking, or more likely he was used to getting his way with his charm and that smile. Well, it didn't matter how much he affected me. Putting my suddenly reignited libido before my other customers wasn't going to happen.

And I wouldn't rush through the baking process when it came to any of my recipes, for anyone, no matter how sexy.

"I am sorry about that, Mr. Snow—"

"Zane," he said.

"Zane. I'll call Noel and explain to her—"

"No! I mean, that's not necessary. I'd rather not let her know about this. I mean, I already spoke to her husband, TS, about. I'm not sure what she was like during her pregnancy with my nephew Carson, but if at all possible, I don't want to upset her. She's been looking forward to your shortbread *all day*. Can't you just mix it up and bake it now? I could go run an errand and be back in like half an hour."

Carson was Noel's four-year-old son, and I knew neither of Noel's brothers had been around when he was born, so they weren't aware of her intense cravings the closer to her due date she got. And by his reaction, it was fair to say he didn't have his own kids, and he wasn't wearing a ring, which might mean there wasn't a Mrs. Snow? And, there went my traitorous mind again. I didn't have time for flirting. But it wasn't such a bad idea, and it might get Kiersten off my back if I gave it a try.

"Look, I'll make you a deal. There are certain parts of the recipe that can't be compromised, but if you help me finish the last few steps before I have to chill the dough, an extra pair of hands would shorten the prep time. If you can help out, then I'd be willing to give you the last two dozen cookies I set aside for another customer."

Zane's expression went from neutral to another dazzling smile. He asked, "What do I need to do?"

"Follow me." I didn't wait for his answer. Turning on my heel, I walked back into my kitchen wondering what the hell I was thinking?

CHAPTER 2

ZANE

*D*id the gorgeous pastry chef just ask me to help her bake cookies, then sashay through the double swinging doors, confident I'd follow?

Sashay? *Jesus, Snow, who the hell uses that word anymore?*

It really didn't matter because the subtle swing of her hips had me laser focused on spending more time with her. Getting a chance at a one-on-one time with Holly was too good to pass up, even if it meant doing something I'd never done before. But I needed to find out if she was as interested in me as I was in her. From the moment I stepped up to the counter, one thought kept racing through my head. *Mine.*

Her sweet smile, sexy curves and sugar-laced scent were like a beacon to a drowning man in an ocean full of perfection obsessed women who had lost their appeal years ago. Plus, she didn't just give me the cookies meant for someone else. She was going to make me earn them.

I just may have found the perfect for me woman.

I've had more than one ex-girlfriend complain that I was too wrapped up in my business, never taking time off for them or being more spontaneous. I'd stopped a long time ago worrying about finding a woman who'd understand how much time it takes to build my businesses. And because I'd yet to find a woman who understood what drove me, I remained a bachelor.

But Holly's dark brown eyes, full lips and hourglass figure ignited something deep in me that had me doing something very unexpected. Following her into the kitchen to bake cookies. For my sister, no less. I had a strange feeling this could turn out to be the best challenge I'd ever accepted.

"As I mentioned, I was just about to gather all the ingredients for the shortbread, when Kiersten told me you were here, but it will just take me a minute, and thankfully the butter is already room temp. So, I'll need help with separating the wet from the dry and, of course, zesting the lemons." Holly tied on an apron, cinching it under her full breasts. I caught myself from releasing a groan at the vision in front of me. I covered it with a deep inhale. "Wow, it smells incredible in here."

She grinned and tossed me an apron. "Put this on. There's a sink behind you so you can wash up. I'm thinking I could put the finished dough in the freezer. I've never tried it, but it might work cutting about thirty minutes out of the total time needed before I pop the shortbread in the oven for forty."

I liked how her mind worked, finding a solution to a problem she'd never expected to have. Showed willingness to work with her customers to provide superior customer service. It was something I found sadly lacking in some of my business partners and…why was I thinking about work when I had this woman all to myself? I should be coming up with ways to find out if she was single and interested. Because I certainly was.

In fact, I couldn't remember one woman from my past that I'd been this eager to find out all there was to know.

I aced measuring out the ingredients, and she seemed very pleased with how efficiently I worked.

I began peppering her with personal questions, happily finding out she was single, had siblings and her parents were local. "How long have you been in business?"

"It's five years this month. Doesn't seem that long, though. I still look forward to coming in every day."

She held out a handful of lemons for me to take, but I was caught up in the joyful expression on her face. It was nice to meet someone who genuinely liked what they did for a living.

"Okay, so take these and run them under the faucet, then lightly rub them dry. When you're done, I need you to zest them over this bowl and after that, dump them in here, then I'll fold them into the dough and *then* you can help me divide it up into the pans over there." She pointed to a spot behind me, but I kept my gaze on her.

"What?" she asked. A small smile lifted the corner of her mouth.

"You really enjoy this, don't you?"

Her laugh was light, almost musical. Before she answered, she placed the lemons in my hands, turned and stared into the largest mixing bowl I'd ever seen, pausing so long I didn't think she'd answer me.

Holly shook her head and quickly wiped away what looked like a tear beneath her right eye and began adding ingredients. "I hope so, otherwise why do it?"

"Hey, I didn't mean to make you sad."

"Oh, you didn't. I was just thinking how lucky I am to be doing what I love and how if it weren't for my grandmother, I'd never have my own business. Now, let's get moving, so Noel has her treat tonight."

At that moment, I was a bit jealous of what Holly had built here. She obviously cared about her customers. If she didn't, I wouldn't be standing here with no clue on how to zest a lemon. But I knew I'd never shed a tear over any of the businesses I'd built, bought, and sold, including the sale of my signature company that would be taking place the day after Christmas.

Sure, I'd celebrate the achievement, and the windfall that came with nurturing the multi-million-dollar corporation that'd become number one in the home improvement sector, but to shed a tear over it?

Unlikely. It would push my net worth up and over the billion-dollar mark and I had no plans to celebrate it, let alone shedding any tears over it. And maybe the saddest part was I won't have anyone other than my immediate family to help me acknowledge the accomplishment.

"Zane, you okay? You look, I don't know, a little sad."

Giving myself a shake, I looked into her hazel eyes, becoming lost in the concern I saw shining back at me. "Um, yeah. I think I need a hand or some guidance. How do you use this thing?" I held up the wickedly sharp zester she'd placed on the countertop.

Holly's cheeks pinkened. Then she bit her lower lip before stepping to my side. Lucky lip. I fought the urge to dip my head to find out what she tasted like. I didn't think she'd go for a kiss so soon after meeting.

Shifting my weight from one foot to the other in an attempt to hide and relieve the pressure of my erection, I angled my body as much as I could without catching her notice.

"It's pretty simple, although you'll want to make sure you don't scrape it against your skin because it will draw blood." Demonstrating, she glided the zester over the lemon, and once a fair amount of the yellow flesh from the fruit built up, she tapped it against the glass bowl and handed both items back to me.

"Just like that. Easy, peasy, lemon squeezy." She sing-songed the words, then laughed.

Our hands brushed and I swear an arc of electricity ran between us. For a moment, time stopped and neither of us moved. When she finally looked up at me, Holly did the cutest double take I've ever seen. Shaking her head, I watched fascinated by the myriad of emotions cross her face. Desire, shyness, confusion before controlling her features and looked away.

Pulling her hands from mine, she cleared her throat and stepped back over to her section of the gleaming steel top workspace. "Um, so keep doing that around the entire lemon, making sure not to scrape off the white part, the rind. You just want the yellow zest. That's where the lemony oil goodness lives and we want that for this recipe."

I'm not sure I'd ever caused a woman to be so flustered. I liked catching her off guard.

"You, um. Nothing. Okay, if you think you've got it, I need to finish combining the rest of the ingredients and…what are you looking at?" Holly paused and asked.

"What do you mean? I'm looking at you. If that makes you uncomfortable, I apologize. But when I see something beautiful, or someone, I can't help but take time and admire."

"Oh. Well, I…thank you." Her cheeks went from a light pink to a deeper shade, and I couldn't hold back any longer.

"I like that color on you. I'll have to compliment you more. How about I take you to a late dinner?"

Holly dropped the large spoon she was holding, then flattened her palm over it to keep it from tumbling off the counter. "That's sweet, but we need to focus on getting this shortbread made for your sister. Besides, didn't you say your family is having dinner together tonight?" She avoided looking at me as she made quick work of the already measured ingredients in front of her.

"I did. That's right. Okay, how about breakfast tomorrow? I'd really like to get to know you better. I'm here for five more days, and I'd like to spend as much time as I can with you. As much as you'll give me. I'll meet you anytime, anywhere."

Holly's eyes had gone wide, staying that way as I made my bid for her time. It made me wonder if she was this expressive in bed. And with that thought, my fingers itched to touch her again, sending another surge of need straight to my cock.

"What?" I asked. "You don't think I'm serious?"

REGAINING HER COMPOSURE, she let out a snort-laugh. Could she be more perfect?

"What I think is…is you're insane. Cute, but insane. First off, we just met. And second, you don't live here. And third, this is my busiest time of year. If it were next week, I'd agree to a dinner, at the normal time. Maybe. But you're Noel's brother, she and I are friends—"

"I'm flying out early on the twenty-sixth. And I don't think it matters if I live here or not. I'd really like to spend time getting to know you better. So, think about breakfast tomorrow, okay?" I flashed her a hopeful smile, then went back to zesting.

We finished the dough in silence. She wrapped the pans and placed them in the freezer, then set a timer, washed her hands, before finally facing me with her arms crossed, a serious look on her face. Up to this point I thought my bid for a date, scratch that I'd need more than one, and possibly my charm, would win her over.

"Look—"

"Uh-oh. Nothing good comes from a sentence beginning with 'look.' Give me another shot. I may not be living here now, but I'm making plans to spend more time in Pineville. After all, it's my home-town. My sister is here, and my brother, Hayden, just bought his first home not far away as well. There's something about you, Holly, some-thing that clicked between us. And I think you feel it too."

I felt my chances slipping and I couldn't leave here without getting Holly to agree to give me a chance. "Do you believe in kismet?"

"Hold on. What? Do I believe in kismet? Okay, look--"

Throwing up my hands, I said, "Don't say that word."

She laughed.

I grinned.

And there was hope.

"Zane, I'm sure you're a nice guy."

"I'm a great guy. I'm fun and I've been told I'm a good kisser. I also tip well, I can ride a unicycle and…you're the most intriguing, gorgeous woman I've ever met and—"

She blushed again, but she held up a hand, stopping me. "Thank you for all those, um, accolades. You know I don't know what exactly is it you do for a living but I've never seen someone negotiate for a date with me with quite so…fervently."

"I'll take that as a compliment." I said.

The swinging doors opened, and Kiersten barreled through. "Oh, sorry. Forgot you were still in here. I've got the front secured. I'm off to the hospital. Pray for me."

My manager grabbed the order of shortbread, leaving as quickly as she entered and, for the first time, the silence between us turned awkward.

"She, uh, has this thing going on with an ER doctor. No one understands it, but I think she likes him even though she always complaining about him."

Without knowing what or whom Holly was talking about, I felt a curious kinship with the good doctor in regards to the women in Pineville; they all seemed to be a bit on the stubborn side.

"Anyway, wait, can I begin a sentence with 'anyway?'"

Holly smirked. "I don't think it's a good idea for us to go on a date, but I'm flattered." She checked the ovens while I stood there grappling with being shot down.

I was prepared to use any angle I could to change her mind. I walked over to her and waited until she returned her gaze to me. "Noel would want us to give our connection a shot." I may have crossed my fingers, but Noel really wanted to see both Hayden and I find love and if it was with a friend of hers, I didn't think she'd disapprove.

"Do you always get what you want, Zane Snow? Do you pester all your dates until they agree to go out with you?"

Grinning, I shrugged my shoulders. "I have a pretty good track record of getting what I want. In business. But as far as my private life goes, I've never 'pestered' a woman like I've pestered you since I've never met anyone quite like you. And if you say yes, I guarantee you'll be my last."

Another long pause filled the air, and I almost broke it. She'd hit the nail on the head. I was used to getting what I wanted. And right now, Holly was at the top of that list.

"All right, we'll have our first date right now. After I put the shortbread in the oven, I'll make us some hot chocolate and we can get to know each other better while they bake. It's the best I can do on short notice. How does that sound?"

Two hours after Noel had talked me into picking up her favorite cookies, she met me at her front door. One hand on her hip, the other cradling her baby belly.

"Where have you been? Did you make them yourself or what?"

"You're not far off." I mumbled. Stepping onto her porch, I handed over the coveted treat and kissed her cheek. "There was a bit of a mix up, but it got straightened out. Dinner ready?"

My sister followed me through the house to her kitchen full of delicious smells, giving off a feeling of home we never had as kids. TS and their oldest, Carson, were sitting at the counter thumb wrestling. "Mommy, I won again!" My nephew was the spitting image of his father, poor kid, but there was always the hope baby number two would take after Noel.

"Hey, where's Hayden? Didn't he say he'd be here by now? I'm starved." I hadn't realized how much being dumb struck by love could work up an appetite. Or maybe it was because I skipped lunch. Either way, meeting Holly had set off not just the obvious physical pulls, but a feeling I'd never encountered—that she was what I never knew I'd been missing.

Spending time watching her do what she loved, teasing her into displaying that sweet smile of hers while keeping my hands off her except when I "accidentally" brushed up against her, had me expending a herculean amount of energy to resist dragging her off like a caveman. Never in my life had I experienced such an immediate, intense attraction and if I hadn't had to come back to my sister's house, I would have done my best to talk Holly into a late dinner, a goodnight or more.

"Of course you won, Carson. You're getting so big and strong." Noel set the cookies on the back counter and walked over to her son, dropping a kiss on the top of his head. Turning to look at me, she lanced me with her sharp gaze. "Zane, what's with the goofy grin? And why'd it take so long at Holly's shop?"

"Hm? Oh, yeah. Sorry about that. I ended up helping her make more cookies after she said she'd need to stay past closing to finish them."

Noel shared a look with TS over the top of their son's head, who'd begun chanting "cookies" when I mentioned what I'd been doing. TS picked him up under the arms and carried him to the dining table. "Later you can tell us how you persuaded her to do that, but first dinner. Mama's got to eat, so baby sister gets stronger for her big day." He tickled Carson after he placed him in the booster seat.

Looking around the kitchen, I asked, "What can I do to help? Dinner smells great?"

"Well, aren't you just a Santa's little helper? And when does Holly Cameron let anyone into her kitchen? I knew her for two years before I was invited into her inner sanctum." My sister gave me a pointed stare full of more questions.

"Noel, give him a break. He brought the cookies, and you need to sit down and eat, babe." TS put his hands on my sister's shoulders, guiding her to the table, then went back to the stove, grabbed the dishes warming in the oven and began serving his wife and son.

If I hadn't noticed it before, it was pretty obvious my brother-in-law was the perfect partner for Noel. The real estate developer and Outlaw baseball team owner took excellent care of my strong-willed sister. She deserved nothing less than the best, and he was it for her.

I'd always believed in a certain amount of serendipity, as our great aunt used to call it. I relied on it when it came to making major decisions. And with the upcoming sale of my business, it wasn't too big of a surprise to find the one thing that had been missing in my life, love, at the right time.

I always wanted someone to share my life with. And not just anyone, the right one. The perfect woman for me. And after spending the last two hours with Holly, I knew she was the one.

"She couldn't say no to the Snow charm and good looks. And we got to know each other while waiting for the cookies to bake and cool. She told me how she got accepted to culinary school and worked back east before her grandmother passed and she opened her own shop. She told me about her family; a sister and a brother, which I hear you know her brother, TS. She's super proud of Brock. Funny how small Pineville is. I'm looking forward to meeting him. Too bad he's retiring.

He's a hell of a player for the Outlaws. Oh, and did you know she's thinking of expanding her business? Seems she's outgrowing her current location. Anyway, I'm going to see her again tomorrow and the next day and the next. I hope you're okay with that, Noel?"

"Wow, seems like you learned a lot about Holly in a short amount of time. What's gotten into you, Zane? I've never seen you so interested in a woman. Not that we've met many of your girlfriends, but you know what I mean."

I did know. And I knew that I sacrificed a lot in my personal life. But that was over.

I always knew I'd eventually find someone to settle down with and it'd happen in its own time. But even I didn't think it would happen as quickly as it had. But as soon as I laid eyes on Holly, I knew. She was the one. Now to ease my family into my big news.

Finishing our meal, I pushed back from the table and began clearing dishes. And as if on cue, Hayden, my fraternal twin, pounded on the front door, rapping out an old, familiar rhythm from our youth before walking in, his big personality and two potted poinsettias proceeding him into the room. "Merry Christmas!"

"Uncle Hay! You're here!" Carson scrambled down from his booster seat, beelining for his second favorite uncle.

"Yeah, you're just in time to hear all about the woman I'm going to marry." Yeah, maybe I could have finessed that better, but oh, well. I was too keyed up to keep my feelings a secret from them.

Stunned silence filled the room. Then all three adults and one very loud toddler began bombarding me with questions.

Now all I had to do was convince Holly. I wonder if she'd agree to elope on New Year's Day?

CHAPTER 3

HOLLY

I want to see you every day till Christmas. Give me four dates to prove what's happening between us is as real as it is special.

Zane's words had made it difficult to get much sleep last night. Well, that and my body's response to him. Sure, he was movie star handsome. His lean, muscled body and wide shoulders had me sighing, but he was also nice. Almost too nice.

And he listened to me when I went on and on about growing my business and needing to find a bigger location. He talked about his family, particularly his twin brother, Hayden. They were fraternal and as opposite as night and day, but they stayed close. Noel hadn't mentioned that Hayden was *the* Hayden Snow, host of his own adventure show. Although I should have guessed as Snow wasn't a name you heard often. He'd recently bought a place on the lake in neighboring Cedar Ridge.

Zane had used that as a selling point in accepting his request because he planned on staying at his brother's until he found just the right piece of property for himself.

He'd also mentioned he had to go back to LA to sign papers for the sale of his business, which he was surprisingly vague about. He owned a home restoration business that grew pretty fast and became larger than what he wanted. He was still deciding on his next steps, but mentioned the money he'd make from this sale would afford him the time to pick his next project.

My alarm blared. I rolled out of bed, padding to my kitchen. I may have gotten a total of four hours of sleep if I was lucky. The shop didn't open until seven, but I made a habit of being there by six even though the staff I'd hired over the past couple years could handle the morning rush without me. There was nothing like getting in early and preparing the delicate pastries my customers loved.

Coffee'd up, and my body still humming from imagining Zane naked while I showered, I greeted Savannah in the bustling kitchen. We caught up on the orders she'd created overnight. Sending her home for some much-needed rest since she agreed to come in the next two nights, which I generally only needed her a couple nights a week, then I went in search of Kiersten.

"Hey, you. How'd it go at the hospital last night?"

"Uh-uh. You first. What happened between you and the hunky Zane Snow last night? Please tell me you finally let loose and had sex in the kitchen after I left."

I choked on the latte she'd made for me and scanned the room, looking to see if anyone had overheard her. "Yeah, that would be a big no. And even if I did, I wouldn't tell you. You'd probably shout it from the roof of the building. 'Holly Cameron finally got laid!'"

"Oh, my god, that's a great idea. I'll tuck it away for when it happens. You know, have sex sometime this decade."

Yeah, that would be nice. It'd been way too long since I had an orgasm with a man instead of my B.O.B.

"Kiersten, what would I do without you? You're good for my ego, but I'm taking my coffee and myself back to the kitchen. There are some pecan butter tarts calling my name."

"You're no fun." Kiersten's words followed me into the kitchen. "Promise you'll tell me all about him later."

I might, but I kind of liked keeping what was going on between Zane and I to myself. Barely twenty minutes went by before she came into the kitchen, calling out my name. Without looking up, I said, "Later, Kiersten. Anyway, there's nothing much to tell."

"I'm not sure if I should be offended by that or encouraged that you can keep a secret."

Zane's words and his husky tone sent a zing of electricity through me. How did he do that? It'd been a while since I had sex, but that didn't explain how turned on I was simply from hearing his voice. And when I looked up to find his hot gaze on me, I began wondering if maybe I should stop being concerned about keeping him at arm's length.

I wasn't used to such attention from a man, but maybe once the holidays were over…

"No offense meant. My manager's just worried about my personal life. She thinks I'm going to turn into an old spinster before I'm forty." Said manager had made a quick escape while my other employees found other things to pretend an interest in. I'm sure I'd be bombarded with questions later.

"Well, I would have to disagree with her. I definitely see no signs of that happening any time soon."

I watched as his hot gaze traveled over me before his eyes settled back on my mouth. It took every ounce of strength within me to not lick my lips.

His mouth formed into a crooked smile. Dammit, he knew. He knew what he was doing to me simply with a look. What would it feel like when he touched me? Would he want to undress me or watch me as I stripped in front of him? Or maybe he wouldn't be able to wait as I unbuttoned my blouse, and he'd tear it down the middle, push my bra down and take a nipple into his hot mouth and…*oh, shit*. What was he saying?

"…and I'm sorry for interrupting. I know we agreed I'd call you later today to see if you had time for dinner, but I wanted to stop by and see if you could break away for an early lunch?"

I looked around the kitchen, what for I could honestly say I had no idea. He scrambled my thoughts simply by standing there.

"Um, I haven't had time to look at the afternoon schedule. I can't do lunch, but I should be able to break away around five-thirty?"

"Great, give me your address and I'll pick you up at six." Zane took his cell from his jacket, then stepped closer. So close I could feel the heat from his body. "Okay, I'm ready."

"Hmm?" Lord, he smelled good. A citrusy scent with a hint of musk. Or maybe it was all him. Either way, I wanted his arms around me so I could take another hit of it and then maybe lick my way from his collarbone to his navel.

"Jesus, Holly, you're going to have to stop looking at me like that, otherwise I'm going to haul you against me and kiss you until I hear what kind of sexy sounds are buried deep within you. But I don't think you want your employees to witness that, and I want you alone and willing the first time I finally get my hands on you."

All I could do was nod. Because I wanted nothing more than the exact same thing. Decision made, I marched over to my desk, grabbed a pencil and paper, scribbled my address, and handed it to him before I could change my mind.

"Make it 6:15 p.m."

Zane's eyes turned near black. He took the piece of paper without a word, but his gaze raked down my body. Lighting a fire, there was no way could be banked until later tonight. After he left, I spent a long time staring at the spot he'd stood, trying to pull myself together and wondering was that really me who just all but agreed to let the sexiest man I'd ever met, and who miraculously wanted me, find out what kind of sex noises I made?

Yes. Yes, I was.

CHAPTER 4

ZANE

The anticipation of dinner tonight with Holly was killing me. I wasn't sure I'd be able to make it through even an hour of sitting across from her in a public place without wanting to drag her back out to my car like some caveman. These feelings for her were so different from anything I've ever felt toward a woman, and I didn't want to screw things up with her.

So, I arranged to pick up dinner on my way to her place, then worried the whole way over that she'd take one look at me with takeout bags and slam the door in my face.

Before I knocked on her door, it opened. Her eyes took in the bags in my hands, and a huge smile split her face. "I knew there was a reason I was so drawn to you. I love Salvatore's. Get in here."

"Yes, ma'am. Where do you want me to put—"

Holly took the bags filled with lasagna, two salads and garlic bread, set them down on the island in her kitchen, then grabbed my jacket with both hands, pulling me down and gifting me with the hottest kiss of my life. Bar none.

It was all-consuming and the sounds I waited all day to hear filled the room. Soft at first, then louder, demanding, and my dick responded. Rock hard didn't do justice to how my body responded to Holly's. Desperate to be inside her. I ripped my coat off, lifted her up against me. She wrapped her legs around my waist, rubbing her hot core against my erection.

"I'm not going to make it to your room if you keep doing that." I gritted my teeth as she did it again.

Never taking her lips off mine, she mumbled, "Don't need a bed. Right here."

What the lady wanted; the lady got. I scanned the room, spotted a thick rug in front of her Christmas tree.

Running my hands down her sides, I realized she'd answered the door in nothing but a long sleep shirt. Spread out before me was the best present I could have dreamed of. Tunneling my hands under the soft material, I discovered she didn't have any undergarments on.

"Have I told you how perfect you are for me?"

"Later. Much later. You have too many clothes on." She lifted the shirt over her head, and she was gloriously naked. The lights from the tree played over her skin, highlighting and shadowing her curves and valleys. Her nipples puckered, waiting for my atten-tion. But when let her legs fell open, I knew where I wanted to begin.

Moving quick, I shed my clothes, and grabbed my wallet. Hopeful and prepared, I took out the condom I'd put in there less than an hour ago, placing it within reach. Dropping kisses between her breasts, I licked and sucked first one nipple, then the other before moving down her body. I caressed her hips before gripping her thighs, spreading them wider. The first taste wasn't nearly enough. Her soft moans ringing in my ears, I licked her wet folds slowly until she begged me to go faster.

"Zane, please!"

Her hips lifted, seeking her release, but I wanted another taste. Plunging my tongue deep in her pussy, I thrust in and out, then slipped a finger inside her slick channel.

"So wet, baby." My voice, raw sounding, and husky as it rang out in the room.

She met each thrust with a roll of her hips, her cries now drawn out and desperate. When she came on my tongue, I pressed my thumb onto her clit, rubbing circles, prolonging her orgasm.

But I wasn't done. Not even close.

I started all over again, bringing her back to the edge, then easing off before I lifted her legs on to my shoulders and with short delicate strokes flicked her swollen bud over and over until she came, collapsing onto the rug beneath us.

Mine, this gorgeous woman, was all mine.

I grabbed and quickly rolled on the condom; my arms braced over her. I asked, "Tell me what you want."

Her breathing was heavy and quick. She laughed. "That was… perfect. And I want, no, I need you inside me. Now!"

My cock twitched as she curled her legs into her body. I lined myself up to her entrance and thrust myself home. Her inner walls clamped down on me, sure that I'd spill too soon, but I took a deep breath and pulled back not quite all the way out but enough to pound back into her searching for the right spot to send her spiraling once more.

Later, after we'd had something to eat, I carried her to bed and made love to her slowly for as long as we could both hold out. The second time was just as shattered as the first. Nothing or no one had ever come close to making me feel this way. I wanted to find out if she felt the same, but also wanted her to tell me without thinking she had to reciprocate. I could wait.

I hadn't ever been interested in talking after sex, but since this was more than sex to me, I found myself giving in. "You're the first woman I've wanted to cancel all my plans for. If I could, I'd stay through next week. Just ask my family, that's unheard of. I live and run my business by the calendar. And there's just no way I can cancel this trip. I'm selling my business and I need to sign papers making it official. Come with me. You said you're taking time off. It's perfect timing, kismet even."

Her body stiffened, and she pulled away. I felt the mental shift. She wasn't buying it, but I didn't know what else to say to her.

"This can't be any more than what we've already had. There're reasons I'm still single, Zane. No, it's okay. I decided to put my business first, like you, but I'm beginning to suspect unlike you, I did it because of a bad relationship. I may be over him, but to be honest, my heart is still bruised. It's safe to say that I'm more than cautious with my feelings. And I don't want to discount your feelings, but I'm not sure I believe in kismet or fate or whatever you think is at play here. All I can offer you is the next few days. And I'll think about LA, okay?"

She snuggled deeper, her backside to my front, stroking my arm lightly as I tightened my hold around her soft curves. I lay there for a long time, simply holding onto her before my body gave in.

My last thoughts were I wasn't giving up. She was too important to let go. She may have thought warning me off would save me from heartache, but she had no idea that when I found something I wanted, I never gave up until it was mine.

Including her.

CHAPTER 5

HOLLY

*I*t had only been three days since Zane had walked into my shop. Every thought I had in between creating, baking, and interacting with my customers was full of him. Tomorrow was Christmas day, which meant today would be my busiest day of the year, and yet I felt unnaturally calm about all the last-minute things that could go wrong, had gone wrong in the past.

I'd given more responsibility to Kiersten the last few months and until last week, she'd been reminding me I hired her for a reason. I baked, she ran the day-to-day operations and marketing for Just Desserts. She'd been checking my temperature all day, sure that I was coming down with something.

"You're sure you're feeling okay?" For at least the dozenth time, Kiersten stood across from me in the kitchen. Concern lacing her features.

"Yes, Mom. I'm fine. And like I told you the last eleven times, I'm concentrating on what I do best and letting you do the job I hired you for. Which you're excellent at, by the way. Now, go." Waving her off, I grabbed my cell out of the pocket of my apron. It had vibrated a few moments ago, but I was in the middle of rolling out some puff pastry. Scrolling to open the message from Zane, I read it and sighed.

Forgetting that Kiersten was still standing there, I jumped when she shouted. "I knew it!"

"What do you think you know?" Grinning, I re-read the NSFW text.

"You had sex." Kiersten shouted.

"Keep your voice down." I peeked behind me, praying that no one else heard her outburst. No such luck. Two of our delivery guys stood near the back of the room, staring at Kiersten.

Waiting until they left, I finished scoring the dough, then put down the fork and grinned. "Okay, so I may have seen Zane a couple of times over the last few days."

"Wow, he works fast. What did he do to get you to say yes during our busiest week? I mean, this is unheard of. Wait, this is more than just sex, isn't it? Do you like him? I mean, like, really, really like him?"

I couldn't quite look her in the eye. Nodding and humming, I turned away and washed my hands.

"Holly, come on. This is big. I'm happy for you. You deserve this. And he's hot. What does he do for a living?"

"He develops commercial property and owns a company that specializes in home restoration. Bringing older homes back to their original condition. He's in several states, I think."

Kiersten sent me a goofy grin. "You think, huh? Spending more time between the sheets learning all the other things about him, hopefully. Anyway, he must be doing well."

Feeling my face flame at her statement, I said, "Yeah, he must. He did mention this is the first vacation he's taken in years because he finally felt comfortable leaving someone else in charge."

"Have you talked to Noel recently? She good with you hooking up with her brother?"

I know Kiersten wasn't slamming me, but her question shook me. I felt zero guilt over what Zane and I were doing. But was it simply hooking up? When we're together, he'd spoken about things we could do together beyond this week. I'd answer noncommittally and change the subject. Did I want more than just this magical week with him?

"Wait, I recognize that look."

"What are you talking about? Shouldn't you get back out front?"

"No, they work better when I'm not hovering." Kiersten wasn't budging.

I checked my list and began pulling ingredients for the last special order of the day. "Why don't you take a long lunch? You deserve it. I can't remember when Christmas week has run so smoothly."

"I know what you're doing, Holly, and I'm not letting you get away with it. This guy really has you all tied up in knots, doesn't he?"

"What makes you say that?"

"If you just wanted a little scratch, and that's all it was, I don't think you'd have given him a second date. But here you are, checking your phone, blushing, and I've never heard you hum. You've been humming and oh, my…you're in love! This is what you look like in love." Kiersten clapped and did a little jig. "Oh, and if you guys get married, you'll become Holly Snow. And you guys met at Christmastime. This is so great."

"Kiersten!"

"This is so great. I'm so happy for you, Holly."

"Kiersten. Stop. I'm not in love with Zane. I just met him, literally. Like three days ago. That's not how love works."

She stopped hopping in place. "How do you know? C'mon, the last guy you were in love with, you caught with your best friend and you knew him since high school. I'm sorry to say it, but you've been hiding yourself away from the possibility of love. I think you're in denial."

"Really, you want to talk about denial? How about Jack, Dr. McSteamy, hmm? What's going on with you two, Ms. Love Expert?"

Kiersten's face fell, but she recovered quickly. "Okay, that's fair. But right now, we're talking about you. And Zane. You can't tell me you don't have some real feelings for this guy, right?"

Maybe she was right. Maybe I was hoping what we had could go beyond just this week, beyond the amazing sex, but love? I knew just enough about him to know I liked him. To know that I loved him would take more time. Maybe he had an annoying habit he was hiding from me, or he left his dirty clothes lying around his room, or he didn't want kids? Those were the things I needed to know before I even considered being in love with someone.

"Holly?"

"Um, yeah, feelings. I mean, I do like him. But I'm not in love with him. That would be…" I couldn't bring myself to say crazy, because maybe I was—just a little. Crazy about Zane. But it came with a bucket of uncertainty and the need to keep my heart from getting broken again.

Kiersten finished my thought, the one that I couldn't quite believe. "It would be wonderful. Didn't you tell me your parents got married just three months after they met and now it's been what, forty years? I wish you'd forget about that jerk who didn't have a clue about love or that you were the best thing to ever happen to him."

"We're just spending time together for the holidays. He'll be gone the day after and I'll be taking next week off, napping, and reading all the books I've been hoarding all year."

My manager threw up her hands. "Sure, that sounds nice. You deserve time off to do whatever you want or nothing at all. But maybe you should take a closer look at how you feel when you're with Zane. Love doesn't have to take weeks or months, sometimes it does. And sometimes it happens in the blink of an eye, in the brushing of hands and the tripping of your heart when you see the one that makes you sigh and say, 'Oh, there you are.'"

Shocked at her words and even more shocked at how they rang true, I stopped what I was doing, walked over to her, and hugged her tight. "Kiersten, I don't know what to say other than thank you. And I hope things work out for you, because I know you think you're talking about me and Zane, but maybe there's a bit of your own story in there."

When she didn't answer me right away, I knew what I said was true. She had her own inner debate going on with the hunky doctor, but she also opened my eyes to accept maybe that what I was feeling shouldn't be written off as mere physical attraction.

I had so much to think about before I saw Zane tonight. I'd been giving myself a pep talk all morning to prepare for it being the last time I'd see him. Could I undo years of conditioning myself that I may never fall in love again and open my heart to the possibility that after a handful of days, I'd fallen hard?

CHAPTER 6

ZANE

The days had quickly fallen into a routine with Holly. She needed to work, and I needed to see her, so I'd bring dinner to her place. We'd eat, make love, or make love first, then eat. I'd spend the night with her, then wake up as she kissed me goodbye before leaving for work.

Since today was Christmas, we spent it with our families, planning to get together later.

My brother complained I wasn't listening to him when he went on and on about his new show or our upcoming twenty-year high school reunion. Claiming he didn't want to attend, but I knew him. High school had been tough for him, so showing our former classmates that the chubby nerd had turned into the sought-after world traveler with his own show and an honorable mention in the last year's People's Most Beautiful edition would guarantee he'd be there.

And so would I, with Holly on my arm.

Then there was Noel. She was doing some major nesting and wanted all the furniture in the house moved. TS had volunteered me, claiming I needed to do more brotherly things with my sister. Which proved how smart he really was because she changed her mind at least five times before she was happy.

But tonight was all about Holly. I didn't want to fly back to LA not having told her how I really felt. In fact, if she agreed, I planned on taking her with me.

Ringing Holly's doorbell at six, I patted my jacket pocket. After I finished up with Noel and moved the baby's crib one last time, I visited a local jewelry store, the owner happy to open up once I gave him the number to my Black Card. The necklace I bought was perfect. I wanted to give her something special to mark our first Christmas together. And after she agreed to be my wife, I'd take her back, and we'd design the perfect ring.

"Hi." My cheeks had begun to hurt from so smiling so much lately, but it was worth it and so was she.

"Hi." She looked distracted, but I had a plan for that. "You look beautiful."

"Thank you. You do too. I mean handsome. But you always do."

She turned back into her front room. There were candles lit and music playing. She'd set the scene perfectly without even knowing what I had in mind.

"This looks nice. Do you want to eat first or…?" I wanted her to choose our activities for tonight. Sensing a goodbye in her eyes, I had to tell her how I felt before she pushed me away.

"I was hoping maybe we could talk first. Then eat later. Much later." Holly gave me a shy smile, then held out her hand.

I joined her on the couch. "What's up? You have this look on your face and it's got me worried."

"Zane, this week has been wonderful—"

"Don't say, but. Anything else, please." My heart began to pound.

"But, you're leaving for LA and—"

"Come with me." The words tumbled out of me. Not exactly how I'd planned to ask, but desperate times and all. Tucking a piece of hair that had fallen forward behind her ear, I placed a hand on her cheek, rubbed her full bottom lip with my thumb, then kissed her. I meant it to be quick and light, but she pulled me back and deepened it.

And just like all the other times I had her in my arms, I didn't want to let go. I didn't want to stop and perform the speech I'd practiced all day. I just wanted to love her.

Holly leaned back, breaking the kiss, then placed a finger over my lips. "Can I give you my answer later? Right now, I need you inside of me."

She didn't have to ask me twice.

We stood, and she led me to her room. Undressing each other, I memorized every line, every freckle on her gorgeous flesh. With a gentle push, she tumbled onto the mattress. I covered her body and for the next several hours took my time, wringing the cries of her desire from her until it we were both satisfied.

Sometime around one a.m., I woke from a dead sleep, groggy, but happy, and realized I hadn't given her the words or the present I'd intended. I gathered her back into my arms and settled in. I didn't need to wake her to find out if she would go with me in the morning. The way she took me into her body told me everything I needed to know.

She may not have admitted it to herself yet, but Holly had fallen just as quickly. Now all I needed to do was show her that love didn't need a timeline to be real.

CHAPTER 7

HOLLY

"**W**hat is this, Zane? Why are we headed to a private jetway?" I'd agreed to go to LA. I couldn't bear to see him go, and I had a whole week off to be with him before saying good-bye. It was an adventure and maybe I would find the answers I needed to decide if what I felt was more than a thrilling fling with great sex, easy conversation and…yeah, I probably didn't need more time. I just needed to get over my years' long aversion to letting myself be vulnerable enough to fall in love again.

"Because we're flying on my plane."

My mouth fell open. "Wait. Hold up. Your plane. Like you own the plane?"

"I own the plane. Well, technically my company does, but I own the company, so…"

"Wow, I didn't realize the home restoration business was so lucrative." I sat unmoving as the driver pulled up next to a sleek jet, a set of stairs already in place next to the open door.

"Is there anything else you haven't told me?" I'm not sure why I was so surprised. There had been hints that he had money, but I didn't really push since his sister was married to a billionaire, but TS was low key about his wealth. They lived well, but never flaunted it.

"Let's get settled inside." He exited the car, rounded the back, and opened my door.

Taking his hand, I did my best not to appear shocked as I wondered what else he was keeping from me. "So, you're rich. Like, you own this jet and can fly anywhere in the world, rich?"

Zane greeted the pilot and an attendant who asked for our coats. "I guess you could put it that way. Is that a problem?"

Problem? Nope, but it would have been nice to know the man I was seeing, and spending all my free time naked with was a freaking billionaire. "Why didn't you mention it?" I asked.

"My wealth has become a hinderance in my personal life. I never know if a woman would be with me if I weren't wealthy, although in the last five years it's a pretty good bet that was the main reason. Anyway, it was nice to know you had no idea who I was besides Noel's brother. And I'm going to have to thank her for not telling you."

How could I argue with that? "That sounds logical, but if you're keeping a secret family from me, then I'm outta here." Grinning, I squeezed his hand.

"Nope, no secret family. I plan on one wife, and hopefully a couple of kids. One day. Soon I hope."

My heart went into double time and my hands began to sweat at the mention of "soon." Zane Guided me to a pair of oversized seats toward the middle of the plane. He stowed my handbag, then took my hands in his.

"Last night was perfect, but there was one thing I didn't get a chance to say before you fell asleep. No, I'm not complaining. Watching you fall apart in my arms is something I never want to end. You're perfect for me, Holly. You're smart, compassionate and you make me laugh. I love your lemon shortbread and the joy you bring to your job. But most of all, I love you."

Emotion bubbled into my throat. I didn't think it was possible. It had felt too soon when Kiersten said she thought I was falling in love with Zane. I knew he believed in kismet, but to hear him say the words was overwhelming.

Tears fell onto my cheeks, but Zane brushed them away. Dropping feather light kisses on my forehead, he hugged me close, then whispered. "I've loved you from the very moment you smiled at me. I knew you were meant for me." He pulled out a jewelry box from his pocket, opening it to display a dazzling diamond set in the middle of two entwined hearts.

"When you know, you know. You have my heart. This necklace is my promise to you that you're my forever."

Butterflies exploded in my lower belly, and I let myself believe the truth radiating in his eyes. My entire being had never felt more alive by his touch and his words. This was crazy, and yet it felt right. Releasing a sigh, I let myself say out loud what it had been begging to tell him since last night.

"I love you too." A bit overwhelmed, I laughed and cried as tears streamed down my face.

"Oh, sweetheart. Don't cry." Zane bent, swept me into his arms, settling me into his lap. "Be mine forever?" His whispered plea against my neck had me squirming in his arms. I hope I never stopped reacting to him like it was the first time. Lucky didn't begin to describe how I felt every time he showed me how much he wanted me. Loved me.

"Is there a bed on this plane?" I wanted to begin our forever now.

"Is that a yes?" Zane's eyes were suspiciously shiny and filled with humor.

"It's more than a yes. It's that and a thank you for showing me there is no timeline when it comes to love. You are mine—forever."

I managed to render Zane speechless. I watched with fascination as he opened his mouth, shut it, then repeated the pattern two more times.

Finally, instead of responding, he framed my face, dipped his head, capturing my lips in a deep, slow kiss, sealing our love.

Who knew my grandmother's lemon shortbread recipe would lead me to finding the man of my dreams?

TANGLING WITH THE MOUNTAIN MAN

A PINEVILLE WORLD CHRISTMAS NOVELLA (TANGLING SERIES)

ABOUT

TANGLING WITH THE MOUNTAIN MAN

Being an Army Ranger hadn't prepared me for running, *literally*, into the curvy, beautiful chef.

I didn't plan on moving to Pineville, Idaho, but after finding the half-brother I never knew I had, he and my best friend convince me it's the perfect place to settle down. And if there's one thing I crave after spending twenty years in war, eating my weight in dust and sand, and living out of a duffel bag, it's peace and quiet—which I find in a mountain cabin that needs a bit of TLC.

Meeting Taya changes my plans. I cannot get enough of her musical laugh, sexy curves, and yes, even her choice in an ugly Christmas sweater.

My new focus is convincing the beautiful single mom that taking a chance on a grumpy former ranger is more than an instant connection and friends with benefits. It can be the love of a lifetime.

CHAPTER 1

TAYA

*I*t was a week and a half until Christmas, and I had so many things left to do, like find the perfect gifts for Dylan and Lauren before they left tomorrow for their grandparents' place in Canada. This year they'd received plane tickets from their father's parents to spend the holiday with them and I was a little weepy about it, even though they'd been with me the last two weeks since their break from college started.

I repeated the thought again as I stood in front of the prep area of the kitchen where I worked. The fact that I had children old enough to attend college often surprised people. And when we were often mistaken for sisters, it secretly gave me a thrill.

But when they turned nineteen last year, I can't lie, my anxiety increased big time over them repeating my own life choice at that age, I refused to label my kids as a mistake. The thought had me stress eating the truffle-laced French fries my customers kept coming back to O'Malley's Pub & Grill where I was head chef. I was still trying to work off the extra ten pounds I'd gained since we added them to the menu.

But big things were coming. Soon my catering company would launch, and I'd be too busy to think about the possibility of becoming a young grandmother or eating my weight in fries. In fact, I had a couple of events lined up before Christmas as sort of a soft opening that I was planning new dishes for that would keep me busy while the girls were away.

I'd still help out at the Pub, tweaking the menu for Maverick and Luke when they wanted new items, but I was so looking forward to the change of pace. Not that I didn't love working here but owning my own business had been my dream since graduating culinary school.

I'd raised the twins on my chef's salary, and even with my ex's child support, I still had to work for someone else in order to afford health insurance. But now, at forty-one, I could finally afford to go after my dream. Thankfully the girls' stellar grades had earned them both partial scholarships so, along with working part-time jobs and scrimping and saving the last two years by working all the hours I wanted, come the new year Full Plate Catering would be up and running.

Dylan and Lauren's father may have pulled back emotionally from them, the bastard, but I couldn't fault his parents, their grandparents, especially since they helped out over the years with extra funds and now helping pay for their living expenses at college. It would be a lonely two weeks without them, but they'd be back in time to help me with the launch of my business.

I carried their lunch order out myself. It was Wednesday and the mid-week crowd was slower than normal, so I snuck away for an extended break with my girls.

My sous chef shouted my name as I crossed the threshold between the kitchen and the pub. I answered his question, then without looking, began walking again, right into a brick wall. One plate stuck to my chest and the other and all its contents smashed against the wide chest of a shocked patron with the darkest eyes and broadest shoulders I'd ever seen.

Before I could form an "I'm sorry," large hands latched onto my hips, holding me steady from the impact, followed by what sounded suspiciously like a low, impatient growl.

"I've got you. Are you okay?" A deep, rumbly voice asked.

The question confused me. I opened my mouth, but no words came out. At five-four, I was used to being shorter than a lot of men, but this one seemed to have almost a foot on me. Carrying the scent of fresh cut pine, he had muscles everywhere. Encased in a form-fitting thermal shirt, the bearded mountain of a man narrowed his eyes at me. I felt my cheeks heat from under his grumpy yet interested gaze.

"Mom, you okay?" Dylan appeared behind the grumpy but also incredibly handsome man, a look of humorous concern filled her face. "Whoa, what a mess. Was that our lunch? I'll go get some towels." She sprinted off behind us, disappearing through the swinging door.

Lauren appeared from the other side, walking away down the hallway where the restrooms were located. "Mom, oh my gosh, what happened?" She took a long look at the hot guy between us then continued. "I'm sure you didn't have to dump food on him to get his attention." Cracking up at her own joke, Lauren stood next to me, her gaze flicking between me and the still grumpy looking man who apparently was still waiting for me to respond to his question.

My heart raced, and my palms were sweating, so I shoved the plates into Lauren's hands. "Here, take these and find your sister. She's getting towels." Looking back into the poor man's eyes, a shock of awareness flitted down my spine. I may be forty-one, but I was far from dead and this guy had some serious magnetism going on. Still not sure if he found the situation amusing or aggravating, I began wiping my hands on his mid-section, trying to remove the food I'd just smashed onto him.

My fingers met solid steel. Holy wow, this guy was built. Maybe he's a bodybuilder. "I'm terribly sorry. I rarely carry dishes out of the kitchen. There should be a rule against me doing it, and here, let me...."

Dylan arrived with towels, but she was no help. She stood there next to her grinning sister. They watched with way too much enjoyment as I further made a fool of myself. "I, uh, can wash your shirt in the sink. And your meal is on me. Oh, um no, that's…okay. Let me begin again. What can I do to make this right?" Yeah, stupid question to ask with my hands full of pasta primavera loaded with extra garlic and white wine sauce. If it wasn't so funny, I'd probably break out in tears. Thank goodness he wasn't yelling at me. Instead, he was still patiently watching me, waiting. Oh, yeah. He asked me if I was okay.

"So, I'm fine. Are you? I mean, obviously you just had a plate of hot pasta dumped on you, but other than that, did I hurt you?" So maybe that last part wasn't needed. This man probably wouldn't get hurt if a bomb went off in the pub. He had a rough yet ready and very capable look about him that screamed *protector*.

"I'm good. My shirt is fine. I'll take one of those towels now." He kept his hands on me despite his declaration. And he never looked away from me. Not once, even as other employees arrived to help.

One of my girls let out a nervous giggle. The sound broke whatever spell held us together and his hands dropped to his sides. I felt a wave of disappointment while still feeling the heat from his touch.

Before he could leave, I grabbed a towel, wiped the food from my hands. He took one as well, and everyone else left us alone. The busboy had already used a mop to clean up the floor, and the girls reluctantly returned to their table after I gave them my mom glare.

"Again, I'll pay for your meal and anyone you're with. Where are you sitting?" I asked.

He nodded and waved a hand. "Over there in the far corner. I'm here with a buddy. His wife used to work here. Maybe you know her?"

Following the direction of his hand meant tearing my gaze away from his, and I was having a difficult time getting my brain to re-engage and follow directions. When I did, my gaze landed on Cole Nolan, who was married to Scarlett, one of our former servers, a close friend of mine. Cole waved at me and smiled.

"You know Cole and Scarlett?" As soon as I asked it, it sounded dumb. *Of course he does. That's what he just said, Taya.* "I mean, how do you know them?"

"Cole and I served together. I moved here recently after visiting them last year. I'm Beck. Beckett Rivera. And you must be Taya Davis, the chef I've been hearing about."

He'd heard of me? Had he eaten here before? His attention, although far from uncomfortable, was something I wasn't used to. I dated sporadically, but after beginning my fourth decade, I did mention to Scarlett that I would definitely get myself back out there if only to find a friend with benefits situation. Probably. Maybe. In the new year, for sure.

Scarlett had been on my case lately about my lack of male companionship. Could I be so lucky that this man is single?

As much as I wanted to learn more about him, now was not the best time. The girls were waiting, and I needed to get back in the kitchen, grab them two new plates of pasta and then get back to work. "You're Beck? Oh, that didn't come out right. She told me you're staying with them. Well, I hope it was only good things. That you heard about me, I mean." Groaning inwardly, *could I be any more awkward*? "I'll let you go to get cleaned up. Don't worry about the bill. I'll go take care of that now. It was, ah, nice meeting you."

"It was. I hope we can see each other again. Without the plates of food between us. I enjoyed the special, by the way. Now I have more reason to come here than just the great food."

"Oh, what's that?"

The pub was fast filling up and people were coming and going around us, but all I could do was stand there, mesmerized, as Beck smiled. At me. All his attention was on *me*.

"The beautiful chef, of course." He answered then looked me up and down.

Wow. I mean, wow, wow, wow. What had just happened? I watched him walk down the hallway. His long strides holding me captive while my own daughters catcalled me from across the room.

I'd been caught checking out Beck's ass.

CHAPTER 2

BECK

*D*riving up to my new home, thoughts of Taya ran through my head. Figuring out a way to see her again had started not five minutes after I left the pub a few days ago, but I hadn't found a good way other than appearing like a stalker.

I wasn't a guy who dated. Hell, lately I was a man who'd barely had sex in the last couple of years. Small talk and dinners over candlelight were not in my wheelhouse. One-night stands were all I could handle when I was on leave. I'd never had the urge to settle down with one woman. I contributed most of my outlook on relationships to not having been raised with a father. I never witnessed my mother in a healthy relationship with a man, so I figured it wasn't in the cards for me.

And if anyone had asked me six months ago who Beckett Rivera is, that would have been an easy answer: Army Ranger, now officially retired, my mother's only child, and a friend you could call on in the middle of the night for help with just about damn anything.

But now, I'm somebody's brother, Thomas "TS" Scott's, to be

precise. He's one of the main owners of the United States Baseball League's local team, the Idaho Outlaws and a real estate magnet. Talk about life throwing you a curveball. After my mother passed away earlier in the year, her dying wish had been for me to track down the father I never knew. She'd never told me who he was until she'd been diagnosed with cancer.

And when I began the journey to discovering my background, one coincidence after another kept popping up.

First my buddy Cole had moved to the Pineville. The same city where my mother had worked all those years ago as a maid. After a brief affair with her boss, she became pregnant with me. With a check for ten grand, he sent her away. His only request had been not to tell me who my real father was. So, she began a new life thousands of miles away as a single mom never marrying.

When I'd made a first brief visit to Pineville for Cole's wedding to Scarlett, I received word from the private eye I'd hired, that my father had passed long ago, but his only known child was living here. It turned out to be TS who Cole and Scarlett knew through her former employers at O'Malley's, Maverick Jansen, and Luke Garibaldi, two current players for the Outlaws. And Cole's sister Evie was engaged to Sam Campbell whose mother, Lois, is TS's executive assistant.

Man, I needed a scorecard just to keep up with all these new names and faces.

What a small fucking world it is.

After I got TS's name, I'd debated contacting him, but with Cole's encouragement I reached out, and then we did one of those DNA tests and *Bam!* I was thrust into an instant family.

And now I was the owner of ten acres on a mountain with an almost finished three-bedroom cabin. In finding the brother I never knew I had, I'd also found the spot I longed for and the solitude I'd always dreamed of after spending half my life overseas.

Shortly before I took off for Sherman Mountain this morning, where my new place is, Scarlett surprised me with the news that she and Cole are hosting a holiday slash housewarming party in a few days and as luck would have it, Taya was invited. How had that gotten by me? So wrapped up with getting to know my brother and his family better, I hadn't paid much attention to anything else.

The most recent bombshell had been TS' informing me he was giving me half of the inheritance from his, I mean our, father. It still hadn't sunk in. When I tried to refuse it, he'd called his wife Noel into his office. I learned fast that you couldn't say no to her. She also talked about all the great things I could do with the money: I could start a foundation for veterans, give back to kids from broken homes, the list went on and on. For the first time since I turned in my papers to retire from the Army, I felt a new purpose to my life beyond serving my country.

Arriving at my place, I pulled under the carport I'd added just last week. I planned on waiting till spring to have a garage added plus a shop where I still didn't know what I'd do with it, but I had a vague notion of finding a new hobby, like woodworking.

I'd only moved in the bare necessities like a bed and refrigerator, having camped out a few nights here and there while I did most of the renovation work myself. I had a decent wood pile going for the new wood-burning stove I'd installed and built a shed before the snow hit. I'd also cleared away what felt like a ton of debris and slash from around the house that had been half built a few years ago, never having been lived in since the owners ended up filing for divorce. Their loss was definitely my gain.

A half mile off the main road, I wasn't even sure how many other people lived up on this mountain, and that suited me just fine.

"Yo, Rivera! Where are you?" Cole's loud voice rang throughout the empty house.

The echo from his words reminded me I needed to do something about furniture and everything else that went with outfitting a new home.

I'd been glad to take Cole's offer to stay with them while I finished my place, but I couldn't wait till the county signed off on the final test from my underground well, so I could get settled in by Christmas Eve. Then my buddy could spend the holidays with his family without my grumpy ass in the way.

"There you are. You took off so quick. What's lit a fire under you?" Cole asked.

I was in the mud room installing hooks plus the fittings for the washer and dryer that'd be delivered tomorrow. "What do you mean?" I didn't bother to stop, just kept working. "Two more days and I'll be out of your hair. I'm sure you can't wait so you can walk around in those boxers Scarlett likes."

I felt the whoosh of a flying object pass over my shoulder. Finished, I dropped the wrench and snagged the wadded-up painter's tape Cole had thrown and with a fake left; I pummeled him in the chest as I turned to face him.

"You tell no one, or I'll be sure to share your number with the next woman who hits on you at O'Malley's." Cole chuckled then rubbed his left thigh. He'd lost the lower half of the leg almost two years ago now after stepping an IED just days before he'd been set to come home.

There was no one I admired more than Cole. He'd been through hell, and after losing three of our unit's men that day, he'd persevered, did the hard work of recovery and then found a good woman to love right here in Pineville. He deserved every good thing that came his way and more.

But the coincidences that kept popping up around here, made me wonder if there was something about this place that connected lost souls with their better halves.

"I'm just kidding. Besides, I have a feeling you already have a woman in mind to give your number to."

"Is that right? You think you got me figured out do you?" He probably did, I thought. We'd spent plenty of time over the years talking about what we didn't want, that it made it easy for both of us to spot the things, or the person, that'd be a perfect fit in our lives.

"I do. And it begins with 'T' and ends with 'aya.' She's a really good friend of Scarlett's, and an incredible chef. But as much as I hate being that guy, if all you want from her is a quick spin around the proverbial dance floor, then I'd ask you as a friend, as a brother, to stop looking her way." Cole crossed his arms. He wore a look on his face I hadn't seen since we'd first met.

"Are you really warning me off Taya?" I decided to make him sweat a little before I reassured him. "C'mon, you're really going to deny me a chance with her. Have you seen her curves under that frumpy chef's jacket she wears?"

Cole's eyes flashed. It was the only warning I had before he took a step and poked a finger in my chest. "You play around with her, then you will have me to deal with. No one, not even you, bro, messes with Taya. She's as close to a sister as Scarlett has ever had, and I don't want to see my wife upset."

Damn. I couldn't hold it together, letting out a laugh. "Good to know since I don't plan on anything less than getting, hell begging if I have to, to get her number. There's something about Taya, something I've never felt before and I know it sounds corny, but…when I was watching her after we collided the other day, I heard this ding in my head go off. Like 'pay attention Rivera, she's yours.'"

Cole let out a bark of laughter and shook his head. "Damn. That's not corny or crazy. That's a lot like I felt when I met Scarlett. And it explains why you've been wearing a non-stop grin on your typically grumpy ass face the past few days. I should have known it was because of a woman."

"Does that mean you'll get her number from Scarlett for me?"

"I don't think that's going to be necessary. She's catering TS and Noel's party tonight. You can ask her yourself."

His words released a weight I hadn't realized I'd been carrying over when or how I'd see her again. I wasn't looking forward to attending the party tonight, mainly because I'd have to talk about myself and how TS and I were half-brothers. But knowing I'd see Taya again, well, I'd walk through a roomful of unknown threats and endure a dozen plus conversations filled with small talk and nonsense just to be close to her. If that made me a sap, then give me a nametag because Taya was going to be mine.

CHAPTER 3

TAYA

*T*hree days had passed after my unexpected introduction to Beck, and I was still thinking about him. I'm not sure I ever stopped. Not even as I made sure the girls made it to the airport, following their flight on an app then making them text me when they arrived at their grandparent's house. And definitely not now, as I diced and sliced my way through the final prep for my first event as Full Plate Catering.

Noel and TS were having a party for their close friends, family and about a dozen of the players who lived locally from TS' baseball team, the Idaho Outlaws. It was almost party time, and I was in their dream kitchen alongside the new sous chef I hired and half a dozen servers. I was putting the final touches on the hors d'oeurvres along with the mini Wagyu beef sliders I'd created for O'Malley's menu. A sense of pride filled me that so many of my friends and customers enjoyed my food and this particular dish that I did a little dance as I cleaned up.

Not all of my current mood was due to finally beginning my dream. At least half of it was because of how Beck's rock-hard chest and smoldering dark eyes had made me feel. And even though I had no reason to believe he was actually attracted to me besides my hope that he felt a similar way after our meeting, my heart raced every time a bearded, tall man entered the party. Who knew so many baseball players wore beards. My poor heart couldn't take much more.

"Taya, it smells incredible in here. And the food looks great too." TS winked at me as he walked through the arched walkway that separated the kitchen from the large dining area where several pub height tables were decked out with tea lights and sparkly pine boughs and snowy white tablecloths. Guests milled about with drinks in their hands, murmured conversation and laughter drifted into the room.

"You and Noel certainly know how to throw a party. Thank you again for choosing Full Plate to cater—"

He waved a hand, then grabbed a slider off a passing tray. "For these alone, I would hire you full time, but Noel is very protective of her kitchen. Which reminds me, I have an idea for our anniversary. It's in February, so I'm booking you now."

"Of course. Email me the details. Valentine's Day, right?" I double checked, although I was pretty sure. The story of their whirlwind romance was something I'd heard about soon after I started working at the pub. In fact, their oldest, Carson, was in Scarlett's son Matty's kindergarten class.

"Great. Now, if you'll excuse me, I need to go make sure the kids aren't stealing anymore of Holly's lemon shortbread. I hope you don't mind that we brought it in from Just Desserts? Noel's been craving it for weeks."

"Not at all. I may have already swiped a cookie myself. By the way, I'd love to see Carson. I'm sure he's changed a ton since I saw him over the summer." I finished plating the last items and handed it off to the nearest server.

"Sure. He and Matty are roaming around trying hard not to pester the players. You're going to come in and join us, right? Noel wants to show you off to our guests. Oh, and I need to introduce you to my brother, well, half-brother, but I don't think he's here yet."

Two separate thoughts collided in my brain. TS's second statement made me excited for the future customers I could meet tonight, but his comment about Matty being here had me immediately flashing to Scarlett and Cole's friend, Beck. Would he be here as well?

Unbuttoning my chef's jacket, I tossed it on the counter behind me and, with shaking hands, smoothed wrinkles from the gold silk blouse I'd worn underneath. Noel had made me promise I would join the party and mingle, so I made sure to put on a nice outfit with low-heeled pumps which were both cute and comfortable.

I'd splurged on the tea-length skirt of dark green velvet that had a layer of lycra around the waist. It was my new favorite as I had ample hips and it kept me feeling snug and supported my plus size curves. And bonus, it had pockets!

Taking a moment to calm the butterflies in my lower belly, I lowered my hands over my middle, then took a couple deep breaths until I felt confident enough to walk into the party. I couldn't remember being this worked up over the possibility of seeing a man. Not since junior high when the hormones were raging. It could be for nothing. Just because the Nolan's were here didn't mean they'd bring their houseguest.

The next thirty minutes were full of introductions, two glasses of champagne, and praise for my food. Feeling flushed and full of hope for my business, I snuck off to a corner where I noticed Matty and Carson along with a few other children beginning a game of pin the nose on Rudolph. I needed a break from the grown-ups and from craning my neck, hoping to get a look at Beck. So I offered to supervise the kiddos.

There were easily seventy people in attendance, and I felt overwhelmed by all the attention and noise. I realize how odd that sounds since I'm currently hanging out with half a dozen grade-schoolers, but their energy was different, and it reminded me of when my girls were this age at Christmastime.

Stepping out of my shoes, I wiggled my toes, then perched on the edge of a wingback chair, encouraging Maverick and Kelsey's little girl, Mari, that it was okay to put on the sleep mask we were using as a blindfold because she didn't want to mess up her hair. I told her that her curls would survive the minute or so she'd be wearing it.

"So not only are you an excellent chef, but you're a pro at kid-wrangling. What else can you do?"

The raspy drawl of the man who'd kept me from sleeping the last few nights shot straight to my spine before turning into a tingle between my thighs, then deep in my core. Oh. My. He was here. The children forgotten, our gazes locked and like in the movies, for me at least, sound dimmed, replaced by a low hum. Everyone else in the room faded as nearly all my senses were overcome by the sexy former Ranger and newly minted mountain man, if the rumors were true.

Yes, there were rumors, but all I cared about was could I break out of my typical mode of burying my true feelings when attracted to a man? And this man had taken over the number one spot of my wish list. Remembering Dylan's advice to "Go for it, Mom. He's a hottie," I decided to do just that.

"Well, my kids would say I'm a decent bowler. I have a knack for origami, but to be honest, I spend most of my time cooking. I've always loved seeing people enjoy something I've made for them." *Wow, bowling. My skills at flirting needed an upgrade.*

"And you're one of the best chefs I've had the pleasure of not only enjoying the taste of your food but wearing it as well." His teasing smile enhanced his chiseled features, while his smoldering gaze signaled a different story altogether. Could he really be feeling the same intense need that I was feeling for him?

"It looks like the reindeer games are wrapping up. I was wondering if you'd like to—"

"No, he's my uncle!" Matty's shouted words rang throughout the room.

"Nu-uh! He's mine. My daddy said so." Carson's young face was scrunched, his arms crossed, and the two friends stood toe-to-toe, neither one willing to back down. Scarlett appeared followed Noel.

"Boys, what are you doing? What happened to your promise to behave tonight?" Scarlett whispered, but her tone held the full force of the patented mom-voice given to each woman upon the birth of her first child.

"Carson says Uncle Beck is his uncle, but he's mine. I knew him first." Matty lifted his chin toward the now silent man standing next to me.

Confused, I looked away from the sweetest little boy I'd ever met, stood up and looked up into Beck's embarrassed face. He rubbed the back of his neck and seemed to be looking for an exit. I didn't blame him. This was a conversation better held in private, but Carson wasn't having it. He ran from the room screaming for his dad. Noel didn't attempt to follow, instead she came over and offered Beck a small smile.

"So how do you feel about being fought over by two six-year-olds wanting the new shiny toy all for themselves?"

Beck chuckled, then looked at me. Again, everything else faded, and I wondered for a moment what I could do to convey to him silently that I was interested in finishing our conversation later. With the looks he'd been giving me before the kids began arguing, he'd done what no guy in recent memory had been able to do: make me feel petite and pretty. And it had me wondering how'd we fit—without clothes. If I had my heels on right now, he wouldn't have to bend too far down to kiss me or maybe with the size of his biceps alone he could lift me up, then I'd wrap my legs around his waist, which would line up our fun parts…

But instead of a kiss, he leaned toward my ear and whispered. "I need you to stop and save that look for later, otherwise I'm going to kiss you in front of our very avid audience, and my sister-in-law. If you'll excuse me, I need to go talk to two best friends and explain that they both get to call me uncle." He started to move, then stopped. "Oh, and when I kiss you for the first time, it's not going to be quick, and hands will definitely be involved."

Beck's gaze and words had an immediate effect. A very frustrated one. I nodded wordlessly as he followed Scarlett, leaving me with Noel, who wore a smirk on her glowing face.

"Wow, you work fast. I had no idea you knew Beck. Although

we're still getting to know him, he's obviously won over Carson. And Matty. Don't go anywhere. I'll be back soon, and I want to hear *everything*."

Yeah, me too.

I nodded to Noel's retreating form as she waddled after Beck. Feeling a bit dazed, my fingers were still tingling from the brush of Beck's hand right before he walked away.

It appeared there was more going on here than just the crazy hot connection between Beck and I. And I couldn't blame it on the champagne or my girls' telling me to "go for it" after I spilled pasta on him two days ago.

No, this was all me and the voice that was inside my head screaming, *"He's the one!"*

Stepping back into my heels, I went in search of answers.

CHAPTER 4

BECK

$\mathcal{W}$ho knew I'd use the negotiation skills I'd honed in the Army would be put to good use over which six-year-old loved me more?

It was humbling, overwhelming and something I'd never would have guessed about me. That I would instantly become connected to two little souls, three if you counted Matty's new little sister, Olivia. Hell, there'd be a fourth one soon as well. Noel was due any day with a girl. Instant family and on top of it all was the instant connection I felt for Taya. And it was more than her looks. Her curves and the hands down best food I'd ever eaten.

It was her empathy, the way she interacted with her adult daughters, but most of all, I think it was the mutual realization I saw in her eyes. That moment of knowing. You're my other half. My reason for being and sure, the need to rip each other's clothes off.

Over the last hour I reassured Matty and Carson that I would be there for each of them and yes, I would take them up to my mountain and look for bears. That last part I promised out of earshot of both their mothers. Even though I was new to Idaho, I knew enough about hibernation to be pretty sure running into a bear was pretty low this time of year. I made a mental note to check on my ATV order. Any trekking we'd do after Christmas would be done safely strapped into the off-road vehicle with helmets for the boys.

Cole pulled me aside before he bundled up his new family. The baby had stayed behind with Scarlett's grandmother. "You coming with us or…"

I let the question hang between us. Cole may think he knew me well, but if he only knew what was really in my head, he'd be taking me to the VA for a check-up. Hell, I was half tempted to make an appointment myself. Taya had knocked me on my ass, and I hadn't even kissed her or touched her outside of almost knocking her flat. But she'd stood as tall as her five four frame could and in the middle of chaos charmed me, took responsibility for her an accident that was equally my fault. And in the middle of that pub while covered in pasta that I one day I hoped to try sitting down, I felt struck by lightning or more accurately a knowing that I'd discovered my person.

Over twenty-plus years as a soldier, eating sand, discovering the humanity among the shittiest of situations, seeing hope among the displaced, and seeing the life force leave too many brothers in a foreign land not to believe in signs. Call it fate, serendipity, or divine intervention, but I believed that life was too damn fragile and short not to ignore when the universe shouted my name.

Eighteen-year-old me would have scoffed at the woo-woo of soul mates. But I was open to finding not the perfect woman, but the perfect woman for me when I least expected it, at the right time. And Taya was that woman. I could feel it all the way to my bones.

I went looking for her as people began to leave the party and naturally found in her in the kitchen where she was quietly speaking with a server who couldn't have been older than twenty. "Anytime you need some extra cash, call me. I'll give you as many hours as you need. Don't give up on your studies. If it's what you really want, you need to go after it."

Excellent advice and I planned on using it with her.

"Hi. Hope I'm not interrupting."

Taya's eyes had gone wide, then her full lips lifted into a slow smile.

"Not at all. How are the boys?" She said goodbye to the last server before giving me her full attention.

"I think I got them to understand that I care about them equally. Plus, I bribed them with a ride on my new ATV next week up on my mountain."

"Do their moms know about that?"

"Yes. They were right there. I'll need to track down some child size helmets, and then the bear hunting can begin."

"Um, yeah, you're on your own there. You must not have any kids."

"Not that I know of." I grinned.

She paused at my statement, then laughed. "You had me going for a moment. Well, I hope you don't either. It'd be a shame not to know your own kids or grow up without a father."

"Yeah, it's tough. But I turned out all right."

"Oh, I'm sorry, I mean…dammit, I didn't know. That was insensitive of me." She was so cute when she was flustered.

"No worries. You couldn't have known. And besides, when I did find out about my father, it was too late to meet him. But at least I've got TS now. Never thought I'd want a brother, not after having spent my career in the military where I had plenty of found brothers, like Cole, but so far things have been going pretty well." But I didn't come in here to talk about myself. I wanted to get her out of this kitchen and somewhere more private where we could spend time getting to know each other.

"So, it's true. I'd heard gossip, but I try not to put much stock into things that swirl around the pub. How did you find out?"

"How about you let me buy you a drink, and I'd be happy to tell you all about it?"

She glanced around the kitchen. There were several small bags on the counter, but other than that, I couldn't see anything else she needed to attend to.

"I, ah. I need to get my things out to my SUV, then I'm good. And yes. I'd like that."

"Great. Since I'm new to the area, how about you choose where we go? It's late, but I'm sure there's something still open."

While she thought about my suggestion, I had an idea. I knew the perfect place. It was a clear if a bit cold night and what I had in mind the view would be unobstructed, and the seating intimate; we'd have the place to ourselves. On my mountain.

CHAPTER 5

TAYA

I can't believe I agreed to this. Following Beck up to Mount Sherman along a not too twisty road, with packed snow, my little SUV was handling it pretty well. But, I mean, I really didn't know Beck. Yes, I knew who he was, who his friends were, and now I knew that he was TS's half-brother. And that he was a sucker for six-year-old boys, and every woman at the party tonight had her eyes on him, even the married ones. But if he was a player, I didn't see any signs of it earlier when each time I looked around the room, his eyes were always on me.

We decided neither one of us wanted to be around other people, and this late on a Saturday night, if we went to a bar, most would be loud and full of rowdy patrons. No thank you. Forty might be the new thirty but when I was thirty, I was raising two girls on my own, flipping burgers in a food truck after last call to put as much money as I could into Dylan and Lauren's college fund. The bar scene had never appealed to me even if I wanted it to.

Beck's truck lights flashed on a wrap-around porch before he pulled under a carport. I stopped right behind him, turned off the engine, and sat staring at his tall, muscular form as he stepped down from the new Chevy pickup. I couldn't help but compare the hard metal of the truck to the hard muscled veteran. The man fit the vehicle and vice versa.

His long strides toward me had my toes curling and my palms itching to find out what the rest of him felt like. Beck opened my door and held out his hand.

"Technically, I'm not supposed to have anyone in the house till I get the final sign off on the well, but there's nothing that says we can't sit in the porch swing, have a beer and count the stars while we get to know one another."

Damn. It wasn't poetry or a fancy dinner, but the way he spoke gave me shivers and made me think this might be more than a night of fun. And by fun, I meant getting tangled up in the sheets and each other.

It's what I'd hoped all those gazes across the room we shared were leading to.

"I've got some blankets inside and some beer stashed in the snow out back by the woodpile. I'll be right back." He led me up the stairs to the porch and waited till I settled into the swing. I may have checked out his ass when he unlocked his front door and disappeared inside.

Sighing, I rubbed my arms and looked around the yard that was buried in about three feet of snow. The moon was almost full. It shone over the treetops and beyond. My gaze locked onto the inky black surface on the lake below. It was so peaceful out here.

"It's pretty great, isn't it?" Beck placed a blanket over my lap, handed me a beer, and settled in next to me. His large thigh brushed against mine, and I was instantly warm and toasty. My nipples puckered, and my breasts began to ache for his touch.

"Beck, this is all very…romantic. And I'm happy you invited me here, but I don't need this." I waved an arm around, indicating the fabulous view. "Maybe I'm wrong, but I guess I thought…well, you know that we would…." I couldn't finish. Maybe I wasn't as confident in my sexuality as I thought.

"You mean you thought once we got here, I would drag you inside, strip you and we'd have wild sex all night till we collapsed, then begin all over again in the morning? Am I close?"

Nodding, I took a long drink of a very excellent beer, opened my mouth, then closed it again.

Beck draped an arm around my shoulders, pulled me close and nuzzled my ear.

"Believe me, I'd like nothing more than to do all of that. But first, I'd like to know a bit more about you. Then we can have all the swing from the chandelier sex you want."

"Wow, that's an upgrade. Isn't chandelier sex something we'd need to work up to?"

His eyes blazed hot as he gave me a slow once over. Um, so I think that was a no. Oh, my.

"Okay, so if this is about getting to know one another, I need to be honest. And really, I don't think I've been more honest with anyone in such a short amount of time as I have been with you…" I took a deep breath, then continued. "Beck, I'm not even sure I could pull off wild sex. I have never done this. Followed a man to his home with the unspoken agreement the night would end in bed. I mean I'm forty-one, mom to two college-aged girls…women…oh, and if you were to ask me the last time, I dated…had sex…I'd have to look at my calendar from about two years ago, because it was that unforgettable. And please stop me, I can't seem to stop this word vomit and—"

Beck placed a hand on my chin, pulled me toward him. Everything seemed to happen as if in slow motion. His smoldering gaze turned me into a pool of vibrating need at a level of anticipation I almost couldn't stand, and it also brought out a blast of plus-sized insecurity. How could this gorgeous man be looking at me like he wanted to eat me up and follow through on his promises of hot wild, and or chandelier sex? What did he see in me that other men had overlooked while choosing one of my thinner friends to ask to dance or go out to the movies?

"Beck, what is this—"

He swooped in, kissing me hard and deep. His hands tunneled through my hair, then he absolutely devastated me with his full lips and oh, what a wicked tongue he had. Every swipe ignited sharp sparks of pleasure that felt like fireworks. When his lips lifted away from me I wanted to weep. Resting his forehead on mine, our heavy breathing created white puffs of air between us. The urge to crawl onto his lap became too great to resist.

Shifting, I tossed the blanket off then bent my right knee and on the upswing bumped the hand that held my beer, splattering it all over his face and chest. Stunned, I fell back into the swing, slapping my hands over my mouth. The ping of the bottle ringing out as it spun on the floor of the porch.

"Oh, my god I can't believe I did that. Again! Beck, I'm…such a klutz and so sorry." Closing my eyes, I let out a long groan. Of course, this would happen. The first time I decide to be spontaneous and naughty with a super-hot guy who was into me, if the bulge I briefly felt between his thighs was any indication, and I messed it up in style.

"Taya, it's okay. Really. Actually, it's kind of flattering that you totally forgot you were holding the beer. This thing between us is… intense. And I know it's fast, but sometimes that's how it happens." He tugged my hands down and brushed loose strands of hair from my eyes.

"Really? This happens to you a lot?" I asked, my voice coming out in a squeak.

His deep laugh filtered through me, but I wasn't sure if he was confirming or denying my accusation.

"Never. But I've heard it can and obviously that's what happening between us. And hey, since we're alone instead of at a bar or restaurant, no one has to know, okay?"

Nodding, I smiled and said, "Thank you. Truly, your kindness just makes you more attractive, and I'd really like to get to know you better."

"How come I hear a but coming?"

"Because there is one?" Scrunching my nose at the disappointment I heard in his voice; I stood and lifted my hands. "It's late. Definitely later than I usually stay out. I'm going to head home. Thank you for the beer and sharing this incredible view with me."

Beck stood but didn't make a move to stop me. Part of me wished he'd pick me up and take me inside, so we could have some of that hot chandelier sex, but this was for the best. I wasn't cut out for one-night stands.

"Don't forget about our kiss. That was more than incredible. And I understand if you want to go home, but Taya. I want to see you again. Soon. Are you free for dinner tomorrow?"

My heart started pounding double time. The fact that he wanted to go on a date with me after twice spilling food and drink on him seemed like a gift. But the timing sucked.

"I'd love to."

"I hear another but coming." Beck said.

"Yeah, well. I'm going to be honest with you some more. The party tonight was the first one for my new catering business. Dating is not something I can do right now. That's why I agreed to come with you tonight. I decided to take a chance, do something I never do and go home with a handsome man and have—"

"Wild sex." He grinned. And bonus he didn't look upset.

"Right. I just want to be up front and not lead you on." Had I ever said that phrase to a man before?

"Okay. I get that. But I'm not giving up. I'd like to see you again. Explore this attraction between us--."

"It's crazy, right? I've never been so drawn to someone before." It was my turn to interrupt him. Then a thought or a phrase came into my head and maybe we could both get what we wanted. "Okay, so what if, as you know, as mature adults we come to an understanding? Like maybe we could have a 'friends-with-benefits' situation between us?" Did I really just utter those words? By the look on his face, yes…yes, I did.

"Huh."

"Okay, hear me out. This is the perfect solution. I mean you just moved here, you're still working on your house and I'm guessing you're not interested in a long-term thing, and neither am I. I've got my new business, my kids, I'm not looking for anything either. And I don't want to pass up what I think could be some really great sex. Just being honest here." I was stone cold sober, and I couldn't believe what was coming out of my mouth, but hey no risk, no reward.

Beck stood looking at me for the longest time without any indication on his face of what he was thinking. Didn't men like salivate over this kind of thing? Sex with no strings was the perfect solution for a lot of guys. So, this is perfect, right? We could have hot wild chandelier sex without getting emotionally involved.

"*Oh-kay*. Let me walk you to your car." He grabbed my hand and led me back to my SUV.

Wow, that was not the answer I was expecting.

"Um…so is that an 'okay' okay? Or more of an 'okay, let me think about it' kind of okay?"

He opened my door, faced me, then kissed me again. This time, it began soft and searching before turning to what I could only describe as a claiming. It was different from the other kiss, equally good, great in fact, but it made my heart stutter and had me rethinking things. Maybe I should want to date him. Maybe I wanted more with him than the promised wild, hot chandelier sex?

Ending the kiss, he helped me into the driver's seat, tucked my legs under the steering wheel, and stepped back. With hands on his hips, he took a deep breath then said, "Taya, I'm more than okay with friends-with-benefits. In fact, I'd like to start tonight, but I want you to go home and think about it. Then I want you to think about me taking off your clothes and worshipping every curve and valley on your gorgeous body. How my tongue is going to taste all of you and then dip between your thighs and taste some more until you're crying out my name before I fill you with my cock, pounding into your sweet pussy as I worship you…all night long." He gently closed my door and walked back to his porch where he turned and watched me until I started the engine. With shaking hands I drove away watching him in the rear-view mirror until I could no longer see him.

Oh. My.

CHAPTER 6

BECK

What the hell had I been thinking last night? I'd woken up to morning wood that wouldn't calm the fuck down. Tossing and turning and thinking of all the ways I wanted to take Taya, make her cry out in pleasure by doing all the things I had described to her last night left me grouchy and frustrated. Why didn't I just carry her sweet ass into my cabin last night and give us both what we wanted?

Because I wanted more. She may think we would only be friends who had great sex, and it will be great, I have no doubt, but that feeling inside that she was the one for me only increased with each minute I spent with her.

After my second cup of dark roast coffee, I checked my email on my cell. The permit I'd been waiting for had come through. No more tiptoeing around Cole and Scarlett's place. I could finally live here and begin to truly make it mine. First, I needed to go pick up the essentials if I was going to bring Taya inside. I wanted her to see this place as somewhere she could see herself living. I needed a kitchen table, chairs, a couch, TV, dishes, all of it.

Making a list, I sent a text to Scarlett asking for Taya's number. I'd forgotten to get it last night. I didn't want any more time going by before I contacted her and made plans to see her tonight. I didn't want her changing her mind, and I wanted her thinking about me as much as possible until we were together again.

After my shower, I got dressed and headed out. Scarlett had come through but had also asked a lot of questions. And she also reminded me about their party tonight. Shit. There was no way I could back out of it.

Then a text from Cole showed up.

COLE: Hey man. Did you spend the night at your cabin or ???

ME: Yes. Headed your way now.

COLE: Why do you need Taya's number? Heard you guys left together last night. We thought well…you know.

ME: I'll be there soon, Mom. I'll explain then.

News travelled fast. Probably Noel saw us leave together, but how would she know that we'd gone to my place? Then it hit me. Small towns, man. Well, it really didn't matter because I wasn't going to settle for being Taya's FWB. Oh, I'd let her think that's all we could be, but I planned on convincing her differently. Just thinking about her had my heart racing and my stomach doing weird flip-flops. Was that what love felt like?

TAYA

I'd been up since sunrise. Drinking all the coffee and working on my computer and laying out the menu for my next event. I answered a text from each of my girls. I was achy, tired, and couldn't stop thinking about seeing Beck today. Tonight.

I texted Scarlett for his number after I realized neither one of us had thought to exchange them. I crossed my fingers, hoping that she'd give it to me, no questions asked.

My cell rang and Scarlett's name and smiling face appeared on my screen. "Hi there. You didn't have to call."

"Excuse me? Of course I did. You can't just text me for a guy's number, especially a guy who has been staying at our place, who didn't come home last night by the way and who I saw ogling you most of the party. What gives?"

What to tell her? I could go with the truth or convince her that it was for something simple, like he dropped a glove at the pub and I wanted to return it. But where was the new confident, honest, go-after-what-I-want me that wanted to climb Beck like a tree and swing for the proverbial chandelier? The new found sexual freedom me? Yeah, the truth was always best.

"We're going to get together tonight and we kind of forgot to exchange numbers. So, do you have it, or do you need to get it from Cole? I'll wait."

I could hear the baby coo and laugh and Scarlett let out a sigh. "I do. But I want to know what you're doing? This is so unlike you, Taya."

Hmm, until she said it out loud, I hadn't thought how my behavior would look to a friend who knew me pretty well. This forwardness toward a guy was new to me. And yet it felt—right.

"I'm done living small, Scar. My business, stepping back from living just for my girls, and pursuing a man who makes me feel alive and sexy is the new me. I'm going after what makes me happy and yeah, I know you're concerned about Beck, that we just met, etcetera, etcetera, but it feels right. And didn't you tell me that when you and Cole were first together, you had very similar thoughts and feelings?"

"I did. And I've never been happier. I want the same for you too. It's just going to take me a minute to get used to the new Taya."

I was so lucky to have a friend like Scarlett. She'd also been a single mom and worked hard to provide for herself and Matty before meeting Cole. The only difference was I didn't want to keep Beck forever. I just wanted to enjoy the off the charts physical connection until it ran its course and then what, I wasn't sure, but it would certainly be a highlight in my life. But I just needed his cell number so we could begin.

She rattled it off in between the baby's fussiness. "I'll see you tonight. I can't wait to hear everything I missed."

"Thank you, Hun," I said.

Darn it. Their housewarming party was tonight. "Um, yeah. Of course. Wouldn't miss it."

"Okay, I gotta go. Little sis is hungry. You're going to love the sweaters I picked out. I was even able to find one small enough for Olivia. Later."

Staring at the piece of paper, I smacked my forehead. I was a sucky friend. I totally forgot about her ugly sweater housewarming party. She'd purposely made it an open house since it was so close to Christmas Day. She wanted to have something fun and laid back as people flowed in and out of their new home.

The day I'd dumped pasta on Beck was the day I planned on shopping for my ugly sweater. That hadn't happened. Since that moment in O'Malley's, all my thoughts had been on him.

I needed another cup of coffee and a shower. I sent off a text to Beck about seeing him tonight at the Nolan's party. I could have called, should have called.

Maybe I wasn't so confident after all.

CHAPTER 7

TAYA

Four hours later, I had an ugly sweater and had finished the menu for the private party Maverick and Luke were hosting for their employees and family on Christmas at O'Malley's. I didn't want to think about it being the last party I'd attend let alone plan for everyone I'd worked with the last five years. They'd all become more like family than co-workers, and I'd be forever grateful to Mav and Luke for hiring me.

I was used to being knee deep in lunch orders by now. This new downtime would take some getting used to. At least until after the New Year, when Full Plate Catering would be up and running. Pacing the house, I wondered what Beck was doing. He'd responded to my text with a sad face, a wink and a "see you at the party" but nothing personal or more descriptive. No, "I can't wait to see you" or a restatement of what he'd asked me to think about last night after I got home. And yes, I thought about nothing else.

His detailed description of what he wanted to do to me, with me, had me unsettled and turned on most of the night. And now that I'd once again imagined him touching me, tasting me, my nipples tingled, my panties dampened, and I didn't want to wait any longer.

Glancing at my wall clock yet again, I made a decision. If the mountain wouldn't come to me, then I would go to the mountain. Quickly changing into my ugly sweater, I packed a small bag with my makeup and toiletries, grabbed my keys off the kitchen counter, and shrugged into my jacket.

I headed toward the door to the garage. A loud knock sounded on the front door. Who could that be? I considered ignoring it. But when another round of knocks rang out, my good manners won out. I'd make quick work of shooing away whoever it was and be on the road in no time to surprise my new friend-with-benefits.

Unlocking the door, I yanked it open.

"Hi." Beck held flowers in one hand and the ugliest Christmas sweater I'd ever seen dangling from the other one. "I finished my errands early and thought I'd swing by and see if you had any questions about the assignment I gave you last night."

"Get in here." I grabbed his heavyweight flannel shirt jacket, tugging him across the threshold. "Seems like we had the same idea. I was just headed out to your place." Shutting the door behind him, I flipped the lock, took both items from his hands and tossed them on the couch. Need hit me hard. My fingers fumbled with my zipper. Beck brushed my hands away, taking over. He tugged the zipper down, peeling the sleeves off my arms and made quick work of his jacket too, tossing both over my shoulder onto the couch behind me.

Before I could second guess myself, I jumped into his arms and wrapped my legs around his waist. He cupped my ass, kneading my flesh through my tights. Squirming to get closer to him, his touch ignited an ache deep within me. Our lips met in a frenzy as I pressed as close to him as I could, twining my arms around his neck. "Bed. Now."

Beck carried me down the hallway, following my mumbled directions as I nestled my face against his neck, inhaling his woodsy scent. Standing at the foot of my bed, he released me, and I slid down his hard body, rubbing against his hard cock, letting out a low moan.

"I'm all yours, sweetheart. Let's get you out of that horrid shirt. Arms up please."

He didn't have to ask me twice. Sliding his hands under the material, he lifted my shirt off, then made quick work of my bra.

My breasts felt heavy with need as he cupped his hands over them, flicking my nipples. His rough, warm fingers igniting a rush of warmth throughout my body, making wet with need. I wanted his mouth on me, as promised.

"I just have one question, sweetheart." He stepped back, took off his shirt, revealing his muscular frame. Greedily, I roamed my hands over his arms and chest. A rumbling under my hands made me look up at his face. His hot gaze full of desire and humor.

"I'm not laughing at you, but damn if you could see what I do. My woman hungry for me…Taya, tell me what you want. Do you want to be on top, or under me? What turns you on, baby?"

"I…I, what?" I couldn't comprehend what he was asking. Past lovers hadn't bothered finding out what I liked, simply took their pleasure, and I had to keep up. Beck was giving me a gift I had never thought to ask for.

"Have you been thinking about what I said? Where do you want me to begin? Tell me where to taste you first." Dazed, I realized we were still half-dressed. Giving me full control to choose what I wanted emboldened me, as did the need I read in his eyes.

It was all for me.

It was all I needed.

I unbuckled his belt, freed his cock, and ran my fingers along his velvety length. He was larger than any man I'd been with, and I couldn't wait to feel him inside me. "I want your mouth between my legs, on my clit. I…I haven't ever been with a guy who wanted to, let alone talked about tasting me there." Taking in a deep breath, I said, "That's what I want, please."

With my hand still wrapped around his erection, he cupped my face and kissed me so softly, emotion bubbling up within me, I held back a sob at his tenderness.

"That was their mistake. I can't stop thinking about how you'll taste on my tongue." Beck dropped small kisses on my nose, cheeks, the corners of my mouth. Slipping his fingers into the waistband of my tights, he yanked them off, along with my panties, in one motion.

He knelt and lifted each of my feet as I stepped free of the material. Naked before him, I fought the urge to cover myself.

"Damn. You are so beautiful. And all mine." He grinned then stepped out of his jeans. I watched wide-eyed as he grabbed a condom from the back pocket and tossed it up onto the bed.

"Lay back for me, baby, and spread those thighs for me. I want to see how wet you are."

Before I did as he asked, I moved toward the light switch. He blocked my path.

"Oh, no. Lights stay on. I need to see you. All of you. Every curve and valley is mine for the taking and the viewing. You don't need to be shy with me. Never with me."

Nodding, I had no words. This man was so much more than I could have ever dreamed. Another surge of empowerment filled me, and I scooted back onto my bed, my legs open to him, my gazed locked on his as he crawled over me.

He began kissing my inner thighs, then lifting me up with both hands under my bottom, he licked me in one long stroke, sucked my clit into his mouth then swirled his tongue over the sensitive nub.

I grabbed the back of his head and rode his tongue as he dived between my lower lips, feasting on me. I opened myself wider, then arched my back as the first tingle of an orgasm hit me. When he slipped a finger between my slick folds and began pumping in and out, I shouted his name from the divine friction. My orgasm hit sharp and unexpected. I didn't want this glorious feeling to end. "Beck! Yes, don't stop." My cries filled the room, and his answering moans wrapped around my heart as he continued giving me pleasure.

After a second orgasm overtook the first, I fell back onto the bed, sure I'd never experience anything as intense as that again.

Oh, how wrong I was.

"So sweet, Taya. Tell me what you want next."

"I want to be on top." Last night I'd pictured impaling myself on his cock, and now that I knew how big he was, I wanted to live it out in real life.

My limbs loose and heavy from two quick orgasms, I rolled to my side, sat up, then straddled him. He watched me intently while I drew lazy circles over his chest before taking him in hand.

"You're playing with fire, woman. But I think you like it."

"I do. So much." I lined him up to my entrance then eased down on his shaft until every inch of him was inside me. Drunk on power, I set a slow pace.

He circled my waist with his hands, and I held on tight to his forearms as I rocked myself closer to a third orgasm.

"Open your eyes, beautiful. I want you looking at me as you cum all over my cock." He slipped a hand between our bodies, rubbed my clit with his thumb, pressing down on just the perfect spot. "Oh, yes." I was getting so close again. It was unbelievable.

Beck lifted his hips, thrusting in and out, slamming against my g-spot. And with a final deep thrust, he triggered a vaginal orgasm that I'd only ever read about, never having experienced for myself. It was beyond any pleasure I'd felt, and when he kept working my clit, I broke again, screaming his name as white lights flashed behind my eyelids. My inner walls gripped him tight. He roared his release, shouting my name, as we continued rocking into each other.

The moment was forever seared into my memory.

I fell onto his chest, panting, smiling. I could feel his heart pounding beneath mine and the last thing I remembered before drifting off, were his arms wrapping tight around me, and Beck whispering he was never letting me go.

CHAPTER 8

BECK

"*W*e should probably get ready for the party." Taya rolled onto her back, her full breasts on display without a hint of shyness.

I flicked a nipple, squeezing it before leaning down and sucking it into my mouth, rolling my tongue over the turgid flesh, then treating its twin to the same until she was writhing under me. "*Beeeck*, we're never going to leave this bed if you keep doing things like that." Her words coming out in between breathy and sexy as hell gasps. She ran her fingers through my hair, holding me in place, contradicting her own words.

More time passed that we didn't have if we wanted to make an appearance at Cole and Scarlett's place. So, with a level of strength I didn't know I possessed, I pulled away from Taya when all I wanted to do was bury my cock deep inside her again, staking my claim and telling her through my actions that I wasn't ever going to let her go.

"Okay, stop tempting me. You hit the shower first but make it quick, otherwise I'll be joining you and we'll never make it." I gave her a playful swat on her plump ass, almost forgetting immediately that I was trying to be the strong one.

"Me? You need to stop touching me like that." Taya's laugh was music to my soul.

I never knew I could feel this way toward a woman. I'd been on the verge of saying things to her I'd said to no other person, ever. Like *I love you, move in with me, be mine forever*. She left the bed, and I instantly missed her. It was crazy how deeply I felt about this incredible woman.

I heard the shower turn on, then what sounded like a cat drowning filtered through the slightly opened door to the bathroom.

Grinning like a fool in love, I listened to her sing and began imagining what a life together would look like.

When I told Cole how I felt about her this morning when I got back from my place, he didn't tell me it was too fast, or I was only thinking with my dick. He got how I felt. Told me it had been the same for him with Scarlett.

Bolstered by his admission, I'd sped through my list of house stuff I wanted to get done before I brought her back to my place later tonight. I also found out for the first time how having a lot of money got things done quickly. I picked out new furniture, set up a delivery for today, and hit the grocery store.

Luck had been on my side, and I cruised through the list just in time to get back down the mountain to pick up the ugly sweater Scarlett had put on hold for me at the local mall before arriving at Taya's.

"Beck, I'm done. The shower's all yours." She peeked her head out, giving me a saucy smile.

I groaned at the sight of her all wet. "Woman, you can't stand there naked and expect me to just take a shower while you do whatever stuff women do after showering."

She let out another one of her musical and throaty laughs. "Fine. I'll get dressed and use the other bathroom to finish getting ready."

"Thanks. Give me a minute to tame this thing between my legs." It took more than a minute to get my erection under control enough that I wouldn't drag her back to bed and repeat everything that we'd spent the last three hours doing.

THE RIDE over to the party was torture. Every time Taya so much as moved or shifted in the passenger seat, she made little noises. Not sure she was even aware she was doing it, she had to be sore from our three rounds of wild, hot chandelier sex.

"I know that smile. And I can't stop thinking about it, about us either. Let's make a quick round of hellos, have one drink, and then we should be good to leave. Deal?" Wearing a naughty smile, she winked at me. If I hadn't fallen already, I would have in that moment.

Leaning over the console of my truck, I gave her a quick, hard kiss. "I think I've created a monster. Can't wait to get me alone again, can you?"

The pretty blush on her cheeks had me rethinking even going in. I wasn't ready to share her with anyone else. The need to take her up to my place and lock us away until after Christmas was strong.

"Maybe. But we can't disappoint our friends."

Getting out of the truck we walked to the front door, hand in hand. Not sure I remember holding a woman's hand, not since high school, if then. Another indication that what I was feeling for Taya went beyond just the physical.

Cole answered the door and took our jackets. It felt strange coming into their home after being a houseguest until just yesterday. Scarlett, with baby Olivia on her hip, met up with us, took one look at Taya and busted up laughing.

"Um, you may want to go into the powder room." She guided Taya back down the hallway. "We'll meet back up with you two in a minute."

Looking at Cole, I asked, "What was that all about?"

He was struggling not to laugh like his wife. "Dude, her sweater was inside out." Cole slapped me on the back. "Let me get you a beer. I'm guessing you guys won't be staying long."

Less than an hour later, I was bundling Taya back into her coat. It was a twenty-minute drive back to my place. I received a text from the delivery service confirming they'd dropped off my stuff. I'd given them the security code to my front door in order to get same day delivery. I needed to remember to change it after we got home.

Wow, I was already labeling us as a couple in my mind. I just hoped Taya would be open to it as well. After today at her place, then seeing how other men were checking her out at the party tonight, I'd made up my mind to let her know tonight how I felt about her. About us.

Turning onto my private road, I reached over and grabbed her hand. "Hey, you went quiet on me. You okay? Sorry, I didn't even ask if you'd come home with me. I just headed here. I can take you back to your place if you want?"

"No. This is great. You must have received the final go ahead to occupy the house, huh?"

"Yeah, I got the email this morning. I thought I told you. I meant to, but when you opened your door today, well, let's just say everything else just disappeared. Part of the reason I was in town today was buying a new table and couch and a few other things. I had them delivered earlier. I hope you like what I picked out."

Her gaze narrowed, but she didn't say anything. I parked the truck, and we hustled inside. The temperature had dropped to ten degrees, and I was eager to get her inside and warm her up.

"This table is really nice. Wow, that couch is huge." She ran her hand along the top of the leather couch. Shit, how could I be jealous of an inanimate object?

Shaking my head, I came up behind her, wrapping my arms around her waist. "Want to try it out?" Nibbling the spot below her ear I found earlier drove her wild, I slipped my hands under her sweater, cupping her breasts. She sucked in a breath, then pushed her sweet ass back into my erection. "I can't believe I even want to have sex again so soon. I never thought it possible, but you do something to me, Beck. You have this powerful pull. I just can't say no to you. And I don't want to. I suppose we'll burn out soon enough."

Her words threw me. She was already looking to the end of us, but I was just getting started.

"Beck, you okay?" She turned in my arms and the concern I read in her eyes slayed me.

How could she look at me like that and yet also anticipate that what was happening between us would be over one day?

Before I stripped her and bent her over the back of this couch, I needed to let her know that I didn't see us ending. That friends-with-benefits just wasn't going to be enough for me.

"Can we sit down for a minute?" Not waiting for her answer, I picked her up and carried her around the end of the couch and settled in the middle section with her cradled on my lap.

"What's going on? Don't you want…I thought we'd…darn it, Beck, don't you want me again?"

"Hell, Taya, is that what you think? No, I'm mean yes, I do. So damn much. I'm not good with words, but I need to make sure things are crystal clear between us because since I laid eyes on you, I knew you were different. That what I felt for you would take more than just a night or a month in bed loving you. That I would never satisfy this ache that's settled right here and refuses to go away." I placed her hand over my heart, covered it with mine, afraid she'd want to pull back from me.

Her eyes had widened slightly at my words, but she didn't try to argue with me that I was moving too fast.

"I realize it's been quick between us, but after twenty years in the service, I've learned a lot of things about myself, what I want. Life is so damn short, Taya. Too short to not go after something I want, or someone, is not an option for me. I agreed to your friend-with-benefits suggestion under false pretenses, and I want to fess up. Make sure there's no doubt what I want between us is so much more than just physical. Although that's a big part of my attraction to you, it's not the only thing."

She still didn't stop me, so I took another deep breath and kept going. "Hell, I'm not a Hallmark card kind of guy and today was the first time I ever bought flowers for someone. And now I get why men do it. I wanted to see you smile when I handed them to you. Weird, right?"

"No. Not at all." She whispered.

"I've been called stoic, closed off, an SOB and plenty of other names over the years and I guess I let the military, the endless fighting harden me, but as soon as I saw you, heard you laugh and smile at me I was a goner. You're perfect for me, Taya. I can't explain it any better than that other than to say I've fallen for you. Hard. And I want to spend the rest of my life loving you. I could tell by how your girls reacted that day what a great mom you are, and everyone I've talked to about you, just thinks the world of you—"

"Wait, you've talked to people. About me?" Taya scrambled off my lap and as much as I wanted to lock my arms around her, I let her go. She paced back and forth, running her hands through her hair several times before she stopped, placing her hands on her hips, a fire blazing in her eyes. I'd never seen this side of Taya, but I liked it. She was sexy as hell when she got all worked up.

"Beck, this is…just, I don't know. It's too soon."

I expected this reaction. Prepared for it. "What's too soon? How long is love supposed to take? Look at Cole and Scarlett. They fell pretty fast and now their married, gave Matty a little sister and they've never been better than together. You can't deny that. I'll be honest, I never expected to fall in love. I was pretty content with my life before you dumped two plates of pasta on me." I did my best to keep my lips from twitching, but the reminder of how she looked after we collided still made me laugh. And feel damn lucky.

She threw her hands up in the air and began pacing again. "It was one plate. We both had pasta all over us. You know how old I am, right? I'm forty-one, Beck. I'm not looking to have another baby. I also was pretty up front about not wanting a relationship."

Lord, she was beautiful when she used that stern tone, thinking it would sway me from what I was determined to have. Her. I planned on telling her that every day, but I just realized I needed a new tactic. "Whoa, okay. So, first, I think your age is definitely a positive. I'm not looking for someone who hasn't lived through a few trials and come out the other side wiser for them. And second, don't you think if I wanted kids, I would have had them by now? I grew up seeing how hard raising a kid on her own was for my mom. I just never had a desire for kids of my own. I like them. They're great for other people. But since you have the girls, I do think I'll be an awesome grandpa, though. It's you, Taya. All I want is you, not what you can give me. Well, except for your love. And maybe a lifetime of wild, hot chandelier sex."

I hadn't realized until I finished my speech that her eyes were all shiny. "Aw, baby. Don't cry. Come back here." I held out my hand and waited for her. I'd wait for her as long as it took.

Luckily, she didn't make me wait.

Crawling back onto my lap, she cradled my face in her hands. A single tear fell, but she shook off my attempt to wipe it away. "What did I ever do to deserve you?"

"I've been wondering the same. How did I ever get so lucky to find you? I love you, Taya." I didn't need her to say it back to me. Not yet at least. I kissed her till my lungs screamed for air, and then kept kissing her until she broke our kiss, leaned back, and gave me the best early

Christmas gift, ever.

"As crazy fast as this is, I agree with you. Life is too short not to live life to its fullest. And we deserve each other. I love you."

EPILOGUE

SIX MONTHS LATER

TAYA

*B*eck lifted my veil and instantly I was transported to that moment six months ago when I recognized my future standing before me, pasta dripping from him. The preacher's words faded and all I could focus on was the loving gaze of my soon-to-be husband.

We were standing outside under an arch of pink and white peonies and calla lilies on a stage near the water's edge of TS and Noel's property. Cole and TS were standing behind Beck, my daughters behind me.

"Mom. Breathe," Dylan said. She was standing directly behind me. She'd been born first by three and a half minutes and therefore had won the good-natured argument with her sister about who would be my maid of honor. Although I knew Lauren was used to losing out to her "older" sister, I made sure she knew I considered them both my Maids of Honor.

Taking in a deep breath, then slowly releasing it, I heard several of our friends and family members chuckle at Dylan's instruction. Beck had finished arranging the veil, then leaned down to kiss me.

The preacher cleared this throat, and said, "It's a brief ceremony, Beck. You'll have all the time you want to kiss Taya—after your vows."

Another round of laughter rang out, and the preacher was right. It went by quick, almost too quick. But I suppose that's been the theme of our relationship. And really, it suited us fine. We'd wanted to elope, but Dylan, Lauren and Scarlett talked us into a small wedding and reception.

I think everyone just wanted free Wagyu sliders and the pistachio buttercream filling we chose for our wedding cake. It was divine. The four-tier white sponge cake iced in ivory and laced with edible flowers, and it was almost too pretty to eat. Holly at Just Desserts pastry shop had outdone herself. There had been a moment when I thought I'd be wearing some of it when we did the cake cutting ceremony, but Beck pulled back at the last minute and instead of smashing a piece in my face, kissed me again.

I loved how he loved me.

Now, sitting next to him at our table as the reception wound down, the sting of tears took me by surprise. Sure, the entire day had been emotional, beginning with the girls telling me how happy they were that Beck and I were getting married and how much they'd come to love and respect him.

Beck brushed away the lone tear that escaped. "Didn't you know, only happy tears are allowed on your wedding day?"

"They're happy tears, mostly. I was just thinking of all that's happened since we met and how I wish your mom could be here." He looked over to where my parents were dancing next to Dylan and Lauren. "Me too. But your mom has done a great job making me feel part of the family. Your dad too, but I think he's still a bit put out that we didn't date longer before you sold your house and moved into the cabin."

"Yeah, but that's the generation our parents are from. Everything had to be done in a certain order. Anyway, it really no longer matters. He likes you. If he didn't, he wouldn't be swapping Army stories with you at every opportunity about his glory days." I kissed him, and for a few minutes it felt as if we were the only two people here.

"Okay, you two, the honeymoon doesn't officially begin until you check in to the hotel." Breaking apart at Noel's words, we both grinned at her.

She stood smirking at us, baby Celia on her hip. Beck had fast become the baby's favorite uncle, even with Noel's two brothers Zane and Hayden vying for the position now that they'd both moved back to Pineville.

Beck stood, holding out his hands to Noel, he took Celia into his arms. "Have my seat. I've got one more dance left in me before Taya, and I leave for the hotel." He held up one of the baby's arms to help her wave at us before he joined TS and Carson, who were having some kind of dance off.

Noel sighed, sitting down. "He's so sweet with her. I'm so happy he's going to get to see Carson and Celia grow up. And I know TS is excited to have Beck in his life. I can't imagine growing up without knowing my brothers existed. Although there were a couple years when they were in high school I could have lived without."

Nodding at her statement, I chuckled. "I hear that. It hasn't been that long ago since my girls were in high school and I remember well all those hormones. Sophomore year was the worst of it when they liked the same boy."

"Ooh, that reminds me. Speaking of high school, did I tell you Zane and Hayden just had their twentieth reunion last weekend? And somebody here may or may not be treating one of my brothers as if he doesn't exist."

"Really? Well, since Zane's engaged to Holly, it must be Hayden getting the cold shoulder. So, who'd he rub the wrong way? I mean, who wouldn't want to date one of TV's most eligible bachelors?" I asked, tongue in cheek. Hayden was a great guy, and I enjoyed watching his show, but according to Noel, he had women throwing themselves at him everywhere he went.

Noel let out a snort. "Yeah, well, his ego has pretty much doubled since that list came out. Believe me, I've been doing my best to remind him that not everyone watches his show and is impressed by his globe-trotting adventures. Actually, I'm kind of glad a woman he's interested in isn't fawning all over him."

As Noel spoke, I'd been dividing my attention between her and staring at my husband still on the dance floor. But this gossip was too good not to find out more, so I tore my gaze away from Beck even though he looked so hot in his black vest and white dress shirt with the sleeves rolled up.

"Okay, now you have to spill. Who's shooting the sexy silver fox down?" I asked.

"First, *eww*! I refuse to think of one of my brothers as a 'sexy' anything and two, you know her as the lovely owner of All in Bloom who designed your gorgeous bouquet and centerpieces. Did you know she's also connected to the Outlaw's through her sister, Thea, who just married Brock Cameron? You know the pitcher who just retired. Anyway, to add yet another connection in this game of *Six Degrees of Separation*, Brock's sister is—"

I held up my hand. "I know, I know. Holly Cameron of Just Desserts, who's engaged to Zane, Hayden's fraternal twin! You know, Noel, this town is turning into a soap opera. Wait, maybe we should pitch a reality show? You know something like, 'Love in the Outfield', or maybe, 'Outlaws in Love?'" We started giggling until tears streamed down our faces.

Beck and TS walked over to the table and stood staring at us; baby Celia now asleep on her daddy's shoulder with Carson standing next to him yawning. "What have you two been drinking? And where can I get some?" TS held out his hand to Noel, and after she grasped it in hers, he said, "As great a time as we've had, it's time I took my wife and kids home, bro. You want me to tell the DJ to announce you two are taking off?"

Beck came around the other end of the table, took both my hands, and pulled me up into his body. Without looking at TS, he said, "Already did. The limo's waiting, sweetheart. You ready to leave?"

My heart began pounding at the look in my husband's eyes. It took little for my body to respond to his and my body had been missing his since yesterday.

I'd stayed at my parents' house last night at the request of my mother. But as nice as it was spending the night with her and my girls, I was more than ready to be back where I belonged, in Beck's arms.

We made a quick round of goodbyes and, to the delight of everyone in attendance, before getting into the limo, Beck bent me backward over his arm and kissed me. It wasn't a quick kiss.

Cradling the back of my head, he deepened the kiss. Taking his time, his lips moved slowly over mine, then with a grin he dropped little kisses over the corners of my mouth, my nose earning us both applause and catcalls that reminded me of the one thing I forgot to ask him after he booked the room at the lake resort. "Did you ask them if the honeymoon suite has a chandelier?"

He threw his head back, laughing, while he pulled me up and hugged me close. Whispering in my ear, he said, "There's one over the jacuzzi tub if you can believe it."

"What?! I was kidding. I can't believe you asked." After we got settled in the limo, I said, "Anyway, we don't need a chandelier. We've been doing pretty well without one."

Beck looked around the interior of the limousine, a sexy smile on his face. "We have, but you know what they say?"

Covering his lips with my forefinger, I said, "Life is too short. Find the button to the privacy divider, Mr. Rivera. We need to cross off an item on my bucket list."

I hope you enjoyed Taya and Beck's story and will consider leaving a review.

What's coming to Pineville in 2025?

Beck's brothers from his Ranger unit are up next in
MOUNTAIN MEN OF PINEVILLE
Series Description:
They're grumpy, possessive and hard living, but these former Army Rangers also have big hearts and an even bigger purpose. In the mountains above Pineville, they offer their fellow veterans and former first responders what they've finally found: a place to rest, reclaim, and reinvent themselves. But what these alpha heroes never counted on finding were women strong enough to match in them in wit, determination and *passion*.
Welcome to Pineville, Idaho, where love always finds a way.

Book One coming April 9th
Pre-order MOUNTAIN MAN SAVIOR now: https://geni.us/
MountainManSavior

Check out the entire Tangling Series
Click here: https://geni.us/TanglingSeries

Want to read Cole and Scarlett's story? Check out WORTH THE WAIT.

** Debra's Newsletter **
Join today and receive a free short story from Debra:
https://bit.ly/DebraEliseNewsletter

RESCUED BY AN OUTLAW

A PINEVILLE WORLD CHRISTMAS NOVELLA (TANGLING SERIES)

ABOUT

NORI

My job has kept me from seeing family during the holidays—but not this Christmas. The wanderlust that's served me well as a photojournalist covering wars and natural disasters has settled and I'm ready to deliver their gifts in person, if I can make it in time.

The need to see my family has me trying to beat a storm by driving through a mountain pass and snowflakes the size of my fist. Out of nowhere, a handsome, if slightly grumpy good Samaritan rescues me from spending a night freezing my patootie off in my rental car.

DEAN

This year I'm looking forward to spending Christmas with my son. I've had it with the media speculating on my dating life. I just want to decompress and work on some long overdue projects at my cabin.

But the peace and quiet I sought is quickly interrupted by thunder snow, and a journalist with an attitude twice her size and a pair of the cutest…dimples.

After years of keeping my emotions in check and guarding my heart, my handsome rescuer shows me the best gift of all may just come in a man-sized package.

CHAPTER 1

NORI

*T*his may not have been my best idea. That thought kept rolling through my head in sync with the falling snowflakes as they grew in size and speed. Driving over a mountain pass in a rental that may or may not have all weather tires had been an impulse decision. I've been making split-second decisions for most of my thirty-eight years, and I've never second guessed myself. Until tonight.

My parents had moved to northern Idaho the year my younger brother had been drafted into the United States Baseball League and I'd yet to visit them. Bad sister. Bad daughter. Now five years into his career, Tyler's star was rising, and I'd stayed away long enough.

Plus, my mother had been on my case and worried that I hadn't settled down. There had been something in her voice during our last phone call that hit me differently than before. I'd accomplished so much in my career the last decade and her concern, along with an itch I couldn't name, had me seriously considering slowing down and to stop running so hard toward that next big story.

An eighteen-wheeler roared past my small SUV, splashing slush and ice onto the windshield. I let out a small scream, then a stream of curse words. Gripping the wheel, I remembered the advice the rental clerk gave me as he handed over the keys. "Whatever happens, don't slam your brakes if you're on ice. Pump them and if you slide, turn into it."

Not sure if the guy was psychic, but it turned out to be the best piece of advice I'd ever received. The glow of taillights faded, but I knew the jerk would have to slow down again soon because there was another incline up ahead. My heartbeat thundered in my ears as I attempted to get my breathing under control. Glancing at the clock, I groaned. I was over an hour behind where I'd thought I'd be.

The gas level indicator lit up on the dashboard. What? The tank had been full when I left Missoula three hours ago. There's no way I was out of gas. Dammit. "Siri, find the nearest gas station." Siri didn't respond, and I didn't dare take my eyes off the road. Cell service was either down or inconsistent this high up. *Okay, Nori. You got this. You've been in worse situations. Just breathe.* For the last twelve years I'd travelled the world interviewing world leaders, insurrectionists, and newsmakers under less-than-ideal conditions. I could handle one little snowstorm.

Flashing lights appeared on the horizon. At least what looked like the horizon. A police officer decked out in thermal gear waved me over to the side of the road. Tiny hairs stood at attention on my neck and along my arms. Same feeling that came over me whenever I was on the edge of a war zone.

"Sorry, ma'am. You'll have to turn around. The pass is closed." He leaned down and peered at me through my open window and rubbed his leather gloved hands. "How much gas do you have?"

Whoa, "ma'am?" My mother is a ma'am. I easily and often passed for someone in their late twenties. And gas? Yeah, I was hoping to fuel up at the next exit, on the other side of the flashing lights and barricades.

"Officer, I have about an eighth of a tank, enough to get me to the next gas station. Couldn't you let me through? I promise I'll come right back and head for that hotel I saw about ten miles back.

The officer stared at me like I had two heads. "There's no gas station up ahead, ma'am. At least not for thirty miles. Besides, the roads are iced up and under at least a foot of snow."

Dang it. "Okay, but I'm not a ma'am. If anything, I'm a Ms. And second, I need to get to Pineville. Tonight." Looking in my rearview mirror, hoping for what I wasn't sure. Backup maybe. Other tired travelers to join the cause and talk the officer into letting us drive on. But all I could see were snowflakes and inky blackness. I waited for headlights to appear behind me. But nothing or no one appeared. *What had happened to all the other cars?*

"Sorry, Ma—"

Holding up a hand, I released a loud sigh. "Please. Please, don't call me ma'am again." All hope of making it to my parent's place faded along with my desire to break the barricade and take my chances on the snow-covered freeway.

"Alright, *Ms*. I'm not sure where you started your journey from, but this storm has been expected for hours and most everyone heeded the warnings on the emergency radio channel. Your best bet is to go back to Exit 14. Woody Forest has a six-room motel attached to the gas station and mini-mart. I'm sure he'd be happy to rent you a room for the night. The plows will be out at dawn."

He had to be kidding. *Woody Forest?* Had to be a made-up name. And there was no way I was going to admit I'd been listening to podcasts instead of checking the weather reports. Usually, I was hyper aware of my surroundings after years on the road and in often unfriendly countries. But the excitement of finally be home with family over Christmas had been hard to tamp down. I couldn't remember the last time I'd spent the holidays with nothing to worry about expect how much snow I could stuff down my brother's ski jacket or how many cookies I could eat without my mom finding out.

The officer touched the brim of his hat and nodded. He waved me toward the emergency road connecting the four-lane highway. It looked to have been recently shoveled as I inched my way over and onto the eastbound lanes of I-90. And just like that I was headed away from a warm bed and my mom's legendary leftovers, back into the fury of relentless snow toward a roadside motel I wasn't sure I had enough gas to reach.

I'd bribed and flirted my way past tougher looking men than him, but this wasn't some third world country, and I knew better than to put myself in harm's way during a storm on its way to a blizzard with rapidly falling temps. In fact, I was pretty much over that period of my life, and I wanted to make sure I stayed healthy and safe for what came next. Even if I hadn't quite figured out what that was.

Twenty minutes later, a road sign appeared showing Exit 14 was less than half a mile up ahead. Scanning the dashboard, I tapped the button on the steering wheel that brought up the digital menu and flipped through till I found the gas level reading. Estimated miles left were three. Well, at least someone was looking out for me.

Slowing to take the sharp right turn from the exit into the parking lot of the only building for miles, my heartbeat stuttered at the neon sign in the motel's office window. No Vacancy.

So much for my guardian angel.

CHAPTER 2

DEAN

"Hey, Dad. Where you at? You get lost in the mountains? I think I have that photographer's number. I bet he could find you." Laughter followed my son's smartass remarks. The voicemail crackled and Heath's next words were garbled, followed by silence. Service in the mountains was sporadic at best, but with the impending storm, it had finally been cut off.

At nineteen, my son's sense of humor definitely didn't jibe with mine. He'd milked my recent spot in the unwelcome limelight every chance he could. A sleeveless workout photo of me at a local gym had gone viral a couple months ago, and it had fed the headlines, becoming clickbait for weeks regarding my private life. My co-workers had had a field day with it even though we were now in the off season.

And by co-workers I meant alpha pumped up athletes who, during time between innings, warming up in the bullpen or strapped into an airplane seat with nowhere to go, loved nothing more than yanking my chain. I was in my fifth year as the head pitching coach for the Idaho Outlaw's United States baseball team.

Divorced for over ten years, there had been constant speculation about the women I dated or why I was still single. It was the unfortunate part of being in the public eye. But at forty-three, I felt I was just hitting my stride in my career, and I had no intention of marrying again. It had become tiresome dealing with all the speculation, and I'd been hiding out at my cabin every chance I could.

I'd thought it had finally died down, but then I'd taken part in a recent charity bachelor auction and the media had stirred it up again. The poor woman who'd won a date with me had taken all the attention in stride. Okay, well, she'd been hoping for a night in my bed, but she was old enough to be my mom and yeah, the night hadn't ended well. But at least she didn't post about it on social media.

I talked Heath into coming up to the cabin for a few days during Christmas. The 1940s structure had turned into a month's long project, and I'd made a run out to it today to make sure the generator and water were working. The previous owners hadn't converted it to full electric, preferring to keep it off the grid, but I enjoyed technology too much to go full nature lover. I'd ended up paying through the nose for the hookup to the local power company, but it was worth the peace and quiet the area offered.

I meant to leave earlier in the day, but the generator had suddenly stopped working after I filled the tank. Two hours later, it was fixed, I think. Checking the weather report, it may be close, but I thought I could make it over the pass before the brunt of the storm would hit.

Grabbing my snow hat, I headed out to my heavy-duty pickup and drove down the winding road toward the highway. I sent Heath a text that I might be a bit late getting home tonight, holding out hope we'd be able to return tomorrow for the holiday.

On his winter break, Heath wanted to hang out with his buddies instead of with me in the mountains with spotty internet. I'd agreed he could spend the first few days at our home in Pineville, but we'd had so little time together between the baseball season with him attending his first year of college in Denver. I wanted one-on-one time so we could catch up—no distractions.

I turned into the parking lot of the gas station-mini-mart and the attached Forest Motel to fill up my tank and grab a couple snack for the road however, the full parking lot of out-of-state vehicles didn't bode well.

"Hey, Woody. Looks like business is good." Nodding at the eccentric owner of the connected three businesses.

"Motel's full up. The pass is closed. You might want to buy more than those mini donuts." The short, wiry man pointed to a row of dried goods.

Before his words registered, the double glass doors blew open, revealing a petite form wrapped up in a knitted scarf. A pair of dark eyes framed by the longest, snow encrusted lashes I'd ever seen frantically scanned the room.

Tugging down the material, the woman revealed a cute, pert nose, high cheekbones, and smudged lipstick. Rubbing her hands together, she blew on her fingers. No gloves and no boots. Well, snow boots. She was wearing a pair of hikers that had seen better days. No local would be caught in December around here without gloves, lined snow boots and a warm winter jacket. She had a jacket on, but it was too thin for north Idaho.

"A sign on the motel's office door said to come in here. Please tell me you have a room left?" Irritation laced her plea.

Woody and I shared a look. Mine was probably more interested in the woman than I had a right to be, considering the circumstances and the touch of desperation I picked up in her tone. I found my gaze locking on her delicate features, taking in her wide eyes and full lips, with the smudged lipstick only added to her appeal, and an unexpected desire to find out how they tasted had me shifting where I stood.

"Sorry, Miss. No room. But if you head back to Missoula, I'm sure you'll find something. Lots of motels there."

The woman's jaw dropped, then quickly slammed shut, her once full lips now spread thin. She looked at me, then at Woody, then back at me as if I could change her fate. In less than the time it took to take my next breath, she squinted her dark brown eyes at me, tilted her head in what felt like a move of recognition, but before I could say anything, she whipped her head back to Woody. "Missoula, *riiight*. Well, thanks." The drawn-out word rang with sarcasm. She let out a long sigh, wrapped her scarf around her neck and lower face and left in a swirl of snow through the double glass doors she'd just entered.

Frozen from the incredible connection with the woman, I stood staring at the spot she'd just been standing. The look she gave me felt as if she found me lacking in some way while also maybe recognizing me. But that sounded a tad egotistical, even for me. Not everyone knew who I was, let alone a woman who was just passing through.

Woody's cackle tugged me out of my stupor. "Spitfire, that's what that one was. Too bad I didn't have a room. Wouldn't mind seeing more of her, no siree." The shorter man peered outside into the night.

Not sure what he was looking at since the snow was now blowing sideways, not even the *spitfire's* taillights were detectable. Realizing no one should be driving tonight in that mess, not even me and especially not the winter clothing deprived woman who'd rendered me speechless, I dropped my armful of food onto the check-out counter and ran after her.

Bracing against the icy wind, I raised a hand to shield my eyes and scanned the lot for a running car. I found the spot she'd been parked in, but no car. Dammit. My chest tightened in worry for her, a perfect stranger that in less than five minutes had rendered me tongue tied and turned on.

The storm followed me back into the quickie mart. I might as well stock up as best I can since it looked like I'm headed back to my cabin with the questionable generator.

"A woman like that'll be fine, Dean. I could tell from the looks of her she's been through worse situations. Don't you worry. She'll be fine. Now, pick up what you need for a few days. I'm shutting down. No one else with any sense is going to show up tonight and you need to get back up that mountain before you're stuck sleeping in that fancy truck of yours."

CHAPTER 3

NORI

𝓜y heart wouldn't stop pounding. My palms were sweating even though it was twenty-five degrees, and my brain was replaying the events inside the gas station/food/roadside motel with whom I assumed was owned by the aforementioned Woody Forest. Counting backwards from twenty, I did my best not to get too freaked out over being up close and personal with my brother's boss.

A man who had no idea who I was and never would have had I not grabbed a flight at the last minute. I'd been under fire, threatened with imprisonment by a third world dictator and delivered a baby in the back of a bus in central America. But none of those events had left me shaking, my heart beating wildly out of control like Dean Jefferson had just done, and he hadn't uttered a word.

Talking myself through the breathing exercise I learned from a monk a few years back when I was covering a story in Tibet, I suddenly realized two very important facts. The first was I'd turned left from the parking lot instead of right, which would have taken me back to the freeway. And two, I was on a two lane, if that, mountain road that was quickly filling up with snow. Snow that would soon be high enough that even this late model SUV wouldn't be able to traverse for much longer.

Unaccustomed to this type of terrain, I did the absolute worst thing. I panicked. Yanking the steering wheel and braking at the same time when I felt the tires slip on the ice, I thought I could execute a U-turn. To my horror, the move sent the car that I thought had been a great choice to handle the mountain pass careening sideways.

At the last minute, I remembered what the rental agent had said if I run into slick driving conditions: "If in doubt, foot off the gas and the brake—don't fight the wheel, turn into the slide until you can regain traction." Yeah, that was brilliant advice unless there also happened to be a fast-approaching tree in the direction of your out-of-control car.

Squeezing my eyes shut, I sent out a quick prayer to the Universe and slammed on the brakes. My head bounce-checked off the steering wheel at the same time the right corner of the car clipped the tree before it rocked back and settled.

With my white-knuckled hands gripping the wheel, I watched snow fly out outward from the car just before an enormous pile of it dropped onto the top and the hood. Huh, it was true about moments of terror happening in slow motion.

Slowly, I turned my head to see how far from the road I ended up and was greeted with the same sight that had been plaguing me the last hour, sideways snow against an inky black night sky. No lights, no movement and as I hit the button to restart the car, no power to get myself back to the gas station.

Shit. Pounding the wheel, I continued spewing every curse word I could think of in multiple languages. Worn out, I tipped my head back, resting it on the back of the seat. Feeling somewhat back in control, I went over my options. Try my cell to see if I had a signal. If that didn't work, hike back to the gas station and beg the owner to let me sleep on the floor of the motel office. *See, Nori. You got this. Every problem has a solution.* I just needed to take things one step at a time. And don't worry about freezing my ass off. I hadn't driven too far away from —

"*Ahhh!*" A sharp knock on my window made me jump, but the

seatbelt yanked me back. The door swung open, and Dean Jefferson leaned in. Sexy Dean Jefferson. My brother's pitching coach. The handsome, leanly muscled coach who I may have spent more than one lonely night waiting for a glimpse of in the dugout as I watched an Outlaw game on my laptop from whatever overseas location I found myself.

Um, lord, he smelled good. A mixed scent of sandalwood, man and maybe a hint of pine, tickled my nose as I took in another deep breath.

Swiping hair out of my eyes, my fingers ran across my forehead. "Ow!" There was a lump square in the middle.

"Hold on there, easy. There's no rush to move." His calm voice was deeper than I expected. Goosebumps broke out on the back of neck and upper arms from his touch as he unbuckled my seatbelt. Kneeling on the floorboard, he cradled my face in his large, warm hands and gazed into my eyes. Holding back a moan at the feel of his rough skin against mine for a moment, I wondered if maybe I'd died and this was heaven?

"Your pupils aren't dilated, but that doesn't mean there's no concussion. How's your vision? Blurry?"

Snow piled up inside the car and the wind cut through my nylon jacket, but the concern in his eyes left me wishing this moment would last forever. Silly, I know. In a blink, my whole body was tuned into him. Not even my last boyfriend had ignited a reaction like Dean did.

And it wasn't as if I hadn't had men in my life since then, but it'd been a while since I went looking for bed partner, otherwise I counted on my vibrator. Wait, why was I thinking about all of this now?

"Let's get you out of here. The temp is going down quick." He helped me out of the SUV, grabbed my bag in the back seat, locked it, and stuffed the keys into my backpack.

"I have a cabin a couple miles up the road. My name's Dean, by the way. Woody, back at the gas station, can vouch for me. Anyway, you're welcome to stay until this blows over."

Still not sure if any of this was real, I smiled and held out my hand. "Nori. And thank you. I appreciate the rescue."

Watching him from the corner of my eye, he helped me into the passenger side and buckled me in, then tossed my things in the back.

He disappeared for a moment and my heart stuttered at the thought that he fell and knocked himself unconscious and I'd have to help him into the truck, then I'd have to drive a stick shift and I've never driven anything except an automatic.

A moment later, he pulled himself up into the cab, put the truck in gear, and started off up the mountain.

Jeez, maybe I'd hit my head harder than I thought. My mind wouldn't stop rushing through different scenarios of how being alone with Dean in a snowbound cabin would play out. And in each one, they ended the same. With Dean and me on the rug. In front of a roaring fire. Making out.

"We're here." He put the truck in gear, pushed open his door, then stepped into snow up to his calves. He kicked a path from the truck to the porch steps before heading back to open my door.

The gesture touched me. Something so simple yet practical. It had my heart fluttering as if he'd handed me a bouquet of roses. Shivers ran up my spine that had nothing to do with the cold and everything to do with the man who had no clue how he affected me.

"Thank you, Dean. I didn't realize how suddenly the weather can change. Although it is magical out here, I'll be forever grateful you stopped for me."

Holding out a hand, his gaze landed on mine, then he smiled. I wasn't prepared for the flurry of butterflies let loose in my abdomen at the simple brush of our hands. Wondering if I was the only one feeling this instant connection, I followed him up the steps.

"Give me a sec. I locked the door when I left."

My gaze fell onto his very firm backside, then traveled up and over his broad shoulders encased in a thermal pullover.

Maybe being stranded with the handsome coach wouldn't be so bad after all.

CHAPTER 4

DEAN

I stepped into the cabin with Nori on my heels. The day hadn't gone as planned, but as I've learned from letting go of old wounds, the unexpected often proved to be the most rewarding. I wouldn't say I believed in fate, but her smile and touch of something indefinable yet familiar settled in me and I found it uncharacteristically comforting.

Along with the over-the-top physical attraction, maybe being stranded with an attractive woman wouldn't be so bad.

Crack!

Boom!

Nori crashed into my back and let loose a scream. "What was that?"

"Thunder snow," I said. Her nails were digging into my waist, but I enjoyed having her close, so if I had to subject myself to possible blood loss, I was good with that.

"Thunder. Snow. You're kidding me right now. It sounded more like a canon going off." She must have realized her hands were still on me and snatching them back before wrapping her arms around her waist and rolling her eyes.

"I never kid about thunder snow." Facing her, the difference in our height became clear and yet I knew if I gathered her in my arms right now, we'd be a perfect fit. Clearing my throat, I rubbed the back of my neck, then took a step back, ensuring I didn't follow through on my thoughts. I was pretty sure she didn't want to be hit on minutes after walking into my cabin.

"There's, uh…moisture out there and pockets of warmer temps, same as when you get thunder and lightning during a rainstorm, so if the conditions are right, you get thunder snow."

She kept looking at me as if I'd grown a second head. "Thanks for the lesson, Al Roker." A smile appeared on her face and any attempt at a quick comeback froze in my throat.

I thought she was pretty after first seeing her at the gas station. But the smile took her beauty to another level, and I thought I heard someone say "wow." Before I could figure out if I'd said the exclamation out loud, another boom rocked the windows.

Nori jumped, and I swore. Not the best sign when the hope was for the storm to blow itself out soon.

"Okay, I believe you now. Thunder snow is real." She walked over to one of the two windows in the front room while I checked the front door, making sure I securely locked it. Walking over to the kitchen, I waved her toward the oversized couch in front of the fireplace. "I'll get the generator going. Why don't you make yourself comfortable until I get the heat turned back on? There're a couple of blankets inside the chest behind it. Need you to rest until I'm sure you don't have a concussion." I'd bought the oversized piece mainly because it converted to a bed so Heath could use it when he visited. Which, if this storm kept up, was looking less likely.

She let out a nervous laugh then sunk down into the dark brown microfiber covered couch, covering herself in a large, knitted blanket. I wondered what she would do if I offered to warm her up. My body heat and hers, together. Naked

Trudging through the snow that had accumulated in less than an hour since I left, I flipped the switch again as I briefly closed my eyes and sent out a prayer it would start to whomever was listening.

The damn thing started, sputtered, then died. I tried again and this time there was barely a whir from the engine, followed by a loud click. *Dammit.* I should have never taken the prior owner's word that the generator had been properly maintained.

Resisting the urge to kick the damn thing, I went to the woodpile and grabbed as much as I could hold. Snow stuck to my eyelashes, but I was able to get back inside before I was fully covered in snow.

Kicking the door shut behind me, I delivered the bad news. "Generator's dead. But there's plenty of wood. I'll have the fireplace going in no time. You doing okay?"

I waited for her to nod, but all she did was stare at me with her mouth open. It was the oddest reaction I may have ever received from a woman. There was a twinkle in her eyes as she quickly closed her mouth, covered it with a hand, then finally nodded. "Um, yes. Peachy." I heard a snicker escape her pretty lips. Okay, now I was thoroughly confused.

"Sorry, it's just that your hair is completely covered with a layer of snow, and it's stuck to your eyelashes and your beard and...well..." Releasing a long sigh, she fidgeted, twisting her hands together. "You look like a *se...x..*, er, I mean you look like Jack Frost. I'm sorry, I laughed. It must be the storm, ending up here, just days before Christmas...and I didn't tell anyone I was coming. And now you have to spend time away from your family with a stranger. I guess it's just made me a bit off."

Sadness shadowed her beautiful features, mixed with a sweet blush of embarrassment along her cheeks.

Wow. I wasn't expecting her to admit an attraction toward me and I couldn't let her think she was a nuisance or an unwanted guest. Not when my body was telling me, for the first time in a while, it wanted a woman. This woman. "You have nothing to feel bad about. My son can fend for himself. He's nineteen and in a house with a well-stocked pantry. I'll try reaching him after I get this fire going. And thanks for the compliment. I'm not sure I've ever been compared to a...well, Jack

Frost, but I'll take it. So, get warm and I'll be back in no time with more wood. Then I'll get the stove and the fireplace blazing and we'll figure out dinner, okay?"

Her lips upturned in a grin. I watched as she spun around and cuddled back up on the couch under the blanket. Struck by how comfortable I felt with her, I went back outside and quickly filled my arms again with the remaining split wood.

There was just something familiar about Nori I couldn't put my finger on. I knew we'd never met, and it made little sense, but it was like I'd met her once but couldn't remember where.

It had to be the circumstances of being stranded together by the storm, but it didn't matter since I was feeling like Jack Frost the longer I was outside. Getting back inside to the woman fate had placed in my path quickly became a priority.

CHAPTER 5

NORI

*D*ean finished stoking the fire and once it was roaring and filling the small area with warmth, he stood and walked into the kitchen and began pulling items from the grocery sacks he'd brought in earlier, along with my two bags. My gaze greedily ate up his every move.

"I picked up the basics at Woody's after he told me about the road closure, so we've got bread, cheese, soup and eggs, plus a few other things. Nothing fancy. But I grabbed a six-pack of Hart's Pass finest."

"Hart's Pass?" I asked.

"It's not an actual mountain pass, but Luke Hart, the football player who grew up near here in Cedar Ridge, opened a small batch brewery and pub a couple of years ago. He finally found a distributor, so now we can enjoy his signature brew at home." Dean pulled out two bottles and handed me one. "They're still cold."

Eyeing the offering, I debated accepting. I wasn't a huge fan of beer but when in Rome, plus after the day I'd had, enjoying a drink even if it was beer along with the literal man of my dreams was an offer I couldn't refuse.

Nodding, I reached for the bottle. Our fingers brushed during the exchange and a rush of warmth surged through me. Another jolt of electricity hit me, like what I felt earlier. I hadn't had a sip yet of the beer, but I was already feeling flushed. Dean Jefferson was potent with merely a touch. What would happen if we kissed?

Turning away from his questioning gaze, I took a deep, cleansing breath, twisted off the cap, and took a long sip to settle my nerves. I couldn't remember, if ever, a man making me feel this way. Even as a teenager when the hormones were raging, I couldn't recall being this turned on by my high school boyfriend and at the time I thought he was the hottest boy in our class.

Wandering the small space between the living area and the small kitchen and eat-in dining area, I scrambled for something safe to discuss before I did what I really wanted to do…forget we just met and find out what would happen if I kissed him. "So, this cabin. Has it been in your family for a while?"

I chanced a look back over my shoulder and he was staring at me as he drank from his beer. Shivers ran down my spine at the interest I saw in his gaze.

"Um, no. Actually, I just bought it a few months ago. As a getaway of sorts. My son and I were going to spend the holiday up here. That's why I was here earlier, to double check the generator. This snowstorm wasn't supposed to dump this much snow. From what I've been told, the area doesn't see real snowfall until February. Guess Mother Nature's getting the last laugh this year."

He moved toward the sturdy pine table, sat on its edge as he dangled his beer in his hands between his wide legs, and rubbed his chin. "I should probably try calling him again. Cell reception is spotty up here, even on a clear day."

Dean set his beer down, then made that move that men did, and women drooled over. He reached behind his head and pulled the Outlaw embroidered sweatshirt off, revealing a short-sleeved shirt molded perfectly to his lean, muscular frame.

My mouth dried up at the sight before me. My brain—scrambled. It had to be the situation, forced to be together in a cozy space that was making me so aware of him. I'd been in close quarters with attractive men before and had never been this turned on. Searching for a safe subject, I struggled to find one.

My parents. Aha, yes! Thinking of them was an instant cold shower. I could try calling them, but they didn't know I was this close. Should I let them know? Or save them the worry and just show up when I was able to get back to my rental car and have it pulled out of the snow berm and the tree?

They were used to me being in war zones and long ago gave up asking me to keep them informed of my travels. All it did was cause undo worry. Sometimes it was better not knowing that your child was in a dangerous situation until after they were safe. Deciding I'd wait till morning to see what the forecast would be for tomorrow, I sat back on the couch and took another sip of the beer, surprised that I didn't find it as bitter as other beers I've tried.

"You said your son is in college and home for the holiday break, right?" I was seeking anything to talk about other than taking the chance that I'd blurt out how much I admired his arms, his shoulders and, yes, his ass.

"He is. Now that Heath's an adult…man that sounds weird to say, he just turned nineteen. Anyway, he doesn't have to worry about following a schedule for the holidays and breaks anymore between his mom and me, but I'm glad he chose to spend this year with me. I hated he had to go through years of back and forth, but he seems to have come out more mature than I was at that age. I never thought I'd get divorced, but I suppose most people don't."

Dean was quiet for so long, I wondered if he was expecting me to say something about his failed marriage. Yeah, I wasn't going to touch that subject. I'd never been married. My parents were still happily together after forty-one years, so I had no experience with divorce other than I'm sure it sucked even if it turned out to be the best thing for everyone.

His deep voice jarred me out of my musings. Sitting up a bit straighter, I gave him my full attention.

"Anyway, sorry for rambling on like that. I rarely talk about my personal life this much. Heath's mom remarried not longer after the split. So, he has much younger half siblings, which he loves, but right now they have nothing in common. So, the plan was to spend Christmas together, watching football and eating takeout or delivery."

I hadn't thought much about him being a dad. He sounded like a really good one. Caring. And his young adult son actually wanted to spend time with him, which I'm sure was not the norm. I had a couple friends who'd grown up without their dads, so I'd heard plenty of stories of being forgotten or used as a pawn between their parent's issues, but it was nice to hear that Dean was the opposite.

Having a child was something that I thought would happen one day once I found the right guy, but I never did. The obvious love he had for his son came through loud and clear. It sent my overactive imagination into high gear, and just like that, I found myself wondering what our child would look like.

"Hey, there. I lost you. You okay? How's your head?" Dean's face showed concern. He stepped closer to me, peering into my eyes, searching. In my head, I knew he was looking for signs of a concussion, but my heart fluttered at his closeness. Tipping my head back, I said, "Yes, doc. I'm fine. I've had a concussion before. And I feel nothing close to what I felt then." Smiling at his concern, I tore my gaze from his and looked over his shoulder. "Hey, how about I help with dinner and then we can play my favorite game since it looks like we won't have power for the TV?"

I felt him still looking at me as I tossed the blanket off and stood. When I dared a peek at him to see why he'd grown quiet, I froze at the hunger I saw in his eyes. But before I could say a word, he shook his head, stood up straight, and rubbed the back of his neck. His cheeks were flushed, and he looked cute at being caught checking me out.

His interest gave me a boost of confidence. Could I take this opportunity and turn it into something more than two people forced to spend time together because of Mother Nature? Maybe nature's storm was just the boost I needed to live out one of my recurring fantasies.

"Twenty questions, huh? That's doable, but you need to let me check on you throughout the night just to make sure it's not a concussion." Hands on hips, he waited till I agreed.

"Sure. Why not? It's not like I have anywhere to go tomorrow. Unless the snowplow shows up soon?" I asked hopefully, like someone who wanted that to happen, even though I wouldn't mind getting to know Dean better.

He shook his head. "Not with the way the snow is still falling and the wind blowing it every which way. Afraid you're stuck with me for at least the next twenty-four hours."

Stuck? It was more like serendipity. And if I could get over my nerves, I was planning on getting to know Dean Jefferson very well. I just needed to make sure when we played twenty questions that I didn't let it slip that his top relief pitcher, Tyler Yagasaki, was my younger brother.

<h1 align="center">CHAPTER 6</h1>

DEAN

*B*less the former owners for leaving a cast-iron skillet behind. We used it to make grilled cheese sandwiches for dinner, using it on top of the wood stove. Throw in a can of tomato soup and it felt like the good old days when my mom would make it for me after losing a baseball game when I was nine, maybe ten.

"Okay, so you have three younger siblings and no pets. And you already told me your parents live in Pineville. What about hobbies?" I crumpled my napkin and aimed it at the paper sack I set out as a temporary trashcan.

"Nice toss. You should try out for the Lakers." Nori teased.

"Funny." I shot back. "So, what do you like to do when you're not working?" She was sitting on the floor in front of the fire and the light from the flames cast a surreal glow around her, making my mouth water for just one taste. Her arms were wrapped around her drawn-up knees, her head tilted as she bit her lower lip as she considered my question. Lust flowed straight to my cock.

"I like getting myself stranded and saved by good Samaritans, then mooch off their generosity, drink their beer and eat beef jerky."

Her almond eyes twinkled, and my cock took another hit. *Oh, man, she was perfect.* Was she enjoying our banter? The need to know about her grew and so did my erection whenever I happened to catch her checking me out.

I wouldn't turn down making the most of our time together. My first thought to test the waters had been, "Hey, baby, let's get naked," but it didn't seem like the best idea when we were stuck here with no way to leave.

And for the first time in forever, I was truly interested in finding out more from a woman other than if she was single and wasn't looking for anything other than one night together.

I wanted to find about Nori's likes and dislikes. How long was she staying in Pineville? Would her work let her take a longer vacation if I gave her a reason to stay? Oh, yeah, work. I didn't even know what she did for a living.

"A woman with a good sense of humor is a rare thing. But I think it's my turn again. What do you do? For your career, I mean."

Her smile faltered. Wrong question, maybe she was out of a job and that's why she came to visit her parents, or —

"I, um. I'm a writer."

Her face lit up, and I suddenly wanted to keep that smile on her face. All the time.

"Wow, that's awesome. What do you write about?"

Nori shifted her position, then stretched her arms over her head, her breasts lifted, and all thoughts about being a gentleman went out the window.

"Uh, uh…that's two questions. My turn." Nori took a long drink from the bottled water I had already stocked the fridge with the last time I was here. As she swallowed, I felt beads of sweat pop out all over.

"How old are you?"

"Forty-three. How old are you?"

"Thirty-eight? What's your favorite food?"

"A brisket sandwich at O'Malley's pub and the house truffle fries. They have this chef there; I think her name is Taya. Anyway, she can make a flat tire taste like filet mignon. A couple of the players own the place. You should try it while you're in town. Okay, next question for you. What country would you like to visit that you've never been to before?" Nori opened her mouth, then closed it.

"That's a great question. With my job, I've been so many places. Tell me where'd you like to go while I think about it."

How many places does a writer need to visit to write? Maybe she was a travel writer? "Sure. I'd want to go to Scotland or Ireland. Maybe after I retire. I'd take my son with me. Soak up the land of our ancestors. Hit up the pubs. Be one of those annoying American tourists." I laughed because it was true. I'm sure I'd stick out like a sore thumb.

I waited a beat for her to answer, then asked her one last question. It was getting late, and I knew she needed rest, but I was getting the weird feeling she didn't want me to know more about her writing… *that's it!* Suddenly I knew why. Snapping my fingers, I said, "You're a romance writer, right? That's why you acted funny at first when I asked about your job. Hey, you have nothing to be embarrassed about. My sisters consume romances like they were their last meal or something. I tease them all the time that they need to write one together. I've read that it's the most popular genre in the world. You should be proud of it."

Nori did a slow blink, then started to chuckle. Then her chuckle turned into a full belly laugh and she wrapped her arms around her stomach. She laughed so hard her shoulders shook.

"Okay then. Not the response I was expecting. I got it wrong, huh?"

Nodding and wiping the tears from her eyes, she took in a deep breath and settled. "Yes. But the funny thing is, I have a friend who writes romance. She makes pretty good money too. But I'm with your sisters. A good romance to escape into after a tough day is the best way to unwind. I write…essays I guess you could call them. About the people and places I visit. I had a big case of wanderlust as a kid and things worked out to where I combined that with my love of writing."

The panic at offending her diminished and I watched as she covered her mouth as she stifled a yawn. "Okay, next question is mine. If you could do anything other than…whatever your job is… what would you do?"

Her question threw me as I thought she already knew what I did. I thought I'd already mentioned, but maybe not. It'd been a long day. "You know, we could pick this up tomorrow. Not that I'm not enjoying this, it's been fun. I think we need to call it a night. You should get some rest."

She let out another yawn, not bothering to hide this one. "Okay, but you need to answer as we put things away. Then I'll brush my teeth and get settled. Deal?"

"Deal." I answered. I didn't have to think for long. I was living my dream. "I have the best job in the world. Well, actually, I was lucky enough to have two. Baseball is my life. I couldn't ask for anything better than being a coach for the Outlaws. I got the job after I retired from playing five years ago."

We carried our plates into the kitchen. I waited for her to respond. Maybe tease me again, say something about baseball wasn't a job, it was a game. Some people didn't see being an athlete as a real job, just men and women never really growing up, playing a sport for money. I really hoped she wasn't one of those people.

But she was actively listening with a smile on her face and the urge to kiss her right became overwhelming. So much so that I was having trouble thinking up something else to say to cover the awkward silence.

"I have a confession to make."

Oh, man, here it comes. She hates baseball.

"I knew who you were when I ran into the gas station like a madwoman. But I didn't want to come off like a groupie or something. You were famous in your playing days, plus all those commercials you did. And I know the press has been tough on you lately, so I didn't say anything. I'm sorry I should have come clean, especially after you offered your help."

Huh, not the confession I was expecting. "Thanks for letting me know. I appreciate it. The press has been ruthless. I mean, there are plenty of single players, younger players in their prime to follow and write about. Not sure why they're spending their time on an old man like me."

Nori let out an adorable snort-laugh. And even better, she didn't apologize for it. She was the most genuine person I'd met in a long time.

"You're kidding me, right? I mean, look at you. You've still got it, Ace. Besides, I've heard forty is the new thirty. Any woman would be lucky to be with you."

I chuckled. I couldn't help it. This woman was too good to be true and I think I might already be half in love with her and *shit*. Where had that come from? Could it really be love so soon? Lust, sure. I was definitely in lust with Nori, even if I didn't know her last name. But even for me, tonight was too soon to make a move, but all bets were off tomorrow. I knew if we were going to be here another night, there was no way I wasn't going to try for something more with her than playing twenty questions and sharing meals.

"That's kind of you to say. And I won't bore you with the evidence that proves you wrong on that, so I was thinking you take the pull-out bed in here, I'll stoke the fire and the stove and keep the door to my room open to capture some of the heat. I'll check on you every couple of hours. Sound good?"

She nodded, gathered her backpack, and went into the bathroom to change.

Man, I was in so much trouble.

CHAPTER 7

NORI

Waking up in a strange bed was nothing new to me, not in my profession. No, it was the warm, hard body next to me that had my heart racing and my breathing ramped up to almost a hundred. Then there was a pounding pulse between my thighs.

A soft snore sounded next to my ear. Definitely human and male. No wandering bear had made its way inside, searching for a new place to hibernate. Dean had teased me at last night when I expressed concern about that very thing happening. He was quick to reassure me there was next to zero percent chance of that occurring. I chose to believe him because I didn't have any other choice.

I'd come up with the silly thought when I almost found myself confessing to Dean who I was, but then I chickened out. I also hadn't planned on telling him that I knew who he was, but I couldn't keep it from him. Not when I was keeping an even worse secret.

Man, this situation was so unfair. The first real knock-me-over the-head-tie-me-to-his-bedpost-attraction I have for a man finally happens, and he's my brother's boss.

Tyler would kill me if I seduced Dean. That is if I could seduce him. I still wasn't sure he was into me, or if it was just being a forced-to-spend-time-together kind of attraction. At my age, I knew when a man was turned on and I'd noticed the signs with Dean. The shifting and adjusting of his, um, impressive manhood. The widening of the eyes, the intense and darkening gaze as he checked me out.

I mean, I wasn't vain, but I knew I was attractive. Maybe a bit exotic to some men as I was bi-racial, but whatever. I knew how to weed the creeps out. I got my coloring from my Japanese father but everything else was all moms. Curves, big boobs, and an independent streak a mile wide.

But here I was lying next to the man I'd spent more than a few nights dreaming about on lonely nights in a foreign country. He'd done as promised, waking me several times in the night to make sure I wasn't experiencing any headaches or severe pain from the bump to the steering wheel. And he was so sweet. He'd whisper my name, gently shaking my shoulder to wake me.

His husky, sleep-laden voice floated over my body, sparking all kinds of interest along my nerve endings. And if I'd been braver, I would have lifted my face and kissed him until there was no question what I wanted from him.

But I didn't. Instead, each time he woke me, I reassured him I was fine then I'd snuggle deeper under the layer of blankets he'd thrown on top of me and fall back into a dream where he gave me what I wanted, stripped me of my clothes, pleasuring me until I had the best orgasms of my life. Yes, I said orgasms, multiple orgasms because I was sure he was the kind of lover that wouldn't stop until he'd wrung me dry and made me hoarse from screaming his name.

And thoughts like those were the reason I awoke needy, sleep deprived and in desperate need of a cup of coffee. At least I could go take care of one of those things right now.

I took a quick peek over the mound of blankets and noticed his hand was outside the covers, laying near my hip. He was lying on top, but had a blanket bunched around his hips. It looked like he'd put on another sweatshirt during the night.

But why was he in bed with me?

Had he been there all night?

Maybe my subconscious knew he'd been there, and that's why I had all those sex dreams.

The sudden urge to do a fake stretch and snuggle into him was hard to fight. I had two layers of clothes on, thick socks plus at least three blankets, but I'm sure if I got close enough, I'd be able to feel his hard frame against mine and maybe, just maybe, he'd press back into me.

Not a bad way to start one day. Grinning at my wandering thoughts, I let my imagination run wild. How would it feel to have his strong arms around me, without clothes? Were his lips as soft as they looked? What would it feel like to have him buried deep inside me?

Was this fate? I mean, as soon as I began thinking about cutting back on my assignments and taking a long overdue break to reconnect with my family—was this the universe's way of saying, *"Okay, Nori. This is your chance. Don't screw it up."*

I debated what to do next while staring up at the vaulted ceiling with its wide, dark stained planks and as I let my gaze wander, the cozy feel of the cabin made me feel safe and an unexpected sense of contentment overcame me. It was something that had sadly been missing in my life.

For years, I'd loved the excitement of my profession: the travel, the people, and their cultures. I was known for adding a layer of humanity to my stories as I highlighted the struggles of the people I wrote about. It had filled my cup to overflowing, but several months ago something changed, and I'd gotten honest with myself.

I was no longer satisfied with my work, and I wasn't sure why. And the thought that it wasn't enough, scared me to my bones. It was why I came to Pineville. Well, almost in Pineville, but at least I was in Idaho. I needed my parents' wisdom to help me figure out what came next?

An itch began next to my ear, but if I moved to scratch it, I'd have to free my arms, but I didn't want to disturb Dean. Letting out a soft sigh, I did my best to ignore it because I wanted this moment to last. Lying here, it was so easy to imagine that Dean and I were a couple. His deep, rumbly laugh and intense gazes had me tied up in knots last night. Did he know how he affected me? It was crazy how turned on I was by him. And how unreasonably worried that he'd shoot me down, or worse, laugh if I tried to seduce him. But oh, I wanted to.

Soon, two things became equally urgent. My need for a cup of coffee and the use of the bathroom. Easing out from under the blankets, I tiptoed to the kitchen. Still no power. Shoot. Coffee would need to wait until Dean woke up, so I altered course and went to the bathroom. Returning to the middle of kitchen I stood and debated as I glanced over at Dean softly snoring.

I felt bad he'd slept in his clothes, but equally happy at the view his toned backside encased in tight jeans provided. I could go back to bed and get some more sleep or stand here and freeze my ass off, staring at the man I wanted more than a second cup of coffee.

Turning on my heel, I went back to the bathroom, brushed my teeth and finger-combed my hair. I took off as many clothes as I could stand, considering the bathroom was freezing. I then stared in the mirror and gave myself a pep talk. "You're thirty-eight, Nori. You have needs. He has needs. You know he's attracted to you, and you've wanted to do something like this if given the opportunity—live out your fantasy. Grab the bull by horns and have no strings attached, pulse pounding sex with a guy who makes you feel needy and desperate for his touch. Because he's right out there. Now pull up your panties, er, get ready to take off your panties and go seduce the heck out of that man and—"

"Nori, you okay in there? Are you talking to someone on the phone?" Dean's booming voice had me jumping at least a foot.

I grabbed the edge of the porcelain sink and lowered my head. "No, no one. I'm…ah, good. Just thinking out loud is all. Be right out." Releasing a heavy sigh, I opened the door and came face to face with Dean.

He had both arms braced on either side of the door frame. His hair was tousled, and his dark eyes were full of concern. For me. And after a brief but very insightful glance down his long form, he was also sporting morning wood.

When I returned my gaze to his face, time did that funny thing where it seems to stand still and then Dean cursed as his gaze roamed over my body. "Shit, Nori." My name sounded like a plea, and I didn't give him time to take it back. Jumping into his arms, I wrapped my legs around his waist and kissed him.

He grabbed my hips, pulling me tight against his erection, deepening the kiss. Then his hands were everywhere, my back, my ass, then under my thighs. Moaning, I tightened my hold around his neck as he did an about face striding back to the bed. Stopping short of the mattress, the kiss changed as we battled for dominance, our tongues tangling.

Only the need for air had us pulling apart. He leaned his forehead on mine, and said, "Good morning to you, too."

I wiggled against him. "It can get a lot better if you put me down and take off your clothes."

His hands dropped to my ass cheeks and squeezed, wringing another low moan from me.

"I've been thinking about you all night, doing exactly this. I maybe got a couple hours of sleep. You are the most tempting woman I've ever met."

Rolling my hips against his hard cock, I smiled. This. This is exactly what I wanted. "We could either keep talking or you could put me down and—"

Dean let me go. Instead of bouncing, the thick blankets beneath me had me rolling to my side, and then I was sprawled ass up. I heard a zip and the whoosh of clothing followed by a low chuckle as I fought my way free of the covers.

Crawling to my knees, I pushed the blankets to the end of the bed. When I rocked back to face Dean, he was naked and glorious. The wood in the fireplace snapped and crackled, mimicking the electricity between us, and feeding the room with its heat, ensuring we wouldn't have to do this under the blankets.

"I need to know one thing before we go any further."

I froze at his words. Was this where he demanded to know who the heck I really was? Or was he was getting cold feet? Well, from the way his little, er yeah, wrong adjective, the way his impressive cock was standing at full attention, his attraction to me was pretty evident.

Maybe he wanted verbal confirmation that I was all in with sexy-fun-naked-time.

"Um, yes, please. You have my permission to ravish me. Now would be great." Reaching my hand out, I splayed it across his wide, chiseled chest and gave him what I hoped was a come-hither smile or something at least close to looking seductive.

What I received in return had me literally shaking with need and anticipation from the raw desire reflected back at me.

"Just wanted to be sure we both wanted the same thing."

"Oh, we definitely want the same thing. Besides, have you looked in a mirror lately? You're any sane woman's wet dream."

Dean gifted me with the wickedest smile I'd ever received. Oh, my.

CHAPTER 8

DEAN

God, she was perfect. But I also needed to know that this wasn't payback for allowing her to stay in my cabin till the storm cleared. "Thank you. But I just want to be sure you're not doing this as some sort of thank you for rescuing you? Because—" My voice sounded rougher, deeper—evidence of how desperate I was to part her beautiful thighs and bury myself in her slick heat.

"Okay, backup, because I want to be very clear here and it's my turn for a confession." Nori folded her arms under her spectacular tits, and I swear she turned into a naughty librarian right before my eyes when she tipped her chin down with a stern look appearing in her eyes.

"Dean, have you ever made a deal with yourself that if your fantasy ever came true in real life then you'd jump in, no hesitation—just open yourself to what you know will be the experience of a lifetime? We may not know each other very well, but after yesterday I know enough that I want you, in bed, deep inside me, making me scream your name as you pound into me over and over until we both come." She widened her legs just enough to give me a peek at her glistening flesh and all concern that this woman didn't want me as much as I did her disappeared.

"Because that's my fantasy, and I'm more than certain that you'll deliver on all of that and more." Nori's matter-of-fact tone had me barking out a laugh, shaking my head and diving toward the tempting woman I needed more than I needed my next breath. "Well, I can't say that I'd ever put that much thought into making a fantasy of mine come true, but damn if you just didn't describe exactly what I've been thinking of doing to you since last night."

Her eyes flashed in excitement and her mouth opened as if she was going to say something else, but the time for talking was over. I kissed her long and deep until she began wiggling underneath me, lifting her hips up into my cock, grinding her flesh against mine.

She drove me crazy with her soft moans, her nails scoring my back, and when she whispered, "lick me" in my ear, I almost came. Grabbing behind the head of my dick, I pinched it, holding off just in time. "With pleasure."

I took her lips in one more deep kiss, flicking my tongue against hers, a promise of what I was about to do to all her pretty pink parts. Trailing open mouth kisses down her neck then between her full breasts, I sucked a nipple into my mouth, pinching the other one between with my thumb and finger and then she let out the sweetest cry of pleasure urging me lower.

Nori ran her hands through my hair, over my shoulders and arms. Her touch lit flames everywhere. Trailing my lips down her stomach, she let out a sigh. "Please, Dean."

"Don't worry. I'm going to take very good care of you."

The first lick made her back bow. The second had her moaning, and I was just getting started.

NORI

Floating. I felt like I was literally floating after two, no three, intense, firework producing orgasms. Dean was sprawled on top of me, and I didn't want him to move, ever. It was perfect. Even our breathing was in tune. My fantasies had been poorly directed because what just happened far exceeded my imagination.

And one thing I discovered was Dean didn't do shortcuts. No, he took his time and knew how to use his tongue.

I giggled at the direction my mind had gone, then quickly slapped a hand over my mouth to muffle the sound. Laughter after sex that spectacular wouldn't earn me a repeat performance, and I planned on more than just another round. More like ten at least.

"What's so funny?" Dean stirred, then raised his head, looking me in the eye.

Damn, he was handsome. Sleepy-eyed, hair a mess from my hands, and a very satisfied grin lifted his full lips.

Yeah, there was no way I was going to let him in on my inner dialogue. Didn't want to feed his ego or make him think he was anywhere done.

"Oh, shit!" He flipped himself over, landing on his back. "Nori, I didn't use any protection. I'm clean, I swear. It's been months and… dammit, you must know I'd never put you at risk."

I curled onto my side, facing him, and placed a hand on his chest. "I know you wouldn't. In the short time we've been together, I've learned you have a good heart. I'm on the pill, and it's been longer for me. Almost a year, in fact."

He captured my fingers, pulling my hand up to his lips and placed a soft kiss on my palm. When his breathing evened, he said, "Not to get too deep here, but that was…great, right? I mean…heck, I'm no poet, or good with flowery words, but tell me I'm not alone here when I say that was off the charts."

This man was a definite boost to my ego. And he was right. Our connection was incredible, but what did that mean? Was it because we were in this cocoon where our inhibitions were no longer an issue and, like an idiot, I told him he was my fantasy come to life? Would he think I was looking for more than just a good time? A really good, spectacular time that in less than twelve hours, I was thinking about how to make this work between us once we're back in our real lives.

He was waiting for a response, so I needed to keep it light and not scare him off. "Well, if my screaming your name over and over was any indication, I would say most definitely." I couldn't remember the last time I had pillow talk with a lover, but something tugged at my brain, telling me to guard my heart. Unbelievably, I found myself wishing for this storm to keep us snowbound and cut off from the outside world.

"Ready for some coffee? Breakfast?"

I nodded and before I knew it; he was kissing me hard but way too short, then bounded out of bed, whistling. I watched him walk toward the bathroom and sighed. Yes, that man had one fine ass.

"I'll get some water boiling on the stove, then take a quick shower. Wait, no hot water. Sponge bath it is. You stay in bed and rest. I have plans for you."

"You're pretty bossy in the morning. Was that the awesome sex or are you always this way?" Doing as instructed, I snuggled deeper under the blankets. I could get used to being waited on.

The only answer I received was a rumbly chuckle. Then the bathroom door shut. Smiling to myself, all sorts of naughty things came to mind for our next time.

I must have drifted off because the last thought I remember having was I'd let him boss me around anytime, especially if my reward was more toe-curling orgasms.

"Hey, sleepyhead. I've got your coffee and scrambled eggs."

Cracking open an eye, I woke up to his smiling face and a steaming mug of happiness. "Please tell me you have creamer."

"Powdered. I put in two teaspoons."

I accepted the coffee and took a long sip. Oh, my, that first sip of the day was always the best. I grinned at him and said, "Be careful or you're never going to get rid of me. Coffee, scrambled eggs, and multiple orgasms. You really know how to treat a girl right. Thank you."

Dean inhaled a quick breath and let out a short laugh. "You're welcome. I'm going to go chop some more wood. It looks like the storm finally broke during the night, but there's got to be another foot of snow since we got here." He backtracked to the kitchen and shoved his arms into his jacket and opened the door in the kitchen that led to what I assumed was the backyard.

He was acting...weird. I forced a smile onto my face. "Okay. I'll go wash up and help you bring it in when you're done. Did you check to see if we have cell service?"

He shook his head. "No luck there. Don't worry. With the break in the weather, the plows should be out. It may take a while for them to reach us, but I don't think it'll be more than a day. We should be out of here by tomorrow."

He disappeared outside, and I was left chewing on the fact we'd be here another day. I flopped back and groaned. *Good job at spooking him, Nori.* I needed to remind myself that what happened between us was nothing more than chemistry. It wasn't going to lead to some romantic happily ever after. It couldn't be anything more than two strangers enjoying each other as long as it lasted.

CHAPTER 9

DEAN

$\mathcal{N}$ori's words played over and over in my mind as I chopped wood. It was effing cold, and the wind was biting, but I needed to get as much done before the snow began falling again. The cell service may be down, but I was able to tune in a station on an old radio I found under the sink and the weather report called for another front to move in mid-day.

Working on the generator was a no go since I didn't know what the heck I was doing, anyway. I should have just bought a new one before making plans to spend Christmas up here with Heath. At least he was back home, safe with his Xbox and pizza delivery. Mm, pizza. And bacon, hamburgers, and fries. Damn, I had to stop thinking about food. But I did have one thing my son didn't have, and that was Nori.

What happened between us had hit me like a freight train. There was something about her that felt like we'd known each other forever, while at the same time, I wanted to learn so much more before our time was up and we'd have to go back to reality.

I set down the ax and filled my arms with wood and went back inside. She was lacing up her boots, and her expression fell when she saw me. My heart took a hit at her disappointment. What was this woman doing to me that her reactions were already affecting me?

"Sorry I took so long. I wanted to help."

"If you really want, you can go grab as much as you can carry. Then we should be good until late this afternoon."

Her face lit up, making me feel ten feet tall. In that moment, I knew I was going to spend the rest of our time together doing everything possible to keep that look on her face. I'm not sure why it was so important, but my heart and my head seemed to be in agreement: this woman could very well be the one I had given up hope of ever finding.

We worked in silence for the next half hour, getting both the fireplace and the wood-burning stove in the kitchen blazing to the point it was comfortable enough to no longer wear our jackets.

"So, what made you buy this place instead of building something brand new?"

Our earlier awkwardness faded. We'd made the bed, folded it back into the couch, but nothing much else needed attention since it was just the two of us and we'd already cleaned up the dishes in the kitchen. I'd found some packets of cocoa I'd brought with me from home and we each sat staring into the fire, sipping on the chocolaty treat.

"It has good bones, and I wasn't looking to put the time in on new construction. I wanted something I could use this year. This storm wasn't supposed to be this bad, so I convinced Heath we should hang out here for Christmas. Surprisingly, he agreed. And I am glad I decided to come up a few days early to check the place out and bring a few things from home."

Nori tucked a strand of hair behind her ear and all I could think about was leaning over and kissing the delicate skin she'd exposed. Man, I had it bad.

"You did good on the decorations. I was curious about that when we first got here, but that makes sense you'd want a bit of home here. Good call on being prepared."

"Well, I'm not sure about being prepared. If anything, this storm showed me how unprepared I really was. But one good thing did come from it."

"Oh yeah, what's that?"

"Meeting you." I leaned in for a kiss but stopped less than an inch away from her lips. "I know things have moved pretty fast."

She licked her bottom lip, and I was instantly hard. Well, harder. It seems my natural state around her was sporting wood. "Tell me what you're thinking, Nori. You were all in on living out your fantasy, and I'm so thankful you did, but now I'm getting this feeling that maybe you're wishing you hadn't."

Shaking her head, her long hair fell around her shoulders, framing her face, and all I could think about was tugging her hair back and devouring her lips in the hope of convincing her that what we shared shouldn't cause regret.

"No regrets, Dean. I told you I wanted it, you. But after, it was just so unlike me. I guess I didn't know how to act is all. And we don't know much about each other, not really. Except this incredible physical connection and I don't know what to do with that. Does that make any sense?"

Smiling, I took her mug and along with mine placed them on the side table, then gathered her in my arms, sinking deeper into the cushions of the couch. "It does. So, how about this? We finish playing twenty questions, then we'll have lunch and then who knows? We could get naked again, or there's a five-hundred-piece puzzle in the closet we could put together until the roads are plowed."

"Hmm, decisions, decisions. More orgasms or a puzzle? I'll give you my decision…after lunch, but right now I'm dying to know what your favorite color is?"

"Dark brown."

"Um, okay. Unusual choice. I'm sure there's a story there."

There was, but she was pretty quick, so I'm sure she'd figure it out. I asked, "What's your favorite meal?"

"Ugh. That's so hard." She pouted.

"Not as hard as I am right now."

"Yeah, I noticed. But if you behave and play the game, your odds of more naked time will increase." She grinned.

"My mother makes the best pepper steak with garlic mashed potatoes."

"Dean, it's my turn."

"I know, but I'm just trying to move things along. Is it lunchtime yet?"

"You're the one who suggested this then lunch."

"Right. Okay, what's your favorite?"

"Anything I don't have to cook myself."

"Really?" I was surprised. Not that I thought every woman liked to cook, but that she sounded so adamant about it. "Is there a specific reason for this aversion?"

"Probably because I've been traveling non-stop for over ten years. I never really learned, so I eat out a lot, or if I'm somewhere…remote, I rely on protein bars and jerky or others to cook meals."

Didn't sound like the life of a romance writer. "What type of writing do you do that has you traveling so much?"

"Ok, that's two questions. My turn. What was your favorite memory as a ball player?"

"That's easy. My first game as a pro. I thought I was going to throw up but once I reached the mound and turned, settled into my stance I imagined playing catch with my dad every night when he got home from work and how much he and mom sacrificed so I could play when I was a teenager, then college. Next, I looked up in the stands and there they were, about five rows back behind home plate. The crowd's chattering, but I tune them out. The catcher throws me a couple of signs. I nod at the one I like. I let it loose and that first pitch is a strike. You'd have thought I was in a championship game. My dad jumps out of his seat, pumps his fist and my mom's crying. We lost that game, but I spend the night walking on air. I was being paid to do the one thing I loved to do, pitch a baseball."

I looked down to see why she was so quiet and found her staring at me with tears in her eyes. "Hey, what's this?" I wiped away a single tear as it began to fall.

Smiling said, "You are really something aren't you Dean Jefferson? Just when I think I've got you pegged as this protector type, taking care of me, you go and tell me one of the sweetest stories I've ever heard. You must really love your parents."

"I do. But sweet? Don't be spreading rumors like that about me. The bull pen will never let me live it down."

She lifted herself onto my lap in a move so quick my head spun. And just as fast, I let out a moan as she wiggled her sweet ass against my cock, which had been patiently waiting for attention. Lucky me, I was going to see some before lunch.

CHAPTER 10

NORI

There was no way I wasn't going to let this once in a lifetime opportunity pass. Our first time together had been fast, desperate, explosive, and yes, it had me thrown me with its intensity. Now I wanted slow.

I wanted whatever Dean would give me for whatever time we had.

"No touching. Not until I say." Pulling my shirt off, I tossed it over my shoulder, unhooked my bra, dangling it to my side before I dropped it on the floor.

Sucking in a deep breath at my strip tease, his eyes had gone wide and dark. His gaze was full of heat that had my body responding with a zing of electricity from my sensitive nipples to the rush of warmth in my core.

"You make me wet with just a look, Dean. But you'll have to wait a few more minutes before you can dive inside. It's my turn for a taste." Even though it killed me, I got off his lap and wiggled out of my jeans and panties. No longer worried about him seeing all of my imperfections, stretch marks and soft belly, not after last night. I crawled back

343

onto his lap. The move made me feel empowered, even more so when he groaned and threw his back to rest on the top of the couch.

"You. Are. Killing me right now, Nori."

"Good. That's my plan. Now arms up." He moved swiftly, holding my gaze as I tugged his shirt over his head. Running my hands over his muscled chest, defined abdomen and up the ridges and valleys of his arms onto his broad shoulders, I was mesmerized. A little bit of drool may have escaped my mouth at the sight of his toned body. And it was all mine.

"Nori, you need to stop looking at me like that, or I'm going to break your rules, baby."

For just a moment I wanted that too, but I quickly recovered and, moving my hands to his waist, I unzipped his jeans, freeing his thick cock. Running my fingers over it, I marveled at the velvety skin over hard steel as I pumped its width. The sounds he was making from my touch thrilled me and the thought of impaling myself on him made me wetter, hungrier, for him to be inside of me. I wanted to give him the same pleasure he'd already given me.

"Lift your hips." He complied. I tugged his jeans down over hips and with strength I didn't realize I had, I pushed the denim over his thighs and off his legs.

With nothing left between us, I sat back on his lap, stretching my legs wide. I took him back in hand and ran his cock over my clit. I watched him as his gaze locked on the space between us. He let out a low growl as I rocked against him once, then twice more.

"I'm not sure what your plan is, but I'm not sure how much longer I can last. When it comes to you, I'm weak. Let me touch you. Let me inside."

His plea thrilled me. I was so close to coming that I gave in. "Next time, we'll go slow. Right now, I need the same thing." His hands were on my hips before I finished the sentence and then his thumb was circling my swollen bud. With a few swipes, my orgasm rolled through me. I cried out his name, but I wanted more, so I lifted myself over his cock, sliding down over his rigid length as he stretched me inch by inch with another orgasm building.

Bracing my hands on his shoulders, I met each of his thrusts as he slammed into me. The sounds of our flesh slapping filled the cabin. "Yes!"

Dean cupped my face, tugging me down, and captured my lips in a deep kiss that mimicked the thrust of his cock. Somewhere in the back of my mind, I had thought that last night was as good as it would be, but this moment made me weep with from the pleasure he was creating.

"I'm coming." Dean shouted my name as his fingers worked my clit, pounding into me over and over as we came together, our bodies shaking with our release. Whispered words of satisfaction mingled between us, and in that moment, I knew.

I knew that there would be no one else for me. Not after this.

But how was I going to tell him I'd been keeping a big secret from him and hope that we could maybe figure out a way to be together? Would he be able to forgive me? Would I be able to forgive myself for not being honest with him from the start?

DEAN

We never did get around to eating lunch. Spending the rest of the day in bed, we dozed off at some point, then around four in the afternoon I woke up chilled. I'd forgotten to stoke the fireplace, so I left Nori softly snoring, and tugged on my jeans. I fed the fireplace and the stove, then padded over to the front window. A light snow had started to fall again. Earlier, before we'd fallen asleep, we'd both decided to check our phones. Mine was dead, but Nori's had one bar and about five percent battery left, so she sent off a text to her parents, letting them know where she was just in case we couldn't get out until after Christmas.

For a quick moment I wished we'd be stuck here for the rest of the week, but we had little food left and the last forecast I was able to get on the ancient radio was calling for clear skies tonight. The county plows would definitely be out in full force by then.

My stomach rumbled, so I went about putting some food together for dinner. More soup and the jerky that Woody insisted I buy would have to do.

"Hey, handsome. What you doing over there?" Nori's sleep-filled voice called out.

"You wore me out, woman. Need to refuel. How does clam chowder sound?"

"Mm-good. But I need to shower first." She sat up in bed, her glorious hair a mess around her face and shoulders. She sent me a grin before she threw the covers off and quickly dressed. With no guilt, I watched as she put her clothes back on, booing after she covered up her curves. I'd spent quite a bit of time tracing every inch of her, learning how she liked to be touched, where she was most sensitive. I was just getting started with her, but she didn't know it yet.

"I see that look on your face. I'm not sure I'm ready for more amazing orgasms right now. Wait, I can't believe I just said that. Okay, how about this? Food and maybe another nap, then I'm all yours." Laughing, she closed the bathroom door. I waited a beat for her to realize there still wasn't any hot water.

"Dammit!" she shouted.

I stood outside the door. "Sorry. I could heat up some water on the stove?" I heard some muttering, then a heavy sigh.

"No, that's okay. I'll do a quick sponge bath and be right out."

Chuckling at her pouty tone, I responded. "Well, at least the toilet functions. Best fifteen hundred I ever spent." Walking back to the kitchen to dish up the soup, I sent out a quick thanks to the salesman who talked me into buying a composting toilet.

An hour later, after filling up on soup and bread, we were back in bed. But Nori kept her word and as we spooned, we shared the funny and mundane things from our lives before she fell back to sleep. I was happy to just hold her go over the things I'd learned about her in such a short amount of time.

Like the stuff you find out over months of dating. Our time together had pretty much turned into one long super date. Where typically you'd see each other a couple times a week for a few hours during the early part of a relationship, we'd had non-stop time together and the more I learned, the more I liked about Nori. She was funny, independent, and sexy as hell, and I was hooked. I didn't think at forty-three I'd find someone like her, someone I could see myself growing old with.

Watching the flames dance in the fireplace, my brain worked out different scenarios for after our time here was up. First, I needed to find out why she was hiding her last name from me. Although, I had a pretty good idea of why I'd like to hear it from her.

But the real challenge was figuring out how to convince her I'd fallen in love with her and how to keep her in Pineville.

Later that night, not sure what time it was, I felt icy fingers digging under my shirt. "I'm cold. I need someone to warm me up."

"There might be another blanket around here somewhere. Hold on, I'll be right back." I faked getting out of bed, but she threw a leg over me. I wasn't going anywhere, and she knew it.

"Clothes off, mister. I need you." The raw hunger I heard as she quickly undressed and welcomed me into her arms buoyed my confidence that she wasn't ready to see this end any sooner than me.

What we had was more than sex.

I would not waste whatever twist of fate that had put us both in that gas station at the exact right time, at least not.

I took my time loving her. Slowly. Deliberately. Drawing out her pleasure. Feeding off her, I wrung her dry until her voice was hoarse from screaming my name, and only then did I fill her up and take mine as well.

Somewhere around three a.m. the sound of snowplows woke us. Holding each other tighter, we knew. Spending another day, hiding out from the world, wasn't meant to be.

CHAPTER 11

NORI

Moving on autopilot, I shrugged into my winter jacket, then laced up my battle worn hiking boots. They'd seen plenty of endings, but this one wasn't one I was looking forward to leaving behind. I'd just had the best three days of my life and everything within me was screamed for more time. Stupid mother nature and snowplows.

"I'm ready when you are." Standing, I looked around the space even though I had no other belongings to worry about. Just me and my pounding heart. Dean was standing at the kitchen sink, his back to me as he stared at something out the window.

He hadn't reacted to my comment. What was he thinking? Could he possibly want the same as me? To find out if this whirlwind of connection stood a chance at becoming something more.

Before I found the courage to walk over to him, to wrap my arms around his waist and sink myself into his now familiar form—to tempt him to stay just a few more hours, he broke out of his musings then rubbed his hands together and turned to me with a distant, but friendly smile on his face.

"Ready? Let's go see if those plows buried your car." He made quick work of securing the cabin and held the front door open for me. It was happening all too fast, but I couldn't think of the right words to keep him from marching forward.

So, I did my best to match his light mood. Brushing past him, I made sure not to bump into him because I knew if I so much as grazed him, I'd throw myself against him—begging for more time.

The drive down the mountain was over before I was ready, and then flashing yellow lights greeted us as Dean approached the spot where my rental had been buried. A tow truck operator was pulling it free from its frozen nest, and my heart fell. My stomach dropped at the last hope that maybe, just maybe, I'd have an excuse to spend more time with Dean.

Usually, I couldn't wait to be alone, back in my own headspace. Dean had flipped that record and shown me what it was like to be cherished, not only for my body but for my mind, and my terrible jokes. He managed to get me to share the real me where no other guy had really tried. And now, minutes away from being thrust back into the real world, I was on the verge of experiencing my first ever panic attack.

"Looks like your rental survived with just a dent on the front-end passenger side. Did you sign up for insurance?"

Did I sign up for insurance? That's how he was going to play this? Oh. Hell. No. This man had shared almost three days with me, cut off from all distractions, we shared our intimate thoughts and the sex. My god, the best sex of my life had been with him.

He did not get to blow me off this way. "Um, yeah. I did. I've been thinking that I'd like to see—"

"What the hell is Tyler doing here?" Dean's question sent me over the edge into the panic attack I'd been fearing. He didn't sound at all pleased to see what I could only assume to be my brother. How many Tyler's did he know?

Although he didn't know the Tyler that was on the Outlaws was my brother, so maybe I was just projecting my own guilt, which at this very moment rode heavy on my shoulders.

"Tyler? Where?" Whipping my head from Dean's frowning profile to out the front window of his truck, I saw an unfamiliar dark Jeep parked a couple of car lengths behind my rental. Then I saw someone jogging up the road toward the tow truck that was idling on the side of the road, facing us.

Shit. Shit. Shit. It was my brother. But what was he doing here? I chanced another look at Dean from the corner of my eye as I counted slowly, taking deep breaths. I was not going to freak out. Nope. No freaking out. I could handle this. Maybe.

The realization I had made a huge mistake in not telling Dean who I really was produced a weight the size of an elephant squarely on my chest. *So stupid.* I was stupid to think I could wait one more day to tell him had me hyperventilating.

"Nori, you okay. What's wrong, sweetheart?"

Dammit, why'd he have to call me that, sound so concerned? Instead of warming me from the inside out as it had the last few days, I began gasping for breath. Shaking my head, I kept my eyes closed, breathing through my nose, out through my mouth. As if in a wind tunnel, I heard Dean exit the truck, then come to the passenger side and open my door. He placed his hands on me, rubbing my arm and my leg, attempting to help calm me down. I did not want to end things like this. Karma was a real bitch.

Finally, I got my breathing under control. But before I could say anything to Dean, I heard my brother call my name.

"Nori? What are you doing with Coach Ace?" He stopped short of the front of Dean's truck, confusion marking his features. "Coach, what's going on?"

Bracing myself for a long explanation I gently removed Dean's hands and slid from the seat onto the pavement and quickly walked away from the man I was certain I'd fallen in love with toward the brother who wasn't going to be very happy with me.

How was I going to explain to Tyler that after just a few days in a cabin with his coach, I'd fallen in love?

"Tyler, what are you doing here? How did you even know where to find me?" My whole body shook. Stepping closer, I opened my arms for a hug, but he continued to look from me to Dean and back again. I could see his mind working things out.

Crossing his arms, Tyler settled his gaze on me. "Mom and Dad. They called me and said they got a text from you. Said you were not far from the Forest Motel and gas station off Exit 14. And that you'd wanted to surprise them but got caught up in the snowstorm two days ago."

Three, but who was counting? "Um, yeah. They'd closed the pass, and I wanted them to know where I was in case…you know, something happened. But then I ran into Dean, and he offered to let me stay at his cabin and…." I stopped explaining when I saw Tyler's eyes narrow even more as he looked at Dean.

This was exactly what I'd been afraid would happen. Creating a rift between my brother and his coach now seemed inevitable. I was a horrible sister.

Sensing Dean's body heat, he'd stepped up directly behind me. Was it his way of assuring me he had my back? Or was he planning on confronting me about keeping my last name from him?

"Ty, before you get worked up. I recognized Nori was your sister. She was totally safe with me. She had a slight bump on her head from when her car slid into the berm of snow, but other than that, she's fine. I just bought a cabin and was headed back down to Pineville to pick up my son. I found out the pass had been closed when I stopped at Woody's where your sister tried to get a room for the night, but he was full up. Unfortunately, or fortunately, she ended up going in the wrong direction when she went to get back on the freeway and I found her here, stuck, and offered my help."

Thankfully, Tyler's features relaxed into relief and my little brother, who stood six inches taller and outweighed me by at least seventy-five pounds, engulfed me in a bear hug. "Sis, I'm so glad you're okay. Thanks, Coach, for looking out for her. Me and my family really appreciate it."

Not sure what to say and afraid to look Dean in the eye, I pulled out of Tyler's hug. Years of finding myself in sticky situations had me bulldogging my way through the awkward situation. "I'm going to grab my bag, get the rental warmed up and I'll follow you to Mom and Dad's. Sound good?"

"You sure Nori? We could have it towed, and you could ride with me. I'm sure after everything you've been through, you don't feel like driving."

Keeping my body turned toward Tyler, I said, "I'm good to drive. I've never felt better. Lots of, uh, naps the last few days." I scooted around Dean, still not ready to face him, grabbed my bag and dug out the car keys.

While the two talked, I cleaned off the windows of the car while it warmed up. "All set, Tyler?" I'd tried to eavesdrop on their conversation. Dean didn't say anything about me being Tyler's sister. Instead, they talked about offseason workouts. Feeling relieved he wasn't going to cause a scene, I waved at him, opened my car door, and said, "Thanks for everything, Dean. You were a real lifesaver." It killed me to keep all emotion from my voice. But I wasn't going to throw myself at a man who obviously hadn't been looking for anything more than what we'd had.

A good time. No strings. Like two adults who knew the score. But it was more than good. It was amazing, and I knew deep down that I'd never meet a man that would hold a candle to Dean Jefferson.

His face was unreadable. No indication about what he was thinking. Zilch. Nada. I couldn't believe this was how it was going to end between us. He made no move to come over and speak with me. He waved back, patted my brother on his back, then got in his truck and drove off.

And just like that, he was out of my life.

CHAPTER 12

DEAN

Well, that didn't go according to plan. My nerves had kept me from telling her how I felt on the drive to pick up her car. That I wanted to see her again—actually, that wasn't right, because as unbelievable as it seemed, I was in love with her.

Nori was mine. She had my heart and if she wanted, she could have it and me forever.

I'd figured out early on who she was. And had a pretty good idea why she'd kept her identity a secret from me. If the situation was reversed and Tyler had wanted to be with one of my sisters, a long discussion would have to take place. But life was too short to be that person who stood in the way of two adults who wanted to be together.

The first thing I needed to do was speak to Tyler alone and let him know I was in love with his sister.

Arriving home an hour later, I walked into my kitchen. Heath was using his favorite appliance, the air fryer.

"Dad!" He launched himself into my arms.

Guess he wasn't too old to miss me.

Ruffling his unkempt hair, I hugged him back. "Whatever you're making, add in another serving. I've been eating grilled cheese, soup, and jerky for three days."

"Pizza rolls?"

"Of course, why change your diet on Christmas day?" Chuckling, I gave him an affectionate punch on the arm, then headed upstairs to shower. A long, hot shower.

An hour later, my son and I finished up our lunch, and I told him I met someone.

"You literally fell in love with a damsel in distress? That's classic." Laughing, he placed a hand on my shoulder.

"Damsel in distress? You been watching old school cartoons while I was gone?" I asked.

"Maybe. Besides, they're a riot." Heath grinned. "So, when do I get to meet her?"

Returning his smile, I said, "I have to tell her first. But my plan is to go see her now and convince her that no matter how quick this is, it's real and I can't imagine my life without her now that I found her."

"Whoa. You're serious?"

"What did you think I meant when I told you I loved her?"

"Well, I guess you were…you know, just really into her. You don't tell me about your dates or when ,you know, happen to get lucky. Hey, don't act surprised. It's not like I don't know about sex, Dad. I'm nineteen. We've had *the talk*. A while ago and anyway, I've never seen you so worked up about a woman like this—ever. But I'm glad. Really glad. You deserve to be happy."

"Well, thanks. That means a lot, son. Okay, I'm headed out. Next time you see me, if everything goes well, you'll get to meet I Nori."

NORI

"Mom, how long did it take you to know Dad was the guy, the man, for you?" We were setting the table for dinner, and I'd been avoiding Tyler all afternoon. I needed some time alone with Mom before I broached the subject of me and Dean with my brother.

Luckily, he and Dad were downstairs in the man cave watching football. But avoiding my sisters, not so much. Sabrina and Mika were fraternal twins and were as different as their names but were the best of friends. Sometimes I envied their relationship and although I was the oldest, I relied on them for guy advice. We had a video call a couple of hours ago since both their flights had been cancelled and they couldn't reschedule until the day after Christmas.

When they found out who I'd been stranded with, they wanted all the details. But things got tricky with Mom listening in. So, I ended up texting them a few details with a promise to catch them up when they arrived.

Mom set a bottle of wine on the table, then gave me a long look before she answered. "Well. I guess it didn't take too long. Why? Are you dating someone? Did you and Kyle get back together?"

"No. And I haven't dated Kyle since last year, Mom. No, I was just curious. I've been thinking a lot about my future. I wanted to run some things by you and Dad before I make any changes, but I'm pretty sure I'm done travelling. Overseas for sure."

"Oh, Nori! That's wonderful. Let's tell your father."

"Mom, wait. I wasn't going to say anything until after Christmas. It can wait." Darn it. I wanted to ask her more about her and Dad and see what she thought about my feelings for Dean. I couldn't stop thinking about him, and maybe I could still salvage the mess I made. But before I could push mom for more specifics, Tyler interrupted.

"Hey, Nori. You got a sec?" Walking into the dining room, he swiped an appetizer from the tray mom was attempting to keep away from him.

She rolled her eyes. An expression I've seen her give Ty at least a thousand times. "It's not time yet. And I didn't make extra since your sisters aren't here. Didn't I put enough snacks downstairs for you?"

"Do you ever?" Ty grinned, sidestepping her as she playfully slapped his arm.

"Go on, Nori, take your brother somewhere else to talk, otherwise all the food will be gone before dad gets up here. I'll let you know when the roast is ready."

A bottomless pit. Even at twenty-nine. Tyler smacked his lips. "Mm 'mm. You should sell these, Mom. I'll be out front, Nori."

Out front? That was weird. But I had one more question before I followed him. "Mom, when you said it didn't take long with Dad to know that you loved him. How long before you knew?"

"Okay, what's going on? Is there a man you're not telling me about? I swear if you tell me it's for a story you're writing, I'll ground you from dessert." Laughing, she placed her hands on her hips and stared me down, well she had to look up since I had a couple inches on her.

There was no way I was missing out on dessert. My mom's cooking was the best and it would be unheard of for me not to eat two desserts when at home, so not getting a piece of my mother's triple chocolate Yule log cake wasn't going to happen.

"Promise me you won't go overboard, okay? Okay, so hypothetically, let's say I met a man I really like. Would it be weird to, you know, be in love with him after a short period of time?"

Please say no, please say no.

I could tell by the way my mom's eyes went wide and biting her lower lip that she was doing everything she could to keep from screaming in excitement. She tried her best to stay out of all her kid's love lives, but we knew she and our dad wanted to see us happy and settled with someone of our own. And they wanted grandkids. She loved to remind me that by the time she was twenty-eight, she'd already had all four of us.

Mom sank into a chair, folded her hands on the table, and smiled at me. "Hmm, well, I guess all things considered; love doesn't happen on a timetable. It just…happens. For me, at least, because I can't speak for your father, I guess I knew after our first date. Now, I'd only had one kiss from him, but oh, what a kiss. And he was so charming and attentive. And he brought me flowers. I couldn't wait to get home and tell my sister."

A day. One date and mom knew my dad was it for her. But was that love?

"Wow, that's pretty fast. When did you say it to him?"

"Oh, um. I guess right after he told me he loved me. That was probably a month later. Then he proposed a month after that. We got married six months later and then you arrived ten months after that." Sighing, she rested her chin in her hand and stared off into the distance.

Leaving her lost to her memories, I gave her a quick kiss on the cheek. "Thanks, Mom. That helped. I'm going to go see what Ty wants." Grabbing my cardigan on the way out, she called me back.

"Wait. So, you didn't tell me. Who is this mystery man?"

"Oh, well, like I said, it's all hypothetical." Avoiding eye contact, I gave her a little wave as I left the room.

"I'm not buying it, Nori Maire Yagasaki. This conversation is not over." Her voice rang out through the house. I stepped onto the front porch. Tyler was leaning up against one of the pillars, speaking to someone standing in the late afternoon shadows.

"Hey. Who are you talking to?"

Tyler straightened, walked over to me, and placed his hands on my upper arms. Whomever he was just speaking too was effectively blocked by his large frame as he stepped close.

"I want you to know, I'm okay with any decision you make." Tyler bent his knees so we could be eye-to-eye. "Your happiness is all that matters to me."

"What are you talking about?" I took a sniff of the air. "You been into Dad's peppermint Schnapps?"

"Nope, although that's a good idea." Chuckling, he dropped his arms, then swept his left one toward the walkway. I followed his movement and came face to face with Dean.

"Thanks, Ty." Dean nodded at my brother. Stepping onto the porch, he took my hand.

"Okay, I'm confused. Ty, why is he thanking you?" Turning to where my brother had been, I found nothing but empty space. The sneak had disappeared back into the house. What were they up to?

"So, why were you thanking my brother? And why are you here?" Nerves mixed with a touch of pissed-off made my tone sharper than it should have been, all things considered. Plus, I wanted to be the one to go to him first and explain things.

"I'm here to see you. I thanked him for not punching me in the face after I explained how I felt about his sister." Dean took my other hand in his, bringing both up to rest on his chest.

"Before you say anything, I wanted to tell you how much being with you these past few days has meant to me. And to make a confession."

"Wait, I should go first."

He kissed me soft and quick then started speaking again. "I feel like we've had this conversation before. The sexy version. But for now, I'd like to go first, please?"

Nodding, I mimed zipping my lips closed.

He tossed his head back and laughed. Lord, I loved that sound.

"Okay, I knew who you were pretty quickly once we spent some time together. Ty has a picture of you and your family in his locker. Plus, you have the same smiles. But I got the impression you didn't want to let me know who you were, for obvious reasons, right? Worried how whatever was going on between us would affect our working relationship."

I mumbled my answer without opening my mouth, then nodded.

That earned me a grin with dimples showing.

"Now...since neither one of us acknowledged how we were connected by your brother—which you have to admit that in a kind of perfect, low stress way—it allowed us to get to know each other without any weirdness."

I waggled my eyebrows, which was hard to do outside in almost freezing temps.

"Stop making me laugh. I'm attempting to be serious here, Nori."

One nod. No laugh inducing hijinks. But I did begin feeling the stirrings of hope.

"Okay, so back to the elephant in the room. Your brother, my pitcher slash employee, could have been a real obstacle if we had met any other way. But we had almost three whole days to ourselves, playing silly games, finding out what made the other tick, and the crazy hot sex was, of course, the icing on the cake."

I nodded vigorously, then had to stop because it was making me dizzy.

"So, what I'm trying to say is I'm not ready to end what we found stranded in my cabin. And I was planning on telling you that on the drive to get your car, but then I changed my mind. No, don't pull back. I didn't change my mind about you, just where I wanted to tell you. And telling you that I love you in the cab of my truck after everything didn't feel like the right place. And then Tyler showed up and ruined my game plan and—"

"Wait!" I may have shouted a little too loud.

"What?"

"Why do men always bury the lead?" I threw up my hands, then put them on either side of his handsome face. I couldn't believe this was happening.

"Bury the lead? What are you talking about…oh, you mean the L-word."

"Yes. Tell me again."

"Man, you're bossy."

"You like it," I said.

Dean gave me a sexy smile, tugging me in closer. "You know I do. I love you, Nori Yagasaki."

"And I love you. As crazy as it seems, I have fallen in love with my brother's coach and I'm not one bit sorry about it. He'll just have to get used to sharing you, although I'm the only one you get to kiss."

"Um, yeah, thanks for putting that picture in my head." He tickled my ribs. "I'm going to have to come up with something equally gross to make things even."

"Stop. Stop tickling!" Gasping for breath, I placed my almost frozen fingers under his shirts, trying to get him to stop. "I promise I'll never, ever-ever say anything like it again. Just, please stop tickling me."

He stopped and then he made up for it and kissed me until we were both out of breath and Tyler was yelling at us to get in the house. Well, first he shouted, "get a room," then he told us to get in the house because mom and dad wanted to meet the man kissing their oldest daughter on the front porch on Christmas day.

But even with all that, it was the best damn kiss ever.

Until the next one, of course.

EPILOGUE

TWO MONTHS LATER

DEAN

*N*ori was stunning in her ankle length wedding dress. Tears gathered in my eyes while I watched her father walk her down the aisle of the small church on the Saturday before I was officially due back at work for Spring Training.

Our family and close friends attended the intimate ceremony. We decided we didn't want to wait until after the season to get married: it was too long to wait when we wanted to start our life together now.

My bride made me the luckiest and happiest man alive not once, but twice in less than a month. First, when she said yes and then just last week when we were back up at our cabin, buried under blankets on the bearskin rug in front of the fireplace. She placed a hand on her lower abdomen and told me we were having a baby.

She was scared. I was scared. We hadn't planned for it, although I knew from the way she doted on my nieces and nephews at our engagement party that she would make a wonderful mother. At thirty-eight, she was in excellent health but she was considered her high risk because of her age. So, with plenty of reassurance, the said he and his nurses would keep a close eye on her and our baby during the entire pregnancy.

Heath was beyond thrilled, well as much as a nineteen could be about becoming a big brother, again. And since he was grown and didn't need her to mother him, they bonded over her foreign travels, developing a fast friendship. He now wanted to visit some of the countries she'd been. I negotiated it to one trip a summer as long as he was in college and kept his grades up and definitely no war zones.

Nori's father gave me her hand. Emotion welled within me, and a tear finally fell down my cheek. At that moment, I didn't care who saw how this woman affected me. Her shining eyes met mine and…screw it. I was going to kiss my bride no matter what the reverend said last night at the rehearsal.

But I did wait until her father sat down, however.

"Dean, I know that look in your eyes. You can't kiss me till after he says, you know, '…husband and wife.'" Nori whispered.

"Too bad. Can't wait and you look so beautiful. A dream wrapped in a song, or maybe it's the other way around. Either way, you're too irresistible."

The kiss was a huge hit, and the reverend didn't say a word. At least not until the third kiss before finally beginning the ceremony.

WHAT TO READ NEXT? Check out the rest of the Tangling series which can be read in any order HERE.

Join my newsletter today and receive a free short story from Debra also set in the Pineville World, https://bit.ly/DebraEliseNewsletter

TANGLING WITH SANTA

A PINEVILLE WORLD CHRISTMAS NOVELLA
(TANGLING SERIES)

ABOUT

His unexpected kiss has me wanting to be on Santa's naughty list— maybe forever.

Timing is everything.

A few months ago, I thought he was into me. Then nothing but friendly smiles and nods. I miss the sultry gazes, the swoon worthy smiles that left me hot and bothered.

Now, a week before Christmas, I'm mingling with friends at our favorite pub when my phone jingles, *"All I want for Christmas,"* filling the air as I scramble to answer. Santa has bailed. Slade swoops in offering to be my, I mean, the party's Santa.

Needing a Santa for the party I'd been planning for months was one thing. My need for Slade Johansson, one of Pineville's most eligible and mysterious bachelors, was another.

Months of wondering turn into days, moments of spending time together planning the Christmas Eve party for the Children's Club where I work. Instead of sugarplums dancing in my head, my dreams turn naughty, with images of Santa offering me his special "package" of joy and giving.

Is this just a holiday hook-up or can we find a way to make the magic of the season last forever?

CHAPTER 1

KARA

"*N*o, you can't do this to me!" The man I'd hired to play Santa at the Christmas Eve party was no longer on the other end of the call that threatened to ruin my first major event at my brand-new job. I'd been hired at the Children's Club to assist the Executive Director on special projects and community outreach. My dream job.

This could not be happening. Not five days before the party.

"Kara, are you okay? What's wrong?" One of my best friends, Miranda, set her drink down and grabbed my arm. Tonight was our last girl's night of the year at O'Malley's Pub. Our two other friends, Evie, and Heather, looked on in concern as I tried to hold it together. *I need another beer.*

Frustrated, I shoved my cell into my purse then run my fingers through my hair, messing up the blowout I'd paid a fortune for earlier in the day. "Oh, nothing. Just Santa leaving me high and dry. Where am I going to find another one? I mean, this guy wasn't even my first choice. I'm so screwed."

"Ladies, thanks for coming in tonight. It's great seeing your beautiful faces again." Slade Johansson, the pub's new manager and our favorite bartender, well, my favorite, placed a pitcher of the house ale on the table and was wearing the sexiest smile I'd ever been lucky enough to receive, even if it was directed all of us.

Last summer, I'd thought he was into me. He'd asked Evie if I was single, then nothing. And now the guy I continued to lust after from afar was now front and center to witness one of the worst moments of my career. I couldn't let the kids down, and I wasn't about to let him see how upset I was.

"The table in the back sent this over. Typically, I don't indulge guys like them, but since two of them claim to be your husbands, I decided to play along." He flashed another smile. Goosebumps erupted all over my body. For a brief, hopeful moment, I thought he was flirting with me, but then he turned to my sister, Amber. "This is for you. Royce wanted to make sure you didn't feel left out." Slade placed a soft drink in front of Amber. And I swear, she blushed. Yeah, Slade had that kind of effect even on happily married women. Pregnant with her first baby, my sister took a drink, then lifted it up, winking at her husband across the room.

I sighed. Tonight wasn't supposed to be about my friends flirting with their husbands.

We hadn't planned on being here the same night as them. Unfortunately, this close to Christmas tonight was the only time everyone had free. My plan was to figure out if Slade was still interested.

Well, at least there was plenty of beer to drown my sorrows. How was I going to explain this to my boss? Rod had been looking for someone he felt comfortable giving more responsibility to, and I couldn't let him down. He'd been running the club almost single handily for the past few years and was only able to hire me thanks to a recent large donation. He was planning a big reveal with the donor at the party. Busy working on expansion plans I know had to let him know our Santa had bailed and I might need his help after all.

Darn it, who could I find this close to the party and who could fit into the suit I'd already rented?

"So, what are you ladies up to tonight?" Slade's silky voice pulled me from my brooding. A voice that had me squirming in my seat and my cheeks heating at all the naughty images of us together that had been playing in my head.

Suddenly my ringtone blared, *"All I want for Christmas is you,"* and I felt my face grow warmer. I quickly took my cell back out of my purse and silenced it. Another junk call. Could the timing have been worse? Because truth be told, Slade is exactly what I want for Christmas.

Another image of Slade from this past summer in his board shorts flashed. His ripped body on full display made me internally combusting. Being so close to him was endangering my ability to think straight. Taking a long drink from my beer, I mumbled, "Sorry about that. I, uh, really like Mariah Carey." *Sheesh, could I sound more like a dork?* Sinking down into the booth, I glanced at Miranda and mouthed, *"Help me."*

She grinned, then chuckled before doing the exact opposite. "Hey, Slade. What are you doing on Christmas Eve?"

Oh no, she just didn't. Taking another sip of my beer, I looked at him from the corner of my eye. Was it my imagination, or did his smile slip just a little? If it did, he recovered quickly.

I knew where Miranda was going with that question, and I didn't like it. Not one bit. Turning my head enough so Slade couldn't see, I glared at her.

Returning my attention back to him, he did that thing where men widen their stance and cross their arms. Oh. My. He gave his full attention to Miranda, which gave me the opportunity to ogle him unnoticed. For months, I've spent a good amount of time imagining what those arms would feel like wrapped around me. And here he was, standing inches away, giving me a front row view of his muscular biceps and forearms.

His gaze flicked down to mine before landing on my mouth. Time stopped. Was I imagining things, or did I see desire fill his eyes? Either way, his intense look made me squirm in my seat once more. *Oh, my gawd.* I had to bite my lower lip to keep myself from moaning out loud. His nostrils flared when my tongue soothed my bruised lip. The moisture dried up in my mouth. If he wasn't into me, then he was doing an awesome job at pretending to be interested.

Someone at the table giggled, breaking me out of the fog. Covering my mouth, I let out a fake cough to cover my embarrassment. I'm sure I was misreading the situation. Inhaling, I took a deep breath, hoping to settle my out-of-control pulse. Big mistake. His spicy, unique scent made hit me at the same time. It, and him was addicting, intoxicating. *Pull it together, Kara.*

After another sip of beer, I turned to Miranda and asked, "Hey, weren't we going to talk about this new guy you have a crush on?"

She didn't take the bait. Just smiled sweetly at Slade, ignoring me as I shot imaginary daggers at her through my now blurry eyes. Stupid beer. I was such a lightweight. "I'm sure Slade is very busy. He probably needs to get back to work."

"Not at all. And I like that song too, Kara."

He winked at me, and I was torn between being embarrassed and turned on.

"Things have slowed a bit and I've got some time to chat with you beautiful ladies. So, what's happening on Christmas Eve?"

My friends and sister all stared at me with expectant looks on their faces. Oh, they were so going to get it later. Another deep breath and I counted to five. Could I ask him to help me out? To be Santa. There wasn't an ounce of fat on his six-foot two frame, and he'd have to use a lot of padding to pull it off, but since the loser who bailed was about the same height, the suit would probably fit him with a few adjustments.

But could I spend time around the man who put me in the friend zone last summer?

"Wait, I think I know what this is about." Slade gazed around the table before he settled on me.

"You do?" I squeaked. Darn it, I sounded like a lovesick, pimple-faced teenager instead of a thirty-three-year-old, mature woman who, if I had the nerve, I'd ask him what happened after he asked my friend if I was single last summer.

And I would.

If I wanted to.

But not right now. Because I had a bigger problem and possibly too much beer, too fast.

Besides, why would he want to help me out by wearing an itchy, ill-fitting suit and having kids sit on his lap the night before Christmas? He probably had a date all lined up and ready to sit on his, er, lap and…*oh, my god I didn't just say all of that out loud, did I?*

"I do. Did I hear you saying something about needing a Santa?" Slade responded with no indication that he was aware of my crazy inner monologue and freak out.

I let out the breath I didn't realize I was holding. "Yes, that," I nodded. "The guy who I booked just called and told me he had a better offer and bailed. Do you know of someone who'd be willing to spend the night listening to kids list what they want for Christmas who are hopped up on sugar and, oh also have a fake beard and hair yanked on non-stop?"

Did I just sound halfway normal? I hope so. Crossing my fingers that he knew someone, I smiled and made direct eye contact. I could no longer avoid looking directly into his eyes and I prayed he didn't pick up on the need in mine. And possibly the fear of rejection I'd been carrying with me.

Taking a chance that he'd call me, I'd turned down dates for months, thinking he might finally ask me out. But when he hadn't, I'd convinced myself that Evie must have misunderstood him. After all, a man like him could have any woman he wanted, so why would someone like him wait so long to ask me out?

"Sure. What time do you need me there?"

"Oh, I uh. That's kind of you, but you're uh, what I mean is I need someone who's a bit more…fluffy?"

Everyone laughed, easing my anxiety.

"Kara, he'd make a great Santa." Heather jumped into the conversation. "I'm sure we could find some padding for him. The kids won't care if he's…fluffy or not. As long as Slade can act the part and throw in some 'ho-ho-hos', he'll be great."

What were my friends doing to me? Slade was just being nice. I'm sure he had better things to do on Christmas Eve than help me out with a bunch of kids. "You know, what was I thinking? I know just the guy that could do this. How about if it doesn't work out, I'll call you. Okay?"

Slade's handsome face was unreadable. Darn it, I hope I hadn't hurt his feelings. Reaching up to my throat, I grasped the locket I wore, rubbing the cool metal. My breath caught in my throat at the transformation on his face. His eyes darkened and his lids lowered. His gaze was focused on my hand as I rubbed the face of the locket over and over. It was a nervous habit I'd never been able to break.

Dropping my hand into my lap, he slowly lifted his gaze back up to mine, then nodded. "Sure. But let me know if things don't work out. I'd love to help. The kids."

"Yes, I will. And I really appreciate the offer. Thank you."

For a moment, it felt as if we were the only two people in the room. Then someone shouted his name. He excused himself and left to deal with an employee who needed his help.

Watching him walk away, I began to doubt myself. Maybe I shouldn't have shot down his offer. Could it be that he was being more than nice?

CHAPTER 2

SLADE

 I walked back to the bar, limping from the semi-hard on being so close to Kara always seemed to ignite.

Staying away from her for the last few months had been difficult, but necessary. I hadn't anticipated her changing jobs last summer to begin working at the Children's Club. I'd begun the process of setting up an endowment fund using my grandfather's inheritance and the club for disadvantage youth was at the top of my donation list. To pursue her while I was also working with Rod, her boss, could have made for a sticky situation before the donation was finalized, and we made the announcement. On Christmas Eve during the party she now needed a Santa for.

I'd been waiting to make my feelings known to Kara because I didn't want there to be any doubt about how I felt about her.

From the moment she came into the pub, I wanted her with a desperation that was new and exciting, and I did not want to screw this up. Working as a bartender may seem strange to those who know I have enough money that I don't need to work, but I had my reasons.

Having a lot of money that I did nothing to earn had been a burden. But it was hard to explain to friends and coworkers. And when they did find out, they would treat me differently.

It was one of the reasons I'd moved to Pineville. Fresh start and all that.

One of the things I like about Kara was how smart she is. Her looks and curvy body only added to her appeal. I continued to keep an eye on her table as the night went on. And now that I knew she needed help, I'd make sure she could count on me.

"Hey, Slade. How about a couple of beers over here?"

The voice belonged to Nolan Cole, a former Army Ranger who'd quickly become a friend when he'd married one of our best employees, Scarlett. Sitting beside him was an even larger guy than Cole, someone I never seen in the pub before today.

Nodding, I made my way down the bar and set them up with two drafts. "Scarlett, let you out, I see. How's she doing?" Between them, they had Matty, her son from her first marriage, and recently announced they were expecting a baby.

"Hey, I can come and go as I please." Cole chuckled, then added, "And today I decided to please my wife. You'll do the same one day. Anyway, she's been craving Taya's sliders and fries. We're having a beer while we 'wait' for the food."

Laughing at his air quotes around the word wait, I slid my gaze over to his buddy, who was checking out the table where Kara and her friends were sitting.

"Hey, this is my friend, Beck. He recently moved here after retiring from the Army. We were in the same unit."

Beck turned away from my woman, smart move, and held out his hand. The guy was straight out of central casting. If someone was looking for a jacked former military turned mountain man, he was it. "Nice to meet you, Beck. Welcome to Pineville. You're in for the best food in town. Taya is a genius in the kitchen. You wouldn't believe the number of other restaurants who've tried to steal her from us."

Cole chuckled and took a long drink from his frosted glass. "I believe it. And she's pretty easy on the eyes too. Is she seeing anyone?" Cole tipped his head toward Beck ever so slightly.

"What was that?" The mountain man growled.

"What? Nothing. I like to tease Slade about Taya. They're good friends. By the way, why haven't you asked her out?" He narrowed his gaze on me and I think I knew where he was heading.

Cole was up to something with his buddy. "She's great. Actually, the best. But you know, we're good friends. And her kids are great. The youngest is in college now too, so Taya's an official empty nester."

I looked between the two men, and decided I needed to stay in my lane and worry about how I was going to convince Kara how serious I was about playing Santa.

"You two enjoy your beer. I'll see you around, Cole. And give Scarlett my best, okay? We sure miss her around here. Beck, nice to meet you." Moving away to fill another order, I scanned the tables at the front of the pub and watched as Kara and her group gathered up their things to leave. She turned my way, then quickly looked away. She was so cute when she was flustered. One of the things that drew me to her was her lack of calculation when it came to men. She didn't overtly flirt whenever she and her friends would come in for their girl's night out. She was simply herself: confident and funny and with no idea how much she affected me whenever we were close.

Considering I didn't pursue her after the party at my boss' place in August, she was probably confused by my offer, and I wanted to catch her before she left. I finished filling another pitcher, wiped down the bar and looked over again to see her and her friends winding their way between the tables toward the exit.

It was then I noticed Cole and his buddy, Beck, leaving with their food. They arrived at the door at the same time Kara did. Even from where I stood, I could see the interest on Beck's face as he held the door for Kara. The guy's perma-frown lifted into a smile as he checked her out.

Oh, hell no. Not happening.

I tossed the towel down, jumped the bar and reached the door in record time. "Hey, Kara. Let me walk you out. I had a thought about our earlier conversation."

I ignored the burly ex-Ranger's lifted brow and low grunt at my intrusion.

Kara's her beautiful face was marred with confusion, but she let me take her arm. Leading her out of the pub into the snowy night. There was no way I would let some newcomer, or anyone else, near Kara.

CHAPTER 3

KARA

"Slade. Slow down, please." Out of breath from the pace he was keeping, I wiped snowflakes from my eyes and stopped a few feet from my car. "What's going on?"

Releasing my arm, he looked back at the pub, then down at me. "Do you know Beck?"

"Who? Oh, you mean Cole's friend? No. I've heard he's related to TS somehow, but we haven't officially met."

Thomas Scott, TS to friends and family, was the owner of the Idaho Outlaws and married to my friend Noel Snow. She was also a big supporter of the Children's Club.

Slade seemed to relax at my response, then smiled and ran a hand through his sandy blond, snow covered hair. My fingers itched to touch the collar length wet strands that had become stuck to his polo shirt. I watched in fascination as steam rose off his body from the cold air where it touched his bare skin.

Light snow swirled around us, creating an atmosphere of intimacy. And the light from the nearby streetlamps lit the area in a soft glow. It was romantic and my mind began to wish for things to be different between us.

"Kara, I'd really like to help you out with the party and be your Santa. For the kids. You don't need to call your friend. I'll do it." His tone was full of urgency and something else I couldn't define.

Unable to control my constant blinking caused by fat snowflakes, I lifted my hand to shade my eyes. "Oh. Okay, if you're sure. I guess that'll be fine." *But would it?* I'd make it somehow.

"Definitely. I'm sure and I already have the night off. So, do you need to know how big I am?"

Lust slammed into me. I couldn't help it. The man and his words had me turning this moment into something way sexier than it was.

"Pardon me?"

"My size. For the suit."

I almost let my gaze fall to where my thoughts had initially gone—the juncture between his thighs, but I held strong. He had to know the effect he had on women. A man who looked like he did was more than aware of his appeal. But I didn't want him knowing I was far from immune to his charm. Besides, he'd put me in the friend zone. I wasn't going to try for a shot at getting out of it or let him know how much that had hurt me.

"Right. Yes, for the suit. I do have one. And knowing your size would be helpful." The cool air began clearing the fog from my brain. "I'm pretty sure it'll fit, but we could take it to a seamstress since you're leaner than the other guy. I'll make some calls tomorrow and get back to you."

He reached into his back pocket and pulled out his phone. "Here, put in your number and I'll text you. That way, you'll have my number for tomorrow." Our fingers brushed as I took his cellphone, and goose-bumps erupted throughout my body. Shaking my head, I tapped in my number and quickly handing it back to him. I caught myself just in time from leaning into his warmth, praying he hadn't noticed the movement.

Then he did something unexpected. Lifting a hand, he used a thumb to brush snowflakes from under my eyes. Frozen in place, I thought he was going to kiss me. Wished for it desperately. Instead, he took a step back, tucking his hands in his pockets. "Great. I'll be waiting. You good to drive?" Slade nodded at my car.

I was stone cold sober at that moment and more turned on than I'd ever been in my adult life. Trying to speak, I couldn't. Instead, I returned his nod. Then, not to appear like a total dork, I lifted my hand and jangled my keys. "I'm good."

At my response, his gaze narrowed and landed on my lips. Fighting to keep from licking them, I waited for his next move.

"I have no doubt about that. Goodnight, Kara. Sweet dreams," he whispered. Bending toward me, he kissed my forehead, then jogged back to the pub while I stood watching his tall form disappear through the double doors. A bit dazed, I spun on my heel, unlocked my car door and slid bonelessly into the cold leather seat.

So much for staying away from Slade Johansson.

I WASN'T LOOKING FORWARD to calling Rod the next morning. Telling my boss that the first major event I'd been assigned was close to having no Santa wasn't what I thought would be something even remotely possible. I'd had this guy lined up for months. He was a sought after and highly recommended Santa in the community and to have him back out on us was unacceptable. I just hoped Rod with roll with the change and wouldn't have any objections to Slade stepping in.

"Hi, sorry to call you on the weekend." I paced from one side of my condo to the other.

"No worry. Just got in from my run." Rod barely sounded out of breath. He'd been a defensive end in college and was in better shape now than he'd been ten years ago. He claimed he had to just to keep up with all the kids.

"I didn't want to wait till Monday to let you know the Santa I hired called me late yesterday and cancelled. But I have a substitute all lined up. So, no worries."

"Okay."

Okay? I wasn't expecting such a quick acceptance. Sinking onto the closest piece of furniture, I let out a relieved laugh. "Thanks for that. Honestly, I was a bit worried, considering the first Santa had come highly recommended."

"I'm sure whomever you found to replace him will do a great job. Even though the other guy bailed, that's not your fault. And I trust your judgement. It's one of the main reasons I hired you."

I accepted his compliment even though a part of me wanted him to say he'd be our Santa, but the kids would no doubt recognize him and there'd also be questions about why he wasn't at the party.

"So, who'd you get?" The noise of a blender came over the line.

"I'm not sure if you've ever been to O'Malley's Pub, but he's the manager there, Slade Johansson?"

A clatter rang out, then a curse and finally silence.

"Rod? You still there? Everything okay?"

"No, I mean yeah. Sorry. So, um yes. I've been there. I know Slade. I, uh, guess, I don't picture him as the Santa type. But you just never know, right? Anyway, I'm glad he stepped in to help."

Maybe it was my imagination, but Rod's long-winded response sounded...off. I'd only worked for him a few months now, but I thought I'd come to know him fairly well. Could it be that Rod and Slade didn't get along?

I set the worry aside because I just didn't have the time to search for a new. And my next call had to be to a friend of a friend who knew a seamstress that might be able to fit Slade into her schedule.

"Thanks for being so understanding. I'll see you on Monday."

Rod said his goodbye just as my call waiting chimed. From one call to the next, I spent my Saturday morning checking in with all the people I'd hired for the party to reassure myself that no one else would be backing out and to double check they still had us on the schedule. There was a band and a caterer and two college kids I'd hired to be elves. Everyone confirmed they were all set for Christmas Eve.

The last call was to Slade. But first, maybe I needed some advice. So I started with Evie.

I got her voicemail. "Hey, Evie. Call me back. Thanks." She and her new hubby, Sam, were probably doing cute couple stuff.

On to the next. "Hey, Miranda. Could you call back when you get this message? Thanks." Then half-way through, I remembered she had an extra shift at the hospital today. Dang it.

"Amber, I'm desperate. I really need you to call me back. I need some advice on men." After the third message, I debated trying someone else, then decided I needed lunch. Or maybe a nap.

Halfway through my chicken salad sandwich, my cell pinged. My stomach did a weird flip-flip when I read the notification. Slade had texted me. Darn it, I wanted to be the one to reach out first.

I really wanted to handle this in the most professional manner, but last night's dream starring the sexy bartender had my palms sweating and my nipples standing at attention. Should I text him back or call? Do I offer to pick him up and drive him to the seamstress' shop or tell him I'll meet him there? It was like I'd been teleported back to being a teenager and all the uncertainties of talking to a boy I like bubbled to the surface.

Appetite gone, I put the remainder of my sandwich in the fridge, then went to the bathroom. I fixed my hair, then snorted at my reflection. This was lunacy. He wouldn't be able to see me. Marching back out to the kitchen, I picked up my phone and stared at his text again.

Let me know when and where you need me. S

Okay, not anxiety inducing or blood pressure rising at all. Well, maybe a little. The temptation to read innuendo into his words was too much to handle. Because I wanted this man more than anyone I'd ever met. And it was so frustrating because I thought I had rid myself of the hope he may one day want me as well. And now, there he is in my life in a big way, stirring up all the hormones I'd thought tamed. *You can do this Kara.* It's just business. For the kids and the club.

Grabbing my cell, I quickly text out the address and time of the appointment and tell him I'll meet him there. Done.

Before I can set it down, he texts back.

Can't wait. See you soon.

He then added a wink face. Ugh, this guy was killing me.

CHAPTER 4

SLADE

*T*he drive through downtown Pineville was not as busy as I expected days before Christmas. We'd received another couple of inches of fresh snow this morning and the road crews were still clearing it up. The business district had decked out the old-fashioned lampposts with twinkle lights and three-foot-tall white bells. Even a bachelor like me who never decorated much for the holiday, I had to admit it all made the area feel magical.

Scratching the short stubble on my jaw had me wishing I had time to grow my beard out. Hopefully, I could find a fake one that would hold up to the tugging Kara had warned me about. Simply thinking about her raised my blood pressure and the closer I got to the shop where we were meeting up, the more my excitement grew.

I was looking forward to keeping her a bit off balance and showing her what I'd been holding back. At thirty-four, dating had become practically like a chore. It was weird how quickly the shift took place. For years, all I cared about was having a good time, never really planning out what I wanted my future to look like. I took for granted that I would find someone who'd I want to spend the rest of my life with. When that hadn't happened by thirty, I wasn't too concerned. I figured it would happen.

And when I first met Kara, it was like, "Oh, there you are." It was the damnedest thing because if you'd have asked me, I never believed in fate, but there she was—the perfect woman for me, and I realized she was everything I didn't know I was missing.

Then my grandfather passed, and I had all this money I needed to figure out what to do with, and when I did, I discovered I'd waited too long to make my move because now she worked for the organization I chose for a large donation. I didn't want there to be any question about why I was pursuing her. And I didn't want to put Rod Davis, the Executive Director, and Kara's boss in an awkward position. And then fate stepped in on the day my donation went through, and Kara needed a Santa. And now I fully believed in it—timing was everything.

But how did a guy let a woman know he wanted more than just a good time, or a short-term hook-up? I'd never gone out of my way with small talk or finding out what the woman I was with had any goals or dreams or anything serious.

But Kara was different, and I planned on going all in today. Parking my car, I practically ran down the street.

"Hi, I'm here to see Marion." The shop was wall to wall clothing and costumes.

"She's in the back. I'll let her know. Have a seat." The employee waved me to a couple of chairs by the street facing windows. I smiled and walked over, but I didn't sit down. My gaze landed on the curvy, dark-haired beauty walking down the sidewalk. Kara. Even wearing a knitted hat and bundled up in a scarf and jacket, I knew it was her. My dick perked up. Shifting away from the window, I walked over to a rack of sport coats and pictured my third-year psych teacher who, at the time, was pushing eighty and wore support hose and orthopedic shoes. She was a nice woman but was better than a cold shower when I needed one. And I did. Desperately.

In unison, Marion and Kara entered the front of the shop. I turned my attention to the seamstress first and extended a hand. "Hello, I'm Slade and here's Kara." I turned toward Kara, grinning. "Let me get your coat."

Kara blushed, and I found myself wanting to find out if the flushing of her creamy skin went below her neckline.

Marion cleared her throat. "I only have thirty minutes. Slade, follow me. You too Kara. You can help."

She led me back to a changing area, handed me the suit, and pointed to a curtain. "Change in there, then come back and stand over here."

I took the bundle of red and flashed Kara a grin. She was holding in laugh as Marion stood, arms crossed with measuring tape hanging around her neck. "Hurry up. We don't have time for you to flirt." She waved her hands at me. I turned and did as instructed.

Ten minutes later, Marion had what she needed, told me to change again and leave the outfit in the changing room. She had another last-minute customer to deal with. Then I had an idea. I stuck my head out and looked around. "Kara, could you help me? I seem to be stuck."

Kara had been scrolling on her phone. At my request, her head snapped up. It looked like she was debating on calling for Mary, but I had plans. "Please, it'll take just a second."

She tucked her phone into her purse and stepped inside the changing room. I slid the curtain closed behind her.

Kara's stomach growled. I grinned. She blushed. Pretty and flustered, I wanted to reassure her. "Did you miss lunch? Because I did. After we're done here, let's go grab some dinner."

A flash of something appeared in her dark chocolate eyes. Maybe uncertainty, but I wasn't going to let it deter me. Tucking a long shiny lock of hair behind her ear, I backed up a step to give her space. "I'll keep my hands to myself. Promise." Crisscrossing my heart, I held her gaze until I saw her shoulders relax. I wanted her comfortable with me, not thinking I was trying to score and get into her panties. Although I did want that and hopefully sooner than later, but I'd settle for a dinner date and getting to know her better.

"I'm not sure that's a great idea." She didn't sound convinced. Maybe I needed a different approach? Being direct had always served me well in the past, and I didn't want her confused about my feelings for her.

"I can see the wheels spinning, Kara. You're all about keeping things professional, and I admire that. But you can't deny there is something between us? A spark whenever we're together. I'd like to spend more time with you. It's not like you're my boss and I'm your employee. Besides, I'm volunteering, and if you try to pay me, I'll just donate it back to the kids and the club."

Her expression softened at the mention of the kids, and I said, "You really like your job, don't you?"

"I do. Quite a lot. That's why us being seen together right now isn't a good idea."

"Hmm, okay. What if we label this a 'working' dinner? We can discuss the schedule for the party and if we happen to learn a bit more about each other, then that's bonus."

"Why now?" Kara was staring at me intently. A little furrow appeared between her brows. Shifting again to keep myself from touching her when all I wanted to do was take her in my arms and kiss her pouty lips to reassure her that I've wanted her from the moment my eyes locked on her months ago, I rubbed the back of my neck and sighed.

"Maybe I should finish changing and I'd be happy to tell you… over dinner." There were certain moments in your life when control over something you wanted was given to someone else, and you had to roll with it. So, I would. Didn't mean I liked it, but she was worth whatever short-term obstacles I had to overcome.

"Oh, yeah." Her gaze roamed down my chest and the cute blush she had earlier returned.

I couldn't wait to reverse our status, and I could gaze at her flesh.

Her silence had me sweating, but I held her wide-eyed gaze, flashing her a hopeful smile.

Backing out of the dressing room, she broke eye contact and let out a nervous laugh. "Okay. Dinner. Salvatore's is just down the street. I'll wait out here." She released the curtain.

I heard the patter of her shoes as she walked away, and I let out the breath I'd been holding. Swiftly, I put my clothes back on before she changed her mind and remembered that I had asked for help. The only thing I had needed help with was getting her to agree to going to dinner with me.

CHAPTER 5

KARA

One glass of wine and I may end up agreeing to anything Slade suggested because he was charming my socks off and I was letting him. He was also doing his best at avoiding the question I asked him earlier, when we were up a close and personal in the changing room.

So damn close. Full of want, I almost threw away the promise I'd made to myself and forgive him for not pursuing me. Oh, how I wanted to plaster my lips onto his full mouth I still wasn't sure how I kept from giving in to the urge to press myself against his deliciously hard, chiseled chest and beg him to take me had been something I'd never felt toward a man *ever* in my life. Being in that changing room had been equal parts thrilling and scary. But instead of going after what I wanted—him—I froze.

And why? Hurt feelings were one thing, and in the past, I'd been able to get over other guys not being into me pretty quickly in the past. But with Slade, who I'd been fantasizing about for months, I had hit a brick wall in getting past, or was it over him? All I really knew was that I wanted to be under him.

Maybe what I really needed to figure out was: could my heart survive if things didn't work out between us? Would it be worth the price of a hookup, learning what his touch felt like, how it would feel to be filled with him, by him, taking the chance that I might be left with only memories after he moved on to someone else?

"Penny for your thoughts?" Slade's smooth baritone snapped me from my worrying.

"Hmm, you might need to take out a loan. I have so many and I'm pretty sure they're not Slade-friendly, considering we don't know each other very well."

"That's why I wanted to take you to dinner."

I finished off the merlot, pushing the glass away, then immediately began drawing a design on the base with my finger. Still not ready to look him in the eye, I brought up the question that had been nagging me for longer than just the hour we've been sitting sharing bits and pieces of ourselves. We'd quickly run through the details of the Christmas party. I mean, all he needed to do was show up on time, act like Santa and more important have a ton of patience with the kids. I knew his patience capacity was high. Being a bartender and manager of a restaurant practically demanded you hold a degree in it, and I've seen firsthand how he dealt with difficult patrons. He was a pro and a magnet for people. Especially women.

And there was the real reason I was hesitant. Deep down, I was worried about his reputation, whether it was real or not. But I'd witnessed first-hand women come on to him, and rarely subtly. He seemed to enjoy it, but maybe he was looking for more than just a short fling? I hope so because I was now ready to find out.

"Okay, Slade, I need to be straight with you. Ever since you said you wanted to be Santa…and can we be honest here?"

"I want it all. Hit me." Slade finished his wine and gave me his full attention.

"First of all, stop with the sexy eyes."

"Sweet Kara, I only have one set of eyes. I can't control how they appear to you, but if you think they're sexy, then I don't want to be wrong. Or would it be right? Doesn't matter because either way, my eyes are yours."

"Stop. Oh my god, you don't want to hear me snort." Grabbing my stomach, I leaned to the side, taking a deep breath. It didn't work. And he was still looking at me like he wanted to eat me up. "Okay, stop."

"Stop what? You're so cute when you giggle." Slade leaned over the table and held out a hand, palm up.

Instant sobriety hit me. "Babies are cute. I'm an attractive, thirty-two-year-old woman. And I'd like us to get serious for a moment." Sitting up straight, I put my shoulders back and dug deep for the truth I wanted, no needed to share.

His gaze followed my movement, then resting on my chest for a moment before slowly lifting to my overheated face. His blue eyes darkening from glacial to a smoky blue. Damn those sexy eyes with the faint crinkle lines at the corners.

"Slade."

"Kara." Soft and sweet. He was going to test me the whole way. Alright then. Onward.

"I'd like to know why three months ago at Noel & TS's end of summer party you told Evie, I mean asked her, I mean—"

"If you were single? And then, like a bastard, I didn't follow-up, follow through or try to hook up with you?" He asked.

"Yes. That. All of that. Well, maybe not the bastard part." Butter-flies, moths and maybe a few crickets were thrumming inside me. He lifted his palm and waited. Before I could talk myself out of it, I placed my hand in his. His large fingers engulfed my hand, and he rubbed his thumb back and forth over my sensitized skin.

"Answering in detail would take too long. But know that I had a good reason and I'm here now. And I'd like more than a hookup."

Too long? Was he trying to piss me off? "Look—"

"Damn. Nothing good follows 'look,'" he interrupted, grimacing.

"You're right. Sorry, let me try this again. I know it sounds…silly, or maybe high-schoolish, but I was, I am attracted to you—"

"Good, I feel the same." Another sexy grin.

"Would you stop interrupting me?" Pulling my hand from his, he held on tight, making it difficult to retrieve my hand without more force. I didn't want to let go of him. I just wanted him to take me seriously. Why was this so hard?

"I'm sorry. I'm listening."

He was. I searched his eyes, and finding what I needed, understanding and empathy, I continued. "At this point in my life, hooking up may be fun at first, and who doesn't like a good orgasm now and then, but I'm looking for something more. A relationship beyond an incredible physical attraction. I'm not a prude or anything, but if all you're looking for is a night of hot and sweaty sex, then we need to end the night here. I'm still grateful that you want to help at the party, and I hope you'll still be Santa for the kids. We can be friends, whatever or however that looks, but no naughty times, okay?"

Slade's face remained unchanged, unreadable, and I had no idea what kind of reaction was coming. I gave him a half smile, my heart pounding as I waited him out.

The first indication he wasn't going to be mad was his thumb resumed its feathery glide over my skin. The simple touch sent a zing straight to my clit. Oh boy, maybe I'd been too hasty in putting the kibosh on sexy times between us. But that wouldn't last, and I was done waking up alone with no one to share my thoughts and feelings. I wanted someone to hang out with and be happy and content doing absolutely nothing expect sharing time and space—together.

"I don't blame you for thinking that's all I had on my mind. In fact, till recently it's all I thought I needed from someone. But—"

"There's always a but isn't there." Letting out a heavy sigh, I readied myself for his agreement on my 'let's be friends' request.

"However,…is that better?" He grinned. I grinned, then he continued. "However, if all I wanted from you was a hookup, then I wouldn't have asked Evie about you. I would have waited until you were alone and approached you myself. So what I'd like from you, hell it's a need at this point and so brand new to me I'm having trouble naming it, but it's something that didn't go away over the past several months. And I'm sorry for leaving you questioning my intentions."

I felt my body begin to tremble. Where had this version of Slade been hiding? Was he saying he wanted a shot at a relationship with me?

"I like the sound of doing nothing with you. Learning more about you. Being silly or boring with you. Hell, I also want to touch you, find out what makes you moan my name, and that's the truth and I wouldn't be here if I didn't want those things. If your original Santa hadn't bailed on you, believe it or not, I was ready to ask you out."

Wow. Like double wow.

"I have the day off tomorrow and I'd like to spend it with you. How about a movie or we could go to the ice-skating rink?"

The thought of him on skates, for some reason, made me chuckle. Did he throw that out there because he thought it was something women secretly wanted all their dates to be into? "Do you skate?" I asked.

"It's been years, but the weather's supposed to be clear tomorrow and it's what people do on dates in the winter, right?"

"I appreciate you wanting to do something typical, but I've never skated, and I'm not going on our first official date and try standing on skinny blades for the first time in my life. A movie sounds good."

Slade still hadn't told me the *why* of it all and I stubbornly couldn't stop thinking there was something he wasn't telling me. But the way he was opening up to me had my thoughts ping-ponging inside my brain, desperate to land on a solution. Needing to move past the doubt and insecurity from failed relationships, I was willing to take this chance on him. On us.

We ended the evening by agreeing on a time for him to pick me up tomorrow, and he did keep his hands to himself as we walked back to where I'd parked my car on a side street a few blocks away.

There was no awkwardness or an attempt at a goodnight kiss and as I drove home, I wished that I hadn't made such a big deal about hooking up. Hours later, lying in bed, my body still heated from the few touches we shared, I spent the night dreaming of Slade.

CHAPTER 6

SLADE

The thing about movies is you don't really get to know a person. There's little chance for a meaningful conversation. Times that by ten when the room is packed with holiday out of towners and the only thing you learn is what makes the person you're sitting next to laugh, cry or look away from the action on the screen.

I learned all those things and more sitting next to Kara in the dark megaplex surrounded by strangers. The most important of which is how hard she makes me and how difficult it was not to use the age-old move men have been using since the dawn of movies, the stretch and reach around while snuggled up close to the person you can barely stand *not* to touch.

I resisted. But it was torture. My knee bounced through most of the comedy, and I wouldn't be surprised if she guessed what I was battling. Hell, all anyone sitting within a few feet of me had to do was look in my lap to see the evidence on my body's reaction to Kara. So yeah, I'm sure she knew exactly what was running through my mind and noticed my cock straining to escape my jeans.

"That was funnier than I thought it would be. I'm glad we came." Kara flashed me a bright smile, her eyes still adjusting to the light.

"It was." I took her hand in mine, leading her through the crowd. A wave of frigid air hit us on our way out of the warm building. Thanking the weather gods for the reset, I widened my stride and the pressure against my zipper eased. Able to think with my brain again, I asked,

"Are you up for a drink, or…?"

Kara took her time in answering. Walking in silence, I helped her into my car. Settling into the cold leather, I flipped on the heat before turning to look at her profile. Suddenly I felt that if I didn't move faster, she'd slip through my fingers, and I couldn't let that happen.

Shifting toward me, she wore a tentative smile. "I think I'm ready to find out why now? I mean, was it just my imagination, or havn't we had this flirty back-and-forth thing going on for months ago?"

"We did. Really, I've been attracted to you since you started coming into the pub even when you had that annoying boyfriend. What was his deal, anyway? Every time I saw him, he had on a different pair of glasses."

She let out a laugh. "That was Jonah. He's an optometrist. He had an eyewear fetish, probably still does. I could tell you stories, but I won't. He was nice, just…not for me."

"I'm glad. He wasn't for you, that is. And I promise, I don't have any fetishes that I know of anyway." I couldn't hold back any longer. I leaned closer to her over the console and cupped her chin. "But maybe we could discover some together. Because I could quickly become addicted to you, Kara. I told myself I'd take this slow, but sitting next to you in the dark gave me too many ideas."

Her eyes went round at my words. "Why…why have you been holding back?"

"For one very good reason. You matter. Maybe we haven't spent a lot of time together, but I want to change that, and I don't want to mess this up with sex."

Her lids fluttered, and her breathing increased at my words and oh, damn, she wasn't making this easy.

"What do you want? Why did you agree to dinner last night? The movie today? And if you tell me you're doing it because I'm helping you out, I don't think I can—"

Kara moved in and pressed her lips against mine, cutting off my rambling. I grabbed her arms and lifted her over the console onto my lap, burying my hands in her hair and deepened the kiss. She let out a low mewl. It hit me first in my gut, then my dick. She wiggled against my growing erection, and I cursed that this was happening in the front seat of my car. I wanted her naked and in my bed.

The sound of teenagers passing my window and laughing broke the spell I was under. Dammit, I didn't want our first time to be in the front of my car, where anyone could see us. She deserved better. And so did I.

Gently, I ended the kiss, framing her face with my hands. "I want you, Kara. Have no doubt. But I want you to be absolutely sure this is what you want. Please forgive my stupidity for staying away from you. And I hope you don't feel you owe me for helping you. I'll back off if you want. I can't believe I'm saying that, because there is nothing more than I want then to take you to bed and spend hours feasting on you, but—"

Fingers pressed onto my lips; Kara stopped my rambling. "I feel like the tables have been turned here. I don't want to pressure you either. But Slade, we're old enough to not play games. Tell me why you all but ignored me for months and months because for the first time in my life, I'm considering having sex in the front seat of a car."

Reluctantly, I helped her back into her seat and put my car in reverse. I needed a distraction and driving was the best one I could come up with.

"Slade?" The hurt in her voice almost had me pulling over and taking her back in my arms. Almost.

"I'm the donor." The words rushed out and an unexpected weight of what now seemed to be the dumbest idea I ever had lifted.

"Wait. Donor? As in the million-dollar donation that Rod was bouncing off the walls over, then swore he couldn't tell me who it was until it was finalized because the donor wanted to remain anonymous. That's you?"

"Surprise?"

CHAPTER 7

KARA

A bit dazed, Slade pulled into my driveway, jumped out as if on fire, then helped me from the car. Standing on my front porch, instead of digging out my keys, I turned to him and said, "I wish you would have told me."

"I know. But I learned a long time ago money makes people do weird things. And after they find out how much you have, well, let's just say things get awkward real fast. My intent was to make sure no one had any doubt about why I was with you and why you were with me. That might not make sense right now, but my grandfather was a big deal in the city where I grew up. And although my parents kept us away from the society stuff, I saw up close how different those who have money are treated versus the have nots and how it can ruin all kinds of relationships."

Not the explanation I'd been anticipating. I began to shiver, and his hands came up and rubbed my arms, keeping me warm in the cool night air. My body reigniting with need at his touch, I squeezed my thighs, hoping to ease the ache, but it only increased it. "Okay, so you work at a bar, but you're rich. And now you're richer thanks to your grandfather, and able to give a million dollars away?"

Slade shifted, letting out a long groan. He huffed out a frustrated breath, and I so got it. We were both fighting against the need to give in to our lust, yet getting the truth out was important.

"Don't forget, I'm the manager now, more than just a bartender like I was for years. Originally, I did it in college to rebel, I guess, but then I found I really liked working with the public. Plus, it's a good profession for someone who likes to travel and move around. Which I did. I never stayed anywhere for long. Until Pineville."

He stopped speaking. His gaze on my lips. What more did I need to know? Do I wish he'd told me sooner instead of leaving me hanging? Sure. But he had a good heart, and he thought enough of me to not want anyone to think I was with him just for the donation, the money he apparently had more than enough of to give away.

"Kara Wyatt, you make me want to stay. You're like no other woman I've known. I want a chance to show you I'll take care of your heart and these gorgeous curves of yours." As he spoke the words, his hands grasped my hips, pulling me closer to him.

A fresh wave of sparks curled up my spine, cementing my body's vote. Months of wondering what it would be like in his embrace faded as the reality became a hundred times better and we'd barely begun. "I want you to stay." My whispered words echoed between us, and it was now a race to get where we both wanted to be—tangled up in each other.

Tearing into my purse, I dug out my keys and miracle of miracles, even with shaking hands, I unlocked my door on the first try.

Frantic movements had us closing the door, ripping off outer clothing, then racing to my room. Slade wrapped an arm around my waist, pulling me up against him, hard and tight. His hands diving into my hair, holding me still as his lips, his tongue, consumed mine.

When air became a necessity, heavy breathing filled the air. Slade grinned and said, "Clothes off now!" More than eager to follow his command, I took a step back, bumping into the end of my bed, then steadied myself. Bolder than I'd ever been, I stripped out of my blouse, slacks, and bra in record time. His eyes blazed, but he didn't touch me.

Slade's gaze had followed my movements and when I paused before slipping out of my panties, he let out a groan that went straight to my clit.

"You're still dressed." It wasn't the same command he'd given me, but it was enough to have his arm sweeping behind his back as he tugged his shirt over his head in one smooth motion. Oh. My. I felt my jaw drop, and it was my turn to stare. Unbuttoning his jeans, he pushed them off along with his briefs, freeing his cock. I reached for it, needing to touch him, but he backed away.

"You touch me now and this will be over before I can make you scream my name." And just like that, he pushed gently on my shoulders, and I tumbled onto the mattress.

Slade bent a knee and climbed over me slowly, never breaking eye contact. "So many nights I've imagined what you taste like, how tight you'll feel wrapped around my cock. This almost doesn't seem real." His gaze swept over me, lighting me up. I felt desired and a bit wanton as I shimmed my hips then arched my back, offering myself. He didn't disappoint, taking a tight nipple into his mouth while he caressed and flicked its mate, dragging sounds from me I had no idea I was capable of. He captured my lips in a deep kiss. Time stilled.

Dropping hot, open mouth kisses from my neck to my collarbone, then down the center of my stomach where he placed the tip of his tongue inside my belly button and swirled. My hips shot into the air at the feathery contact. Liquid heat pooled in my core. I was on the verge of begging him to taste me where my pulse was now throbbing.

"You like that, baby?" Slade's words freed me.

Inhibition gone, I cried out, "Yes, lower. Please. Lick me."

"With pleasure." His first swipe made me grab my bedspread, and the second brought me to the sweet edge of a climax. I wanted, needed, more. "Slade." Was that my voice begging him for more?

He didn't make me wait. Lifting my thighs over his shoulders, he began feasting and wringing from me frantic, explicit words of praise. A light flick of my swollen clit brought white stars behind my eyelids.

I rolled my hips, seeking more. More pressure, more Slade. In short, quick strokes, his tongue drove me to my peak, and I crashed in waves, his name ringing out as I silently gave thanks for finding a man who knew how to bring me pleasure beyond what I thought possible.

The sound of ripping foil filtered through my brain as it floated back to the moment. I opened my thighs wide, welcoming him, then watched as he guided himself into me, filling me. I clamped my inner walls around him, greedily taking all of him as he pounded into me. Pleasure overrode everything. Desire ruled. And his thrusts drove me wild. When I felt the rush of another orgasm, he roared my name. We came together. The moment…perfection.

I wanted to draw it out, I didn't want it to end. My inner voice, the naughty one that hadn't been confident enough to show itself until him, promised me that this was only the beginning.

EPILOGUE

ONE YEAR LATER

KARA

*T*he children, even the teenagers, were laughing at Slade's performance. He took his role of Santa very seriously with equal parts playfulness. It was only the second year of donning the tailored suit, but he worked the room as if he'd been doing it for years. As the last notes of the Christmas carol sing-along ended, our daughter chose that moment to make her presence known.

I was standing in the corner of the gym that had been transformed into Santa's workshop, the best view in the room. I rubbed the spot where I'd just taken a double kick to the ribs. If I didn't know better, I'd think she was expressing her thoughts on not hearing her favorite song, *"All I Want for Christmas is You."* Actually, Slade had dubbed it her favorite.

Patting my belly, I assured her, "Later, little one." We had Mariah's Christmas album on a loop at home. I didn't have the heart to tell Slade

I couldn't wait for Christmas to be over so we could change our playlist.

"You doing okay, Kara?" Rod handing me a cup of punch then nodded at Slade. Even with the distance, I could tell he was wearing a concerned look hidden beneath his snowy white beard.

"I'm great. Don't you worry too. Slade's been on me all week to relax. Just because tomorrow is my due date doesn't mean she'll show up on time. First babies rarely do, you know."

"Yeah, well, I wouldn't know."

Rod was a confirmed bachelor, or so he proclaimed, but I had the feeling if he found the right woman, or the right woman found him, he'd change his tune.

My sister Amber and her husband Royce, holding their six-month-old daughter, came up to say goodbye. "Hey, sis. You look like you need to sit down. We're headed out. Give me a call in the morning, okay?"

I let out a long sigh. Did every pregnant woman go through this? I don't remember being such a worry wort over Amber when she was ready to pop. "You bet. Now go on. I'm fine. Get my niece home so you two can get some rest, too."

An hour later, the kids were gone, and most of the staff had left as well. Slade and Rod were making the rounds and locking up the center. So much had happened in the last year. I took a moment and marveled at how far both the Children's Club and Slade and I had come.

Slade's donation had been more than enough to add on an addition to the center, which helped serve more kids in the community after school and on breaks.

We had a small wedding on New Year's Day, just our family and close friends. His sister, Kelee, who was now living and working over in Cedar Ridge just an hour away, was one of my bridesmaids, along with Evie and Miranda. I may have aimed my bouquet toss directly at Miranda. She deserved to find her happily ever after soon. I suspected she was carrying a torch for someone at the hospital, but I hadn't figured out who—yet.

And even though Amber was a little put out at having to wear a form fitting dress at four months pregnant, she made a gorgeous Matron of Honor. And tonight, exactly a year later from the night Slade and I were together, we were ready to become a family of three.

"Kara, put that down. Please?" Rolling my eyes, I ignored my husband and finished what I was doing. "Slade, it's a folding chair. I'm pretty sure putting it away isn't going to put me into labor."

"Just because you're the one carrying our daughter doesn't make you an expert. This is your first time, too." His voice had gone all growly, reminding me that I had some plans for him when we got home.

I loved his overprotective nature. And he looked sexy in his Santa suit, more so now that he'd removed the fake beard and padding. The jacket was open, revealing the tight-fitting undershirt he wore. My fingers were itching to explore the abs I knew oh so well.

"Uh, uh. You just cool that look, Mrs. Johansson. You've had a long day, no sexy times for you tonight. But if you promise to be good and go to bed as soon as we get home, Santa will fill your stocking first thing in the morning."

My heart skipped, and I grinned. "Oh, how I love you, Mr. Claus." I tucked my hand through his offered arm and wrapped my arm around his waist. I lifted my gaze to his and sighed.

"I love you more, Mrs. Claus," Slade whispered. Bending down, he captured my lips and kissed me breathless. There'd be no waiting till morning.

My husband knew me all too well. Tangling with Santa every year had become my favorite holiday tradition.

TANGLING WITH THE GRINCH

A PINEVILLE WORLD CHRISTMAS NOVELLA (TANGLING SERIES)

I had a feeling this was the year I'd finally fall in love—I just didn't know it would be with the grumpy, grinchy single dad who takes over running the Pineville Christmas tree farm.

Mazie

I've never been worried about not finding "the one." I've always believed I'd recognize him the moment I see him, so as my friends got married, I continued to build my pop-up gift business until he shows up. Now at 35, I've checked off two of my top three goals: purchasing my first house and opening a storefront. And I'm confident the third one will happen just in time for the holiday season.

But first, I'm committed to one more pop-up at the tree farm. He'd given me my first shot ten years ago, and I would not let the aging owner down.

Only this year, Sheridan's son is running the farm and I literally run into him on the first day. Not a great way to make a first impression, but oh, what an impression he made on me.

Walker

I never wanted what my cantankerous old man spent more time working on than with his family, so when he leaves me his tree farm, I scramble to make it work until I can find a buyer and fast.

Christmas is my least favorite time of the year and I only tolerate it for my young son. Now, I just have to get through the next four weeks of non-stop *Santa Claus is Comin' to Town* and pine-scented *everything*.

Then a whirlwind of peppermint-scented sunshine slams into me as I inspect the barn where my father rented out space for holiday treats and over-priced snow globes.

Every day I try to ignore how my body aches for her, but what I don't expect is how slowly but surely, she gets under my defenses with her smile and yes, her non-stop holiday spirit.

When she discovers I'm selling the farm, will I be able to prove to her I'm not the total grinch she believes me to be?

Walker kissed me first, well kind of, but then denies our instant connection. But I'm not worried. He's The One and I'm determined to be the last woman he ever kisses.

CHAPTER 1

WALKER

The crackle and crunch of dry leaves filled the air, mocking me as I strode toward the old red barn on my old man's tree farm. Scratch that my tree farm. Dang it, my Christmas tree farm.

"Dad, this is the best day ever!" My seven-year-old, Devon, had found the tire swing.

The ancient oak stood out in a sea of evergreens, with its gold and red-orange leaves. Well, the leaves had all fallen, but the childhood memory of watching the tree turning colors was one of the positive memories I had during the months leading up to our father's all-consuming passion—and it wasn't spending time with his four kids, well at least with me.

Mason Sheridan hadn't passed along his love of farming to any of us. Oh, he'd tried. Maybe a bit too hard. The farm hadn't always grown a variety of fir and blue spruce trees. When dad first bought the land, the crops were mainly mint, wild rice and barley. That was before he sold off chunks of it over the years to developers in order to pay mom's medical bills. Now all that's left are those darn trees.

And surprise, surprise, instead of making things easy on his kids, because whenever did he do anything that was easy, he put a stipulation in his will just for me. Besides the one where he named me executor and manager of the farm. He decreed that there would be one more tree season no matter what time of the year he passed, and I was the one who had to run it.

And now I had to meet some lady named Mazie who ran the holiday gift shop in the barn where I'd had my first kiss when I was twelve. Her name was Jessica, and she was an older woman of thirteen. We'd snuck away from our job of helping customers pick out their trees when things had gotten slow. She'd moved away the following year and broke my heart. The first, but not the last woman to do so.

I can still hear my dad's disappointment ringing in my ears as I get closer to the barn that's seen better days. We were staying in the farmhouse I'd grown up in, which held even more memories, mostly of mom. It was bittersweet for sure, but Devon was having a blast and that's all that counted.

"Devon, I'm headed inside. Don't get too crazy on that thing. That rope has been there since I was your age." Standing with my back to the barn doors, I knew I was stalling. I knew that once I entered, then this whole debacle of overseeing the Christmas tree farm that had made me run as far away as an eighteen-year-old could get would become real.

Dammit, I don't have time for this. Spending six weeks away from my business back in Seattle and taking my son out of school was more than inconvenient. It was my dad's way of having the last word one final time.

Jeez, why'd he have to pick me? He knew how pissed off it would make me to come back here. And I guess I had my answer. I needed to shake off this mood for my son. He was so mature for his age, sensing when I wasn't fully present in the moment. And that was the last thing I wanted for him. It was how my dad was with me, and I swore I'd never be that way if I ever had kids.

So here I was, all tied up in knots over something that can't be changed, but that didn't mean I had to like it.

So distracted by the memories this place stirred up, I wasn't paying attention when I turned around to head inside that instead of the wooden handle, I found myself holding a soft, warm peppermint-scented female a good eight inches shorter than me.

"Oomph! Oh, my." The surprisingly sexy voice traveled directly south to the territory behind my zipper and settled, sending signals to my brain, rerouting blood flow. A signal I hadn't received quite so quickly, at least since my teenage years.

Holding her upper arms, I kept her from falling backward. Her head snapped up at the change in direction and I was face-to-face with a decidedly younger and sexier version of the woman I thought I'd be meeting.

While my long-neglected appendage attempted to stand at attention, I took in a deep breath and tried my best to untangle myself from the gorgeous, curvy brunette wearing garland around her neck like a scarf and a dusting of green glitter on her chin.

"Are you okay, ma'am?"

"I'm so sorry I wasn't paying attention to where I was going."

Speaking at the same time, I took a large step back, putting as much distance between us as I could without making her feel self-conscience about how quickly I removed my hands. Her breathy voice was like another hit of adrenaline I wasn't sure my zipper could withstand.

This reaction was the strangest damn thing. I was a long way from my twenties when a strong wind would have made me instantly hard, so what was it about her that had me wishing we were alone and close to a bed?

"I'm good. Just, uh, embarrassed. Anyway, you must be Mr. Sheridan's son, Walker. I'm Mazie Cameron. I'm so sorry for your loss." The expression on her upturned face was so sincere and if it were any other moment in time, I could get lost in her dark brown eyes. But it wasn't. And I couldn't.

The mention of my dad was the bucket of cold water my out-of-control libido needed.

Mazie held out her hand. It was dwarfed in mine as we shook, and I swear electricity sparked.

"Thank you, Ms. Cameron. I'm sure the lawyer informed you that this will be the last year you can run the gift shop. I hope it doesn't hurt your business, but running this tree farm was our dad's dream and none of his children want it. I'm just here to fulfill what was laid out in our his will, then I'll be putting this place up for sale come the new year."

Her expressive eyes narrowed then she released a long "hm" which sounded awfully like "yeah right, buddy." Although I realize I came off a bit harsh, I wanted to make sure she understood what was what right up front so there'd be no false hope of changing my mind.

"Really? That'd be such a shame. This place is such a big part of so many families' holiday traditions. I'm sure once you see how much the community loves this place, how the children get a thrill from hunting down the perfect tree, cutting it down themselves or watching the staff bundle it up, and then there's the gift shop. Did you know we have at least a dozen local artisans who sell handmade items from wooden toys to holiday home décor and unique gifts found nowhere than right here in Pineville and the tree farm has always been their showcase?"

The challenge in her tone should have put me off, instead it fanned the fire already lit inside me. The one that had flared to life the moment we bumped into each other.

And her excitement over everything Christmas and this farm should have had the opposite effect on me. Instead, as I watched her talk, focusing my gaze on her full, cherry red lips, all I could picture was the two of us rolling around naked and me dropping kisses along her flushed pink skin.

Nope, not going to happen. Besides, she wasn't my type. Anyone who loved the holidays as much as she obviously did was not someone I needed in my life. I was just going through a sex drought, is all. One of my own making, sure, but since gaining full custody of Devon four years ago, there wasn't much room in my life for dating.

And no matter how pretty and tempting Mazie was, I would not be sucked into her orbit.

"Are you feeling okay? You look as if you just sucked on a lemon? Oh, hi there. What's your name?"

A lemon? That's a bit harsh. So focused on Mazie I hadn't realized that Devon was standing next to us, his gaze bouncing between us.

"Hi, my name's Devon Sheridan, ma'am. What's yours?" Devon had lost both his front teeth last week and had refused to smile ever since. But not today. His toothless grin filled his face as he gazed up at Mazie.

Rolling my eyes, I let out a long sigh as I took in her reaction to my son's interruption. It was both a blessing and a curse, the Sheridan charm. And my son seemed to have found his. I needed to remember that and make sure I held mine in check. I'll let Devon be the good cop while I, as usual, play the bad cop.

"Nice to meet you, Devon. Are you excited about the opening of your grandpa's, I mean your dad's, Christmas tree farm? We'll have free hot chocolate and cookies every day. I was just checking the supplies for the gift shop. I bring in items crafted by local artisans each season and help out with the wreaths that are made right here on the farm. Maybe you could help me out? If it's okay with your dad." Mazie's smile rocked me back a step. It rivaled Devon's in wattage, but it had a whole different effect on me than my son's.

I had to hold firm.

Releasing a low whistle, I placed a hand on my son's shoulder. "You act fast, Ms. Cameron. We just met and you're already recruiting. What's next? You going to ask me to wear that ridiculous Santa suit my dad wore every Christmas Eve?"

Maybe there was too much rude and not enough tease in my tone as I'd meant because by the height of her eyebrows just now, I could very well be on her naughty list. And with that thought, my mind took a left turn to a decidedly sexier naughty list than the one ol' Saint Nick ever checked.

I tried again to sound a bit more neutral. "Neither one of us is here to participate in any of the holiday activities, Ms. Cameron. I'm just here doing my duty, then we'll be heading back to Seattle.

Better she knew right from the start where I stood about my son taking part in the holiday activities on the farm and with her. The last thing I needed was to be around her tempting body every day.

Mazie's smile disappeared as I spoke. She crossed her arms under her firm, and perfectly sized to fit in my palms breasts. It took every bit of effort to keep my gaze on her face and I prayed that she didn't notice the bobbing of my Adam's apple as I swallowed a moan at the alluring picture she made. Did she have any idea how she was affecting me?

"You're awfully young, Mr. Sheridan, to be so…grinchy."

"Young?" I let out a scoff. "I'm forty-two. Old enough to know better. How old are you? Twenty-five, twenty-six? There's more to life than running a tree farm that's only useful for a handful of weeks of the year. I'm only here because I have to be, not because I want to be. Not because I have joy for the season or whatever good tidings it's supposed to bring. My son will not be working anywhere on the farm and that includes the gift shop. I, on the other hand, have no choice, so if you have any issues, you've got my number."

Instead of arguing with me, she stared me down. Not in defiance, but in speculation. No, that wasn't right. It was like she could see right through my bluster. For a moment, I saw what might have been a flash of empathy, then interest, but that too disappeared in an instant so I wasn't sure.

But I was mesmerized either way as her luscious lips thinned out, and she gave me a slight nod.

I was being a dickhead, and I knew it. Instead of arguing with me, her gaze dropped from my face to the tip of my battered cowboy boots and back up again. Not only did I feel the heat from her perusal, and perhaps some mutual interest, I also felt her disappointment.

Rarely do I let what others think of me bother me. I'd long ago developed a thick skin toward other people's opinions, and it had become even thicker when my ex took off. But with Mazie, as ludicrous as it seemed, I wanted her to like me even knowing nothing could come between us. I refused to let another beautiful woman lead me around by my hormones.

"Oh, I have your number all right, Walker." She dropped her arms and gave Devon another smile. "It was so nice meeting you. I hope you visit me next week after we open. I've been known to hand out candy canes." Her smile disappeared when she looked back at me. With a quick nod, she spun on her heel and walked back inside the barn.

"Dad, she was nice. Why'd you have to be like that?"

"Like what?" I knew what he meant but instead of answering me, he rolled his eyes, turned and ran back to the tree. I was left alone, staring at Mazie's heart-shaped backside as she bent over a box of holiday ornaments. She'd effectively dismissed me. But my body wasn't getting the memo.

If anything, her standing up to me made me harder, and more interested than I should be considering what I'd said. The only thing that saved me from further embarrassing myself was my mid-thigh jacket covering the evidence of a less than five-minute interaction with a woman I just met.

Apparently, my body and my brain were ready to do battle, and whether I wanted it or not, I had a feeling Mazie Cameron would be more than worth breaking my self-imposed hiatus.

CHAPTER 2

MAZIE

I couldn't get home fast enough. The first person I needed to speak to was Natalie, my best friend and, as of last April, my sister-in-law. "I met him, Nat." The words rushed out of me even before she finished saying hello when I called her.

"You mean old man Sheridan's son? Which one is taking over the farm, again? Hunter or Walker?" I could hear Ellie cooing in the background. She was just a couple weeks old and her husband Easton, my brother, had left today for a road game. He was in his last season as a wide receiver for the Washington Sentinels. I'd been helping out when I could and will probably end up at her house later, but I just couldn't wait to tell her.

"Walker. And he has a son, Devon. But let me say this again: *he's the one*, Nat. *The One* I've been waiting for." My head was still buzzing from the events of the day. Running into the man of my dreams, literally, had my heart racing pretty much non-stop since. There was just the little matter of his attitude toward Christmas, but I'm sure once he gets settled in, meets with the employees and sees how valuable the gift area in the barn is, not to mention profitable, he'll change his mind about selling the place. At least that's what I kept telling myself the entire drive home.

I knew my guy would show up this year, and he did. Just in time for my favorite season. And bonus. The moment we touched, okay, ran into each other, I swear my ovaries exploded and every follicle on my body electrified, making every hair stand on end.

Natalie let out a noisy yawn and mumbled, "Well, wasn't that the plan? To meet at the barn at one o'clock."

My poor sleep deprived bff. She'd been doing her best to get Ellie on a feeding schedule, but the baby had her days and nights messed up. Oh, the joys of motherhood. It was something I couldn't wait to experience myself.

"Okay, I know you're tired, but I need you to focus. Six-foot something, silver at the temples with the sexiest dimpled chin, a few days growth of beard, and a bit, maybe slightly okay pretty grumpy Walker Sheridan…Is. The. One." Out of breath and shaking, it hit me that I forgot to eat lunch. But somehow, I didn't think my low blood sugar was totally to blame for how I was feeling. No, Walker had had quite the effect on me.

"Mazie Cameron, you better not be pulling my leg. I've had two hours of sleep in a row in the last couple of days and I'm not playing."

I laughed at how stern she sounded, but I couldn't help it. Oh, how I loved her and was so grateful to have her as my best friend.

"Wait, are you sure? Absolutely, one hundred and two percentage positive Walker is, *The One*? I can't recall much about him since he's older than us and left for the service the day after he graduated. I'm not even sure he's been back home since. I seem to remember having a conversation with his sister Stassi that his ex-wife did a real number on him and basically deserted him and their young son when the kid was only three."

We'd been saying one hundred and two percent since we were kids, and I could always count on Nat for good intel. And now things made a bit more sense. But I suspected there was more there-there with Walker's father, I was sure of it. But figuring out how to deal with my slightly, okay, a lot grinchy guy would have to wait. I had an equally grumpy momma to feed and a niece to cuddle while Natalie ate and took a much-deserved nap.

IT WAS NEARING midnight by the time I made it back home. In between numerous diaper changes and reassuring Nat that yes, I was more than capable of taking care of Ellie while she slept in the next room. I mean, I babysat most of the neighborhood kids through middle and high school. I could definitely take care of one sweet, angelic newborn.

But who knew such a tiny thing could produce so much poop? I removed my stained top and put it in the washer, then headed for a nice, long, hot shower. After finishing my nightly routine, I settled in and let my mind wander. Of course, it wandered to the grumpy new owner of the tree farm.

Walker Sheridan hit me in all the right places. However, the unexpected attitude toward Christmas, which I hadn't expected considering he grew up on the farm, plus his father's love of the season, was something that could be overcome. I hoped.

And then there was his son, also unexpected but in no way an issue. Funny how I never considered that my Mr. Right would have a child.

As I snuggled even deeper under my favorite comforter, in the king bed that I'd bought last year with the intention of sharing it with *The One*, my mind raced with ideas on how to convince Walker not to sell and how I could spend more time with him.

There was no way I was going to let him get away now that I'd found him. I saw the shadows behind his eyes as he tried to convince me the tree farm didn't mean anything more to him than a duty he had to see through to the finish. Well, whether Walker Sheridan wanted it or not, he was going to get a continuous drip of holiday cheer between now and Christmas Eve, so powerful that, like the classic cartoon character, his heart would grow large enough to let me in.

And the first step would be figuring out how to get him to kiss me the next time I see him.

CHAPTER 3

WALKER

hanksgiving was a whirlwind of family and going through our dad's personal items and stuff of our mom's we had no idea he'd held onto all these years. My brothers Roman and Hunter, along with our younger sister, Stassi, were in Roman's office after dinner, while his wife Miranda entertained Devon. She'd offered, claiming she needed the practice. Plus, we'd all agreed to clean up the kitchen before leaving which only seemed fair since we ate all of her delicious food.

My son was in heaven, he'd never experienced a family holiday, and it hit me how wrong it was of me to stay away from Pineville. But no matter how much my siblings wanted it, I was not changing my mind about the farm. I know their relationship with our dad was much different from mine, but I couldn't let that sway me.

I guess as the oldest I got all the parenting mis steps and even with Roman telling me about how my dad regretted his ultimatum before I left for the Marines, it still didn't change the years of me feeling my dad cared more about the farm and those damn trees than he did me.

"Hey, Walker, you keep frowning like that and Santa's gonna leave you coal in your stocking. Again." Stassi chuckled. Instead of going through the box in front of her, she was typing on her cell. "I'm making my Christmas list. What should I get Devon this year?"

"Legos." I mumbled, then went back to searching through the box I'd been assigned. But instead of focusing on the task at hand, my mind flashed to running into Mazie yesterday and the Christmas cheer radiating off her. Well, until I acted like a jackass.

The interaction had unsettled me more than I'd like to admit. And when combined with my instant attraction to her, well, it just made me grumpier than usual.

She made me feel things I hadn't in years. Every time I closed my eyes last night, all I saw was her thousand-watt smile, and that led to me stripping her and kissing every inch of that sweet, curvy body.

Damn, I needed to get laid.

"Walker, you have to see how much the farm means to the community. And to dad's employees. I think selling to another developer is a mistake. Aren't there enough cookie cutter houses on the land he sold after mom died? I mean, isn't it kind of our duty to Pineville and the surrounding towns to keep the tradition going?" Stassi had been bending my ear about tradition for the last thirty minutes and if Devon wasn't down the hall, I'd have cut her off a long time ago.

I didn't want to be the grinch, not really. I just didn't know how to be anything else from the beginning of November through December twenty-fifth. "Alright, you run it." I did my best to keep the bite from my words, but from her wide-eyed response, guess I failed.

"Listen, sis. We may have grown up in the same house, but for you it was all twinkling lights and hot cocoa when dad added those trees. It consumed him, and I didn't have a choice at twelve-years-old. And for all the years until I left, he chose those damn trees over me. You know how many of my basketball games he went to? None. He always had an excuse and claimed he was ensuring our future. Well, all I wanted was for him to just once be there and sit on those uncomfortable bleachers and watch me play. So, if you're so committed to keeping it open, it's all yours." I ran my hand down my neck, instantly regretting the rough sound of my words.

"Hey, Walker, we get it, but don't take it out on Stassi. She was only in kindergarten when the trees were mature enough to open the business for customers. It's all she knew growing up." Roman, the negotiator of the family, answered for our sister.

"It's okay, Roman. I can handle Mr. Grumpy Pants. Maybe I should run it, but what would I do the rest of the year? We need to decide as a family what to do, Walker. You're not alone in this, you know?" Stassi sat down next to me on the couch and punched me in the arm. "I'm sorry things were different for you." She rubbed the spot where she hit me, then patted me on the knee and stood back up.

"Okay, who's hungry for pie?" She clapped her hands together, then called out to my son, "Devon, your dad says you can have two pieces of pie!" Sticking her tongue out at me, she giggled, then ran out of the room.

Hunter busted out laughing. "You, my grumpy pants brother, deserved that." He hadn't said a word the entire conversation, and he hadn't seemed very happy about what I said to Stassi. That was my baby brother. He thought things through before making an ass of himself. Hunter got up and followed our sister, and I was left with Roman.

I knew he wasn't afraid to stand up to me. He was just smart enough to do it in private. "So, we don't have to make any decisions tonight, or next month, for that matter. Let's see how this season goes, and if we can keep it profitable in order to pay the employees at the very least. I'd really like to hold off till after the new year after Miranda has the baby, okay?"

Roman was so like our dad in some respects that I had a hard time not taking out my old issues with him. But he was happier than I'd ever seen him now that he married Miranda and their first kid was on the way. I just hope things work out for them unlike they did for me and Devon's mom.

"What if I don't want to wait? It looks like I'm the only one in this scenario that loses. None of you can drop what you're doing to run things for the next month. I'm it, Roman. And I don't want it."

"What about Devon?"

"What about him? He's just excited he doesn't have to go back to school next week."

"I mean, how does he feel about being on the family farm? Seeing where you grew up?" Roman asked.

"Is this the guilt trip portion of the evening? Because if it is, I have no problem telling you where to shove it."

Roman puffed out his chest, then yelled, "Hey, Dev. Your dad just told me you're getting a new bike for Christmas."

Sounds of excitement rang out down the hall.

"What the hell was that about?" My whole family had lost their minds.

"Don't you think you owe him, us, some time to come to terms with dad being gone? And I'd like some time to get reacquainted with my nephew. Since you have to be here, I suggest you take a hard look at how happy that kid is and try not to make the same mistake dad did with you. Stop being such a hard ass, and enjoy yourself, Walker. C'mon, what can it hurt?"

Roman held out his hand, and I took it. He pulled me up, and we stood toe to toe. "I know it's hard this time of year for you to be back home, and I appreciate what it took for you to be here. More than the other two are aware of. And I also know that it's not just dad's passing that has you so freaking grumpy. Am I right?"

Damn, I hated when he was right. Staring him down wouldn't do much good. We were pretty evenly matched size wise, so wrestling him to the ground would probably end up in a tie. It just sucked that the time of year my ex chose to desert Devon and I was approaching and added to my dislike of Christmas.

"The past is past, bro. That little boy needs to see his dad, if not jumping for joy all the time, making more of an effort to not be so grumpy about everything all the time."

I let out a grunt instead of using my words, which only made Roman laugh harder.

"Man, you really need a woman."

For the first time in a very long time, I busted out laughing. He had no idea just how right he was. And if I didn't want to turn into a sexless single dad any longer than I already was, I needed to take his advice.

But how was I going to get another chance at making a better impression on Mazie so she wouldn't laugh me out of my own barn the next time I saw her?

CHAPTER 4

MAZIE

$\mathcal{I}$t had been a week since Walker and I ran into each other. When I was on the farm, I'd only seen him from a distance. He'd done his best to stay out of the barn whenever I was there. His behavior made me all the more determined though. I had plans for the sexy grinch, but I needed him to at least be in the same space as I was.

Fortunately, I had the pleasure of seeing Devon every day. He was on the tree swing at every opportunity, and I'd bring him a cup of cocoa before I got too busy with customers. I'd thought about quizzing Devon about his dad, but that felt all kinds of wrong, so we talked about his school, his friends, and what his favorite shows were.

Today I put the finishing touches on the gingerbread cookie station that had become a yearly tradition. It kept the kids busy while their parents shopped, plus they were my favorite Christmas treat when I was a little girl.

Carla, one of the farm's part-time employees, came in shortly after we opened. "Hi, Mazie. The place looks amazing this year."

"Thank you. Oh, my gosh, I love your elf ears. Are all the employees wearing them?"

She accepted the treat, unwrapped it, and popped it into her mouth. "Yes, and it was quite a battle with the new boss to let us have our fun."

Digging into my apron pocket, I pulled out a mini candy cane from my stash. "That deserves a reward. I'm still trying to figure out why he's so anti-Christmas."

"Yeah, it's kind of weird, huh? In fact, I just overheard him arguing with one of his brothers. Walker wants to throw out a box of his mom's decorations from when they were all young. I mean, who would do that? Anyway, thanks for the treat. I was hoping you could set aside one of those cinnamon stick three-wick candles and one of those gorgeous little carved trees for me? I don't have anywhere to keep them right now since my shift started. Well, two minutes ago. I promise I'll come back when I'm done to pay for it."

And this is why I need to pull out all the stops this year to show Walker what an important part of Pineville the tree farm and this shop are. Not just the employees, but I'd been getting texts all morning asking about the items I'd posted on social media last night.

This place was needed and special. And whether Walker wanted to admit it, I just feel that deep down he knows it too. And Carla's bit of unintended intel just gave me the perfect excuse to track him down.

I let the cashier know where I was headed, and that I'd be back in ten. On my way out, I saw Devon in his favorite spot. "Hey, bud. Do you know where your dad is?"

"Hi, Mazie. Do you have hot cocoa?" Devon's face lit up with hope.

"Oh, shoot. Not right now. But when I come back after talking to your dad, I have something fun for you to do in the barn. You like gingerbread cookies?"

His cute little face scrunched up, then he hopped down off the swing. "I like cookies. What's gingerbread?"

"You've never had a gingerbread man at Christmastime?"

"Nope. Just Santa, and reindeer, and snowman cookies. No ginger men. What do they taste like?"

I can't believe this poor child had been deprived of the best holiday cookie ever. Now I had two missions for the day. "They taste like, well, heaven and Christmas. Don't go anywhere and I'll be back soon and we'll decorate and eat some together."

"Alright!"

Devon's cheers followed me as I made my way to the Sheridan farmhouse where Devon had pointed. I'd never been inside and always wondered what it looked like. Every inch of the outside had always been lit up with twinkling lights and pine boughs wrapped with ribbon on the railings and pillars during the season. It had been a picture postcard. But not today.

No lights or decorations to be found.

Yeah, this grinch must be stopped.

And I was just the woman to change his mind.

Hopefully.

Stepping onto the porch, I knocked on the front door and waited. And waited. So I knocked again, then turned around to look at the view. The house was situated on a slight incline. There were several elves running back and forth, helping customers and holiday music blasted from several speakers. At least there were lights strung above the pre-cut tree lot. Now all that was needed was a dusting of snow.

Where could he be? I scanned the lot again for his tall frame and his handsome, if perma-frown-wearing face amongst the cheerful tree buyers and merry elves. I did see his sister, Stassi, helping out and I think Hunter, the youngest brother, was helping a family get their tree tied down on top of their SUV. But no Walker.

Was he really so grinchy he couldn't even help out his family? Well, my ten minutes were almost up, so I turned back to the front door with my hand raised for one more attempt. Instead of wood, my fist knocked on a very firm, very muscular chest.

"What the…oh, it's you," Walker growled.

The rumbly vibration of his words traveled along my hand and arm before landing and zapping my lady bits. *Oh, my.* I opened my hand, then flattened my palm and rubbed in a lame attempt to soothe his bruised flesh. That's my story and I'm sticking to it.

Instead, what happened as I absorbed his body heat and lost myself in his heated gaze was further confirmation that he's *The One.* The way he was looking back at me with his pupils blown wide in desire and the feel of his hand on the back of mind as he held me in place instead of pushing me away made me sway into him.

The moment was like a movie. Our connection, explosive.

For a split second, I thought he was going to lean in too and kiss me. Then someone shouted his name, and he pulled his hand away from mine and I swear I heard him let out another growl.

"I, uh, I'm so sorry I wasn't paying attention." The words rush from me. My heart was racing from that almost kiss and I just prayed I didn't sound like a fool.

"Yeah, well, no harm done. What's up? You have a knick-knack emergency or something?"

And just like that, the desire I'd thought I saw radiating from his gaze disappeared and Walker's face morphed back into that stupid frown.

"No, I uh, heard you had some childhood decorations you wanted to unload, and I thought I could help you out with that." I ginned, trying to ignore my still humming body need to touch him again.

"Um, yeah. No. Now, if you don't mind, my knuckle-headed brother, Hunter, is waving like a loon over at the bundling shack. Excuse me."

And before I could step out of the way, he grabbed my upper arms and shifted me to the side. He stepped around me and jogged down the steps, leaving me staring after him. It all happened so fast I was left staring at his very cute ass in a well-worn pair of jeans, not one bit ashamed that I was checking him out.

Because as fast as he seemed to want to get away from me, I heard him sucking in a hiss of air as he touched me and felt what I knew was an obvious bulge behind his zipper as he brushed past me.

Oh, yeah, there was no way he could pretend there wasn't something happening between us now.

CHAPTER 5

WALKER

Spending the afternoon at half-staff hadn't happened to me since I was a pimple-faced teenager. It was damn distracting as I, under much protest, helped Hunter with the customers who needed their trees tied on top of their cars.

"What is your problem, bro? Is it really that hard to lend a hand around here? These trees," Hunter flung his hands out, "these trees paid for my and Stassi's college, man. I know you and dad had your issues, but can't you just set all that old crap aside and make this last season on the farm a positive one?"

I looked around to see if anyone was near enough to overhear us. Shit, he was right, but that didn't make the negative reaction I felt to this place just go away. "You're right. I'm acting like a jerk. It's just been tougher than I thought, you know?"

Hunter stood a couple of inches taller than me and looked so much like our dad. It was sometimes a gut punch seeing him again after being apart. I knew he was different than our dad, plus he had no interest in taking over the farm as he built his own career. It was strange that he was the one checking my attitude and giving me advice.

"I know. Well, at least I think I know since I was more interested in video games than what was going on between you and dad. You're just lucky your kid seems unaffected by your constant scroogy personality."

Talking about Devon always brought a smile to my face. "He's the best thing that came out of my marriage, so I do my best to hide how this place really makes me feel."

"Yeah, well, I say you're walking on a thin line there. I think you need an infusion of holiday cheer. Maybe some spiked eggnog later?" Hunter looked at his watch. "We've got another forty minutes till we close. How about we head over to O'Malley's Pub? I'll call Roman to see if he can pry himself from the hospital, and maybe Miranda can watch Devon for a couple of hours. How does that sound?"

It was tempting, but I had an apology to deliver. And maybe get a chance for a do-over with Mazie. I've only been around her twice, but my body was begging for a taste of the lusciously curved and peppermint-scented Mazie Cameron. See if she was interested in a short-term fling because if I was going to be around her for the next few weeks I knew I wouldn't be able to concentrate on anything else, including finding a buyer for the farm, until I worked her out of my system.

"Maybe another time. I, uh, promised Devon, I'd meet him at the gift shop and he could pick out presents for Miranda and Stassi. He hasn't had a lot of interaction with women outside of teachers and that's my fault. He's so excited to be around his aunts and get some much needed and deserved female nurturing. It's become crystal clear to me that he needs more of what I can give him."

We walked back to the shack to finish up. Hunter threw an arm over my shoulder, then said something that stopped me in my tracks.

"Maybe I should tag along. Mazie is one fine piece of *ahhhh*…hey, what the hell, man?"

I dragged Hunter around the back of the shack and pushed him against the aging pine. "I don't want to hear you ever speak like that again about her."

Stepping away before I decked him, I wiped my hand down my jaw and tried to get myself under control. *Jeez, where had that come from?*

"Walker, I was just going to say, fine piece of holiday candy. I'm just teasing, bro. I'm not the total douchebag toward women Stassi makes me out to be." My brother straightened his jean jacket and waited me out.

"Right, and reindeer really can fly. Look, I'm sorry. I don't have a good reason for my reaction. Let's finish up so I can go meet up with Devon." I tried to control my accelerated breathing while I tried to figure out why I responded like a jealous lover. I may want Mazie under me, or on top, or anyway she'll have me for the matter, but that was no reason to try to take Hunter out.

TWENTY MINUTES of searching for Devon had my blood pressure at code red levels. He couldn't have gone far. I'd specifically told him to stay in the house once it got dark out. That kid never disobeyed me, so there was only one place that held the kind of fascination a seven-year-old couldn't resist.

The closer I got to the barn, the doors still wide open even though we'd closed down ten minutes ago, was a signal that Mazie was still inside. And from the laughing that filtered out, my son was with her.

"Devon, your dad is going to love it. Let me find some tissue paper and a bag so you can get it home without him seeing."

One thing from the Marines that still came second nature to me was my ability to enter a building quietly, using stealth tactics that had me standing in Mazie's path not two feet away from her. Spinning on her heel, she looked up and let out a startled cry, but she was moving at full speed and once again she ended up in my arms.

"Where-where did you come from?" Low and breathy, her words hit me below the belt and with her trying to untangle herself from me and Devon snickering behind her, I did my best to adjust myself without using my hands. Dammit, what is it with this woman? I was forever and immediately hard.

Unable to find some relief without drawing Mazie and my son's notice, I grinned and bared it. The best I could hope for was neither one of them to look below my belt.

"I'm here for Devon. Sorry to keep running into you. You okay?" I watched closely as she smoothed her clothing and I noticed her face was now flushed in a pretty rosy hue.

"Oh, not a problem, really. I mean, it's not like you're trying to purposely scare me to death, right?" Mazie's gaze landed on my crotch and her blush deepened. Clearing her throat, she turned back to Devon. "Hey, can you bring me the ornament I decorated so I can tuck it away behind the counter?"

Devon's face morphed comically. "Huh?"

Mazie laughed nervously. "You know," she pointed to an object on the table next to where my son was standing, "that one."

Hmm. Something was up. And someone was trying to keep me from seeing what they'd been working on. Who was I to spoil my son's surprise? Not me. I'd prove to them both I could be less grinchy. "Hey, I should check the wiring for the extra lights you added. I'll be over by the circuit breaker box. Devon, once you give Ms. Cameron her ornament, I need you to run back to the house and clean up for dinner. I'll be there as soon as I discuss something with Ms. Cameron."

"But dad, you said I could pick out some gifts for Stassi and Miranda." My son gave me the saddest looking puppy dog eyes I'd ever seen.

Who was this kid?

"Right, well, we'll do that another day. We still have some time. Now, please do as I say." From the corner of my eye, I watch Mazie swipe an object off the table and hide it under her apron, then walk toward the checkout counter.

"Can we have burgers?" Devon asks.

"I picked up a frozen pizza."

"Woo-hoo! I'll see you tomorrow, Ms. Cameron."

"Bye, Devon. Thanks for all your help." Mazie stood watching me with an unreadable look on her pretty face. A face that was still slightly pink.

With a wave and a hop, my son made a beeline for the old house that could use some renovating if we had any hopes of finding a buyer. Just one more thing to keep me in Pineville longer than I wanted. But now that I was alone with her, maybe my time here wouldn't be wasted.

Waiting a few extra beats to make sure Devon was truly on his way to the house, I opened the circuit box and flipped everything off except for the lights along the roofline of the barn.

"Oh, but I'm not ready to go yet." Mazie's tone was more than a little put out.

I closed the distance between us until I stood less than a foot away. She seemed a bit unsettled by my closeness, so much so that she backed up until she bumped into the wall.

Well and expertly trapped, I leaned an arm above her head, dipping my chin until we were eye to eye. "Three times now I have had you in my arms and I know you've seen how you've affected me." Taking a long sniff of the scent I've come to associate with Mazie, peppermint, and something else I couldn't identify, I leaned closer to her neck and whisper, "I don't ever operate this way when I'm attracted to a woman, but there is something about you that has me perpetually hard. If I don't kiss you now—"

And her reaction reassured me I didn't need to worry about her being attracted to me. Mazie cut off my words with her plump lips. She let out the sweetest moan and I took advantage of the opening, slipping my tongue into her hot, silky mouth and drank like a starving man.

And I was. It had been so long for me but that still didn't explain this intense reaction to her. Because if it were anyone else, I know I wouldn't come within fifty feet of a woman whose business revolved around Christmas.

Yet, here I was swallowing her up. I couldn't get close enough and when I pressed my lower half against hers, grabbed her hips and pulled her up tight against my aching cock, she released another moan. This one rough and needy and I was effing lost in her.

I banished the words "too fast" from my mind as we began to grind against each other like a couple of horny teenagers. Hell, I was never this into any of the girls I dated in high school or the ones I hooked up with in the service before I got married.

The noises she was making spurred me on, and I took a hand from her hip then tunneled it under her shirt, finding her warm flesh. I feathered the back of my fingers up her soft skin until I reached the full underside of a breast. I cupped it, then squeezed lightly and was rewarded for my efforts with a throaty sounding, "yes."

I'm not sure how long we were wrapped up in each other, but the thought of taking her against the wall began to filter through my brain. Reaching for the top button of her slacks, my fingers fumbled in their haste and I let out a short chuckle and mumbled against her lips, "Guess I'm not as smooth as I thought I was."

Her minty breath tickled my nose as she sighed. "Oh, you're very smooth." Pressing her lips back onto mine, she hooks a leg around my waist and presses her full tits against my chest and I lose whatever coherent thought I still thought I had.

"Dad! I'm hungry. Can I turn on the oven?" Devon's words were as effective as a bucket of snow dumped down my pants. *Shit!*

Mazie jumped off and away from me, her breath coming out in little gasps.

"No! I'll be right there." I stayed locked on Devon until he turned and ran out.

"I'm sorry, Mazie. I picked the absolute wrong time for that. I'm sure you understand that he comes first?"

She nodded quickly, sending her hair bouncing along her shoulders. Lord, she was beautiful. Even hidden in the shadows as we were with light from the roofline shining outside on the packed snow, I could see the glow on her face and her eyes bright with desire. I'd done that. And I couldn't wait to do it again, plus a lot more.

My chest felt tight as I kissed her on the forehead. I knew if touched her lips again, my son most likely would turn the oven on and we'd soon be hearing sirens for the local fire department. How she'd wrapped me up so quick in all-consuming need was better left untouched. At least for now.

"I, ah. Maybe we could grab a bite to eat one day or something?" Those were not the words I meant to say. I'm not looking to date Mazie or woo her, well, except into bed. I'm past wanting something permanent with a woman, and the ex leaving me and Devon when he was barely three-years-old had convinced me I'd never let anyone else back into our lives.

"You don't look too sure about that? You want to try that again. This time with feeling?" Mazie looked almost as confused as I felt.

"Well, I didn't think you'd like it very much if I asked for a, what do the kids call it these days, booty call? It's just I'm not here permanently and I kind of forgot that as I was holding you up against the wall just now."

Mazie shook her head, then stormed away and grabbed her things. "Yeah, I almost forgot, you're too old for Christmas, so knowing the correct hook-up lingo shouldn't come as a great surprise. Look, Walker. We obviously are attracted to each other, and I'm no prude and if all I wanted was sex with you, well, let's just say I'd text you directions to my house in a heartbeat. But I don't."

"*Oh-kaay.* Maybe I read this situation wrong, but you just had your tongue down my throat minutes ago, so you can't put this all on me. You wanted that," I waved my hand behind me to the spot where I'd just had her pinned to the wall, moaning my name, "just as much as I did. There's no need to get all prissy about hooking up." I air quoted, "hooking up," then rubbed my hands down my face.

Shit, how did this get so turned around so fast?

"Look, I'm sorry. I need to get going and feed my kid. Maybe tomorrow we can start again?" I wanted to wait to see what her answer would be, but she stood holding her things in front of her like a shield, not saying anything.

Walking away was the easy part. Wiping how she tasted, how she felt wrapped around me, was going to be one hell of a trick. For once I couldn't wait for Christmas to arrive, so I finish my executor duties and go back to Seattle.

Later that night, after I tucked Devon into bed after his bath and three bedtime stories, I stared at the ceiling of my parents' bedroom long after midnight. When I finally drifted off into a fitful sleep, I dreamt Mazie was laying next to me, sharing my life, helping me with the farm and raising Devon.

That was one hell of a kiss and now I had less than three weeks to forget I ever experienced it. How was I ever going to survive?

<h1 style="text-align:center">CHAPTER 6</h1>

MAZIE

*I*t has been two weeks since, "*The Kiss*," with the man I considered, "*The One*" and I was no closer to figuring out how to get him to see me as more than a potential bed partner than I was when he'd left me standing alone in the barn, needy and achy to take whatever he offered.

But I knew deep down I just needed a bit more time in proving to him that his past Christmases didn't need to define all his Christmases, and by this Christmas Eve I vowed to show him exactly how good we could be together even with his grinchy attitude. But then again, I could see Devon's excitement at being on the farm and all the events on the tree lot had begun to slowly chip away at the wall Walker had put up after he'd left Pineville.

I also came home most days burned to a crisp from Walker's smoldering gazes. Oh ,he looked at me like he did that night in the barn and often. But he never touched. Well, if things went according to plan tomorrow night, I was ready to change that.

Business had been booming, and it had seemed to thaw Walker's attitude toward selling the place. Part of the success had been from increasing the social media marketing and partly because people were curious to see if Walker had changed his dad's operation.

I'd been dividing my time between the tree farm and my store front on Main. I'd hired two part-time employees to help me out knowing it would cut into my profit for the season, but I wasn't going to have my last year running the gift shop be anything but the best ever.

Just about every day, I managed to find a reason to get Walker to stop by the barn.

From approving the carolers we'd hired to roam the pre-cut lot to donning the Santa suit one Sunday afternoon when there were two dozen kids waiting to see the jolly old elf and share their wishes. He'd grudgingly accepted, but the joy on Devon's face when he found out his dad was one of Santa's helpers had gone a long way in making the time Walker spent with the kids not just a positive experience for all the kids, but I think for him too.

"Hey, Mazie. The place looks so great. I'm surprised you have anything left in here. I've heard so many of my friends gushing over the new artisans you've brought in."

"Hey, right back, Miranda. Wow, thank you. That's so nice to hear. I'm so glad you were able to make it out. How are you feeling?" Walker's sister-in-law used to work as a nurse at Harmony General. She was now happily married and expecting her first baby with Roman, who was just a couple of years younger than Walker.

"I'm ready for this little one to be here, but I've got a few more weeks. Could you show me a few things? I've got just a couple more people to buy for than I'm going up to the farmhouse and pick up Devon for a sleepover. I finally convinced Walker to let us take our nephew for a night of pizza and Pixar movies."

Hmm. Walker's going to be all on his lonesome tonight. I may just have to pay my favorite grinch a visit later.

I'D NEVER CONSIDERED myself to be forward when it came to sex and men. Meaning I didn't show up on a guy's doorstep wearing sexy lingerie with seduction my goal. But when opportunity strikes, especially when the man I wanted to seduce was a single dad, you need to go for it.

When I visited Natalie for a quick hug and a snuggle with baby Ellie, I told her what I was going to do.

"I wish I could meet him first, but I get that you feel like you need to move now. I'd just hate for you to be disappointed come the beginning of the year if he decides to sell the place and go back to Seattle. But if you're sure he's the one, then go get him." She gave me the hug I really needed and, with her words playing over and over in my mind as I drove back out to the farm, taking a chance on love was all that mattered to me.

I'd waited so long for him that for me there was no turning back. It wasn't like I was going to jump his bones the minute he opened the door. My plan was to talk first, then seduce. But now that I was sitting in my car outside his house, I had a moment of uncertainty and self-doubt.

What if he only wanted one-night? Would I break down? Would I beg him to give me—us—a chance? Would he laugh at me and call me crazy for believing I'd fallen for him the moment we met?

"Mazie? You okay?" Walker knocked on my car window.

I jumped, screamed, then covered my face with my hands. *Great way to begin the most important night of your life, Mazie.*

The car door opened, and Walker reached his hand inside to help me out. I grasped him and let him guide me to stand next to him.

"What's going on?" His gaze captured mine, a look full of questions.

"Um, hi. I was wondering if we could talk?"

"Sure." He didn't move toward the house, but patiently waited for me to talk.

"Could we go inside?" I asked hopefully.

"Mazie, are you here for a hook-up?" Walker's eyes darkened, his pupils blown wide as he finished the question.

Biting my lip, I knew I had two choices, but the way he was looking at me and after weeks of fantasizing about our kiss and what it would be like to roll around naked with him had me thinking maybe the talk could wait.

"No, not a hook-up in the traditional sense. I was hoping maybe you could tell me why you've been avoiding me first?"

He released a heavy sigh. "Maybe we should go in and talk. You've got to be cold in that thin coat and," he looked down my legs and raised his eyebrows, "no pants or nylons. Um, Mazie, what are you wearing under there?"

Grinning, I locked my car, then scooted around him and walked toward the porch steps. "You'll find out. After we talk." I put more swing into my strides and was rewarded with a loud groan. I waited patiently for him to catch up and open the door.

"You're playing with fire, Mazie. I hope you know what you want because I'm ready to throw you over my shoulders and take you to my childhood bedroom and fulfill some of my favorite teenage fantasies."

"That's big talk for someone who kissed me like he was dying a couple of weeks ago, then spent the time since treating me like a stranger and getting no more than five feet close to me."

Walker closed the distance and stood so close behind me without touching that it was as if I was standing in front of a furnace. Every nerve ending came alive within me, my girly parts pulsing, and if he wanted to take me right here in the December freezing temps, I'd strip in record time.

"Maybe I had to think about things before submitting to the easy part."

Walker threw me for a loop on that one. "What's the easy part?"

"Sex. Hot and furious, and most certainly unforgettable. I'm sure it would have been spectacular that night if my son hadn't interrupted us, but I'm glad he did. It woke me up, some parts more than others."

I giggled nervously at his joke. Oh, there he was. The person I'd suspected he'd been hiding behind old hurts and long-held beliefs.

"You think that's funny? Wait until you hear what I've come to realize." He rested his chin on my shoulder and sniffed me.

"Did you just sniff me?"

"You know I did, sweetheart. The better question would be, why?"

Why? How could a girl think when the sexy, hard bodied man of her dreams was pressing his obvious need for her into her soft backside?

He made me so aware of myself and my need for him that all thought of explaining what my plan had been—vanished.

"I, um, guess you like me and the way I smell." My breath hitched, then left me all together as his large hands finally touched me. He squeezed my hips, massaging the curves I'd always been self-conscious about until now. He whipped me around to face him and *oh, my,* the naked desire in his eyes for me would be burned into my memory for as long as I live.

"Let's go inside and talk." He reached behind me, twisted the door-knob, and pushed me gently backward over the threshold.

I barely heard the door slam behind us before he scooped me up and strode up the staircase. I'd always wanted to see what the inside of the old farmhouse looked like, but that could wait as everything whizzed by in a blur.

Hanging on tight, I wrapped my arms around his neck. My gaze locked on his. "You, uh, always talk to women like this?"

Walker stepped into a room I'm guessing was his childhood bedroom from the marine posters on the wall and let me go. I bounced once, then twice, on the twin mattress and waited for his next move.

Falling to his knees, Walker placed his hands on my knees and spread them wide, then settled himself into the v between my thighs. My stomach did somersaults at the move, followed by dozens of flut-terings deep in my core.

He cradled my face, so we were eye-to-eye and I never felt more cherished or turned on. "I never talk to women like this. But you're no ordinary woman, are you, Mazie Cameron?"

Again, Walker managed to steal my breath, and all I could do was nod.

"I'm going to apologize now for the small bed, but there's no way I'm taking you to the master bedroom. At least not until I buy a new bed and get rid of all the old furniture that's falling apart. I know you want to talk, but I'm guessing since you haven't yelled at me or left, this is what you want too, right?"

Another nod. My mind was screaming "yes" but I just couldn't make my vocal cords cooperate. This was beyond what I'd imagined being with the right man would be.

"I promise we'll…talk…later. Much later. Right now, I'd rather show you how I feel. Sound good?"

There was no way I was going to just nod again, so I managed a "yes, please" which came out scratchy and low and perfectly conveyed how desperately I wanted him.

From calm to frenzied kissing and clothes and boots and my long overcoat laying in a heap on the floor, Walker was standing next to the bed stripped bare, his erection and the grin on his face vying for my attention.

"I'm liking your little scraps of lace, Mazie, and I appreciate you wearing them just for me, but they have to go."

As bold as I've ever been in my life, I peel my bra and panties off slowly as I watch his lips press into a thin line and one of his large hands wrapped around the tip of his cock.

With his eyes on me, I lean back and wait for him to make the next move.

"Oh, shit. I almost forgot. Hold on."

That wasn't the exact reaction I expected from him considering I'd spread my legs wide for him, so there'd be no question how turned on I was. "Um, everything okay?"

"No, I mean yes. It's just been a while, and I forgot protection. And when I say a while, I mean years. I'm clean, but I think I have a condom in my travel kit."

Releasing a sigh, I laugh. "I'm on the pill and it's been well, not quite years, but it's been more than a while for me, too. Come here." I opened my arms, and the answering grin was all I needed.

The creak of the bed filled the room when Walker climbed on the tiny mattress. But neither one of those things mattered.

"You're so beautiful, Mazie."

He kisses my lips, my neck, and right behind my ear, which makes me even wetter than when I first saw him naked. I run my hands over his shoulders and knead his biceps as I trail my fingers down between his legs.

"Where you headed there, sweetheart?" he growls.

Damn, his growls are the sexiest thing ever.

"Oh, you know, south." I cup my hand under his balls and lightly squeeze.

His low moan sends a thrill up my spine. I lift my legs and press myself against his cock. The sweet pressure takes the edge off my need for him, but I want more. I need him inside of me.

"Not yet. I need to see if you taste like peppermint besides those full lips of yours. Now I've already kissed here and here, but what about..."

Walker takes a nipple in his hot mouth and swirls his tongue around the rigid tip. I press myself closer to him, loving the sensation. He wraps his other hand around my breast and begins to massage, then flicks that nipple. And soon I'm on sensation overload and need him to move.

My arms drop to my sides and I grip the sheet, then lift my hips and grind myself against him. "Y-y-yes." My voice sounds different to my ears. He has me so wound up.

"Patience. I'm almost done, but there's one more spot I still need to taste." Walker pulls away from me, allowing him space to drop open mouth kisses along my torso, beginning another round of intense pleasure.

Then he settles between my legs and nips the top of each thigh, and slowly licks the sting away. I open wider for him, needing him to touch me right....there, ah, yes.

His tongue flicks my swollen bud slow. Too slow. I need want him to go faster and I must have said something because he chuckles and the vibration from his lips on my engorged flesh only makes me want more.

And he doesn't make me wait long. His thumbs spread my outer lips, and he's flicking me again with his tongue until I think I'll pass out from the intense pleasure. When I feel the first sharp tingle of my orgasm, he ramps me up higher by alternating between my clit, then diving his tongue inside me.

"Please, Walker." The cry escapes me as I crash over the blissful cliff. He continues stroking, prolonging the orgasm until I'm a writhing under him now screaming his name.

"I need…want…you inside me. Now!"

Once again, Walker is a step ahead of me. On his knees, he notches himself at my entrance and pauses. His gaze captures mine as he cradles my face and gives me a slow, sexy smile. Locked on to each other, he enters me, filling me, then pulling out and repeating the process until my body is shaking.

"You're the one, Mazie." He says my name and slams into me. This time, his strokes are short and fast, and I'm on the edge of another orgasm as his thumb presses between my slick folds.

I squeeze my eyes, throw back my head and call out his name again as bright white lights bursts behind my eyelids, my body vibrates from another orgasm.

He shouts my name as he climaxes after me and we ride the wave until he collapses on top of me. Raining kisses along my jawline, he wraps his hands under me, pulling me on top, holding me close.

"That was…." I couldn't finish. Because I know I didn't need to. He experienced it as well.

"Yes, it was. And I was right."

What?

"Okay, I'll bite. What were you right about?"

"You taste like peppermint, everywhere."

EPILOGUE

ONE YEAR LATER

*M*AZIE
"You've got something right here." I pointed to the side of my face to show my husband where some icing from his gingerbread cookie had become stuck in his whiskers. My husband. I loved saying that phrase even if I only thought it in my head.

I watched as he brushed his beard, which only managed to spread it further on his face. Devon burst out laughing from across the table of the cookie station Stassi was running this year for us. She was still working at the accounting firm in downtown Pineville but had agreed to help out where ever she could on the tree farm.

Walker had sold his business in Seattle at the beginning of the year after he told his siblings he was moving home and not selling the tree farm. He and Devon had settled in with me in my tiny two-bedroom home while the Sheridan farmhouse was renovated. We'd moved in just in time for Thanksgiving. Devon loved the old staircase, which had been restored and slid down it every day, proclaiming he would show his little brother how to do it soon. Considering Asher was just two months old, soon would definitely have to wait a couple of years.

"Did I get it yet?" Walker rubbed his face against mine, further smearing the sweet treat onto me.

"Hey, I'm not a napkin." I tried to shield Asher from his father's antics, switching the sleeping baby to my other side.

"No, you're not. You're better than a napkin because now I can lick the icing off your gorgeous face." Walker wiggled his eyebrows, then dipped down and kissed my cheek. "Mm-mm, tasty. And you smell delicious too. Peppermint, my favorite." He laughed.

"Ugh! No kissing!" Devon cried out as he slapped his hands over his eyes.

"Hey, bud, you know that's what parents do, right?" Stassi wrapped an arm around her nephew's shoulder and chuckled.

"But why would anyone want to do that?" He peeked through his fingers, only to see his dad kissing me more.

"I'm out of here." Devon ran from the barn, high-fiving his Uncle Hunter on his way to the tire swing.

"Hey Walker, don't you get enough of that at home? You keep that up and baby number two won't be far behind that little chunk Mazie's holding."

Walker and I look at each and grin.

"No way!" Hunter chuckled. "I was just joking. You can't already be pregnant again. I mean, can you?"

Stassi snickered at her clueless brother. "Um, yeah, she can. What'd you do, sleep through sex ed in high school?"

Walker slapped Hunter on the back. "Someone has to keep the Sheridan name going. Roman and Miranda are doing their best with the girls, but you and Stassi are lagging a bit."

I laughed softly so as not to wake the baby. "Walker, give them a break. When they find '*The One*' they'll know. Sometimes it just takes time. We're proof of that, right?"

Walker picked up the peppermint icing bottle, squirted a blob on his finger, then dabbed it on my lower lip.

Both Hunter and Stassi groaned at their brother's antics. Something my husband would have never done last year or any Christmas before then. "We're getting some cocoa. We'll see you later." The siblings walked away, grumbling about neither being ready to settle down. But I had a feeling they both would in the coming year.

Turning my attention back to my mischievous husband, I ask, "What are you up to, Mr. Sheridan?" Reaching up to wipe the icing off, he snags my wrist.

"Uh, uh, uh. I have plans for that." Leaning down, he licks the frosting from my lip, then kisses me long and slow and oh, my, this man knows how to kiss.

When we pull back for air, I can't help but sigh. The grinch is long and truly gone and in his place is the man I'm so very glad I waited for.

THANK you for reading Mazie and Walker's story. If you have a moment, I would love it if you left a brief review on the site you purchased your copy.

WHAT TO READ NEXT?

Any of the other books set in the Pineville World.
Check out the Tangling Series >>> https://geni.us/TanglingWebsite

-OR-

Love mountain men romances? I have a brand new series set in Pineville.

Check out the MOUNTAIN MEN OF PINEVILLE >>> https://geni.us/MountainMenPineville

Want to stay up to date and informed of my upcoming releases, special events, and giveaways? Join my newsletter and receive a free short story ---- https://geni.us/DebraEliseNewsletter

BONUS SCENE

*TS & Noel's Annual Christmas Eve Eve Party - One
Year After Tangling with Santa's Epilogue*

NOEL

"Holly, what are you doing? Where's Zane?" I rushed over to my sister-in-law's side. "Here, give me that tray." I take the dessert filled platter and carry it to the buffet. Our yearly party was nearly set to begin but I was worried about Holly and the precious babies she was carrying. She and my brother had been trying to get pregnant since they got married and now the twins were almost ready to make their debut.

"Noel, I've got this. If I can survive three rounds of IVF and your brother's henpecking, I can handle toting a measly two-pound tray of pastries." Holly rubbed her baby belly and grinned.

"I know, I know. Humor me, okay? I just want to make sure you don't go into labor tonight." Grasping Holly's shoulders, I pull her in close for a hug. This woman who'd started out as my go-to pastry chef when I needed an event catered or one of my favorite treats, had

446

become more than a friend over the last few years. She'd become the sister I never had. Zane had surprised us all with his whirlwind romance with Holly and now they were going to be parents. I couldn't wait to see my high-powered brother brought to his knees by the twin girls they'd begun to believe they'd never have.

"You two aren't conspiring in here, are you?" Zane walked into the dining room and went straight to his wife's side.

"Maybe. So, how are TS and the kids doing? Did Carson talk you into playing Mario Kart again?" I asked, grinning.

"Your son is a tough competitor, but I managed to beat his a—." Holly elbowed her husband.

"Ow! Hey, the kid usually wins. Let me have this." Zane rubbed his side, then dropped a kiss on his wife's cheek.

"Zane, he's your nephew. Be nice. Was Willow still on her tablet?"

"No, *Mom*. TS managed to talk her into a game of UNO. Now if you'll excuse us, I'm taking my wife for the last bit of alone time we'll have for a while and, uh, show her the Christmas lights outside." Zane wrapped his arm around Holly's waist and led her from the room.

Watching my brother and his very pregnant wife sneak off for what was sure to be more than looking at lights had me smiling to myself and wondering when I could talk TS into doing the same. Although knowing my husband, it wouldn't take much convincing.

The doorbell rang, and for the next hour, our guests arrived. Our house was once again filled with laughter and the sounds of kids hyped up on sugar and the anticipation of Santa delivering their most wished for presents.

"Taya, could you help me out in the kitchen?" Beck's wife sent me a quizzical look, but she happily followed me from the great room where most everyone was still hanging out.

"So, what's up, Noel? You have an appetizer emergency?" Taya chuckled. "Or do you just want my recipe for my crab cakes?" We both settled in at the kitchen island as I refilled our champagne glasses.

I'd been bugging Taya since her wedding to TS's half-brother, Beck, to share her secret ingredient, but she hadn't given in. "Actually, I want you to bring those famous crab cakes to the New Year's Eve party. I think this year Hayden and Brenley are hosting, but I need to check in with her before I officially hand it over. She's been having a difficult time with potty training Landon. Unfortunately, with Allie still getting over the flu, she's had her hands full this past week."

Taya's eyebrows shot up at my statement. "Oh, no. I was wondering why they weren't here. But I suppose it's nice having your brothers married and with families of their own, huh? No more being the default holiday organizer. And yes, I'd be happy to bring the crab cakes. Beck has been asking for them, so now I have a reason to hold him off another week. I swear that man still has the appetite of a teenager."

"Oh, my gosh. TS too. Must be in their genes. There are days I curse my husband's faster metabolism. It's really not fair, especially at the holidays, and with my lovely sister-in-law's being such great chefs it's a losing battle." Sighing, I twirl the stem of my glass and let Taya in on the real reason I called her into the kitchen.

"Tell me what you think of Archer King? I hear Beck and his business partner Cole are doing the finish carpentry on Archer's new facility."

Taya pauses, then rests her chin in her hand. "I don't know that much about him other than what I've read in the newspaper. But his is a bit, what's the word…unsocial. Why?"

"He's been in Pineville for almost a year, and I haven't seen him with anyone, and I was thinking he seems a bit lonely and—"

"Uh-oh. You're getting that matchmaker itch, aren't you? Isn't it enough that Zane and Holly are adding to the family's headcount? Plus, Slade's wife, Kara, is pregnant with their second and they're pretty much like family. Then there's Dean and Nori finding each other during that bad snowstorm. Plus, me and Beck. I mean, we're all just a pack of happy couples around here.

Although I'm just glad neither of my girls are ready to settle down yet or taking after me and having a baby at barely twenty and oh, no you don't Noel Snow-Scott. Dylan and Lauren are too young for Archer King."

Taking a sip of my drink, I think about her comment. Yeah, her girls are too young for him. He's forty, and they just had their twenty-second birthday and beginning their careers. The last thing either of them need is a grumpy older man even if he is loaded and gorgeous. Besides, money isn't everything and it definitely can't buy you love.

"Okay, so who do we know that is single, ready to settle down and wouldn't mind a slightly moody, but really hot billionaire?" I ask. And yeah, the matchmaker in me was looking to fix him up.

"Are you two talking about me again?" TS walked into the kitchen with Beck and then right behind him was Dean, the Outlaws pitching coach and his wife Nori carrying their little girl.

"There's that ego again. You think your wife has nothing better to do than talk about you twenty-four, TS?" Dean slapped my husband on the back and pulled out a chair at the kitchen island for Nori.

"Of course not. She sleeps, doesn't she?" TS answered with a grin.

Everyone let out a collective groan.

"Alright, if it wasn't me you two were discussing, then who was it?"

Shoot, I was busted. "Oh, no one you know."

"Archer King." Taya replied at the same time.

"I've met him. He seems nice." Nori settled baby Skylar on her lap. The toddler let out a huge yawn, then popped her tiny thumb into her mouth and closed her eyes. Kids were amazing. They could fall asleep just about anywhere. Well, most of them. Our daughter Willow still wasn't a good sleeper, and she was almost five.

"Oh, when did you meet him?" I ask.

"I got a freelance assignment with GQ earlier in the year to interview him. He's super driven, so I think he comes off as aloof, and maybe grumpier than what he is. But he was pretty tight-lipped about his personal life. I couldn't find any information about who he was currently dating."

TS squeezed my shoulder lightly. "Noel, don't. Leave the man alone. No guy likes to be set up, let alone have his private life discussed by people he really doesn't know."

"I agree. A hundred percent. That's why I've been thinking we need to have him over for dinner. I mean, most of you are in the same club and all." I say in a matter of fact tone.

A sudden silence fell over the kitchen. Taya and Nori were both looking everywhere but at me, and the men were looking at each other as if I'd lost my mind.

"Okay, so not an official club. But successful people generally hang out and discuss…things. You know, like stock options or what professional sports team to buy next. So why not add him to our circle of friends?" I wasn't going to be talked out of this, so I didn't mind bringing up TS's latest venture to make my point. Although even I knew I was on thin ice with my theory.

Just then, Slade and Kara walked into the kitchen saving me from a debate with my skeptical husband. "So, this is where the real party is. We turned on a movie for the kids and they seem to be settling down. What's everyone talking about?"

"Archer King." Nori replied.

"Slade, you must know a woman who'd be a good fit for him?" Taya grinned as she put her former boss on the spot.

"Taya!" Both Beck and Kara said at the same time.

Taya held up her hands. "C'mon. He manages a pub. He knows a lot of people. And when I worked there it seemed to draw a fair share of women so, Slade may know of someone, right?"

Beck took Taya's glass of champagne and set it out of her reach. "I think you've had enough cheer. And I agree with TS. This is not something any of us need to be sticking our noses in. Give the guy a break. When he's ready, he'll find the one. I mean, look at all of us." Beck opened his arms wide. "We all seemed to do okay, right, guys?"

Over the next hour, we all talked about how each couple met. Then it hit me. "Hey, Slade. Is your sister dating anyone?"

Slade and Kara shared a look. The kind of look only a married couple could share. There was some serious, silent debate going on between them before he finally sighed and said, "Yeah, she's single. But she, uh, kinda has a history with the guy over a land deal near Cedar Ridge. So, I'm thinking she's a hard no."

Kara rolled her eyes at her husband's words, then ran a hand over her protruding belly. She was also close to her due date, and for a moment, panic took over. *Please don't let either woman go into labor tonight.*

"I wouldn't say it's a hard no. I've seen him in the pub when I'm visiting Slade at lunchtime, and there was this one time when Kelee came in with her friend Jana and Archer was already at a table eating. And well, I think there might be some there-there, you know."

"Kara." Slade whispered his wife's name, a warning tone in his voice. "Not you too?"

"Lord, help us from happily married women who want to see everyone else happily coupled up." TS ground out.

"Amen." Beck, Dean and Slade's voices mingled in unison.

"Hey, Mom. Uncle Zane just told me to tell you that he's taking Holly to the hospital. The babies are coming!" Carson, our oldest, skidded to a halt next to his father. "Dad, can we go and see them?"

TS and I looked at each other and laughed. Of course, the babies are early. Holly's doctor had warned her about a twin pregnancy and had wanted her to stay close to home this week.

"Uh, not yet buddy. These things can take time. Your mom will go, and she'll keep us updated. Right, honey?" TS scooped up Willow as she ran into the room. "Babies are coming!"

"Yes, sweetie. Your cousins have decided they need to be here for Christmas too."

I gave my kids a quick squeeze and a kiss, then looked toward my husband. "You sure you'll be okay with them? They've had a lot of sugar."

"No sweat. I got this. They'll crash as soon as the next holiday movie starts, then I'll put them in bed and wait to hear from you. Go. Give Zane and Holly my love."

Everyone else chimed in and the house was buzzing with activity and excitement over the soon-to-be newest additions to the family.

With a promise to all to catch up on Christmas Day, I drove over to Harmony Hospital. The ride gave me time to think about the conversation we had about the mysterious Archer King. The longer I thought about it, the more determined I was to set something up between him and Slade's sister, Kelee. And I knew Taya, Nori and Amber would help.

JUST AFTER ONE the next morning, Zane and Holly became the proud parents of Ivy and Clara Snow. They may have arrived early, but they were healthy and loved and had a bunch of cousins anxious to meet them.

I ARRIVED home with dawn just making its presence known. A fresh layer of snow had fallen and with it, that magical feeling of joy filled me as I drove through Pineville. Once home, I snuggled into bed behind my cozy warm husband then squeezed my freezing feet between his legs and resting them on the back of his calves.

"You're going to pay for that." TS's sleepy growl filled me with another type of joy as he turned over and covered my body with his.

"Oh, I hope so." I grinned into his handsome face and sighed. Just as he dipped down to kiss me, a knock sounded at our door.

"I'll pay you a thousand dollars to ignore whichever child that is."

"Babe. Money is not going to keep me from taking care of our kids," I whispered. I kind of want to take him up on it and continue with our grown-up time, but deep down I also kind of want to snuggle in with whomever had a nightmare after seeing my brother holding his newborn daughters.

"They know this is my time. I get you when it's dark outside. That was the agreement, Noel." TS fake-whined.

Another knock and a not so quiet "Mommy" filtered through the door.

"As I keep reminding you, the agreement was written in crayon and never notarized. Besides, even if it was legally binding, Willow is not going away. Tonight, you and me. I promise." I throw our comforter off and sit up.

"Promises, promises." TS circles my waist and pulls me back toward him, then begins tickling me. I can't hold back my laughter and it acts as permission for our daughter to open the door and run over to the bed. Carson is on her heels and before I can say "Come in," our bed is filled with two children.

Love may have found us later than most, but we're definitely blessed.

I HOPE you enjoyed this peek into Christmastime in Pineville. If you have a moment, please leave a review on the retailer site you purchased your copy from. Even a short one really helps!

WANT MORE PINEVILLE WORLD STORIES?

Brand new mountain man series coming in April 2025

Check it out here: Mountain Men of Pineville

Join my newsletter and receive a free short story set in the Pineville World
https://bit.ly/DebraEliseNewsletter

ALSO BY DEBRA ELISE

MOUNTAIN MEN OF PINEVILLE

MOUNTAIN MAN SAVIOR **West + Lauren** -

MOUNTAIN MAN PROTECTOR – **Ridge + Addison**

MOUNTAIN MAN DEFENDER – **Lars + Dylan**

MOUNTAIN MAN BODYGUARD - Kane + Chassie

MOUNTAIN MAN GRUMPY SANTA – Sebastian + Zoe - December 1st

PINEVILLE FIRE & RESCUE SERIES

FAKING IT WITH THE FIREFIGHTER - **Rex + Heather**

MORE BOOKS COMING IN 2026

PINEVILLE PROTECTORS

RESCUING ROYCE – **Royce + Amber**

TEMPTING ZAK – **Zak + Harlowe**

CLAIMING SETH – **Seth + Berkley** Nov. 12th 2025

TANGLING SERIES

AMAZON / BN /KOBO & KOBO+ / GOOGLE PLAY

TANGLING WITH THE COWBOY - **Lawson + Jana (99c)**

WORTH THE WAIT – **Cole + Scarlett (99c)**

TANGLING WITH THE PLAYER – **Brock + Thea (99c)**

ZESTING WITH ZANE – **Zane + Holly (99c)**

RESCUED BY AN OUTLAW – **Dean + Nori (99c)**

TANGLING WITH THE MOUNTAIN MAN - **Beck + Taya (99c)**

<u>**IN KINDLE UNLIMITED**</u>

TANGLING WITH THE SILVER FOX **Hayden + Brenley**

TANGLING WITH THE DOCTOR - **Jack + Kiersten**

TANGLING WITH SANTA – **Slade + Kara**

FOR THE LOVE OF CURVES – **Roman + Miranda**

LOVING THE WILDCARD - **Easton + Natalie**

TANGLING WITH THE GRINCH – **Walker + Mazie**

BIDDING ON A COWBOY – **Sawyer + Emma**

CEMENTING HER LOVE – **Colton + Shayla**

GRUMP OF MISTY MOUNTAIN **Finn + Sami**

SECOND CHANCE RANCH 2026

ARCHER - **Archer +Kelee** May 18, 2026

RESCUED BY LOVE: LATER IN LIFE series

LOVE AT EVERMORE & 39TH – **Evan + Cassidy**

LOVE AT SECOND & 49TH – **Kade + Patrice**

LOVE AT FIRST & 35TH – **Sam + Evie**

LOVING GOLDIE – **Ford + Goldie**

LOVE AT FOREVER & 56TH – **Adam + Lois**

RESCUED BY LOVE series

SAVING MAVERICK – **Maverick + Kelsey**

FULL COUNT - **Luke + Lara**

BASES LOADED - **Connor + Reese**

MANAGING BLAKE – **Blake + Caris**

CHASING NOEL – **TS & Noel**

REDEEMING SCROOGE – **Grant + Sophie**

PARANORMAL BOOKS

GODS, MONSTERS, AND MAGIC:

(THE BRETHREN'S LEGACY WORLD)

DRAGON'S GODDESS - Quinn + Britt

WOLF'S MATE - Keir + Rhia

FATED TO THE PHOENIX - Trace + Bex

FATED TO THE GRIZZLY - Mac + Sierra

FATED TO THE PANTHER - Roane + Kara

FATED TO THE SHIFTER - Gavin + Willow, Coming in 2026

ABOUT THE AUTHOR

Debra Elise, a *USA Today* Bestselling Author, writes steamy contemporary and paranormal romance. She lives with her younger trophy husband in the beautiful Pacific Northwest. They also have two young adult sons who have promised to never read her stories.

A self-proclaimed extroverted introvert, when not writing or procrastinating, she enjoys a strong cup of coffee and a good nap.

Visit Debra at www.debraelise.com